"You're not alone in this."

Cassie stood there looking lost and alone and upset, and there wasn't a damn thing he could do to make her feel better. She'd have to ride out this storm or leave town. She'd already mentioned the possibility herself, a reminder that had left him feeling warned.

Knowing he was being a fool, but doing it anyway, he rose and went to gather her into his arms. The instant he drew her close, he realized he might have just made the biggest mistake of his life...

Dear Reader,

I'm sure most of us have been bullied at one time or another while we were in school, if not later in life, as well. Plenty of us probably remember some of it. I know I still remember a few incidents, especially the time a teacher bullied me. I didn't want to go back to school.

The heroine of this story doesn't realize that she carries scars from when she was bullied in school, and it takes the hero's love to help her past them. What's more, as a teacher now, she is again being bullied by someone hiding in the shadows and threatening her very life.

This is a deeply emotional story about caring, about community and about love. But it's also a story of the darker side of human nature and how we triumph. For me it always comes down to love: how we love each other, both as couples and as community. Love is the best answer we have. Sometimes it's the only answer.

Bullying can leave lifelong scars. And while this story is about love's triumph, it also touches on an issue that we as a community need to deal with. Our kids should not be afraid to go to school.

Hugs,

Rachel

RANCHER'S
DEADLY RISK

BY
RACHEL LEE

First published in Great Britain 2013
by Mills & Boon, an imprint of Harlequin (UK) Limited,
Eton House, 18-24 Paradise Road, Richmond, Surrey TW9 1SR

© Susan Civil Brown 2012

ISBN: 978 0 263 90346 1
ebook ISBN: 978 1 472 00696 7

46-0213

Harlequin (UK) policy is to use papers that are natural, renewable and recyclable products and made from wood grown in sustainable forests. The logging and manufacturing processes conform to the legal environmental regulations of the country of origin.

Printed and bound in Spain
by Blackprint CPI, Barcelona

Rachel Lee was hooked on writing by the age of twelve, and practiced her craft as she moved from place to place all over the United States. This *New York Times* best-selling author now resides in Florida and has the joy of writing full-time.

To all the kids everywhere who live in fear of bullies.
You are not alone.

Chapter 1

Cassie Greaves felt the winter nip in the Conard County air as she left her small rental house to head for school. The rising sun to the east cast a buttery glow over the world, and the trees that had fully turned a few weeks ago were now shedding their brilliant cloaks, leaving behind gray, reaching fingers. She scuffed her feet through the dry leaves and almost laughed from the joy of it.

For much of her teaching career, all seven years of it, she had taught in much warmer climes, places where there might be only two seasons, or at most three. Part of what had drawn her here was winter, the idea of being cold, of needing to bundle up, and cozy evenings with a cup of something hot as she graded papers or read a book.

Having grown up in the Northeast, she had found a growing desire to need extra blankets at night, to awake some morning and hear the world hushed under a fresh snowfall.

As romantic as her image was, however, she also knew there would be parts she wouldn't exactly enjoy, but this morning she didn't want to think about them.

She wanted to think about that invigorating nip, the possibility of rediscovering her Nordic skis and the school she was coming to enjoy so much. It was smaller than she was used to, only eight hundred students in the entire high school. And even with budget cutbacks, her classes were smaller. It was easier to get to know her students, and she was beginning to recognize most of the faces that walked the hallways.

Hallways. Another thing she liked. At her last few schools, there had been no hallways, only covered walkways, which meant moving from an air-conditioned classroom out into the heat, only to walk into another air-conditioned classroom. At times that setup had its charms, but she actually *liked* having interior hallways again.

She smiled and hummed to herself as she walked the four blocks to the high school. There she taught math for all four grades, which gave her days quite a bit of variety.

It had also taught her some lessons. A lot of her students had no interest in advancing to college. They were planning to take over their parents' business or ranch and she had discovered a need to rewrite math problems in ways that seemed useful to them. Unlike some other places she had taught, many students here weren't content to just do the work because it was required.

Plus, in perfect honesty, the students' backgrounds encouraged her to find meaningful ways of phrasing problems because there was so much homogeneity in the things that concerned them. Her elementary algebra class didn't look blankly at her when she asked them to calculate the storage space needed for a certain number of bales of hay.

They went home, measured the bales—round or oblong, depending—and gave her answers based on a practical exercise. Now how cool was that?

Discovering the volume of a grain silo, working with board feet of lumber, sketching out plans for a shed, figuring out how many acres of pasture for a herd of a certain size—all those things enlivened them. Consequently she was discovering a new love for her subject herself.

Drawing in a deep breath of the chilly air, she decided this place was growing on her even more than she had hoped.

When she arrived on the campus, Lincoln Blair was standing outside. He was the football coach and science teacher, an absolute stud of a man who had so far remained reserved, even unapproachable, although everyone else seemed to like him a lot.

In her mind she had dubbed him "Studley Do-right" because he was appealing enough to make her constantly aware of him, sort of like an itch in her libido. He had dark hair, astonishingly bright blue eyes and there was something about him that always made her think he must have descended from a long line of Celtic warriors. Square-jawed, weathered a bit from sun and wind, with narrow hips he unconsciously canted in a way that made it impossible for a woman not to notice them.

She gathered from things the other teachers had said that he owned a ranch that had been in his family for generations, and he worked it as time allowed, which probably explained that weathered look. Regardless, while most of the teachers had certainly been welcoming enough, his air of reserve truly set him apart.

Not that she should probably blame *him*. She'd had enough experience with men who wanted nothing but a fling with her, and had concluded there must be something essentially wrong with her. On the other hand, she reminded herself that getting involved with a colleague was seldom wise, and in a small town like this, it might even be a wider problem if people noticed and started talking.

Nor was it as if he were the first man who had ever ignored her. Noticing him amounted to a recipe for grief, judging by her past experience.

He nodded as she approached and opened the door for her with a quiet good-morning, but didn't follow her in. She guessed he had bus duty, the job of standing outside to make sure that no one used the space and time between getting off the bus and through the doors to make trouble.

She tried to shake away thoughts of Lincoln Blair from her mind as she passed other teachers with cheery greetings and made her way to her desk. Unlike other schools where she had taught, she had her own classroom, which also provided her with an opportunity to personalize things. It felt nice to have a space where she could hang up posters or set out cool objects for the students to explore a bit. As much as possible she tried to apply math to real life because it *was* part of real life, an important part. The applications were just a bit different and more focused here.

She prepared her desk quickly, then stepped into the hall to monitor arriving students. This school still had homerooms, a place where students went to have their attendance recorded and hear morning announcements, something she hadn't seen since her own school days long ago. Then fifteen minutes later they moved on to their first classes.

In her last few schools, homeroom had been combined with the first class of the day. It might have cut down on movement, but inevitably it cut into the instructional hour one way or another.

Since it was Friday, her students were a little more restless and less focused than usual, their minds on the many things they had planned for the weekend. Or perhaps they were just thinking of escape into absolutely gorgeous weather.

Either way, she felt some fatigue by the time she was able to close her classroom for lunch. She didn't have cafeteria or study hall duty that day, so the teachers' lounge beckoned.

Bag lunch in hand, she entered the corridor flow as some students headed for the cafeteria and others to study hall.

The wing emptied swiftly and before she reached the end of the corridor she was alone. Or thought she was. As she turned a corner and passed the men's bathroom, she heard a shout that made her pause.

"Stop it! Just leave me alone!"

Without even hesitating, afraid that waiting for a male teacher to arrive could allow something bad to happen, she elbowed the door open.

The five students inside didn't even hear the door. The sight instantly disturbed her. She knew every school had its underside, but what she was seeing now horrified her.

One of her best math students, James Carney, was huddled in a corner on the floor, his arms protectively over his face. He was small for his years, and string-bean thin, and she'd already noticed he didn't seem to have many friends, if any.

Four boys stood around him, taunting him with names like nerd, jerk, girlie, sissy…part of her was waiting to hear "fag," but that epithet didn't appear while she stood there taking in the scene.

She didn't need a mental map to know what was going on. Before she could react, two of the boys spat on James and she could tell that wasn't the first time.

Before the scene could get any uglier, she clapped her hands as loudly as she could and shouted, "Stop this now!"

Four startled faces turned her way. It took a little longer for James to lower his arms from his head.

"Just what do you think you're doing?" she demanded. "You shouldn't treat anyone like this, not anyone. Ever. But this is a violation of school policy. You know what the penalty is. James, are you all right?"

The youth jumped to his feet and hurried for the door. "I'm fine," he muttered as he rushed past her. "You're making it worse."

"Go to the nurse," she called after him before turning to face the four others. As the full impact of what she had just seen began to hit, she could feel herself roiling with anger. For long seconds she simply stared at the four young men who had been taunting James. *Keep it cool,* she reminded herself. It was important to stay calm and reasonable.

"Bullying," she said quietly, "is despicable. It shows you to be small men, not big ones. It isn't tolerated by school policy and you know it. You're coming to the principal with me."

"Make us," snarled one of them, then they all brushed past her, bumping her shoulder as they went, leaving her both livid and helpless. She couldn't run out into the hall after them, nor could she physically stop them.

But there was something she could do. She picked up her bagged lunch, tossed it in the trash—she didn't want to eat it after it had fallen to the bathroom floor—and headed for the principal's office herself. None of this was going to be tolerated.

My God, James had looked as if he expected to be beaten...or as if he had been. She just wished she had recognized the other four boys by name. Apparently they were in Teasdale's math classes. Gloria Teasdale was semiretired, teaching only three classes a day. An elderly woman who wore too much perfume, she was sometimes the object of derogatory remarks from her students, but Cassie ignored the comments. Kids would talk about teachers outside the classroom, and she could see no point in stepping down on it. She was no martinet and she was equally certain some of her students had derogatory things to say about her. The nature of the beast, she thought with grim amusement.

But bullying was a whole different matter, damaging to the bullied student emotionally, if not physically, and most definitely against the school's conduct policies.

She reached the office and asked Marian, the front desk receptionist and secretary, to call the nurse's office and find out if James was okay. Then she joined the principal in his small office. He always ate lunch at his desk, eschewing both the teachers' lounge and the cafeteria.

Sometimes she thought of him as barricaded away from all the possible disturbances in a high school. At other times she thought he just felt like a fish out of water, not sure of his welcome even in the faculty lounge. Or maybe he just thought people would be more comfortable if he wasn't around. She didn't have a good read on him yet.

His round face smiled as he greeted her. He was about fifty pounds overweight, and his lunch consisted of a few slices of lean chicken over a bed of fresh vegetables. He had confided that he was dieting without much success. She looked at that lunch and felt a pang of sympathy.

"Still starving?" she asked him.

"Unfortunately. The doc says I've lost two pounds, though, so I guess it's working. Some days I'm not sure it's worth it."

"I can imagine."

He leaned back, ignoring the dry salad and chicken in front of him, a meal that cried out for a little salad dressing or mayonnaise to help it go down. "Is something wrong? You look…disturbed." He waved her to the seat in front of his desk.

She sat, trying to gather her thoughts, trying to maintain a calm she was far from feeling. "I am upset," she admitted. "I saw an instance of bullying in the boys' room. I stopped it, but when I tried to bring the bullies to you, they told me I couldn't make them and they brushed past me. Les, you know bullying is a violation of the conduct code."

"How bad was it?"

"They were spitting on him and calling him names. He was cowering on the floor in a corner as if he expected to be hit or kicked."

He frowned. "That's bad. That's very bad. All of it. Who were they after?"

"James Carney."

He shook his head. "I can't say I'm surprised. Some people just seem to draw that kind of attention."

"All it takes is being a little different."

"And James is certainly that. Smarter than most, small. Did you know he skipped a grade last year? I don't think that's helped him any but his parents and a committee of teachers felt we couldn't hold him back. Maybe we should have."

"We shouldn't have to," she argued, getting a little hot. "That boy should be free to move ahead if he's capable without four other boys attacking him for it."

Les nodded slowly. "Can you identify the bullies?"

"By face, not by name. They must be in Mrs. Teasdale's math classes."

"If they're still in math at all." He sighed. "How would you prefer to handle it?"

"The rules call for suspension," she reminded him. When he didn't answer immediately, she started to feel both annoyed and nervous. Surely he wasn't going to propose they simply ignore this?

Marian stuck her head in the door. "James Carney never went to the nurse." Then she popped out again.

"So he must be all right," Les remarked.

"That doesn't make this all go away!"

Les lifted his brows and held up a hand. "I didn't say that. I'm just relieved the Carney boy is okay."

"*Physically* okay," Cassie said almost sarcastically. "I'm sure I don't need to educate you on the other effects of bullying."

"Of course not." He sounded almost sharp. "I'm as well-informed as you on the subject. That's why it's against our code of conduct."

She tried to dial back her irritation. "I'm sorry. It just upset me, and then when they defied me that way, I got even more concerned. If they're not going to listen to a teacher, how are we going to stop this? And what are we going to do about it?"

Les leaned forward, shoving his lunch to one side. He rested his forearms on his desk. "I don't think suspensions would be prudent, not yet."

"What?" She was horrified and still sickened by what

she had seen. "We can't just ignore this. And we can't ignore the rules if we expect them to have any force."

"Just hold on a minute and calm down a bit. I understand you're upset and I understand why. You have every reason to be upset. But this isn't a big-city school. I don't favor zero tolerance for a very good reason. Kids will be kids...."

She started to open her mouth but he waved her to silence.

"Just hear me out, Cassie. I'm not excusing what they did. It was wrong. No question. No argument. But we have to ask ourselves what will be the best way to handle this with the least amount of damage."

It took her a moment and a deep breath, but finally she relaxed. "Okay, I'm listening."

"We aren't going to tolerate bullying. You and I agree on that. But we have to ask ourselves how much damage we might do with our response. You must have noticed by now that not many of our students go on to college. Some of that is because they have the family business waiting for them the day they graduate. Some is because folks simply can't afford it. We have a handful who get scholarships and an equally small handful who can afford it. Most of our students who get any further schooling do it at the local community college."

She nodded. All of this had been explained at the time she was hired.

"So we have to ask ourselves," Les said patiently, "whether we want to do something that might make a student choose to drop out, or that might damage a student's ability to get a college scholarship. We've got a couple, I'm sure you know, who are poised to get athletic scholarships. Suspension would take that away."

It was then that she made a mental connection and knew who one of the bullies was. "One of them was our star basketball forward."

Les lowered his head. "Cripes. Now you're talking about the state championship and a boy's entire future. He's looking good to get a basketball scholarship. Recruiters have been here several times."

"He should have thought of that before he started bullying James Carney."

"I agree. But he's still seventeen. You remember being that age? How many times did you think things through, especially when you were with a group of people your age? That's what bothers me about zero tolerance. Why wreck any kid's life if we can handle it another way?"

Cassie bit her lip. She wasn't exactly a fan of zero tolerance herself, understanding that young people made mistakes almost as naturally as they breathed. "But this is a little different," she argued. "This was no mistake. Four of them ganged up on one student. I don't know how far they might have gone if I hadn't barged in. And we have to consider James Carney and what this might do to him."

"I am considering it," Les said. "I want it stopped, but I don't want it to result in additional bullying or anybody's life being wrecked."

"So what will you do?"

"You identify those students. I'll call their parents and make it clear that if this happens again they will be suspended. In the meantime I'll give them detention."

Cassie felt sickened, yet she couldn't rightly argue with what he proposed. He *was* right. They had to be careful not to inflame the situation, and take care that they didn't cause students to drop out or lose scholarships, unless this continued.

"You're not happy," Les remarked. He poked at his lunch listlessly then ignored it again. "I understand. I'm not happy, either. We've always had some minor bullying—what school doesn't? But I don't think we've ever had an incident as bad as what you're describing, at least not in my memory. If you've got a better solution, let me know. Just understand, there are no perfect solutions. If I bring the hammer down too hard, that could result in James being bullied worse. We've got to try to reason our way through this to cause the least damage to all five of those students."

She said nothing, feeling her stomach sinking but unable to argue against his logic. "I hate bullying," she said finally. "It damages the victim well past the incident, sometimes for life. What's more, I hate the thuggish mentality of those who do it."

"Then maybe we need to do something about the mentality. It's not enough to just put a ban on it in the code. Maybe we need to use this as an instructional opportunity."

She perked a little at that statement. "How so?"

"We need to educate our students, maybe their families. We need them to truly understand how bad this is."

She nodded. "What those boys were doing could get them arrested."

It seemed to her that Les blanched a bit. "Oh, let's not go that far. Criminal records for assault? Battery, if it happened?"

"I don't want to do that, either," she agreed. "I'm just saying, if we can't get through with an emotional appeal to a sense of fair play and what's right, we could also list the criminal consequences. Bring it home. Maybe have a law enforcement officer tell them a few things."

Les smiled. "I can see you already have ideas. So what

I'd like is for you to get together with another teacher and come up with a plan for an assembly or two."

Cassie's mind immediately skipped ahead and was already summoning ideas for the assembly and maybe a long-term program. "Okay. Who do you suggest I work with?"

"Linc Blair. He's the most popular teacher with the students and seems to carry a lot of moral authority with them." Les gave a little laugh. "More than I do, certainly. Yes, I'll explain the situation to Linc at the end of the day and see if he's willing. In the meantime, try to get the bullies' names for me. I want to spend some time on the phone with parents."

He paused. "God, I hope this isn't resulting from things that are happening to these boys at home."

It could well be, Cassie thought as she left his office a few minutes later. Bullies were sometimes created.

Why did she feel as if she might be about to overturn a rock and discover some ugly things?

If there was any upside to this at all, she supposed it was that she would at last find out why Lincoln Blair avoided her as if she had the plague.

By close of school that day, she had the names of the four bullies. She had asked for the aid of other teachers, without explaining why she needed to know. List in hand, she headed for Les's office and found he was already talking to Linc. He waved her in to join them and she took the second chair that faced Les's desk.

"Cassie here can give you more detail," Les said, "given that she's the one who broke it up."

She looked at Linc and noted the way those startling blue eyes of his met hers then swiftly looked away.

"I have the students' names," she said quickly, passing her list to Les.

He took it almost as if it might bite him, then muttered a word no teacher was allowed to use within the school. "Ben Hastings," he said. "Damn, why did it have to be Ben?"

"He never struck me as the bullying type," Linc remarked.

Cassie started to bristle. "I didn't make up the names."

Linc glanced her way again. "I didn't say you did. I'm just surprised. As high a profile as he has because of his basketball skills, I would have thought that if he were a bully we'd have known long ago. That's all I meant."

Cassie caught herself, realizing that she was taking everything too personally. She'd been upset about James all afternoon, and if she were honest, she suspected some of that had to do with some bullying she had endured when she'd been a plump adolescent. Boys and even some girls had picked on her weight mercilessly.

"As far as I know," Les said, "the worst cases of bullying we've had in the district have been in the elementary and middle schools. A few fights, name-calling, some blows. But it seems to get better by this age. Or at least less extreme."

"Things have changed," Linc remarked. "We got a lot of new people in town when the semiconductor plant opened, and even after the layoffs there are still a lot of students who didn't grow up around here. That creates a different kind of tension."

Les lifted a brow. "In what way?"

"Outsiders versus insiders. It used to be most of these incidents could be worked out between families who had a stake in keeping things friendly. It's not like that anymore, and new kids make obvious targets. James Carney is a new kid, for one thing, despite the fact he was born here. The family just moved back after years away. He's also a serious student, he's small and he isn't involved in sports. Very much an outsider. He makes easy pickings for a pack."

"So what are you saying?"

Linc leaned forward. "I'm saying we have to nip this in the bud. We can't allow serious bullying to go unchallenged or we'll have more of it. I get why you're reluctant to suspend these students. Hell, it'll probably just make the whole thing worse for James Carney, and maybe even for Ms. Greaves here."

"Cassie," she said automatically, as she waited to hear where he was taking this.

"Cassie," he repeated with barely a glance in her direction. "Look, Les, we have a different dynamic now from anything we're used to around here. We've got new kids, new ones who don't have to go home at night and help in the family ranch or business. Kids who are, relatively speaking, on easy street. They get fancy electronics, most have newer cars, and if they take jobs it's for pin money. What makes you think that isn't going to breed resentment?"

Les's frown had deepened and Cassie felt her stomach turn over. Under no circumstances did she want to see another incident like she had today. The memory still sickened her, the sight of James cowering and those boys spitting on him.

"I've been watching the changes take hold," Linc continued. "A lot of the new kids are going to go to college. They're not going to stay here. The other students know it. Outsiders just passing through. We've been having more and more instances of division, separate groups forming, and some name-calling. Why the hell else do you think I have a zero-tolerance policy on bullying for my football players? I never used to need one, but I've made it clear over the last couple of years that one instance of bullying is enough to get a player thrown off the team."

"You're not proposing we suspend all these students!"

"Not yet," Linc said quietly, sitting back. "But your idea of starting an antibullying program is a good one. We've got to educate before this gets out of hand. And it will get out of hand. The bullying won't just be going in one direction, either. The factions have been forming. We can't let the divisions get any deeper or uglier."

As she listened, Cassie got an inkling of why Linc was so well-liked and respected by students and faculty alike. He seemed to truly have his finger on the pulse of this school.

"How do you know all this?" she asked.

"I pay attention. My students talk to me." He gave her the briefest of smiles. "I've been around a while, too. It's easier for me to see what's happening than it would be for you, or even for Les. He doesn't have as much student interaction as I do."

"So we start a program?" she asked.

"Definitely. As for what happened today, I'm concerned. It's one thing when you see this among third graders or even seventh graders. But these students are on the cusp of adulthood. In the spring or in another year they're going to walk out of here men. They should be past this by now. Sure, they might have little shoving matches, or call a name or two when they get annoyed, but this kind of ganging-up should be well behind them. We're going to have to tread carefully so we don't make things worse."

Cassie spoke. "So you agree with the way Les wants to handle it?"

"We have to do *something*. From the minute you walked in on it, from the instant they ignored your authority as a teacher, we haven't had a choice. There has to be a statement made, punishment doled out. We can't let anyone think they can get away with any of that. But I'd really like it if we could find a way that wouldn't cause more grief for James Carney."

"He didn't do anything," Cassie said. "He wouldn't even talk to me. In fact, he said I was making it worse. If they want to be mad at someone, it should be me."

Les spoke. "We can make the detentions about the way they treated Ms. Greaves and nothing else."

Linc looked at her, really looked at her, for the first time, and she felt an electric shock all the way to her toes. "How *did* they treat you exactly?"

"Well, it wasn't just that they wouldn't come with me to the principal's office. When they passed me to get out the door, they made sure to bump into me, and it wasn't exactly just brushing by."

Linc's dark brows lifted. "That's definitely not good."

Les slapped his hand on the desk. "We can't let that pass under any circumstances. We'll have anarchy."

"But this isn't about me," Cassie protested.

"It is now," Linc answered. "You just got bullied, too." He sighed. "Okay, this is how I see it. Leaving out the gruesome details for now, put the bullies on detention for ignoring Ms. Greaves—Cassie. Make it about ignoring a teacher's direction. We'll get to the rest of it as we go, but for now let's take the spotlight off James Carney. Maybe they'll duck and leave him alone since he won't be the source of their headache for the time being."

Cassie turned the incident around in her mind, remembering the way those students had bumped her shoulder on their way out. It had been a little more than disrespectful. Almost like a hinted threat. Linc was right, *she* had been bullied, too. A little flicker of anger started burning in the pit of her stomach.

"I don't want to make Cassie an inadvertent target," Les said.

Cassie shifted in her chair. "Look, Les, we can't let this go. What do you think those students will do to me, anyway? They can get as mad as they want. Surely you aren't suggesting they'd physically hurt me."

Les looked shocked. "No, of course not. You're a *teacher*."

Cassie didn't think that was much protection, but on the other hand she figured these students wouldn't want the veritable hell that would come their way if they treated her the way they had treated James.

Linc spoke. "Just make it clear to them that it's unacceptable to ignore a teacher, and then add something about how touching her, so much as *touching,* however briefly, is a crime called battery. I don't think any of them is stupid enough to ignore that."

"I agree," said Cassie. "Let's get this program going, give the students detention for ignoring me, call their parents about their behavior and see how much help you'll get. Keeping the spotlight off James is the best thing to do. I don't want them turning on him any more than they already have. He's the one in most need of protection."

"Okay then." Linc rose from his chair, an almost iconic figure in old jeans, cowboy boots and a faded chambray shirt. "I've got to get to the locker room again before the team wonders if I fell off the edge of the planet. We have an away game tonight." Then he turned his attention to Cassie. "Are you okay with this? Really?"

"Being the center of the storm? Of course. Those bullies don't frighten me, they make me mad."

One corner of his mouth ticked up in a smile. "I'll give you a call tomorrow morning and we'll set up some meeting time to get this ball rolling."

He strode out, and Cassie's gaze followed him helplessly. Wow, she thought, he was going to call her. Maybe she didn't stink as bad as she sometimes thought. Les called her attention back.

"If you're okay with this, then that's how we'll handle the matter for right now. But not for too long. I don't want those students to think they're going to get away with bullying anybody."

"I couldn't agree more." Finally feeling satisfied with the direction they were taking, she said goodbye to Les, picked up her book bag and headed out for the weekend.

The day was still glorious, although twilight wasn't far away. Winter nights came a lot earlier up here than she was used to.

But instead of thinking about the glorious weather or the relaxing weekend ahead, she was thinking about Linc Blair again. Dang, he almost acted like it hurt to even look at her. Had she turned ugly since yesterday?

Shaking her head, she tried to think of other things. Despite her reaction in the principal's office, she wasn't entirely easy about transferring the bullies' anger toward her.

She had taught in a school where a teacher had been attacked by a student, and she didn't labor under any delusions that her status protected her. On the other hand, bullies were usually cowards at heart.

It would be okay, she assured herself.

But it would be even nicer to know why Linc seemed so determined to keep such an obvious distance. He didn't even make the normal friendly overtures to her, like the other teachers.

No, it was as if he, or she, were surrounded by some kind of repulsion field. *Keep away* seemed to bristle all over him.

It probably hurt more than it should have because of her bad experiences in the past. Guys seemed attracted to her just long enough to find out if she was willing to jump in the sack with them, and then either way they made a fast exit. It was, one of her friends admitted, weird. But the same friend had reminded her that dating was a series of "noes" followed by one "yes," eventually.

But never before had she met a guy who seemed to see poison every time his gaze scraped over her and then headed elsewhere.

Not that it mattered, she reminded herself. He was just another guy, albeit one who got her hormones racing every time she looked at him. But just another guy.

And maybe the problem wasn't her at all. After all, he had said he would call her tomorrow about the bullying program.

No, maybe it wasn't her at all.

With that hopeful thought in mind, she hurried home to start dinner and get to the homework papers she needed to check. With any luck, all she'd have left to do by tomorrow was some lesson planning.

The thought brightened her mood a bit, easing the memory of the way James Carney had been cowering.

They were going to help him, and other bullied students. Wasn't that all that really mattered?

Chapter 2

Linc headed home after the game. It was late because the next high school was so far away, a major problem for running athletics in this part of the country. Ordinarily they avoided night games because of the travel time involved, but this week had been different because the other high school had some construction work going on over the weekend.

They'd gotten their usual shellacking at the other school's hands, though. Nothing different there. Busby somehow always managed to field a stellar team.

But, as he kept telling his players, winning wasn't the point. Playing the game was. As long as they loved to play, the rest didn't matter. Sometimes he wondered if they believed him. Regardless, he always had plenty of students turn up for spring tryouts.

But after he shepherded them off the buses and toward their waiting parents, making sure everyone got a ride home, he still had a forty-five-minute drive of his own to his ranch, and some animals waiting for him.

The sheep and goats were okay in their fenced meadows, watched by the dogs, who were probably wondering by now when they'd see their next bowl of kibble. He had a couple of horses in a corral he never left out overnight, but always safely stalled in the barn. It wouldn't take him long, but he was beginning to feel weary. He started his days at five in the morning, taking care of livestock, and finished at one-thirty in the morning…well, he was getting damn tired.

As the noise of the game and the racket from the players on the team bus began to fade from his immediate memory, along with a running analysis of how the team could improve, Cassie Greaves popped up before his eyes.

Damn, that woman was stunning. Not in a movie-star sort of way, but more like a…a what? Earth mother? She was full-figured enough to qualify, he supposed, though he wouldn't classify her as heavy. No, she was luxuriously built, exactly the kind of female form that had always appealed to him. With bobbed honey-blond hair and witchy green eyes, she was a looker. Every time he glanced at her, he felt swamped by desire. Amazing, almost like he was in high school himself.

But he'd lived his entire life in this county, and he knew how many people came here, thinking they'd found something wonderful, and then after one winter packed up and left because of the cold, the isolation, the lack of excitement. Hell, even people who grew up here left so why wouldn't people who didn't have any roots?

Some people didn't find enough excitement in days filled with work or with people they saw every day. His own fiancée had headed out after just two years here, swearing she would die from boredom. She probably would have, too, he had finally admitted. Who wanted a life with a guy who was either tied up at his job or working a ranch? Much fun he was.

So he just tried to avoid the whole thing. When it came to a woman who attracted him the way Cassie did, a woman who hadn't even survived her first winter here, his guard slammed up like some kind of shield in a science fiction movie.

But he was getting to the point of appearing rude, and that had to stop. When Les had asked him to work on this project with her, he'd had the worst urge to refuse. Proximity with *that* woman?

But then his better angels had taken over. He and Cassie had to deal with this bullying before it got any worse. And it would if they didn't find a way to get through to these students. Ignoring it because "kids will be kids" was a recipe for serious problems. Yes, they'd do it. Most of them probably had bullied at one time or another, and most had probably been the victims of it.

But the problem still couldn't be ignored. That was one thing educators and psychologists had learned over the last few decades. And with the dynamic he'd been watching develop between the students, he suspected that it could get way out of hand.

As the incident had today. As upset as he was for the Carney kid, he also saw a big danger in the way those boys had treated Cassie. So he'd bite the bullet, keep his guard up and do what he could to get the students to understand that bullying wasn't funny, it wasn't a joke, and it was never permissible.

He was glad, though, to reach his ranch and deal with the dogs and the horses. They centered him, these animals he kept. Reminded him he was part of nature, too, and that a lot of nature was actually prettier than human nature.

After he'd greeted, petted, stabled and fed, he went inside and made himself a bowl of instant oatmeal. It had been a long time since dinner, and while team parents made sure there were plenty of snacks and water for the players, he was usually too uptight to eat at all during a game. He was like a father with thirty sons on the field or bench.

Sitting at the kitchen table, eating his solitary oatmeal, he noticed for the first time in a long time just how silent the house was. He'd noticed it after his father had died eight years ago, and he'd noticed it again when Martha had left her engagement ring on this very table.

Silence, usually a good companion given his busy days, sometimes seemed lonely and empty. Tonight it definitely felt empty.

This big old house had been meant for a large family. Built back around the turn of the twentieth century, he had only to look at old family photos to know how full it had been at one time. His great-grandfather must have kept awfully busy expanding the place as well as running the ranch and farm. But after the Second World War, youngsters had moved away. The G.I. Bill had offered them different opportunities, and only his own grandfather had chosen to remain after returning from the South Pacific.

So the old days of a dozen kids had trailed away, his grandmother had born only one child that survived, and then his own mother had died giving birth to him, and his dad had never remarried.

From many to just him. Sometimes when he walked around and counted dusty, empty bedrooms, and imagined what this place might have been like in its heyday, he felt the lack of human contact. Five years ago he'd tried a family reunion, met some of his great-uncles and cousins he hardly knew, and some he'd never met, and after a rush of "we have to keep in touch" from everyone, keeping in touch had ended when they left town. They felt no ties to this place, or to him.

He didn't blame them for that. Time had moved on, and with it so had their lives, which were so far removed now from this thinly populated county that he was sure most of them couldn't imagine why he remained.

But his roots were very real to him. He felt them dig deeper every time he walked the land, or tended to his livestock, or even did a repair around the house. He was a man of this land and he wanted no other.

Martha couldn't grasp it, either, although for a while she had tried. He just hadn't guessed how hard she was trying. Maybe it had been easier for her when everything was new and fresh. Then it had become all humdrum and endless for her, a routine that never changed. He supposed he was to blame for at least some of that, but the fact was, he had two jobs, one teaching, the other tending this place, and he couldn't simply ignore either one. Animals needed daily care. A teaching job required hours not only at school, but also in the evenings and on weekends.

All work and no play apparently had made Linc a very dull boy, he thought. He needed, he supposed, to find a woman from around here who understood the demands and isolation, someone who could be self-sufficient in more ways than Martha. Someone who would be willing to lend her shoulder to the ranch work and make it part of her life, too.

So far no luck. Judging by his attraction to Cassie Greaves, that was most likely his own fault. He never seemed to be drawn to women who had lived here all their lives. Maybe that was his own form of looking for something different. Whatever, it had left his life very empty.

He rinsed his bowl and spoon and put them in the dishwasher Martha had insisted he install. It was a bit much for just one person, and he could go a week without running it, but it was convenient when he didn't feel like washing up after himself. There were days like that, days that were just too long for one reason or another, especially during football season.

Upstairs after his shower, he stood naked in his chilly bedroom and looked out over the moon-drenched fields. There were no curtains any longer. Martha had taken down the ones that had been there at least since his mother had hung them, and replaced them with something she considered cheerier. She hadn't been gone long when he ripped them down and got rid of all the other reminders.

A childish act, part of him judged, but necessary. He didn't need reminders greeting him everywhere he went. Not reminders of Martha, anyway.

The air was getting downright frigid, but he ignored an impulse to turn on the heat. Once he climbed beneath the quilts he'd be warm enough for the night. In the morning he'd deal with seeing his breath and having to dress quickly in clothes that felt as if they'd been in a freezer all night.

Conservation. He preached it to his students, and practiced it himself. Like the compost pile out near the barn. Nothing wasted. He'd been raised that way, and rightfully so. So had many of his students, though not all.

He figured he had a good life in all, and was achieving some good ends, mostly. But nights like this, when the moon was full and the house so silent, he felt he could howl at the moon for a mate. Man was not meant to be solitary.

He shook his head at the turn of his thoughts and went to climb beneath the heap of quilts on his bed, quilts made by generations of women in his family. Heat tomorrow, he decided as his skin met icy sheets. Definitely. He was not going to be a happy camper come morning.

He shivered for a while until his cocoon warmed up. Closing his eyes against the bright moonlight, he thought again of Cassie Greaves. Why did she have to be such a tempting armful?

But surely he knew better now. Nevertheless, thoughts of Cassie seemed to warm that cocoon of quilts faster than usual.

Cassie awoke in a better frame of mind than when she had gone to bed the night before. As awful as the bullying she had seen had appeared to be, she was confident that with some education and a reminder of penalties they could probably lessen the problems.

And giving the boys detention for how they had ignored her should help remove James from the firing line. They would know it all had to do with what they had been doing to James, but with the detentions arising from their treatment of her, they'd have nothing to add to their scorecard against James. She hoped.

By the time she was eating her yogurt and drinking her coffee, she felt good about the program Les had proposed, even though she and Linc hadn't started to work on it. In her experience, the important thing was to create a culture among students, and if possible among their parents, that frowned on bullying. So the question was not whether it would work, but how long it would take.

From what Linc had said yesterday, she gathered there had been a major change in dynamics owing to the new people who had moved here with the semiconductor plant. She'd already heard that sad story of boom and bust. While the plant hadn't closed down when the recession hit, it had laid off quite a few people. A lot of lives had undoubtedly been hurt or destroyed.

But on the other hand, whatever had brought about the social dichotomy in the school, this wasn't the first time she had seen it. Sometimes it was about race. Sometimes it was about who was a "townie" and who was a "military brat." Sometimes it was just about how you dressed and who you hung around with. Kids could find ample reasons to form cliques and exclusive groups. It seemed to be part of human nature in general.

But it could be contained and controlled. Courtesy, which she thought of as the grease on the wheels of life, could be learned, and could overlay baser impulses.

The problem would be one of motivation.

She hoped Linc would have some idea of what would motivate these students, because she didn't know the student body well enough yet and this was a rather late point in their education to start something that should have begun in the earliest grades.

Linc again. She supposed it would be wise to castigate herself for wasting so much thought and energy on thinking about a man who was making it as plain as day that he'd prefer not to get to know her even casually. Work with her? Yes. Anything else, not so much.

Still, she couldn't help wandering into the bedroom to look at herself in the full-length mirror, something she usually avoided. She was plump, yes, but much as she would have liked to be built like a model or movie star, that wasn't in her genetic makeup. She didn't think she looked *that* bad, anyway. Plenty of guys had made passes at her. Full-figured but not ugly was her pronouncement. Problem was, she didn't quite believe the "not ugly" part.

Stifling a sigh, she bathed and dressed in a flannel shirt and jeans, caught her hair up in a short ponytail, and dug out her planning books. Yesterday had pretty much driven everything else out of her mind, and she needed to come up with some kind of new, hands-on project that would teach math in a real-world way.

It had, she admitted, been easier to come up with things at the start of the year, but as the weeks passed, ideas had become thinner on the ground. She scanned the topics to be covered that week, seeking some fertile soil. Unfortunately, she didn't think most of her students were quite ready to enjoy math for the sake of math.

She was searching around on her computer looking for ideas that might work with at least some of what she would teach this week, when the phone rang. She answered, her heart lifting a bit, expecting to hear Linc's voice.

Instead what she heard was a deep, angry voice. "Stay out of what doesn't concern you, bitch, or you'll pay."

Before her jaw could even drop, the other party had disconnected. At once she pressed the caller ID button, but it told her only that the call had come from Wyoming. Great help.

She sat there, staring at her phone, shaken. Just words, she told herself. Just an empty threat. But she couldn't quite persuade herself of that. Her stomach kept flipping nervously, and she'd have given just about anything to call back and give that man a piece of her mind. It would have relieved her anxiety just to be able to yell at him.

Just as anger began to seriously overtake uneasiness, the phone rang again. Without even looking to see who it was, she snapped, "What?"

There was a pause. Finally Linc's familiar voice said, "Cassie?"

At once embarrassment filled her. "Sorry," she said, aware that her voice had thickened, "I just got a nasty call. I thought it was another one."

A moment of silence. "What kind of nasty call?"

"Telling me to stay out of things that don't concern me, with an implied threat and a bit of name-calling. It's nothing, it just made me mad."

He didn't reply directly. "Are you going out?"

"No, I'm doing my weekly planning."

"I'll be there in forty-five minutes."

Then he was gone, leaving her to wonder what had lit the fire under him. Surely the call, as annoying as it had been, didn't require immediate action. Heck, she didn't even know for sure what it was about.

Then it struck her that Linc was on his way over. She hurried into her bedroom and changed into something more attractive than the baggy clothes she had been working in. Nothing too much, just a more attractive blouse with a pair of reasonably new jeans. Another brushing of her hair, a tiny—just tiny—dab of makeup around her eyes and some gloss on her lips.

Then she started a fresh pot of coffee, since somehow she had managed to drink most of it while working this morning. That much caffeine? It struck her that that might have caused the stomach flips as much as the phone call.

She threw open a window to let in some of the fresh, chilly air, then tried to return her attention to her planning. It didn't work. All she could think about was Lincoln Blair coming here. Imagining him walking through her door. Wondering how he would be able to keep up that shield he seemed so determined to place between them while they were working on a project.

God, was she really thinking like this at the age of thirty? That man had truly gotten to her, yet what did she really know about him? That he looked good enough to model on a magazine? That he was popular with both faculty and students?

That meant nothing, really. Nothing. She gave herself a firm mental shake and told herself to remember that she was simply going to be meeting him to work on a project, something she had done countless times before with teachers she found attractive or not-so attractive. So what the hey?

Despite her best efforts, she couldn't help being a little nervous anyway. If he arrived here packed in his personal brand of refrigerant, she didn't know how she would manage. Yes, she had worked with difficult people before, but there was difficult and then there was *difficult*.

Cussing silently, she waited for her doorbell to ring, giving up hope of focusing on her work. Instead she looked around her little office, the house's one spare bedroom, and decided she liked what she had so far been able to do with it. Little by little she was transforming the place into a home that reflected her love of bright color and handmade crafts. Some items she had brought with her, and some she had discovered since arriving here, at a little hole-in-the-wall place that seemed left over from an earlier century.

Finally Linc arrived. Butterflies fluttered wildly in her stomach as she went to open the door.

Her memory had not exaggerated his Celtic-warrior good looks, not one bit. He stood there in a light jacket, jeans and his usual chambray shirt—it was almost a uniform. On his head sat a felt cowboy hat that looked as if it had seen better days.

"Howdy," he said.

His deep voice seemed to pluck a string inside her and make it vibrate. She very nearly forgot to invite him in, then realized she was in danger of standing there like a starstruck kid.

"Come on in," she said. "You didn't have to race over here, you know." Not that she was exactly objecting.

"Probably not, but we needed to meet anyway." He stepped inside and looked around her cozy living room. He surprised her with his choice of words. "Very inviting," he said approvingly.

"That's what I hope," she said as she closed the door behind him. "Coffee?"

"Love some."

He followed her into the kitchen, and as naturally as if he belonged here, he pulled out a chair at her dinette and sat. She filled two mugs, vaguely remembering from school that he liked his black.

"We could go to my office in the back," she suggested.

"This is fine for now."

As if he didn't want to get any deeper into her life or her house. Feeling a bit stung, she placed his coffee in front of him and sat facing him.

"So I started thinking about this program," she began.

He shook his head a little. "In a minute, Cassie. First I want to hear more about that phone call."

As if a switch flipped in her head, she heard that angry, deep voice again. "What's there to say? I told you what he said. He sounded angry, and threatening, but it was just a phone call. It's easy to make anonymous threats."

"It may be easy, but it's seldom pointless. Somebody's

angry with you, and I doubt that many people know yet about what happened yesterday. The boys involved, maybe their parents if Les has already called them all. Maybe a few people they talked to."

She shook her head. "Nothing has happened. Nobody has been suspended. If this stops, nobody *gets* suspended. Scholarships are protected and so is the almighty state championship. If anyone hoped for anything from that call, it's that I wouldn't push this into a suspension."

He set his mug down. "I agree. Essentially. What's troubling me is the way you got treated yesterday. Your authority was ignored, you were pushed, not just brushed by, and now today a threatening call. That incident yesterday was unusually aggressive for students that age. I'm not saying they never get past name-calling and the occasional spat, but like I said yesterday, by this age they're mostly past ganging up and getting physical. Add that to the way they treated you and I'm concerned, that's all."

She thought it over for a moment. "Then maybe I'm not the best choice to help with this antibullying campaign. If I'm seen as just a troublesome outsider, the message may be lost."

"You're not doing this alone," he reminded her.

No, she wasn't. She had tried to avoid meeting his gaze directly, but now she did, and felt as if she were falling into the depths of the incredible blue of his eyes. An almost electric spark seemed to zap her.

Then he broke eye contact, returning his attention to his mug. "I spent some time this morning exploring the subject," he said. "Unfortunately, I have a dial-up connection out there and the internet moves like molasses."

"I've got broadband. We can use my computer."

"Or go to the school."

She sensed he wanted to be out of her house and into a more neutral environment as quickly as possible. Again she felt that sting, but did her best to ignore it. No point creating a Shakespearean tragedy in her own mind.

"Sure, if you want," she said quickly. "Let me get my jacket."

Five minutes later, with a couple of her travel mugs filled with coffee for the two of them, they stepped outside into a brisk morning. Fluffy white clouds raced overhead in a cerulean sky.

"God, it's beautiful here," she said.

"Really?"

She glanced at him. "Don't tell me you don't notice."

"Well, I actually do, especially out at my ranch." For the first time he cracked a genuine smile.

It almost took her breath away. Of course she'd seen him smile on occasion around school, but never had the full wattage been directed her way. Warmth drizzled through her all the way to her toes, and she had to fight to collect her thoughts.

"What do you raise?" she asked as he helped her into his battered pickup, a truck that might have once been a bright red, but now was dulled with age and liberal applications of touch-up paint.

"Actually my dogs do the raising," he said humorously as he climbed in behind the wheel. "They do a damn good job of looking after my sheep and goats. And I have a few horses. It's not much, but it's all I can handle while I'm teaching."

"Why do you keep on doing it?"

"I enjoy it, for one thing. For another, that place has been in my family for over a hundred years. I'm not going to be the one to give it up."

She could understand that, although it was hard to imagine. "You must feel a lot of loyalty."

A faint smile this time, directed out the windshield as he drove toward the school. "My family invested a lot of sweat in that place. It was *their* place in the world, and now it's my place. Maybe some day I'll have kids and they won't want it, but fact is, I'm rooted here until I die."

"That must be a good feeling."

"Sometimes." He hesitated. "You?"

"Rootless. I have no way to really understand how you must feel about your ranch. My mom moved us around the country a lot. I was lucky to finish high school in the same town where I started it."

"And you've continued the gypsy tradition?"

"You mean because I came here?"

"For one. But what about the past?"

"I've moved a lot, too. You want the truth? It's getting old. I've never known anyone for more than a few years, and then they get left behind. I started thinking about that, and it struck me that's a really lonely way to live."

"So you're looking for a place to stay permanently?"

"If I can find one."

"Why this place?"

"Because it feels right. Because after I'd spent a week here considering the job, I got the feeling that if I stayed long enough to become a part of the community, I could put down some really deep roots. People wouldn't be strangers on a busy street. They'd have names, and I'd get to know them at least a bit. That maybe someday I wouldn't be an outsider anymore."

"So you've always been an outsider?"

"I've never been anything else."

He fell silent, pulling into a faculty parking spot near

the west wing door. From here she could see the freshly painted and repaired roof and side wall. "Someone said a tornado hit the building?"

"Yeah, last spring. What a mess, but at least no one was killed. It just grazed the town, but the thing was a half mile wide. If you get out into the countryside you can still see the scars where it passed. At least no one was killed, although we had some injuries."

"Is that common here? Tornadoes?"

"It's really rare. I won't say never, but what we saw last spring was one for the record books."

"Nobody told me how bad it was."

He gave her an amused glance as he turned off the ignition. "They probably didn't want to scare you away."

"I've lived in tornado country. It wouldn't panic me. I just prefer it if they're not common."

"They certainly aren't here."

As they climbed out and headed inside, she could hear sounds from the athletic fields on the other side of the building. "Practice today?"

"Not until later. I think some youngsters must be playing on the outdoor basketball courts." He unlocked the door and held it open for her.

"Why would the school have outdoor courts? I never got that."

"Only the team and supervised students get to play basketball in the gymnasium. Outdoors is for fun and practice."

"That's really a nice idea." But she couldn't help thinking he had brought her to this side of the school in case some of the basketball players were out there. Or some of the kids she had interrupted yesterday. She doubted he was afraid of any of them, so he must be trying to avoid giving her a moment of discomfort. A generous thought, but really not necessary. She liked to believe she was tougher than that.

They wended their way through virtually empty hallways. In the distance they could hear a janitor working with a buffer, but other than that the place seemed abandoned.

He took her to his office just off the gymnasium, not to his homeroom. She guessed it made sense that he'd have two offices given that he wore two hats at the school.

It wasn't a huge space, but it contained enough room for maybe half-a-dozen students to gather with him, and a counter where he had a coffeepot and microwave.

"This is positively homey," she tried to joke.

"Given their age, high metabolism and activity level, it takes a lot of effort to keep those young men fed. That microwave gets a megaworkout."

"I bet."

He cleared a stack of papers to one side, pulled a chair around so she could see his computer screen and turned on the machine.

"Okay," he said. "You've worked in a lot of different places. How familiar are you with antibullying programs? How much do you already know about the dangers of bullying?"

"Some," she admitted. "In one of the schools where I worked, the program had been in place for at least ten years. It started in kindergarten, actually, and was covered every single year."

"What were the important mechanisms?"

"First, faculty and administration. It's so important for teachers not to ignore bullying, to listen to student complaints about it and do something, and for the administration to be fully involved. You get nowhere if the adults in the school brush it off."

He nodded, his blue eyes touching lightly on her face before returning to the computer screen. She wondered, half-humorously, if he would have liked to dive into the monitor to escape. "And the students?"

"We tried to create a culture where bullying was frowned on. You know as well as I do that peer pressure is more important to youngsters than anything adults do or say. So if you can persuade the students to self-police, to look down on bullies, you can stop a lot of it."

"That's going to be the hard part."

"No kidding. Changing a culture takes time. One assembly won't do it, it'll just get the ball rolling. This is going to have to be an ongoing program."

"Where do you suggest we start?"

She liked that he was looking to her for advice. Even in this supposedly more equal time, she was used to men just taking over and directing projects. She'd always put it down to testosterone or something, but maybe it wasn't. Linc didn't strike her as short on testosterone or manliness, come to that.

"Ideally," she said slowly, "we'd like to get the cooperation of students who are looked up to. The tone-setters."

"Like some of my players."

"Exactly. They can be our first peer-pressure group, the guys and gals most of the other students respect."

"We need to get across how dangerous this really is. It's not just a matter of scaring or upsetting another student."

"No," she agreed. "It can have lifelong consequences. It can cause posttraumatic stress disorder. And have you looked at the rate of teen suicide? A lot of those can be linked directly to bullying."

"We've definitely got our work cut out for us. First to get the staff and a core of students on our side. Once we have the kernels we'll need to help them grow."

Then he looked at her. "Have you ever been bullied?"

"Of course. Most people have been."

"Badly?"

She hesitated then sighed. "I guess. I got picked on a lot for my weight."

He astonished her then. "I don't see anything wrong with your weight. Were you heavier back then?"

"Actually, not by much."

He shook his head. "Amazing. I would have thought most men would have thought you were gorgeous."

Her jaw dropped but he had already turned away. "I wondered," he said, returning to the subject at hand, "because you didn't seem to take the way those guys brushed against you as bullying. Almost as if it were normal."

"I didn't think of it that way," she admitted. "It was a little strong but I didn't feel intimidated."

Blue eyes settled on her again. "Really? But that's what they intended, don't you think? Letting you know that they were bigger and stronger and not afraid to push?"

She bit her lip, considering it. "I guess so. There was no other reason for it. They didn't frighten me, though. I just got angrier."

"Somebody sure tried to frighten you this morning." He frowned then and leaned back a bit in his chair, as if thinking things over. "I don't like this," he said. "Bullying in general, of course, but I don't like the way it seems to have escalated, judging by what you saw and what you experienced. Some element is getting way out of line and we need to yank them back as quickly as possible."

"Maybe it's just the four I caught in the act. Maybe it isn't a trend at all."

One corner of his mouth tipped up, and his eyes scraped over her briefly. "You're quite the optimist. I'm more inclined to think this is the tip of the iceberg. These things don't usually happen in total isolation."

She rested her chin on her hand. "You might be right."

"I hope I'm not," he admitted. "Unfortunately, I've been watching that steady fracturing I mentioned yesterday ever since the semiconductor plant arrived. Little by little a line has been drawn. And when you start drawing lines, how long is it before the people on the other side of the line from you become objects of your scorn?"

"You may be right."

"Basic social dynamics. We've always gone to war over our differences. A school is just a microcosm." He shook his head. "Don't let me start thinking about humanity as a whole. Right now we need to deal with a front-and-center neighborhood problem with as little scarring and fallout as possible."

She gave a laugh. "Yeah, we can't reform humanity in a day, or a school in even a week. How do you want to approach this?"

He took the task of finding the students for his core peer group, and she agreed to set about finding materials that they could use in a more public venue.

Then he rose, stretched and said, "I've got a team meeting in a little while. I'll drive you home."

"I prefer to walk, but thanks."

"Then I'll walk with you."

His words stilled her. "You really *are* worried about that call."

"I wouldn't say I'm worried, but a little caution might be wise until we see if you get harassed again."

She felt an instant of rebellion. She was an independent woman who felt perfectly capable of taking care of herself, and she didn't need a white knight to protect her. On the other hand, it would mean a little extra time with him, which she wouldn't mind. Maybe she could get past the force field a little.

Pulling on her jacket, she remarked, "I thought this was a friendly, nice county."

"It is, mostly. But like any other place on the planet, not everyone is nice."

Outside, the air still had that wonderful crisp feel of fall, and she almost thought she could smell snow in the air even though the sun was bright. After he locked the door, they began to stroll toward her house, carrying the travel mugs. He didn't seem to be in a hurry.

"How do you like living here so far?" he asked.

"I'm loving it, actually."

"Not dying for lack of nightclubs, theaters and huge shopping malls?"

She laughed. "Not at all. I've never enjoyed mall-crawling, for one thing. I'm always looking for little out-of-the way places full of different things."

"We have plenty of those."

"I've noticed. It's one of the things that charmed me. I haven't been in a department store like Freitag's since I was a little kid. I get a kick out of having the wood floors creak under my feet. Besides, if you've seen one mall, you've pretty much seen them all. The homogenization of America. You can't tell what city you're in."

"That's my impression. But what about things to do?"

"There's plenty to do." She glanced at him, wondering

about the line of questioning. "I get together with some teachers to play cards a couple of times a month. We go out for lunch and sometimes dinner. I never liked the club scene. I guess most people would find me dull."

"Not around here."

"And if I ever get an overwhelming urge for a museum or the theater, I can take a weekend and go to Denver. Come on, Linc. You teach. You know how little free time you have."

He chuckled. "You're right. And there's even less with my ranch."

"And football," she reminded him. "Anyway, I really like it here so far. It's different from the places I lived before, but I'm finding it comfortable."

"I'll ask for your opinion again come early March."

She was laughing when he left her at her door, but his smile was faint, and she could almost hear the shield cranking back into place.

What was it with that man?

Sighing, she went inside, taking his advice to lock up behind herself, and decided she would probably never know.

Whatever his problem, Linc had clearly decided not to let her into his circle.

To hell with him, she thought, returning to work on her week's plans. She needed an idea to excite her students more than she needed him.

Chapter 3

Sunday night turned wildly windy and Cassie awoke to a Monday morning with steel-gray skies and air that felt surprisingly warm. The wind had taken the last of the leaves from the trees, and was still blowing them around as she walked to the school.

With no more phone calls, she felt the incident was closed. Over the weekend, though, she'd been texted by Les, the principal, asking that she and Linc speak to the faculty at the weekly meeting at the close of school that day.

Being the new kid on the block, as it were, she didn't feel entirely comfortable with that idea, and as she walked she realized she had a minor case of nerves going, the way she often did on the very first day of the school year. Great. She hoped she'd forget about it during the teaching day.

When she reached the school, she found Linc was still on bus duty. At least he smiled faintly when he opened the door for her.

"About this afternoon…" she began.

He nodded. "I can do most of the talking. I understand you don't want to come off like the new broom."

"Exactly. Thank you."

Another brief nod. "You just fill in when you think I've left something out. I managed to get some of the first few members of our student squad, though. Some of my star players and a handful of the cheerleaders. I didn't make a general approach, just handpicked a few, but no turn-downs."

She turned as she stepped inside. "That's fabulous!"

He grinned, surprising her. "Despite what happened on Friday, most of our students are good people."

She smiled as she walked to her classroom, thinking it was a good start and they'd probably get a handle on the bullying before there was too much more of it. Maybe James Carney and others like him wouldn't have to endure as much.

She unlocked the door of her classroom and stepped inside. Immediately she smelled something awful, something sickeningly sweet. Going to her desk, what she saw made her gasp in horror and back up to the door, where she hit the intercom button.

"School office."

"Marian, I need Les right now. Someone left a dead rat on my desk and I'm not going to be able to let the students in."

She heard Marian talk to someone. "He'll be right there with the janitor."

She stepped outside and locked her door again, standing guard, trying to keep her breakfast down. Ugly. Ugly. The thing had had its throat cut, there was blood all over her desk pad, and from the odor it had been left to rot all weekend.

The message was unmistakable, and almost enough to make her double over and heave. She could feel a cold sweat breaking out all over her body, and the nausea was overwhelming. She wanted to leave and never come back.

She kept drawing deep breaths to steady herself, leaning against the wall for support, and telling herself not to be hysterical. It was a nasty, messy, ugly message, but that's all it was.

If they wanted to frighten her off, it wasn't going to work. She promised herself that even as she felt the urge to leave and not come back. How would she ever sit at that desk again without remembering that rat?

She hated to think what kind of a person would have done that. One of those bullies? God, if it had been one of them, then James Carney could be in serious trouble.

For that matter, so could she.

Several students arrived before Les. "Sorry," she told them, "you'll have to wait in the library or lunch room. There's a bit of a mess that needs cleaning."

Did she imagine it, or did one of the boys actually smirk? Anything was possible, but she told herself not to see everyone as a potential enemy in this. She was likely being hypersensitive.

The nausea had mostly passed by the time Les arrived with the janitor on his heels. Amazingly, Linc wasn't far behind.

Les eyed her critically. "How bad is it?"

"Bad enough that I'm sending my homeroom to the library or cafeteria. Someone is going to have to take attendance. It's a mess."

"Well, let's see it."

She turned to unlock the door. "You'll excuse me if I don't go in there again."

Linc went in, though, and she noticed he took out his cell phone and snapped a few photos. Les gagged. The janitor even paled, and he must have cleaned up some real messes during his tenure.

"This goes way beyond a prank," Linc said flatly. "I think we need to call the sheriff."

Les nodded, putting his hand over his mouth and hurrying toward the door. "Don't touch it. I'll get Gage out here."

"I need to hold class," Cassie said, trying to cling to some semblance of normalcy or routine. Focusing on the one thing she *could* do.

"I'll arrange for a blackboard in the cafeteria," Les said as he hurried up the hall. "And I'll call the sheriff."

The janitor, a guy who preferred to be called Gus even though his name was Madson Carson, just stood there shaking his head. "What's the world coming to?" he asked. "Who the hell got in here?"

"It's been here at least since Friday," Linc remarked. "Let's get out and wait for the sheriff. I doubt he'll find anything useful, but we don't want to contaminate it."

Once the door was locked again, he drew Cassie to one side, holding her elbow gently. "Are you okay?"

"I will be. How could somebody get in to do that?"

"Remember, you can always get out of the building. All someone had to do was lay in wait until the place was empty."

It was true, she realized. All the doors were fire doors, and would open from the inside even when locked. As for her classroom…master keys could be had from several places. Or the lock could be picked easily enough. It wasn't exactly a vault.

She bent and looked at the keyhole. "Someone picked it," she said as she saw some deformation around the lock.

"Maybe." Linc sighed. "Damn, what's happening around here?"

She had no answers. Straightening, she looked at him. "Reality. Like you said, every place has its bad apples."

The hall was becoming crowded with students, and the PA system burst into life, announcing that Ms. Greaves's classes would be held in the cafeteria today.

"It bothers me how fast this had to have happened," Linc said. "The incident was Friday at noon. It's possible that when I opened the school to let the team in someone snuck in with them, but that's still the same day as the bullying, and probably a short time after Les called parents."

"How many people were in here Friday night?"

"The boosters, the team, some other parents, a few teachers. The cheerleaders. There's always a crowd before we leave for an away game."

"In short, too many suspects."

He nodded, but frowned at the same time. "Are you sure you're going to be all right? You could take a sick day."

"And spend all day at home thinking about this?" She shook her head. "No, thanks. What's that they say about after you fall from a horse?"

His frown turned to a faint smile. "You've got some backbone. Okay. But depending on how much of a threat the sheriff thinks this is, maybe you should take care not to be alone."

As if she would have a choice.

The sheriff arrived with his crime scene unit, and Cassie was grateful that the students had all vanished into classrooms. Not that they wouldn't hear about this, not that word wouldn't get out, but they didn't need to be clustered around and hearing gory details, or getting in the way.

The sheriff, Gage Dalton, whom she'd met a couple of times before casually, was gentle and kind with his questioning of her. He started with that morning, but inevitably he worked back to the possible motivation for this treatment.

She looked at Les, who sighed and nodded. "We may as well talk about it all, even though we're going to do our part, perhaps the most important part. You do have plans?"

"We're working on them. Linc and I have both started."

"With what?" Gage asked.

So she explained the bullying incident. Linc refused to let her skip over the phone call she had received. When they fell silent, having explained their plans for dealing with bullying, Gage's face was dark.

"So," he said, looking at Les, "you thought it was a good idea to hang your teacher out on this?" He turned to Linc. "What about you?"

Cassie spoke first. "Our main concern was not to get James Carney into more trouble. We were trying to protect him."

"So you get blamed for the detentions? You become the focus of this gang?"

"I don't like it," Linc said bluntly. "In fact, it concerns me a whole lot, and more now than it did on Friday. The fact remains, the Carney boy wasn't the only one bullied. Cassie was bullied, too. So it seemed we needed to deal with that immediately, without getting Carney into more trouble. We can't have students making implied threats by pushing teachers and ignoring them or we'll have anarchy, and we won't be able to control anything."

Gage hitched his gun belt, grimaced a bit and leaned

against the wall. "You know I could make arrests for what happened Friday. I get the part about not wanting to ruin a young person's life. I completely get it and don't want to do that. But given that you had warning of violence, however mild, this is one bull you should have taken by the horns immediately."

"James Carney..." Cassie began.

"I get it about the Carney kid. Believe me, I get it. But despite these moves against Cassie, are you really sure you've deflected the attention from him? I doubt it. They're going to know what's behind this. All you've done is give them a second object." He shook his head. "Too many suspects now, too. The bullies, their parents, their friends... Unless we find some specific evidence in that mess on Cassie's desk, we're going to be stymied. So keep that in mind. This has escalated. Keep that in mind, too."

Linc walked Cassie to the cafeteria and she got the feeling she wasn't the only unhappy one.

"We were stupid," he announced.

"I don't think so. Les was right about dealing with the infraction against me and leaving James out of it for now."

He looked at her, brows lifted. "You can say that after this morning?"

She bit her lip, then nodded. As nerve-racking as this had become, she didn't want to do anything to give those bullies more fuel against James. "I can protect myself," she said stoutly.

He took her elbow and drew her into a deserted spur of hallway that led to the janitorial rooms. "Don't underestimate this, Cassie. That rat this morning...that's extreme. You'd already been bullied twice. This goes a little beyond that, don't you think?"

She looked up at him and found his gaze steady and

concerned. For once he wasn't trying to look at something else. The impact of his full attention nearly left her breathless. How could he have that effect with a mere look?

She had to gather suddenly scattered thoughts, and that involved dropping her own gaze briefly. "I'm older," she said. "I'm an adult. I can handle it better."

"Even a rotting bloody rat on your desk? Are you so sure, Cassie?"

"Students are different here. Hunting is a part of life for them. This probably doesn't strike them the same way it would if a suburban student were to think of such a thing."

"Now you're making excuses."

"Am I wrong?"

"I don't know," he said forcefully. "And that's what's bothering me. Yes, hunting is a part of life for most of our students, but it isn't usually sport, and it certainly isn't done for reasons of cruelty. A lot of families look forward to deer or elk to get them through the winter. Killing for the sake of killing isn't approved by most folks."

"And rats are vermin to be exterminated," she argued, though he was beginning to make her stomach twist edgily again. Maybe there was no way at all to minimize this. Maybe she shouldn't even try. But she didn't want to walk around the halls of her new school looking on every student as a potential threat. Heck, she liked almost all of her students.

"Cassie," he said quietly, "don't be stubborn. You know this was an awful thing to do to you *and* that rat."

Some bit of her ego deflated. Her hands came together, clasping tightly. "I know," she admitted quietly. "But I've got to get through the day, Linc. I've got to teach, and I have to like my students insofar as humanly possible. I can't let this poison my relationship with them."

He sighed, then nodded. "You're right. I just want you to stay alert, okay? Keep an eye out. Pay attention. Don't go blithely on as if nothing happened until we get this sorted out."

"Blithe is not my reaction to this," she said a little tartly. "Far from it. I wish I could scrub that image from my brain."

"I'm sure you do." He astonished her by reaching out to give her shoulder a squeeze. "Do me a favor. Let me see you home after the meeting this afternoon. Do it for me. I'll feel better."

For a guy who had been avoiding her like the plague, he was getting close awfully fast. He must have a wide streak of white knight in him, she thought. "Okay, thanks," she said finally. It wouldn't hurt and at this point she wasn't exactly as full of confidence as she was trying to project.

But after all her wishing that he wouldn't remain so distant, she wished something nicer had brought them together.

With that gloomy thought, she headed down the nearly deserted hallway to take over her first class of the day, a class that was almost over. So much for great ideas. She'd have to bring them up to speed tomorrow.

She could also tell by some of the looks and whispers as she approached the group in the cafeteria that word had already gotten around. She wondered if they had the details or were going to question her about it all. Twenty-two pairs of eyes fixed on her, but no one said a word.

"Well, it looks like you guys lucked out," she said brightly. "Since I don't have time to cover new material, there will be no math problems for homework. And as for the project for the week, this is your turn to come up with one you'd like using the math and science we cover in class. I want to hear your ideas tomorrow."

At least they seemed eager about coming up with their own projects. By the time they headed out a few minutes later, many were already talking about ideas.

The rest of the day held nothing unusual until she received word that her classroom was once again ready for her. She'd have liked to avoid it at least until tomorrow, but shortly after she was informed, the public address system announced the rest of her classes would be held in the regular classroom.

Damn, she thought, torn between amusement and distaste, which was an odd place to be. She gathered up her materials into her book bag and set out with the migrating students. Gus was waiting for her.

"I got it all cleaned up," he told her. "All of it. Sorry, had to throw out a few things. The school will replace them."

"Thank you, Gus. I'm sorry you had to deal with that."

"I clean up messes all the time, but never one that made me so mad. Don't choke on the air freshener, but that smell didn't want to quit."

She sniffed the air. "You did a good job."

He smiled awkwardly. "You need anything at all, just let me know."

Another white knight, she thought. "Can I be honest? I hope I don't need you again for anything like this."

He laughed and headed out as students began pouring through the door.

In all, the day felt fractured, everything off-kilter, and she was sure she didn't do the best job of teaching. She wound up giving all her students a night off from homework because she wasn't sure she had really explained anything clearly enough. They seemed to be happy about coming up with their own projects, however, and she found herself anticipating hearing their ideas. So at least something good had happened that day.

The faculty meeting after school disturbed her, too. She was tired to begin with, probably because the day had been emotionally stressful, but to get in there and find there were teachers who didn't believe the bullying needed to be addressed left her both astonished and disappointed.

There were a significant number who felt the incident with James Carney was so unusual that it didn't really mean anything. Others felt that kids were just being kids. She was relieved, however, to find that more than half the teachers agreed bullying needed to be addressed firmly and quickly.

She was so glad Linc did most of the talking. Within ten minutes she realized that if she had tried to present the problem and the plans, she would have been dismissed. She was an outsider who knew nothing about their school or their students, and she would have been marked as being hypercritical about things she didn't understand.

Linc's presentation was at least received with respect, if not a hugely warm reception from everyone.

"They don't want to believe it's going on," she said to Linc as he walked her home. "Is it really that invisible?"

"My guess is yes. The students don't engage in that kind of behavior around teachers. At least not when they get to this age. Maybe that's why we thought it was tapering off after middle school. You heard what I said Friday to Les. We usually don't see this kind of extreme bullying at this age. Obviously, that doesn't mean it doesn't happen."

"Obviously." She sighed. "And maybe this really was an isolated incident. But I don't like the way it seems to be snowballing."

"Me, either. I'm really sorry about this morning. That must have given you a distaste for this place."

"Actually, no," she answered truthfully. "There was a while this morning when I didn't want to be in school. I admit it. The hardest part turned out to be trying not to be suspicious of every student in my classes. I like most of them. I don't think any of them were involved, but it still felt like I was attending a lineup for a few hours there."

He cracked a laugh. "I have no trouble imagining that. But you got past it?"

"Of course. It was temporary. The thing is, Linc, I've been teaching for a few years. Bad things happen, students do stupid and ugly things sometimes. It's all a part of growing up. It's not like I'm going to judge this entire county by one incident."

She felt him glance over at her, but she kept her gaze fixed on the street ahead. He might be stepping in right now out of a concern for her, but she had already realized he wasn't interested in any more than that.

"So you're not going to quit and leave?"

That startled her. She looked at him then. "It hadn't crossed my mind. Should it?"

"I hope not. I hear good things about your teaching. Your students mostly don't hate math, which is something approaching a miracle to my way of thinking."

She laughed. "We'll see what happens as the year goes on."

"I suppose we will."

They had reached her door. She had planned to invite him in for a coffee or a snack, but something in the way he said that caused her to pause and face him. "What is it?" she asked him. "You keep saying things that sound like you expect me to leave, or fall flat on my face. Did I do something?"

His face froze for an instant. "No," he said finally. "Most people who didn't grow up here don't like living here for long. Hell, some who *did* grow up here can't wait to leave."

She tilted her head, studying him. "Then I guess we *will* have to see, won't we?"

"That's all I'm saying. Keep your doors locked and don't hesitate to call the sheriff if anything worries you. It's been my experience he'd rather be called over nothing than not be called when he's really needed."

She nodded.

"We'll get through to the holdouts on the bullying," he said firmly. "It may take a little time, but not much. With one or two notable exceptions, the faculty here are primarily interested in student welfare."

She nodded, hoping he was right. "Coffee or a snack?"

He shook his head. "I've got to get back to practice. See you tomorrow."

The shields had slammed back into place, the conversation firmly on business again. Perplexed, she went inside, locked the door and watched him walk away back toward the school. The wind was picking up again, and leaves swirled around the sidewalk and streets.

He looked lonely, she thought, as he strode away into the gray afternoon. But maybe she was imagining that because he seemed determined to keep a distance between them.

One minute approachable, the next as far away as the moon. He was going to drive her nuts with that. Not worth it, she told herself. Maybe he was the most attractive man she'd ever met, but attraction was meaningless without a lot of other important stuff, stuff which he clearly didn't intend to offer.

She needed to think about other things, and quit letting her hormones get the better of her. It was one big waste of time, and she had more important matters to spend energy on.

Like class planning, upcoming parent-teacher conferences and the bullying program.

Then it struck her she hadn't seen James around the school today. Not even in class. How could she have missed that?

Because of a butchered rat on her desk and all the ensuing dislocation. Frowning, she pulled out her class roster, shoved the disk into her computer and called up James's name and phone number. It wouldn't hurt to find out if he was sick. For the moment she refused to consider other possibilities.

James answered the phone on the first ring. "I'm fine," he said, almost truculently. "Just fine. I felt sick this morning is all."

"Will you be in tomorrow?"

"Probably. It's okay, Ms. Greaves. Stop worrying about me."

But as she hung up, Cassie was even more worried than before.

Practice kept Linc pretty well preoccupied until he finally closed up the gym around six-thirty. He needed to get back to his animals, but it was as if the instant he stopped thinking about his team, all he could think about was Cassie. That was so not good on a bunch of levels.

He got in his truck, fully intending to ignore all other

impulses and head home. Instead his truck took charge and he found himself parked in front of Cassie's place.

Hell, he thought, rapping his fingers on the steering wheel. Then with a sigh, he gave up the battle. Climbing out, he walked up to her door and rang the bell. He was glad to see that she peeked out the side window before opening the door. While such measures were rarely needed around here, given that phone call and the rat, a little caution seemed in order.

"Linc!" she said in surprise as she opened the door. "Is something wrong?"

"Not a thing." Boy, this was going to sound stupid. "I just had a wild idea and wondered if you'd like to come out to my ranch with me. You can help me feed animals and see a different part of life around here. Unless you're too busy."

Delight chased surprise across her face. "I'd really, truly like that."

"I can get you home in plenty of time," he offered reassuringly. And maybe if she saw what the rest of his life was like, she'd stop looking at him with those unmistakable flickers of longing, flickers that were definitely getting under his skin. He tried to tell himself it was just because he was a man who hadn't been with a woman in a long time, but that didn't seem to be working.

So he'd give *her* the cold shower, the one he called the rest of his life. He could only listen to his own reasoning with amusement, wondering if he were engaging in a little self-deception, or really so sure this would work.

No, of course it wouldn't work. It had taken Martha more than a year to get totally fed up. On the other hand, Cassie struck him as being a whole lot more honest in her reactions than Martha. Sometimes he looked back at his engagement and wondered if Martha had believed from the outset that he'd sell the ranch, move and support them in a more comfortable lifestyle, one she seemed to want.

The thought now almost made him laugh. Like you could sell a small ranch these days. It wasn't as if there were enough around here to make some wealthy guy from the city want to plant himself here, even for a summer home, unless all he wanted to do was ride horses until he dropped and maybe hunt in the autumn.

He'd seen other places like his sell, but these days they were usually part of a larger buyout of a group of ranches, usually for industrial farming, or subdivisions. No subdivisions likely to be built around here in the foreseeable future, and he doubted many, if any, of his neighbors would want to sell. Most of them, like him, seemed firmly rooted in Conard County.

Regardless, he wouldn't put a dollar value on his way of life, and he wouldn't give up his legacy.

Cassie spoke as they headed out of town. "The shortening of the days is more obvious here than when I lived down south."

"I imagine it would be." It was an innocuous line of conversation, covering a topic they both knew.

"I'd forgotten," she said. "You get used to the difference in latitude quickly and don't even think about it. By next spring I probably won't even notice anymore."

"It's not as remarkable here as some places even farther north. Funny story. I was visiting a friend up in Canada one summer and I couldn't figure out why I was waking up so late every morning. I mean, the day was dang near half-gone. My friend laughed and suggested I look at the time I was going to bed. I was running by the sun and it amazed me to realize a couple of hours after sunset up there was the wee hours of the morning. I was getting to bed around 2:00 a.m. without even realizing it."

She laughed. "I'm not sure I could handle it up around the Arctic Circle. The long days would be one thing, but I think the endless nights might be too much."

"They are even for some folks who grow up there."

She fell silent then, appearing content to look out at the darkening countryside as they passed. A while later she remarked on all the tumbleweed caught in fences. "I had no idea it could get that big."

"Most of the time it gets hung up somewhere on the fences, but if the wind gets really stiff, look out. It can blow loose and be a driving hazard."

"So you have goats and sheep?"

"Yeah. And a few horses."

"Is your ranch a going concern? Or just something you do in addition to teaching?"

He thought about that a bit before answering because it wasn't something he had really settled with himself. "I like teaching. I like coaching football. But I also like working around the ranch. I guess I'm fortunate my spread isn't big enough to really make it full-time. Once it would have been, but not now. Economics have changed for small ranches."

"That's sad."

He shrugged. "The world changes. I get variety in exchange."

He glanced over and saw she had twisted in her seat to look at him. "But if you could make it full-time…?"

"I don't know. I'd have to get some additional land, or find some grazing to lease. Some of my neighbors lease out their land. Others lease it from them. And of course, there are grazing rights I could get on public lands. The thing is, unless you're a really big operation these days, it doesn't take much to break you. So it's best to just do it this way."

"A lot of people don't know it, but not so long ago Florida was the second largest cattle producer in the country."

"So you saw a lot of ranches?"

"Huge ones. Then we had a really bad drought. Maybe you remember it. We had to import hay and feed from all over the country. I never saw so many skinny cattle in my life. Bones sticking out. Water was so scarce the alligators were on the move looking for any pond they could find and sadly many didn't make it. Anyway, after that a lot of the ranches in my area started selling off large parcels for subdivisions and shopping centers. It kind of felt like it was one straw too many for some of our biggest ranches."

He shook his head. "There are advantages to staying small. At least I know I can get through those times. The big guys get into serious trouble fast. I'm sorry."

"It was sad," she agreed. "A whole way of life started vanishing. I can only imagine how hard it was on those families. At least some of them had a way out."

He felt a pang of sympathy for those ranchers. How could he not? But he wanted to keep the conversation cheerful. "Did I just hear you offer sympathy to gators?"

A laugh escaped her, a pleasant, happy sound. "You bet. It's possible to coexist with them, you know. And they were there before we moved in on them. All you have to do is treat nature with respect."

"So I take it you'd advocate for wolves."

"I would. How about you?"

"I'm all for it. They improve the ecosystem. Sure, I lose the occasional lamb or kid, but I was losing them to coyotes long before the wolves were reintroduced."

"How do your protect your herds?"

"Dogs. Big, great, wonderful, furry dogs. Bears hate 'em, wolves avoid them and coyotes run like hell. Be prepared to get jumped on and licked to death. Other than charging them with taking care of the sheep and goats, I pretty much just let 'em be dogs."

She laughed again. "I like that."

Martha sure hadn't. Her idea of a dog was something that could sit on her lap, smell like perfume and wear a bow. She really hadn't been able to handle his dusty, dirty, grubby working dogs.

Well, he'd see how this one reacted soon enough.

It was nearly dark by the time they reached the ranch. Cloud cover eliminated any light at all, so he asked Cassie to remain in the truck while he turned on the security lights. He used them only when it couldn't be avoided and he hated to think about the energy they burned since they were essentially floodlights, much brighter than streetlights.

But they had the predictable effect. As soon as they flipped on, sheep and goats began to hurry toward the fence looking for the additional feed he gave them, and the dogs, who had started waiting joyously probably long before he even reached his driveway, were barking wildly. They knew he'd give them treats after their hard work, chewy stuff that tasted like bacon and turkey, which they gobbled down before even going for their kibble.

The horses were calmer, coming to the pasture fence at a more sedate pace. Of course, they'd probably done a lot more running during the day than the sheep or goats.

He heard Cassie crunch across autumn-dry grass toward him as he watched the gathering.

"You have more animals than I thought," she remarked. "Are goats friendly?"

"A goat would move in with you if she could. At least these would. They come closer to being pets than the sheep, actually."

"How neat! What can I do to help?"

That was a question Martha hadn't asked, not the first time. In fact, come to think of it, he couldn't remember her ever offering to help without being asked.

Cassie, on the other hand, dove right in, seeming glad to do everything he asked. And when she went to feed the dogs for him, the six big gangbusters managed to knock her to the ground in their eagerness. Kibble flew everywhere. She sat on her butt, looking astonished, and he started to race toward her, but then she laughed and accepted all the gentle butting and didn't even complain when she got her face licked.

No, she dug her hands into dusty fur and scratched every animal she could reach. They approved, clearly, and ignored him for the moment.

"A love affair begins," he drawled, leaning against the fence post.

She grinned up at him. "But I spilled their food. How will they eat? Do I need to get more?"

"They'll find it. That's what they have noses for." He pulled a bag of treats out of his pocket and tossed it to her. She caught it. "One each."

The dogs knew what was coming. They swarmed her anew, and her laughter filled the night. He could feel his own face stretching into a grin. He hadn't expected this at all. Not for one second.

She struggled to her feet before opening the treat bag. There was one bit of manners Linc insisted on, and he said,

"Tell them to sit before you give them treats. Just hold out your hand palm down and say *sit*."

She followed his direction and instantly had six dogs sitting facing her. They jostled each other a bit, but kept their butts on the ground.

She giggled again.

"Don't let them snap it from you. If one of them tries just say 'no' sharply."

Barking had turned to impatient whines, but much to his relief they behaved perfectly. They were big dogs, part herders and part other breeds, certainly one that wasn't afraid of bears. He had no idea anymore. These dogs had all descended from the first dogs on the ranch and whatever else they'd mated with over the years. Letting the dogs pretty much have free rein outdoors meant that litters were often indeterminate. There might even be some wolf in there now among the younger dogs for all he knew. He even suspected some coyote. He kept the population down, though, by neutering all but one breeding pair. As it was, he still had plenty of requests for puppies from other ranchers.

"They're good dogs," he remarked. "They do most of the hard work for me."

"The best helpers in the world, I imagine."

She petted them some more, seeming almost reluctant to leave them, but when he moved on to tend to the sheep and goats, she followed along and helped. She appeared enchanted by both, never made a complaint about them being smelly, and then was delighted when she was able to help him stable the three horses.

"Horses are so beautiful," she remarked while he checked hooves then gave them all fresh hay and a little bit of oats. "Do you ride often?"

"As often as time allows. Not so much in the fall, what with football."

"I've only ridden once, when I was little kid, and was led around by a bridle."

"We'll have to do something about that." As soon as the words popped out, he could almost see them written in the air. What the hell was he thinking? He'd brought her out here to turn her off, not offer to see her again.

Instead she'd shattered all his preconceptions about her, and now he was offering to take her riding? He considered banging his head on a stall post to get his brain back into working order.

Too late. Well, he reassured himself, he was busy with football, and they had this whole bullying thing to deal with. He could reasonably avoid having time to take her riding until spring. And by then, she'd probably be crying uncle about this whole middle-of-nowhere place, and pining to have a bagel shop around the corner or something.

The nights were growing chilly enough that he blanketed the horses because they couldn't move much to keep warm. On the coldest nights he could blow heat into this barn, but like everything else, he did his best to conserve by avoiding it as much as possible.

He should have taken her home then, but he didn't like to be needlessly rude, even to protect himself. Instead, he invited her in for a hot drink and light snack. She might as well see the rest of it, the farmhouse that had seen better days, the furnishings left over from earlier generations. There was a difference between maintenance and decorating, and while he was good at the former, he had little interest in the latter. And, frankly, little enough money to waste on nonessentials. Or maybe that was largely his preference. If it served its purpose, it was good enough for him.

The kitchen was an old farmhouse kitchen, huge enough to feed the hands when necessary. The days when this place had been able to hire hands were past, but the kitchen and its long trestle table remained, as did the huge mudroom leading into it.

If he let himself think about it, he could hear better times almost whispering around him. Better times for the ranch, that was. He certainly didn't think his own times were bad.

Cassie stood on the threshold blinking. "Did you guys build for an army?"

He had to laugh as he motioned her to the table. "Families were a lot bigger in the old days. And back then we had hired hands to feed, too."

She sat, watching him as he moved around making some hot chocolate and breaking out some cookies. "What changed, Linc?"

"The times. After the Second World War, everybody but my grandfather moved away. The G.I. Bill helped with that, I guess. Regardless, my great-grandfather also broke up the land, so his kids could have a share. From the stories I hear, it didn't make much difference because everyone was working together anyway. But after the war…" He shrugged. "My granddad bought them back as everyone started moving away. We've still got a few thousand acres but the economics of things now make them almost pointless to put into use. You could call it splendid isolation."

A smile flickered over her features as he turned toward her to put the cookies on the table, but his face looked almost sad. "How do you feel about that?" she asked.

"I'm okay with it. I keep my hand in, I sell wool, I sell lambs, and keep it to a level I can manage."

"Do you ever see it changing?"

He poured the cocoa from the pan into two mugs. "Not anytime soon."

She grew thoughtful and quiet, and he let her be as he joined her to sip his beverage and eat a store-bought cookie.

"It's funny," she said after a while. "Some things are growing rapidly, and other things are shrinking."

"Times change, needs change. Cultures move on."

"I know, but I'm not sure that's always good."

"Right now it's good for the land out there. I didn't just happen into biology by accident. I get a kick out of watching nature move back in."

"Your own little eco-sanctuary?"

He had to smile. "I guess so."

The thermostat had kicked on a little while ago, raising the house from its daytime setting of sixty to a more comfortable sixty-eight for the evening. As the room warmed, he began to detect Cassie's scents—aromas of laundry soap, shampoo and woman. Most especially woman. It was faint, but as it hit him, he knew he'd better get her home soon.

Then she tugged her jacket off and he got a whiff that filled him with an instant longing so strong his jeans felt tight. Not good. Had he been crazy? Had he really thought that bringing her out here to see the reality of his life would cause *her* to put up a wall between them?

Because she wasn't acting as if it had. She had honestly seemed to enjoy it all. Maybe that was its newness, but it certainly hadn't worked for turning her away yet.

Instead he would now have the powerful memory of

her sitting in his kitchen and smelling like temptation personified.

Yep, he'd been an idiot.

But there was no denying he liked having her here. Liked seeing another face across the table, liked the scents of woman that wafted around him. Liked not being alone.

Even though alone was where he was going to wind up. She'd never stay. Never. She might as well be trying life out on Mars.

Something indefinable flickered across her face, yet it communicated some kind of unhappiness. For all he'd avoided looking at her since she started teaching, he couldn't seem to stop looking now. Oh, he had it bad.

"I can't stop thinking of that rat," she said quietly.

That was nearly as good as an icy shower. He found it possible to breathe again and relax a little. "It was pretty bad," he admitted.

"Serial killers do things like that."

"So do stupid kids who routinely kill vermin and hunt."

Her green eyes looked almost haunted. "Seriously? Or are you just trying to reassure me?"

"You can't grow up on a ranch or farm around here without having killed things. It's just life. You shoot coyotes, you kill rats, you even have to butcher deer or elk or some steer that you raised from babyhood. It's a part of life, not a thrill."

"I guess I'm having trouble connecting with that."

"I can understand that. But you said it yourself earlier. You're from a different way of life. I'm just saying that these students are familiar with this kind of thing. It's part of protecting their ranches and feeding their families. No thrill in it, but they'd sure be able to guess it might give *you* the willies."

"Because I'm an outsider."

"Because you weren't ranch-raised. Kids in town find it repulsive, too, which makes them the butt of jokes sometimes. But killing a rat? That's nothing. They kill them all the time to keep them out of feed and out of the barns. I would almost bet the sheriff finds this one was caught in a trap before they killed it. And once it was in a trap, killing it would have been a mercy. Chances are it had a broken neck or back."

She shuddered. Well, he told himself, that was the reaction he had wanted. Too bad that he hated to see it.

"Okay," she said, appearing to stiffen herself. "I get it. I've trapped mice in my home upon occasion."

"Same thing. You're lucky if the trap kills them cleanly, but it doesn't always. And most folks around here don't want to put out poison for them."

"That's odd, because I've heard of poison bait being used to get rid of coyotes."

"It's allowed, but it's dangerous. Your dogs might get it. Your cats. And when it comes to rat poison, the problem gets bigger. So most of us try to avoid those methods. Cats and traps in the barn are preferred."

"I guess I've got a lot to learn."

He tried to smile reassuringly. "Everyone does. Look, I'm not defending what that culprit did, putting that rat on your desk. But while it was intended to upset you, and maybe frighten you, I doubt anyone meant it as a serious threat. Chances are some numskull thought it would be funny."

"God!" Worse was that she had taken this very sensible attitude only this morning, and now she was resisting the very reasoning she had offered herself. Why were her thoughts shifting like quicksand? Maybe she had felt braver at school, but the prospect of being home alone at night now didn't seem quite so safe. Harder to be above it all.

"There's no explaining the humor of a teen."

She knew he was right: the grosser, the better. They'd certainly achieved a total gross-out for her. "Then maybe we shouldn't have called the sheriff."

"Why? It may have been just an ugly prank but it remains it was vandalism and possibly another attempt to bully you. Having the sheriff investigate may have put an appropriate fear in certain people. There comes a point, Cassie, when you've got to realize that stuff you got away with as a child is no longer acceptable or even legal."

He paused, realizing he must seem to be going around in circles. Well, he probably was, between her damned scent and his own uncertainty about what was happening.

"I'll be honest with you," he said slowly. "I'm not really sure what's going on here. I'm wondering what's been bubbling beneath the surface at the school that I'm not aware of. That makes me uneasy. Obviously, something has been getting out of control. On the one hand, I'm trying to paint it in the best light because I know these kids. Or thought I did. I don't want to think the worst of any of them. On the other hand, I guess I shouldn't minimize it. There have been three transgressions we know about with you. Four if we add James. I'm not going to dismiss it, but I'm not going to be Chicken Little yet, either. The mind of a teenage male is impenetrable."

She surprised him by losing her haunted look and actually laughing. "You're right, it is. And girls aren't much better at that age."

Girls weren't much better at any age, he thought a little while later as he drove her home. He'd certainly never figured them out.

"Thanks for a wonderful time," she said as he walked her to her door. "I really enjoyed it."

"So did I," he answered more truthfully than he would have liked. He had to bite his tongue to keep from suggesting they do it again.

"And thanks for the reassurance," she added as she unlocked her door and opened it. "You're right. I know perfectly well that youngsters that age aren't always thinking clearly. They get a wild idea and follow through."

"Still, we have to put the brakes on it. And we will."

She was still smiling as she said good-night and closed the door.

He walked back to his truck, keys jingling in his hand, and thought about it all, from the bullying to the rat to the evening just past. The thoughts were still rumbling around when he got home.

Something wasn't right. Something. He'd grown up here, gone to school here, been away only during his college years, and now had been teaching for a decade.

His nose was telling him something was wrong. Very wrong. The question was what. And who. He didn't want Cassie to be needlessly scared, but he couldn't lay his own concerns to rest.

Somehow, in some way, a scale had tipped, leading to some ugliness against a teacher that was so unusual around here it couldn't be ignored.

What happened to James Carney concerned him, of course, but that fit better into the parameters of the kind of ordinary ugliness people were capable of. It had a frame of reference, one they needed to put a stop to, but well within the range of "normal," however wrong.

Threatening phone calls and dead rats. If it had just been the rat, he would have been almost positive it was someone's bad idea of a prank. But added to that phone call, he couldn't begin to dismiss it.

Nor could he stop wondering if the real problem wasn't students at all now.

Chapter 4

Cassie's apprehension eased over the next few days. Nothing untoward happened, James was back in class looking all right, if a bit edgy, but when she tried to talk to him as he was leaving, he gave her an angry look and hurried away. Things were still not right in his world, and that troubled her. She wondered if he was still being hassled, but she had no way to know.

On the bright side, her students had come up with some interesting ideas for projects. As she taught them math with some physics mixed in, she enjoyed their pleasure and growing interest.

Success was sweet. She hoped it lasted.

So maybe the worst of the dustup was over, at least for her. Maybe whoever had been mad at her had finished venting. The detentions were scheduled for Thursday afternoon and Les had insisted on supervising them. After Monday, he said, he didn't want her involved with the disciplinary action.

She was, however, involved with Linc in a meeting with the students whom he had approached to become the vanguard in the antibullying campaign.

As she would have expected of the students who were most respected among their peers, they were all good-looking. At that age, appearance meant a lot. But as she listened to them talk with Linc, keeping mostly quiet herself, she was impressed with how good-hearted they were and their quick grasp of the problems.

She knew they'd been handpicked by Linc, and there were probably other student leaders he hadn't chosen, but this group was great.

"There's always bullying," said one of them, a petite blonde named Marcy. "Always. But not like what they did to James Carney. What's wrong with James, anyway? He's just a nerd." And from that statement, Cassie realized the story of what had been done to James had made it all over school. The students were talking about it, so they needed to turn that talk to a positive end.

Linc responded. "There's nothing wrong with James. The question is what is wrong with people who would treat him that way, and whether the student body is going to allow bullying of any kind to continue. The teachers can crack down, but you know where that gets us."

"Yeah," said Bob, a young linebacker from the football team. "It just goes under the radar or happens out of school. That's no good."

"So," said Linc, posing the question, "how do we make bullying uncool?"

"Speak up and speak out," was the first answer from another of the girls. "And we've got to get our friends to do it, too."

"Police it," agreed a boy. "Maybe form a group of students who are willing to step in if they see it."

"Like hall monitors," someone else suggested.

"Diss it," said yet another young man.

At that point, Cassie was moved to speak. "We've got to be very careful not to let our attempts to stop bullying become bullying themselves."

The boy eyed her ruefully. "That makes it harder."

She had to laugh. "You bet."

The important thing was that the conversation had begun, and these students were going to start getting the word out. Specific actions seemed to be beyond reach, other than expressions of disapproval, but that disapproval could spread like ripples.

After the students left, Linc remarked he needed to get ready for practice. "Are you walking home?"

"No, I brought my car today. I need some groceries."

"Okay, then. Have a good evening."

She picked up her book bag and headed out to the faculty parking area, feeling almost amused. No point in feeling hurt by it, but after letting her into his life—even in a small way—on Monday evening, Linc had pulled back like a turtle into its shell.

Oh, he was pleasant, but the distance was back.

How did you figure a man like that? she wondered as she pulled out of the lot. Monday night had been a lot of fun. She'd enjoyed the animals, liked helping with them, and enjoyed his company. Had she done something wrong?

She supposed she would never know. Whatever it was with Linc, she was beginning to think it was his problem, not hers. Which in itself ought to cheer her up. It was a far cry from her usual reaction, that she must be to blame for the way men lost interest.

Heck, she thought with a near giggle, he'd never really been interested in the first place. Maybe she ought to take his aversion as some kind of compliment—aversion was a long way removed from indifference—because clearly she was having an impact on him.

Just not the kind of impact she would have liked.

Unfortunately, Monday night had not just been fun. He'd managed to stir her interest in him beyond being attracted to his good looks, to being attracted by the kind of guy he seemed to be—a man of many talents and interests who appeared to have a good heart. The kind who were usually married with children by the time they crossed her path.

Much as she tried to get her thoughts to behave, to focus on work, teaching, the bullying program and settling into her new place in the world, Linc kept drifting through them. When he did, all other concerns vanished. She'd wander off into some girlish daydream in which he somehow wanted her, wanted to be with her.

Ah, she was getting too old for this. That kind of thinking was better suited to the kids they had just met with, not to a grown woman who'd already experienced her share of dings and knocks from dating. She even had a few permanent dents, so why wish for the unobtainable?

It struck her that wishing for the unobtainable might be a way of keeping herself safe. Oh, boy, she hoped she wasn't that far gone.

She had just climbed out of her car and started walking toward the store when an angry woman approached her. Cassie judged her to be about forty, showing signs of too much sun and wind, with hair almost as dry as straw. A ranch wife? she wondered.

"You!" The woman said the word sharply, taking her hand off the handle of her cart to wag a finger at Cassie.

Startled, Cassie stopped. "Yes?" she said uncertainly.

"It's your fault my boy is on detention today. I know my boy. He never shoved you. You'd better watch your step, lady, because if you want to lie about my kid, you won't be in this county for long."

Cassie's jaw dropped. She didn't know what to say. Les hadn't wanted her to bring James into it, but she hadn't expected him to tell the parents that those boys had shoved her. They hadn't been that forceful, even though the way they had brushed her had felt like a warning of what they could do. She thought Les was just going to say that they had defied her authority.

"Ma'am…" But what exactly could she say? Before she could marshal her words, the woman was storming away, cussing in a low voice.

Well, wasn't that lovely, she thought, her mood souring as she headed into the store. She wasn't going to chase that woman across the parking lot and have a public fight with her, and even if she thought of anything to say that didn't involve what had happened to James, it wouldn't matter. Clearly the woman had made up her mind. She wondered if one of the other teachers would be able to identify her by description.

But did she really want to know?

Damn. Sighing, she pulled a cart from the line, yanking with more force than necessary, and tried to school her face to a pleasant expression as she walked into the store.

She felt a change inside, though. Almost like the way you could feel your ears begin to respond to changes in altitude in an airplane. As she entered it was impossible not to notice that the store was quieter than usual. That people looked at her. That the usually friendly expressions weren't there.

So the parking-lot lady must have been talking.

Her mood sank even more. It would have been nice to just walk out. This would pass, after all, unless those bullies got themselves into trouble again. It was just a detention, no big deal. So she paused to look at a display near the door, one that held no interest for her, and tried to ignore the way her neck prickled with uncomfortable awareness. She could almost feel eyes boring into the back of her head.

Then, as if someone threw a switch, the store returned to normal. Carts started squeaking up and down aisles, a baby cried, women's voices resumed speaking. Employees made noise as they stocked shelves.

Had she imagined that half minute of disapproving silence? Had it even lasted that long? Gripping her cart she set out to get the items she wanted for dinner that night. She had most of what she needed, but when possible she liked fresh vegetables for this dish, and she needed milk regardless.

She received smiles and nods from some of the women as she went, but they seemed tight and forced. She must be imagining it. Surely this many people couldn't be upset about a detention?

Then she remembered the woman's claim that she had lied about being shoved. Well, that would do it, she thought bitterly. If these women believed that, she couldn't blame them.

She was picking through bell peppers, trying to find a few just crisp enough, when a frail voice got her attention. "Honey."

She turned and found a tiny lady, who could have been any age from sixty to ninety, standing there looking at her from faded blue eyes. "Don't pay it no mind, honey," the old woman said. "Most of us know that Hastings boy and when folks stop being mad they'll think about it. And they'll know he probably *did* push you."

"It wasn't exactly..." Cassie started to explain, but the woman cut her off.

"You stood up for my grandson, James," she went on. "That'll get around, too. Count on it."

Cassie caught her breath. "It might make it harder on him," she protested.

"He's been bullied since he first started school. It's just that way for some kids. Never figured out why. Sometimes it's like watching sharks smell blood in the water. Lately I guess it's getting worse."

Cassie faced her, peppers forgotten. "I want to help him, but I don't know how."

"That's the thing, isn't it? We've been trying to figure out how to help for years. Might as well try to stop a flood with a broom. My daughter and her husband moved away from here for about ten years, so James didn't grow up here. But he got bullied wherever he went, so it's not just this place. You keep that in mind."

Before Cassie could say more, the woman turned away, apparently done with the conversation. How was keeping that in mind supposed to help? She'd been teaching long enough to know that bullying was a sad fact of life for most students. What had been learned about it over the past few decades, however, made it something that couldn't be ignored.

Students were often permanently scarred by even minor incidents, and when the bullying persisted they could de-velop posttraumatic stress disorder. It could lead to depression and even suicide, or violent outbursts. In short, it couldn't be ignored as "just being kids."

She was no fool, however. Bullying could never be entirely stopped or prevented, but that didn't mean that it couldn't be reduced.

There was, however, the basketball championship involved here. Remembering her conversation with Les last Friday, she still felt a burst of frustration that he'd chosen not to exercise the full penalty. His reasoning made sense, but he'd chosen to give the students a slap on the wrist and right now she had a sickening feeling that wasn't helping anything at all, least of all James.

But it was clear from what his grandmother said that he had the support and concern of his entire family. They might consider the bullying inevitable for him, but they weren't ignoring it. That was a step in the right direction, she supposed.

She gathered her groceries and headed for the checkout, where she got a frosty smile from a cashier she had dealt with before.

"Trying to change the town?" the woman asked. "You should live here a while first."

Something inside Cassie snapped. "I'm not trying to change the town. I *like* this town. But don't you teach your kids to respect teachers?"

The woman appeared so taken aback that it might have been funny under other circumstances. She looked down at her scanner and started to run the produce through.

"We teach them to respect," she said finally, in a muffled voice.

"I thought so. Sometimes they just need a little reminder. Don't we all?"

The cashier looked up at that, and her smile was a little more genuine. "I guess so. It's just detention."

"Right. And I didn't lie about anything."

There. Feeling better, she gathered her sacks and headed out to her car. Let *that* get around on the grapevine.

She had heard that small towns could be incredibly gossipy, but the reality was beyond her previous experience. In just under a week everyone seemed to know what had happened, and sides were evidently being taken.

Given that she was the new kid on the block, as it were, she suspected most views didn't favor her much. Well, when had life ever been easy?

Cooking dinner for one had been a nuisance until Cassie had wised up and learned to make larger amounts and save some, either freezing the extra or putting it in the fridge for the next night. It made the effort seem more worthwhile.

Consequently, when she answered a knock at her door and found Linc there, she had enough food to feed him and two more like him. "Come on in," she said, no longer caring if he avoided her or she might be smarter to avoid him. Something about the encounter in the grocery store had fed her courage and self-esteem. "If you have time. I have dinner almost ready."

He hesitated. She almost wanted to sigh with impatience. Couldn't the man just make up his mind? It would be easier on them both. But then she warned herself that she didn't really know what was going on with him.

"You must be hungry," she remarked. "You just came from practice, right?"

He nodded. "I wanted to tell you something."

"Well, tell me inside. My pasta primavera isn't going to be very good if the pasta overcooks."

He followed her into the kitchen while she wondered at how he seemed to blow hot and cold. Just as she waved him to a seat, the timer for the boiling pasta sounded. "Give me a minute," she said as she turned off the stove.

Lifting the colander out of the boiling water, she turned it slowly, allowing it to drain thoroughly. Then she dumped the pasta into a waiting serving bowl.

"That's a lot of food," he remarked.

"I cook multiple meals at a time. Unfortunately, this one doesn't freeze well, so unless you help me out, I'm going to be eating this for the next three or so days."

"It sure smells good," he said.

She took that as agreement and pulled two bowls out of the cupboard, placing them on the table with flatware. "So what was so urgent it couldn't wait until morning?" She put the other ingredients in with the pasta and began tossing the mixture. Keeping her back to him made it easier. At least he wasn't distracting her.

"Talk. There's a lot of talk."

"About the detentions? I heard some of it at the grocery."

"I'm sorry."

She sprinkled Parmesan on the mixture, then carried the meal to the table. "Help yourself," she said, offering him the pasta scoop.

He apparently did like the aroma, because he put a healthy serving into his bowl. "I never go to this much trouble for myself."

"I didn't use to, either." She sat, passing a paper napkin to him, and took a smaller portion for herself. "I was confronted by a woman in the parking lot. It wasn't pleasant. She accused me of lying about her son pushing me."

"Damn," he said. He hadn't even picked up his fork, and when she at last forced herself to look up from her own dinner and meet those amazing blue eyes, she saw genuine concern.

Looking Linc in the eye, she decided, was a dangerous occupation. Every time she did, she felt hormones and hunger surge in a tidal wave that wanted to drive everything out of her head. Her thoughts wandered to those broad shoulders, encased by his Western shirt, and her palms itched to touch him.

No, it was safer to look down at her supper. No wonder eye contact was considered dangerous in so many cultures.

"How bad was it?" he asked.

"Bad enough. Ugly. It wasn't much better in the store. A cashier sort of confronted me. I probably should be ashamed to admit it, but I took her on."

"Good for you."

"So is that what you wanted to tell me?"

"In part," he admitted. "Somehow the whole story has gotten out, and it's not entirely accurate. Gossip never is, but you might say lines are being drawn."

"Against me."

She dared to meet his gaze again and saw tightness around his eyes. "Yes."

"Because no one really knows me yet. I heard that today, too. I'm being seen as an interfering outsider. So what exactly did you hear and from whom?"

"Some of my players. I overheard them talking and inserted myself." He shook his head. "I can't believe all this over a few lousy detentions, but I gotta say that I think Les may have handled this all wrong. People want that championship. I know it probably seems like a minor thing to you...."

"Actually no. And especially not here. I've been in much

more populous areas and larger schools where championships became really huge. It wasn't always pretty."

He gave her a short nod. "Exactly. Folks here love this place, they're mostly happy living here, but occasionally they need something to be proud of. Our football team seldom wins, but every so often, amazingly enough, our basketball team takes us to the brink of doing something that will make a lot of chests puff up."

"That's understandable." She ate another mouthful, waiting, and wishing her stomach hadn't decided to start doing flips again. She'd felt pretty good after she'd told that cashier the truth, but now she was definitely feeling the first icy fingers of worry and maybe even fear. Did she really need to be afraid? "So what did Les do wrong?"

"He should have told the parents the whole damn story and explained that he was going lightly. Instead he focused on you. So there's talk running around that you lied about being shoved...."

"I never said I was shoved."

"I know. But apparently Les said you had been. Or made it sound that way. He should have just left it that you'd been defied after giving the students a legitimate direction. Or he should have explained the entire situation. Now nobody has the truth, and speculation is rife. You lied. You didn't lie. These students wouldn't do such a thing. And then somebody put it out there that James was being bullied. God knows who. So right now you look like a troublemaker, and folks are wondering why there's a ruckus about something that all kids do and experience."

She put her fork down, losing all desire to eat. "That's the perception we have to change."

"Obviously. What's worrying me is that we've barely

begun and people are reaching the wrong conclusions. They're finding it easier to blame you for some transgression than to believe these students could have done something wrong. And now parents are starting to rumble."

Her mouth turned dry. "Already? A detention and they're that angry?"

"They don't know you yet, so they don't trust you."

"But surely kids get detention all the time!"

"Some do. Not these four. It would help if they were the usual suspects."

"God!" She'd never been one for drinking. The wines she kept, although good ones, were something she usually reserved for cooking, but now she rose, dug out two wineglasses, and poured some pinot grigio for each of them. "I hope you like wine."

"With a meal like this, definitely."

She stared at her wineglass, wondering if it was a mistake. Her mother had dealt with life's problems by drinking too much, and it wasn't a habit she wanted to fall into. But right now... Sighing, she sipped then put the glass down beside her bowl.

"I can't eat," she said, somewhere between hopelessness and anger. Some middle ground where no matter which way she looked, her stomach did another flip. "Tell me not to make too much out of this."

"I wish I could. I didn't come over here because I wasn't worried."

"Damn it," she said. "Maybe I should just take myself out of the picture. Ask Les to let me out of my contract and find another job."

"Are you that afraid?"

She bridled instantly. "No!" She glared at him. "I didn't

come here to tear this town apart, but it seems to be what's happening from what you say."

"It'll settle," he said firmly. "It'll calm down. I just wanted you to be aware. You might hear some more ugly things."

"I can take people saying ugly things. What I'm not going to be able to take is another dead rat on my desk!"

He didn't say anything for a minute or more. Something in his gaze said he had more on his mind than the talk going around. Something almost sad.

"If you're going to cut and run," he said finally, "do it now."

Startled out of her self-preoccupation, she gaped at him. "What do you mean by that? I'm just talking because I'm upset. Can you promise me no more rats?"

"I'd like to, but at this point I don't know. I wouldn't have expected the first one. I told you. Some kid playing a prank."

"But now you're not so sure."

He threw up a hand. "I'm not sure of anything right now. I've never seen this place polarize so fast. I can't figure out what the hell is going on. Everyone knows bullying isn't good. Everyone. They just turn a blind eye because it's perceived as kids' stuff. Now we have a crazy uproar over you because kids got detention for defying your authority. I can't explain it. It's like someone put loco weed in the water."

She lifted her glass then set it down and pushed it away. That wasn't going to help anything. Rising from the table, she paced the kitchen, trying to get a handle on this.

He was right. It seemed crazy. But she doubted that many people around here were crazy. So what the hell?

"Somebody," she said after a couple of minutes, "must be lying about something. In an inflammatory way."

"I'm beginning to wonder about that."

"But you didn't hear anything from your players that might explain it?"

"Not a thing. Just that folks are talking."

"People talk. If that's all they do, it'll settle down. The detentions were today. If there are no more, it'll go away."

"I hope so."

She stopped and faced him. "What?"

He shrugged. "If someone wants to get even with you for this, they'll try to provoke another situation."

"I'm not that easy to provoke. Usually."

Then she leaned back against the counter, wrapping her arms around herself as if they could protect her. As upset as she had been by the bullying she had stumbled on, she was even more upset now. "I was just trying to do the right thing, Linc. Not infuriate half the town and threaten a championship."

"I know."

Her eyes felt hot as she looked at him. "I'm the one being bullied now. I just hope I diverted them from James."

Linc was touched by her concern for James, but he couldn't deny that she was the victim now. Someone was deliberately exaggerating this entire affair and he couldn't for the life of him figure out why. He suspected at least one of the bullies' parents was mad about the detention and unwilling to believe their son could have pushed a teacher. Parents had that kind of blind spot as he knew only too well, but this seemed extreme. Then, too, the fact that the initial bullying of James had gotten out, when Les had tried so hard to keep it under wraps for the kid's sake, left him wondering about the dimensions of this storm.

Cassie stood there, looking lost and alone and upset, and there wasn't a damn thing he could do to make her feel better. She'd have to ride this storm out or leave town. She'd already mentioned the possibility herself, a reminder that had left him feeling warned.

Knowing he was being a fool, but doing it anyway, he rose and went to gather her into his arms. The instant he drew her close, he realized he might have just made the biggest mistake of his life.

Those luscious curves he'd been trying to ignore felt even better than he'd imagined. Womanly and welcoming, they seemed to meld right into him. She smelled so good and after the briefest hesitation, she leaned into his embrace and rested her head in the hollow of his shoulder.

"You're not alone in this," he said, hating the way his voice had thickened, giving away the surge of desire that roared through him. He tried to keep his hips away from her, afraid his body was revealing too much as he hardened. Damn, he'd meant to offer comfort, and if she felt his arousal she might be completely put off.

Although that would be for the best, said some nagging voice he didn't want to hear. Being deserted once by a woman who couldn't handle life here had been enough. He couldn't endure that again.

But neither could he refuse Cassie whatever comfort he could offer. It wasn't in him to ignore another's distress. He just wished his whole body hadn't started humming with need. It made the comfort he was offering seem like a sham, and it reminded him of his own terrible weakness.

He wanted this woman, had wanted her since he first laid eyes on her. She had begun to haunt his thoughts and sometimes even his dreams. If he could be sure a simple roll in the hay would settle it…

But he couldn't be sure. It wouldn't be fair to her anyway.

She leaned farther into him, almost resting in the shelter of his arms. Then, slowly, her own arms found their way around his narrow waist.

God, he'd forgotten how good it felt just to be hugged. The warmth of her embrace reached deep inside him, adding to the heat he already felt, but even more dangerously filling some empty hole in him.

Damn, life could be unfair, making him want what he was pretty sure he couldn't have. Making him want another woman he probably couldn't trust. Making him want all kinds of things that weren't his to take or enjoy.

A better man would have stepped back then, feeling he'd made his point that she wouldn't face this alone. But he was not a better man. The desire pounding in him weakened him, and drove caution to the background.

He was certain he'd pay for this, but that couldn't stop him. Need brought him to his emotional knees so fast he couldn't grasp at the straws of sanity.

He needed. He wanted. Before he even knew what he was doing, he tipped her face up and kissed her.

She tasted faintly of the wine she had sipped. Running his tongue along her lips, he felt their full, silken smoothness and then, so unexpectedly, she opened to him and he dove in like a bee seeking nectar. Warm, almost hot, soft like her secret depths. The pounding in his body grew until he could hear the throb in his ears.

It was as if hot ocean waves washed over him, carrying him farther and farther from the security of land. Her breasts, full and inviting, pressed against his chest, and his hands wanted so badly to wander her curves, learning each and every one of them. He could have happily drowned in her.

But at that instant, her body wormed closer and made full contact with his pelvis. The ache that shot through him was overwhelming, but just as they made that intimate contact, she gasped and arched backward. His eyes snapped open and he gazed into hers, seeing surprise, seeing his own heat answered.

It was the surprise that tossed him back on shore to safety. This shouldn't have happened. No way. Nor did he need to review his sensible reasons once again.

He loosened his hold on her, slowly so she wouldn't feel rejected, but as he backed away, he couldn't mistake the brief flicker of hurt in her green eyes.

Well, damn him all to hell for a fool. All he was trying was to keep either of them from being hurt, and he'd gone and hurt her anyway.

He didn't know what to say. He couldn't exactly explain that a momentary madness had overtaken him. Couldn't possibly tell her he didn't trust her to stay in this town and he wasn't traveling that painful path again. Couldn't say, "Gee that was nice, how's the weather?"

If he'd ever had any finesse, he'd just blown it.

But then she rescued him. A smile, a bit uncertain, a clearing of her gaze, a toss of her beautiful hair. "Wow," she said. "But I only just met you."

The line was so obviously intended to lighten the moment of near-disaster that he felt a load lift. "True," he agreed.

She walked back to the table and settled as if she intended to eat. "Don't worry about it," she said calmly. "A kiss is just a kiss and I have no expectations."

That, he thought, as he returned to finish the cooling dinner with her, sounded as if it went beyond a dismissal to a deeper emotional truth for her.

She had no expectations? What did she mean by that?

Then he reminded himself it was better if he never found out.

Chapter 5

Cassie awoke in the morning feeling half-dead. It hadn't helped that she'd lain awake half the night bouncing between remembering an incredible kiss and worrying that people were talking about her and that they suspected she had lied about a student.

The worst of it was she couldn't tell which upset her more. Along about two in the morning, she decided it was the kiss. Bad enough to know the man didn't really want to get close, but now she knew indelibly just how his hard body felt against hers, which only fed the fire of desire he awoke in her with such ease. Darn, it had been like opening Pandora's box.

Come morning, she sat bleary-eyed over her coffee, not at all eager to get to school. She tried to sort through an emotional tangle that seemed to be knotting ever tighter. She wanted Linc, admittedly. He didn't want her. The kiss had astonished her, coming after all the distance he had tried to dig between them like a canyon gorge, but it wasn't the first time someone had been attracted to her and then dropped her like a hot potato.

Story of her life, she thought dismally. Somehow she attracted men, and then she turned them off. She didn't know how or why, but they never stayed long. It seemed they found her initially sexy, and then their interest stopped. Boom.

So it shouldn't surprise her Linc had reacted like every other guy who had made an advance. In some way she couldn't discern, and that none of her friends had ever been able to explain, she put men off after the initial attraction.

She ought to be used to that fact by now.

Then there was this mess at school. Sighing, she stared into her coffee and decided to add some milk to it. Her stomach felt uneasy and the coffee was giving her heartburn. She knew better than to try to go without it, though. Coffee had for years been the thing that stood between her and some very bad headaches. A doctor had even recommended it when she didn't want to take something stronger.

So she swallowed her coffee reluctantly with some dry rye toast and pondered how everything could look so different in such a short space of time. At her age that should come as no shock, but it was still surprising.

A week ago she'd been practically buzzing with happiness about teaching and living here. Now she was dreading the day ahead. She had been confronted by a parent, had seen disapproval from people she didn't even know, and now she wondered what she was going to run into in the classroom today. How many of her students would take a cue from a parent or friend?

Well, there was only one way to find out. Rising, she

rinsed her dishes, grabbed her book bag and a jacket and set out.

Conard County offered her another absolutely gorgeous day, although it had grown considerably chillier than a week ago. Ordinarily the air would have invigorated her, but this morning her feet felt like lead.

Lack of sleep, she told herself, only half believing it. Then a thought occurred to her and she quickened her step. It was time to find out *exactly* what Les had told those parents. If he had told parents she had been shoved, she wanted him to take care of it. If he hadn't, then she would know the problem stemmed from elsewhere. How that would help, she wasn't certain, but she didn't want to also wonder about Les.

She knew Gus, the janitor, would be waiting for her outside her classroom. He was there every morning now, a kind of sentinel, and he always checked out the room before she entered. Unlike some around here, he didn't seem to suffer from an overwhelming belief in the goodness of everyone.

That was a cynical thought, and she yanked herself sharply away from it. One person. A small handful. No more than that. If people had heard a lie about her, then their disapproval wasn't a bad thing. They were rallying around neighbors. That was good, right? Eventually, after this mess was over and enough time had passed, she hoped to be one of the neighbors folks around her would want to protect.

Linc wasn't outside. Evidently he'd completed his turn at bus duty and an English teacher, Carl Malone, had taken over. He greeted her pleasantly. Whatever was going around on the grapevine, it hadn't affected him yet.

For the first time she wondered how many of the teachers might start turning frosty, even though the situation had been explained at the meeting this past Monday.

She was not in the best of moods by the time she reached the principal's office and her mood didn't improve when she saw Linc already inside with Les.

Memories of the kiss came rushing back, and with it an unwanted warm weakness between her legs. Damn, she hated that he could make her want him so much when he clearly didn't reciprocate the feeling. He saw her through the glass, though, and waved her in.

She trudged around the large reception desk and entered Les's office.

"I guess you had the same idea I did," he said. "I was just asking Les exactly what he told those parents."

Les, seated behind his desk, looked both annoyed and defensive. "I didn't tell anyone that those students shoved Cassie," he snapped. "I don't know where that's coming from."

"What exactly did you tell them?" Cassie demanded.

"That you had told them to report to my office for a legitimate reason and they refused. Not one word more than that, except to say we couldn't allow students to defy a teacher's legitimate authority."

"You're sure?" Linc asked.

"I'm not an idiot. Details aren't necessary for the very reason you're in here complaining about."

Cassie looked between the two men. "Then what started it?"

"Probably one of the students involved, or one of their friends," Les said. "A lie, pure and simple, exaggerating the matter."

"I still think," Linc said firmly, "that you should have told everything to the parents, including the bullying."

"I was trying to protect James Carney from retaliation!"

"So now a good teacher's reputation is being impugned. You need to call those parents back and tell them what Cassie saw."

"No," said Cassie, surprising herself. "No. It's over as far as those students are concerned. They had detention and the case is closed. Telling the parents about the bullying will only make them madder, and I'll probably be accused of lying about that. Leave James out of it."

Linc faced her. "Are you sure? This thing has been handled poorly, if you ask me. We need to address all the issues involved with all the students involved."

"Of course," Cassie agreed. "But arguing with people over their current presumption isn't going to help." She shook her head a little. "I admit I wanted to know exactly what Les had told the parents, but obviously he didn't say anything to start this kind of extreme talk. So it had to be a student or parent exaggerating the matter, claiming I lied about what happened. No one can prevent that."

"I prefer to take most bulls directly by the horns," Linc admitted. "But you're right. We can't call back the lies. At this point all we can probably do is avoid inflaming things until we get our presentation ready and get the new policy moving."

"We have a policy?" Les said, bridling.

"We're going to try to get students involved," Linc said. "To get some of the most popular students to start frowning on bullying of any sort."

"Oh." Les stroked his chin. "I wonder if that will work."

"It has in other schools," Cassie said. "Unfortunately, it usually starts earlier than high school. It takes time to grow a culture."

"Well, I don't like the one that seems to have sprung

up here at all. I'm going to take whatever action I deem necessary. You guys have a few weeks. If we have another incident of any kind, I'm cracking down."

Outside in the hallway, Cassie started for her classroom, knowing that Gus was probably still standing there like a palace guard.

"So he's going to crack down," Linc remarked. "I don't know how much that'll help."

"I guess it depends on how many get rebellious."

"At this age, that'll probably be quite a few. Cassie…"

She looked at him then and sensed where he was trying to go. "Forget about it, Linc. Things happen. I need to get to my room."

Hard words to say, but the best way to handle it. She left him quickly, striding away as fast as she could walk. Trouble. There'd be nothing but trouble if she got in any deeper with that man. Regardless of whether his reluctance grew from something in him or something about her, or a combination of both, it didn't matter. It boded badly, and it was time to stay away.

"All clear," Gus said cheerfully when she appeared. He opened the door and waved her in.

"Thanks so much, Gus. I really appreciate your concern."

"No problem. I see more than a lot of people would like. What you're doing is right."

Well, at least she had her own cheerleading section. The thought brought the first smile of the day to her face.

Nor was the day bad. While she had expected there might be some trouble with her students, they all seemed to behave perfectly normally. James Carney still looked isolated and a bit pinched in the far back corner, but that wasn't a change. She just hoped that someday soon he would start to appear more comfortable.

For now all she could do was avoid drawing any attention to him that might bring on more teasing.

Unpleasant though it was for people to be talking about her and thinking she might have lied, it was far better for the attention to be on her. She could handle it. Well, except for butchered rats. The memory nearly made her shudder, but then she reminded herself nothing else had happened. The mood must be cooling down now, at least with whoever had killed the rat and phoned her. The confrontation in the parking lot was still fresh in her mind, but she could deal with that kind of thing.

It was shadowy threats from unknown persons that bothered her most of all, and those had stopped.

By the end of the day she was feeling considerably more cheerful about life…well, except when it came to Linc. The memory of his kiss plagued her, popping up without warning, and unwanted.

Damn, she thought, it was just a kiss. Maybe the nicest kiss of her life, the most arousing—how in the world could she explain that?—but it was still just a kiss. He hadn't taken it one step further. Meaningless. Utterly meaningless.

Except she had felt his response to her, and the memory of *that* kept drizzling through her body like warm honey. He *had* wanted her, if only physically. Supposedly that didn't mean much with men, but it meant a lot to *her*. It was good for her ego, if not her peace of mind.

At the end of the day, Linc appeared in the doorway of her classroom just as she was tucking the last items in her book bag.

"Let's go get a bite," he said.

She looked at him uncertainly. "Why?"

"Why not?" He shrugged one shoulder, reminding her abruptly of the strength in the arms that had held her last night. "We go out to Maude's. Everyone can see you with me. That may lead some folks to question certain assumptions about you."

Another rescue mission. God, she thought as she picked up her bag and tossed it over her shoulder, she wished he'd turn up sometime for another reason. Of course there was that crazy trip out to his ranch on Monday night. What purpose had that served?

Only to make her wish she could spend more time there. She'd really enjoyed it. On the other hand, how could either of them be sure she might like it when the novelty wore off? Maybe that was part of what made him keep a distance.

Deciding there was no point in arguing about it, and silently admitting she *did* want to spend more time with him, she accompanied him out to his truck. There must be neutral things they could talk about, like his ranch and his livestock. Anything but school and bullying. Or desire.

He remained silent through the short drive over to Maude's café. One of the things she found charming in this town was that the City Diner, clearly signed and marked as such, was called Maude's by everyone, after its owner. It had struck her as a signpost indicating how well the people around here knew each other. Learning that had been one of the things that had helped her make her decision to accept this job.

She hadn't really thought about being an outsider, and after Maude had taken their orders in her grumpy fashion, she said so to Linc.

"The one thing I didn't take into my calculations when I fell in love with this county..."

He arched his brows, his blue eyes intent. "You fell in love with this county?"

"Of course I did. I wouldn't have moved here otherwise."

"But how could you know so fast?"

She hesitated, then finally decided to admit the truth. "Somewhere inside I've always looked for a place like this. A small town surrounded by wide-open spaces where most folks are friendly. A place where I could actually get to know most of my neighbors. Silly dream, I suppose, but I dreamed it anyway. Until now I've never lived in a place like this, but I always, always wanted to."

He nodded. "Sorry for the interruption. You were saying?"

"There was one thing I didn't realize, that I'd be an outsider. Maybe for a long time to come. I never had to face that before. So..." She shrugged. "I've learned something. Kids whose families came here to work at the semiconductor plant are still outsiders, from what you said last week. How long have they been here, but they're still the new kids?"

He frowned faintly and leaned back to let Maude serve them coffee. "It's easier with the adults, I think."

"Are you sure?"

At that a faint smile appeared on his face. "Well, when you see what Maude puts in front of you next, you may get the message."

"I didn't order anything."

"Around here, that doesn't matter."

Barely had the words left his mouth than Maude slapped

two pieces of pie in front of them and stomped off without a word. "Pie? Why? What do you mean?"

"Whatever Maude has heard, she's letting you know she doesn't agree with it. You've just been welcomed as a regular here. And that means that sometimes Maude decides what you eat."

"Wow." She looked at the pie and felt warmed. "I'm honored."

"You should be. Some folks have been coming in here for years and never been given free pie."

She looked at him and a little giggle escaped her. "So all is better now?"

"Here at least. Maude's making her opinion known, and my experience is that if she hears any talk about you, some steaks are going to get overdone."

Cassie laughed outright at that. "But why would she have a different opinion from everyone else?"

"I doubt it's everyone else, to begin with. Yes, some folks are talking. It worries me, and I wanted you to be aware of it, but rarely does everyone around here buy something like that as gospel. Who was it who confronted you, anyway?"

"I don't know." And she hadn't wanted to talk about this. "I never met her. Can we discuss something else, please?"

"Sure." He sounded agreeable. "So what's on your mind?"

A lot of things were on her mind, and not a single thing she could mention, really. Ask him about that kiss last night and why he'd pulled away? Not likely. She hunted around inside her head for an innocuous topic while covering her silence with a mouthful of pie.

"Wow," she said. "This pie is fantastic!"

"Maude's famous for them. One of the reasons it means something when she gives you a slice for free."

Cassie looked around and saw Maude walking toward a table. "This pie is fabulous!" she called. "Thank you!"

She supposed that grimace was a kind of smile.

"Not the easiest person to get along with?" she asked Linc quietly.

"Depends. I wouldn't want to be on her bad side, though."

She savored another bite of pie, knowing she'd never enjoy it if they came back to the bullying. "Do you ever think about getting more animals at your ranch?"

He smiled. "Often. I like them. But I have to be realistic about what I can handle. As it is, breeding alone gets ahead of me sometimes."

"Like rabbits, huh?"

"Not quite, but sometimes it feels like it." He rolled his eyes humorously.

"I never thought about raising goats. I can understand all the uses for sheep, but goats?"

"I sell a lot of mine. There's a market for the milk, but also for their hair. Mine are angoras, and their hair is something you'd recognize as mohair."

"Really." She smiled at that. "And their meat?"

"There's a cultural market for that, too. So I really have no trouble making enough off them to pay for them with a little left over. But as a major operation?" He shook his head. "I'd need a lot more than two hands."

"Well, I thought they were neat just to have around. If a few is enough for you, there's nothing wrong with that. I actually liked them better than the sheep."

"They're a lot more amusing, to me anyway. Very smart and full of high jinks. It's a good thing I have the dogs to keep them in line."

The diner was beginning to fill up with people. Cassie looked around, trying to make friendly eye contact, but noticed that a few of the people avoided her gaze. She pushed her pie to one side.

"Don't let them get to you," Linc said quietly. "Stick it out a little longer."

"How's that going to help?"

"I'm here with you. More than any of them, I'm in a position to know whether the gossip is true. Hang in there, Cassie."

"I'm not going anywhere," she said firmly. "But my appetite died."

"Just be sure to take the pie with you."

"Must not offend, huh?"

"You got it."

It was hard not to keep looking at him when he sat right across the table from her. Staring down at her cup didn't feel like the right thing to do, either. The people looking her way could interpret that to mean that she was feeling defensive.

Too much education in psychology, she thought with weary amusement. So here she was, caught between the devil and pair of deep blue eyes, to mangle a metaphor. She could send challenging looks around the room, if anyone was staring, or she could give up and just drink in Linc with her eyes.

She knew what she wanted to do. Seizing on the first straw she could find, she asked him, "Do you have a Celtic heritage?"

"Why do you ask?"

"Because that was the first thing that occurred to me when I saw you. Blue eyes, dark hair." Not to mention an incredibly perfect build from what she could tell. She skipped the part about thinking he resembled a warrior, though. That was definitely over-the-top, a female fantasy not to be shared.

"I guess I do," he said. "My mother always said she was black Irish."

"That would explain it. I'm mostly mutt myself."

He laughed. "You look like anything but a mongrel."

She felt her cheeks flush, but only faintly, thank goodness. "I really don't know much about my family. My dad left when I was three, never to be heard from again, and my mother steadily sank into alcohol."

"Damn, that must have been tough."

She acknowledged it with a nod. "There were good times, too. It wasn't all bad. If I can say nothing else for my mom, it's that I always knew she loved me. No matter what."

"I take it she's gone?"

"A couple of years ago. Cirrhosis."

"I'm sorry."

"No need. It's a horrible addiction and I watched her struggle with it. It was sad to watch, because she tried so hard up until near the end, but it was like watching someone in tennis shoes try to scale the steep side of an icy mountain."

"That's some image," he said quietly.

"That's how it seemed. Like no matter how hard she struggled, she could never quite get her footing. That's why I don't drink much. I'm afraid of it."

"I can see why. I guess I've been lucky, because I never really had to think about it. I can enjoy a beer or two on a weekend, or a glass of wine with dinner, but that's enough for me. I got rousingly drunk once in college and the hangover cured me of any desire to repeat it."

She had to smile. "I hear they're awful."

"I got drunk on wine with some friends. I couldn't stand the smell of the stuff for years. And the morning after..." He shook his head. "Never again."

"I don't like things that make my head feel messed up. I prefer it to be clear."

"Then I guess it would be safe to take you dancing at one of our roadhouses." He winked.

Her heart slammed into high gear. Take her dancing? Surely he was joking. He *had* to be. "Why? Because I wouldn't drink too much?"

"You wouldn't trample my feet," he joked. He appeared to hesitate and then volunteered something she sensed was still a sore spot with him. "My former...girlfriend wasn't much of a drinker until we'd go out to do some line-dancing at a roadhouse just outside of town. Then she claimed the dancing made her thirsty. There was more than one occasion when I practically had to pour her into the truck."

Cassie screwed up her face. "How awful. I'm sorry."

"I made excuses for her. She was just cutting loose, and everyone needs to do that at times. But in retrospect, maybe I should have made fewer excuses."

His face darkened, and she lowered her gaze, deciding to leave him alone. Definitely a sore spot, so why persist? If he wanted to say more, he could.

He surprised her with his next words. "I like to dance. Do you?"

"I'm not very good." Mainly because she hadn't had much opportunity to learn or practice.

"I can help you. Why don't we go tonight, if you can stand the country music? And I promise to get you out of there before things get too rowdy."

She almost gaped at him. Last night he'd kissed her

then backed away as if he felt it was a mistake, and now he wanted to take her dancing? Was he asking her for a date?

No, that wasn't possible. Maybe he just wanted to work off some steam dancing. He said he liked it, and while she imagined he could find women to dance with at the road-house, maybe he preferred not to do that. So perhaps he just saw her as a safe dance partner since she was a col-league. "I don't know," she said hesitantly.

"It'll be fun," he assured her. "And it's a part of this county you're not going to see on your own, not if you're wise."

"What does wisdom have to do with it?"

"A lot of people are cutting loose. Like I said, I'll get you out of there before it gets too rowdy."

She got the message, and her curiosity was piqued. She had to admit she wouldn't go to a bar or a roadhouse by herself, and she was willing to bet the flavor of nightspots around here was different than other places she had lived.

Curiosity trumped caution. She had no idea why he'd asked her to go dancing, and feared she might be stepping into something she knew nothing about, but she'd never been afraid to take a little risk. If she had been, she never would have taken this job. "Okay," she said. "But I'm a lousy dancer."

"So are a lot of other people. You won't be alone."

"No practice tonight?"

He shook his head. "We have a game tomorrow. I like the players to have the night off right before when it's pos-sible. I'll pick you up at seven-thirty."

After he dropped her off at home, with directions to wear jeans and comfortable shoes, she puttered around, trying to keep busy while she pondered this strange turn of affairs.

What in the world was going on? Date? Not date? A rescue attempt against the forces of gossip?

She wished she knew.

Linc wished he knew, too. What had possessed him? Last night he'd barely escaped a temptation that had threatened to drown him, and now he was proposing to take the woman dancing?

He'd lost it.

Out in the pastures, tending to his animals and listening to a coyote howl in the distance, he decided he might be getting himself into trouble, which just proved that a grown man could repeat his mistakes, even after painful lessons.

Nor did it make him feel any wiser to remember that she'd been reluctant. Reluctant about dancing, he was sure, but he suspected she was equally reluctant to go with him. He'd had women jump all over such an opportunity before, and he damn well knew when one wasn't jumping.

So maybe it would all be okay. He was doing the neighborly thing, showing her around a bit, at least to places she wouldn't find on her own, like his ranch and a roadhouse. He half expected the atmosphere of the roadhouse would turn her off even more. Smokey, crowded, men talking too loud and telling off-color jokes. She seemed to be the type who'd prefer other amusements. She'd mentioned museums and plays, after all. None of that around here.

So he might as well give her the rest of the county's cold bath: the roadhouse. Which was not to say he had anything against them. After a long, hard week, he didn't see anything wrong with people wanting to unwind in a boisterous atmosphere with a few beers, some twangy music and some dancing. It wasn't as if there was a whole heck of a lot else to do. Church socials if you ran that way, but he didn't, at least not very often. A certain comedian's impression of church ladies hadn't been far from the mark, at least in the church he attended.

Maybe he ought to change that, too.

With goats and dogs nudging him, he almost laughed at himself. Change. That was what he was pining for. At least getting out for a few hours of dancing would be a change from the last couple of years.

It would certainly make some tongues wag in a new way. Everybody around here knew Martha had been his last girlfriend, and everybody seemed to know how it had ended. Martha sure hadn't made a secret of it.

He could imagine the heads shaking as Linc Blair once again took up with an outsider, and by Sunday morning some biddy was bound to suggest he ought to date a local girl. He almost relished the prospect.

Even though the biddy would probably be right.

Aw, what the hell, he thought after he was done tending the animals and had showered and changed. He sat on the back porch for a little while, booted feet up on the railing, and watched twilight take the world.

Almost time to go. He might not know what he was getting himself into here, but there was an unmistakable sense of adventure filling him.

The ranch would never desert him, he thought with amusement. Nor he it. The foundation and cornerstone of his life would always be here, unless he made a stupid financial decision. You really couldn't ask more from life than that.

Everything was chancy by nature, but as long as he had this place, he could take the rest.

Peace filled him, right alongside anticipation. The evening would be fun, even if it never became any more than that. He'd have a chance to watch Cassie in the world she was trying to adopt, and she'd get to see parts of it she might otherwise never really know about.

That might be all it took to snap this fascination he kept feeling for her.

Or not. As usual, only time would tell.

Dropping his feet with a thud, he rose and tugged his keys out of his jeans pocket. Time to go show a lady a good time.

Dusty's Inn didn't look like much of an inn. The large log building was girdled in garish neon announcing any number of brands of beer along with Dancing and Live Music Saturday. The parking lot, consisting of dirt and gravel, held a dozen or so pickups and a couple of cars, leaving room for many more.

"It isn't really busy yet," Linc said as they tooled into a spot next to a pickup that looked older than his. "It'll give you time to ramp up."

She grinned at the expression even though she didn't know exactly what he meant. Excitement and nerves both filled her. "Ramp up?"

"Get used to it. The volume gets a lot worse as the crowd grows. With everyone yammering, Dusty turns up the volume on the music, which makes everyone talk louder. Interesting feedback loop, but I've never been able to convince him there's a point of diminishing return."

Cassie giggled. "Do I need ear protectors?"

"In an hour or two. For now it won't be so bad and I won't keep you past the point where it does."

Keep her? Interesting turn of phrase, she thought as he helped her out of the truck. Did he feel like he was keeping her from something else? Or was that some colloquialism she hadn't yet noticed? Then she reminded herself to quit analyzing and just absorb the experience.

She could hear the music already, even though they hadn't reached the door. The crunch of the gravel beneath her feet made her wish for a sturdy boot rather than her jogging shoes. Judging by the way Linc was dressed, she might well be the only person in the place without a decent pair of boots.

Still it was fun. She was going to a roadhouse in Wyoming on the arm of a cowboy—well, a rancher actually, but tonight she wasn't going to quibble. Not with anything. Some of her old friends would swoon at the mere thought.

Linc always dressed in Western clothes except the couple of times when she'd seen him wearing sweats like the football team. But tonight he'd replaced his battered hat with one in pristine shape, and she thought the toes of his boots looked polished.

Wow. Putting on the fancy duds, she supposed. It tickled her, especially when he had told her to essentially dress down. She had, however, worn her newest jeans, and a satiny green blouse.

She could feel the throb of bass as they drew closer to the building and wondered if it would already be too loud inside.

A plank door opened and a beefy guy in a red T-shirt blazoned with Dusty's welcomed them inside. "It's been a while, Linc." The guy's gaze dragged over Cassie with obvious approval.

"Cassie, this is Glenn. He does his best to maintain order."

Glenn winked at her. "It can be a trial. Nice to see a new face."

They stepped through a second door and the music hit

her like a strong wave. It wasn't deafening by any means, but it was loud. A few couples were already making their way around the huge dance floor, while others sat to one side at tables. A handful dotted stools at the bar that ran around two sides of the room. Through a large doorway to her right, she could see billiard tables.

"This place has everything," she said to Linc.

"Well, it has enough. Let's get a table."

She was glad he didn't immediately suggest taking her onto the dance floor. So few people were out there, she felt she'd be embarrassed. Of course, once it got crowded, she'd probably stick out like a sore thumb.

Then she wondered why she should feel embarrassed at all. Everyone had to learn some time, as she told her students often, and everybody made mistakes.

Linc ordered soft drinks and an appetizer for them.

"You can have a beer," she protested.

"I'm the designated driver."

"And I don't want a beer before I learn how to dance."

He laughed, his eyes crinkling. "A beer might loosen you up."

"How loose do I need to be?"

"For the Cotton Eye Joe? Not a lot. It's an easy dance and a lot of fun. More fun with more people."

"I'm nervous," she admitted.

He reached out and touched her hand lightly. Sparks immediately zinged through her. "It's not hard, I swear. Just watch them dance for a little while and you'll start to feel the rhythm of it. Then I'll show you the steps."

The colas came in huge red plastic glasses, the appetizer in a paper-covered plastic basket. No frills here. She rather liked that. Frills would have seemed so out of place.

"I should have told you to wear smooth-soled shoes," he remarked. "It would be easier."

"Well, I don't have to dance at all."

His blue eyes laughed at her. "You're not getting out of it."

The place slowly filled up with people of all ages. From her limited experience of nightclubs, that surprised her. The few she had visited had seemed to be age-segregated, catering to younger people. This one had the whole range of ages from twenties to sixties or maybe older. She liked that.

As the floor sprouted more dancers, she found her courage. Not that she could have escaped. Linc reached for her hand and pulled her that way.

"It's easy," he said. "Really easy." Keeping her at the edge of the floor, he said, "The first step is stomp-kick-triple step."

She gaped at him, then watched as he did it several times. She could feel eyes on her, but when she glanced around people seemed to be busy with their own companions.

"Now you."

She bit her lower lip and tried to imitate him. The music seemed to help, giving her the rhythm. She made a couple of mistakes, but in a relatively short time thought she had it down reasonably well.

Maybe so, because then he taught her the next part, the shuffle. "Wow," she said finally, "that feels almost natural with the music."

"The whole dance does," he assured her. He slipped an arm around her waist. "Now let's try it. This dance is done side-by-side."

She'd already gathered that part. Feeling a little more

confident, she let him guide her around the edge of the dance floor. With only a few missteps, she made it around the entire circumference. The song changed and they were off again, and pretty soon she stopped thinking about her feet and started thinking about the man whose arm so casually cradled her waist. Stealing a look at other couples, she realized that wasn't a one-way street, so she slipped her arm around his waist.

Wow! It felt so good that she almost closed her eyes with pleasure. Holding him, being held, moving with the music, it all seemed to meld into one wonderful experience.

She was startled back to awareness as she felt an arm link with her free arm. She looked and saw another couple. The man smiled at her and danced alongside her.

Before she knew it, she was part of a line that was pivoting around the dance floor. Then everything shifted, and the whole line was moving straight across the floor, first forward and then backward.

Beneath the loud music, she heard herself laugh. Her head came up, she tossed her hair and grinned at Linc. He grinned back.

She had no idea how long she danced. The songs changed but she didn't count the changes. She was having too much fun. At last, just as she started to feel parched, Linc eased them out of the line and guided her back to the table.

He held out her chair for her, saying, "You're a natural."

"It's fun!"

Fresh soft drinks awaited them, and she drained half of hers in several chugs. He pulled his chair around so that he sat right beside her, rather than across from her.

"So where's this rowdiness that had you concerned?" she asked.

"Later. A different crowd will start showing up, and the beer will flow faster. We'll leave around then."

Just then, without warning or invitation, a heavyset, very large man pulled a chair out and sat at their table. Cassie looked at him in astonishment, wondering if this was another local custom she didn't yet know. She had the feeling she recognized him, but couldn't place him.

"Howdy, Dave," Linc said. "What's up?"

Cassie started to relax as she realized Linc knew him. The relaxation didn't last long.

"So this is the teacher who got the Hastings boy in trouble."

She sensed Linc stiffening, and her own nervousness resurfaced, her stomach feeling almost as edgy as it had right before she'd stepped onto the dance floor the first time.

"I think you got that wrong, Dave," Linc said. To Cassie it sounded as if his voice were edged in steel.

"So she's not the teacher? Everyone says she is."

"What you got wrong is who got who into trouble. The Hastings boy did that to himself."

Dave scowled. "We got a championship to win, Coach. You know that."

It was the first time Cassie had heard anyone call Linc "Coach" except for his team, and she wondered if that word had been chosen for a reason. Of course, in other schools the coaches had been called Coach by everyone. Not here, though, which was odd when she thought about it. Maybe Linc didn't want to be addressed that way?

But her primary concern was Dave. His face was red, and she wondered if he'd had too much to drink. And how far this was going to go.

"I know all about the championship," Linc said. "But the players also know they shouldn't break school rules if they want to play the game. That hasn't changed since your day, Dave."

Dave's expression darkened. "Back in my day, we didn't have no zero tolerance. Kids do things. Kid things."

"That's true. But it's up to us to teach them better."

"Not by blowing the championship. Back in my day, nobody would have risked it."

"Then they were wrong."

Dave shoved back his chair and wagged his finger at Cassie. "You watch it, woman. This whole damn county is going to hold you responsible if we lose because Hastings can't play. And some folks ain't none too sure he bullied that Carney kid or pushed you. Besides, all kids get bullied. I sure as hell did."

He turned and stalked away before another word could be spoken.

Cassie reached for her drink, needing to do something with her hands, only to realize that she was shaking. At once Linc covered her hand with his, and squeezed reassuringly.

"Take a few breaths," he said, the music almost drowning him out. "We'll leave in a few minutes. After we make it clear he's not driving us out."

"I'm not leaving," Cassie argued, hating the tremor she heard in her voice. "I don't like people wagging their fingers at me."

One corner of Linc's mouth lifted. "I'm sure you don't. But Dave is the beginning of the next group of patrons. We wouldn't be staying much longer anyway."

This was the second time in two days that she had been confronted. This thing, she thought, was apt to be like cockroaches. If you saw one, there were probably a quarter million others in the walls. Tip of the iceberg.

The thought almost nauseated her, especially since she doubted that these people would be so angry if she'd lived here all her life. Maybe there was no way to become a real member of this community. Maybe she'd always be an outsider.

She quickly corralled her thoughts, realizing she had edged toward an extreme. Yes, she'd been confronted twice by people who believed she had lied about what had happened. But Maude had given her a piece of pie.

She looked at Linc. "Let's dance again before we leave."

He half smiled. "Sending a message, huh?"

"You bet." Her spine stiffened as she decided that regardless of what came out of this, regardless of whether she began to find it impossible to teach here, she wasn't going to let anyone think she had been cowed. No way.

The dance floor was getting much more crowded, and she noticed the makeup of the clientele had begun to change. More younger people, fewer older ones. The night was just beginning for some.

She also noticed something else: she got pushed. Not hard, not obviously, but unmistakably. Linc, who was on her other side, didn't notice the number of people who suddenly seemed to have developed two left feet, at least when they came near to her. Brushes like the boys had given her last week. Not enough to make her stumble, but they felt like a warning.

She turned her head toward Linc. "Linc?" She had to practically shout to be heard over the growing volume in the room.

He heard, though, and bent his head close to hers. "I'm being pushed. Repeatedly."

His face settled into a frown. "Hold on just a bit longer."

She managed a nod, then realized what he had expected.

Almost as if it were a good-night to the early crowd, the music shifted into something slow and sad. The line dancing stopped and couples turned face-to-face, arms around each other.

Linc pulled her close, an arm around her waist, the other holding her hand up in a traditional dance pose. Slowly he danced her around the floor.

It would have been wonderful if she hadn't been so disturbed. She felt a flare of anger toward the people who had tried to ruin this evening for her, and attempted to think about nothing except that Linc was holding her close, his head bent toward hers.

When she looked into his eyes, she saw blue fire. Regardless of the ugliness, he was thinking about one thing and one thing only. She couldn't miss the message.

Her heart lifted, her lips curved up a bit and she gave herself to the moment, wishing it could go on forever. She reminded herself that he was probably just sending a message of his own, but for the next four minutes that didn't seem to matter.

This time as they left the dance floor to collect their jackets, he didn't hold her arm. He held her hand.

So take that, she thought with weak amusement as she saw a few young women look enviously at her. It wouldn't solve the problem, though, nor did she have the least idea what would.

She just knew that while she wanted to get out of here, she also didn't want to go home.

Chapter 6

Outside in the parking lot, she stopped dead in her tracks, ignoring the steady flow of people around her.

"Is that snow?" she asked, looking toward one of the towering light posts where she was sure she saw a few flakes fluttering down.

"It is," he confirmed. "Just a light flurry, hardly anything at all. It won't stick."

"This is so cool!" she said, forgetting her upset. "I wish we'd get a lot."

A chuckle escaped him as he unlocked his truck and helped her in. "What's the rush? We'll have plenty of winter."

"I want to go cross-country skiing," she said. "I already have the equipment so now all I need is some snow."

"It might be a while yet but the weather around here has been growing much less arid. The last few years we've had more snow than usual, so you might luck out and not need to go up into the mountains to ski."

"Where else would I ski?"

"My ranch is a great place. If there's enough snow."

"No prepared trails?"

"Not around here." He closed the door and walked around to slide in behind the wheel. "Have you ever skied without a prepared trail?" He turned over the ignition and started easing out of the parking lot, avoiding cars and pedestrians.

"Of course, but it's been years."

"I've never had the time to give it any thought. Maybe after the football season is over. You can practice at my place if we have enough snow."

What was going on here? she wondered. After keeping such a distance, he seemed to be closing it awfully fast. Was he just taking pity on her? The question soured her mood, and caused her to reflect on what had happened tonight.

"Those people were pushing me," she said. "Like the boys did last week. Maybe a bit harder."

"But not hard enough that they couldn't claim it was a mistake."

"Exactly."

He wheeled onto the highway and headed back toward town. "I don't like this."

"I don't either, but I can't imagine a thing to do about it. Frankly, Linc, I'm more worried about James Carney. The story of him being bullied shouldn't have gotten out. The fact that it did means someone linked it directly to my complaint. I can't imagine the hell that boy might be going through."

"I haven't seen anything at school."

"Neither have I. He won't talk to me on the phone, either. He told me to just stay out of it. So I have, but…" She bit her lip and looked out the window.

"What can you do, Cassie? We're doing what we can to try to change student attitudes. We'll have an assembly next week."

"Next week? Les didn't mention that."

"Maybe he thought I'd tell you. Regardless, I don't see what we can do. We can't provide protection for James around the clock. We can't follow him to make sure no one bothers him. All we can try to do is make sure these students get it. All of them."

"Do you have any idea how alone he must feel? God, it breaks my heart. His grandmother said he's been bullied everywhere they lived. How much of that can a youngster take?"

"I don't know."

"The statistics aren't good. And can you imagine, everywhere you've lived your entire life being bullied? You'd have to be convinced that something is wrong with you."

"The way you are?"

She gasped, stunned. "What do you mean?"

"Just what I said. Sometimes I get the feeling you think something's wrong with you. Were you bullied a lot?"

She didn't answer immediately, as painful memories flooded back. Had she been bullied a lot? There were all kinds of bullying, some of it as mild as just being excluded. Between being smart and being plump, she'd certainly been made to feel that she wasn't like the other kids. But how much of that was simply normal teenage angst about fitting in? "Some," she said finally. "I don't know if it was a lot. It's not like there's some measuring stick."

"I know."

"Were you bullied?"

"A few times in seventh and eighth grade. It's a rough age for boys. But overall, I'd say not. The fact that you don't know…well, it makes me wonder. How many scars do you carry, Cassie? Do you even know?"

Probably not, she thought miserably. How could she know? She'd had a small circle of friends even at that difficult stage of life. That made her luckier than many. On the other hand, she'd been excluded from a lot, too. Boys hadn't asked her out. Cliquish girls had ignored her. And then there were those who said things about her weight.

"One time," she said slowly, "I was riding the bus back from a basketball game. When it came to a hill, it slowed down and groaned. One of the players shouted out, 'We need to dump some weight from this bus. Make Cassie walk.'"

"Hell. Did that happen often?"

"Things like it, once in a while."

"But often enough. I'm sorry."

She almost said, "But it happens to everyone." That much was nearly true, but that didn't make it right. "There were harder things."

"Such as?"

"My best girlfriend. A lot of the guys wanted to date her, but her parents wouldn't let her date. So they'd ask her on group outings. Her parents wouldn't let her go unless I was there to chaperone. So that's how I got to go."

"You were chaperoning your friend? Good God. That must have made you feel awful!"

"Oddly, I hoped they'd get to like me better if I was enough fun. Being fun evidently wasn't the answer, and I didn't feel too good about it when I realized it."

"You were a lot of fun tonight," he said after a few seconds. "I had a great time. I don't know how you looked in high school, obviously, but I can tell you that right now you're a glorious-looking woman, I was proud to be with you, and you forget those guys who didn't have eyes to see."

Her throat tightened and her eyes grew hot as if tears wanted to flow. She honestly couldn't remember any man saying such a sweet thing to her. "You didn't have to say that."

"No, I didn't. That's the point. I didn't have to say a damn thing."

Now he sounded like he was steaming. She almost said, "You'll change your mind like every other guy," but she held the words in. That was a place she didn't want to go for a bunch of reasons. One night of dancing didn't mean they had a relationship, and she didn't want him to misunderstand what she thought. She settled for "Thank you."

As he pulled in behind her car in her driveway, a few random snowflakes sparkled in the headlights. They were so beautiful. Then she saw her car.

Linc was already quietly furious, though he'd done his best to conceal it. Dave Banks coming up to them like that, Cassie getting pushed on the dance floor, followed by some very personal revelations from her that at once touched his heart and twisted his gut... Well, he was angry. Very angry. When he saw her car he got so mad he almost saw red.

"Don't get out," he said sharply. Pawing around in his jacket, he found his cell phone and called the sheriff's office. Four flats on a car with the back window painted LIAR was not something he was going to ignore. No way. As far as he was concerned, the cops around here needed to get off their butts *now*.

Cassie murmured something. He didn't want to look at her, didn't want to see anguish or fear on her face, not that he would have blamed her for either. He reached out blindly, found her hand and held it tightly.

"Linc, I'm getting scared. Tonight…" Her voice cracked and she didn't finish.

He couldn't blame her. The implied violence in being pushed, however lightly, and now the vandalism to her car would have made any sensible person afraid. "I told you that you wouldn't face this alone. I meant it."

She didn't ask what he meant, and right then he didn't explain. Instead she asked a question that raised every emotional red flag he'd had since Martha.

"What the hell is wrong with this place? I can see people getting angry. I can see people lying, especially when they're upset about their kids. I can see students lying to cover their misdeeds. But to keep brushing me on the dance floor? Those were adults, Linc. And now this."

She had a valid point. "How many people pushed you?"

"Four, maybe five. No more than that. It was carefully done. Some others I was almost sure were accidents."

"Did you see who they were?"

"I saw faces, but I don't know them."

"Younger?"

"Yes."

He turned that around in his mind. "Some people never seem to leave high school even after they graduate. Maybe they were friends of those students."

"I guess."

"I'm just saying that I don't think most people around here would condone that. The vast majority, maybe ninety-nine percent, wouldn't condone that. I'm sorry as hell you met the others."

"Yeah, all in one place." She sighed and turned her hand over so that she was holding his. "Okay, it's probably a very small set. Very small. Most of the people I've met here have been pleasant. And given how many people were dancing when that started, it really was just a few. There must have been a hundred people in that place."

"At least. It's a busy roadhouse on weekends."

"But clearly people around here are mad at me and worried about the championship. Look at that Dave guy."

"So what do you want to do?"

"I don't know. I honestly don't know. But if this keeps up, maybe I should back out of my contract and let the people here deal with it however they want."

He felt an astonishingly strong pang. There it was. "Do you want to leave?" he asked levelly.

"Truthfully, no. But I'm getting scared and I'm wondering what kind of place this really is."

He had no answer for that, especially since she'd only been here a couple of months. How could he defend his county, his neighbors, to her when she had so little experience? It was a relief to see the sheriff's car pull up at the curb.

The random snowflakes continued to fall, almost like a harbinger of things to come.

It would have been so easy, Cassie thought, to decide to pack up and tell Les on Monday morning that she no longer felt safe here. She was sure he would let her out of her contract for that reason.

But even as the desire to get away scrambled around in her head, she had other memories rising up, memories of how pleasant most people here had been to her. How welcoming some of them had been. The pie from Maude today was just one of the incidents that had warmed her since her first day here.

The neighbors who had helped her unload her moving truck, and had been so willing to carry heavy items to exactly where she wanted them. The fellow from two doors down who had mowed her little patch of grass a few times until she found a neighbor boy she could hire. The ladies who had come over with casseroles and other delicacies so she wouldn't have to cook while moving in.

She closed her eyes, focusing on those people and on her fellow teachers who had been nice enough. No, whatever was happening, Linc was right, it involved a small few. While many might be wondering what was actually going on, the truth was, it was only a few who were taking it to the extreme.

But it sure didn't make her feel safe.

The deputy who arrived was a good-looking man in his fifties. Linc introduced him as Virgil Beauregard, but called him Beau. He walked around the car with a flashlight, shaking his head, and squatted down to examine the tires.

"I'm gonna start sounding like our last sheriff," he remarked as he straightened. "This county is going to hell in a handbasket. This about that detention thing?"

"Probably," Linc answered. He sketched the other incidents for Beau, whose frown deepened.

"This seems awfully extreme over a detention," Beau remarked. "It won't keep the kid from playing basketball."

"Nope. Not unless he gets another one."

"Somebody's going to get detention in the county jail if they don't look out." He pulled out a notebook and scribbled. "Whoever they were, they discovered it's harder to puncture a tire than you'd think. Unless there's damage I can't see, they let the air out of the other three after puncturing one. I'm gonna get some other guys out here and we'll talk to neighbors. Maybe someone saw something. It was kind of early in the evening to pull a stunt like this. You all go on inside."

It might be early, but it was also dark, Cassie thought as she led the way inside. Her house also sat in a puddle of shadow between streetlights that weren't terribly bright to begin with.

"Coffee?" she asked, even as she automatically started to make a pot. Somehow she didn't feel as if she were going to sleep tonight, caffeine or no caffeine.

"Thanks." Behind her, she heard the chair scrape as he sat at the table. "You're being awfully quiet about all this."

"What should I do? Erupt? That won't change a thing."

"No, but I wouldn't blame you for being furious."

She started the coffeemaker and joined him, sitting across from him at the table. "Right now I'm frightened. Maybe I'll get angry later. Or maybe I won't. There's nothing that's been done that can't be fixed."

"Except the part about you being frightened."

All too true, she thought, resting her forehead in her hand and drawing aimless circles with her fingertip on the tabletop. "I just wish I knew how far this is going to go, and for how long." Unanswerable questions. "Do you think someone might get violent?"

"A week ago I'd have said no way. I don't even get *this*. A lousy detention? It's not like Ben Hastings can't play because of one detention. If he gets another, or gets suspended, that would be different, but that hasn't happened. All he has to do is behave."

She lifted her head, having noted that he hadn't really answered her question about violence. Her nerves tried to stretch tight, and she drew a deep breath. Violence over a detention? All it would take was one unhinged person. *Stop,* she commanded herself. Get back to reality.

After a minute or two, she spoke again, trying to remain reasonable. "Maybe someone is afraid I'll push the bullying issue. That *should* have got him suspended. He's now on a knife edge, and apparently that's got some people worried." She paused. "One of the teachers must have talked out of school, after our meeting on Monday."

"Why do you say that?"

"How else would everyone seem to know about James Carney? And certainly, having me as part of an antibullying program…. Oh, that was a mistake. I'm the new broom and it probably looks like I'm sweeping through demanding changes, and likely to make a serious issue of future bullying."

"Will you?"

She looked up and saw him smiling faintly. "Yes. I was demanding suspension when I walked into Les's office last week."

"Good. Maybe it takes a new broom to make us realize we need to change some things. When things become too familiar, it's easy to overlook them. Plus, there seems to be a lot of 'kids will be kids' mentality running around. That needs to change about this issue."

She nodded. She had heard the coffee finish brewing, so she went to fill a couple of mugs. "I'm sorry I can't offer much to eat. I don't keep many snacks around and tomorrow is shopping day. Or was. I guess it's going to be car day instead."

"I know the couple who run the auto repair shop. I'll give them a call in the morning and have it all taken care of."

She slid into her seat and made a face. "What if they're on the pro-Hastings side?"

"Whatever side Morris is on, if he's even on one, he'll do a good job for you. Besides, I'll bet most people around here haven't even picked a side. The championship may be important, but most people probably don't consider it important enough to try to mistreat you. I can understand some folks wanting to argue with you, but beyond that..." He shook his head. "It's got to be one person who vandalized your car. The bumps on the dance floor were probably some of Hastings's friends. And I'm trying to minimize this." He gave her a rueful expression. "I guess I shouldn't do that. This is new territory for me."

The doorbell rang. Linc offered to get it, and a minute later he was bringing Beau into the kitchen.

"Coffee?" Cassie asked automatically.

"No thanks. I've had my limit tonight. Okay, neighbors didn't see anything. Some weren't home, others were busy watching TV. As far as they knew, the street was quiet. We're looking around for evidence, but you might as well turn in for the night. Although the floodlights are going to be bright."

"Can I scrape her rear window off?" Linc asked. "I don't want that word there come morning."

Beau hesitated. "I'll do it when we've collected all the information we can." He turned to Cassie. "I'll let you know if we find anything."

"He won't," Cassie said after Beau left. "It's just some vandalism. It hardly requires the sort of investigation a major theft or murder would get."

"You might be surprised. Beau probably feels like you have the entire county on trial in your mind."

"Well, I don't. Not yet. But I may get there if this keeps up."

"Cassie?"

She looked his way. "Yes?"

"You've got a choice. I can camp on your couch tonight or you can come out to my place and use one of the spare bedrooms for the weekend. Either way, I'm not leaving you alone tonight."

She was startled and grateful all at once. "Are you that worried someone might try to hurt me?"

"Hell, I don't know anymore. I never would have thought this much would have happened. But what I do know is you're frightened, with good reason, and that's enough to make me feel you shouldn't have to be alone tonight."

It was all she could do not to gape at him. The turn-around he'd made this week was astonishing. The guy who had tried so hard not to connect with her was now suddenly there, connecting in a myriad of ways. Taking her to his ranch, taking her out to Maude's, dancing and now this?

Part of her screeched to back away before he did. Because he probably would. He must have had some reason for treating her as if she were contagious for the last couple of months. But now he was in her corner, totally and completely.

A white-knight complex? That promised nothing good, because as soon as he felt she no longer needed protection, he might well pull away again.

But she had to admit, the idea of being alone tonight bothered her. She'd lived by herself most of the time since she left college, and never before had it disturbed her, but looking at the night ahead, she really didn't want to be on her own after the deputies finished.

"Pack a bag," he said, making the decision for her. "I've got plenty of room. Plan on spending the weekend. I'll have Morris take care of your car in the morning."

She wanted to object just because she preferred to make her own decisions, but she realized that would be cutting her nose off to spite her face. She *wanted* to spend a weekend at his ranch. She liked it out there. She'd get more of a window on him and how he lived.

And she sure didn't want to stay here. Her home didn't feel as friendly or safe tonight. Nor did sleeping on the couch strike her as very comfortable for him, not as tall as he was.

Finally she nodded and went to pack. Escape sounded so good right now, even if only for a weekend.

The drive to the ranch seemed mysterious along isolated and dark country roads. With the sky clouded over, all she could see was the area illuminated by the headlights and a stray snowflake or two. Even the mountains to the west had vanished, the same inky color as everything else.

"It gets so dark out here at night," she remarked. "I'm used to places where there's at least some light. I didn't know a night could look like this."

"You'll have to come outside with me if the clouds clear out. You probably never saw just how many stars are up there. The first time I really noticed them was when I'd been away at college. Sometimes I think we don't look up often enough."

"Meaning?"

"Maybe we'd realize just how small and unimportant most things are." He paused. "Once we get to the ranch, if you feel like it you ought to sit outside for a while. Let your eyes adapt. With this cloud cover, I can promise you'll see a glow from neighboring ranches. It'll be faint, but you can see it. On a clear night, you can't."

"Maybe I'll try that." Because sleep was the last thing on her mind.

No, with each passing mile her other concerns and fears faded in an increasingly intense awareness of the man beside her. When they had been dancing, there'd been enough going on and enough people around to keep it in check, even during the slow dance when she had wanted to melt against him.

But there was nothing now to keep her mind in check. Not one thing. She was away from town, away from the person or persons who were so angry with her. Safe. And safety awoke a new kind of danger.

Linc felt like throwing up his hands in surrender. He'd failed in every single resolution to keep his distance from this woman. A handful—well probably just a handful, if not just one—of bullies had pushed him right toward her like a plow pushing snow. Nor did he see anyone else stepping up for her. He was still annoyed that Les had put the onus on her for this entire situation. With the best of intentions, he was sure. Who would have expected this kind of reaction?

It remained, his own resolve had failed. He'd known from the moment he first saw her that he wanted her. He thought he knew better, and had made up his mind to stay clear.

Now here he was, taking her to his place for the weekend, a woman who had just tonight mentioned canceling her contract. Leaving. Just like Martha. But even worse,

Cassie certainly had ample reason to wonder if she should remain here.

God, he couldn't fathom this. Not at all. A week ago he would have said this was impossible. People might talk among themselves—well, of course they would. They might even argue about it. Hastings's parents would certainly feel confrontational. But *this?*

He understood the importance of the championship. The school wasn't that big, and didn't have that many students to draw on for its teams. A star came along maybe once every ten or twenty years. In fact, he seemed to remember the last time the school had been in line for a basketball championship had been about twenty years ago. Since then they'd had a track-and-field star, and one football team that had made it to the state playoffs. So yeah, this was a big deal.

Everyone knew scouts had been looking at Hastings. This could be his ticket to college and a very bright future. People were rooting for that kid at least as much as they were rooting for the team. Something bright and wonderful was hovering in the wings, providing a change to the ordinary routine, a few months of pride and something different to talk about.

He could also understand how those who were personally close to Hastings, like his mother and friends, might want to yell at Cassie or even bump her on the dance floor.

But the rat was on a whole different level, as was the vandalism of her car. He'd tried to dismiss that rat to Cassie, even accepting her initial arguments about it, but somewhere deep inside he hadn't been able to shake the feeling they were dealing with a disturbed mind.

Now he was sure of it. People getting into arguments

over the detention, even dismissing the wrongness of bullying the Carney kid, that didn't rise to this level.

Frankly, he admitted to himself, the idea that someone, just one person, was disturbed enough to pull this stuff had him far more worried than if there'd been a mob in the streets. You could deal with a mob. They were out there where you could see them. But one sicko slinking around in the shadows? That's what worried him.

He glanced over at Cassie just before he turned onto his road. She was folded up on herself, staring blindly out the window into the night. It was a good thing the road was bumpy and he had to keep both hands on the wheel. Otherwise he might have wrapped her up in his arms, and then all hell would break loose because he wanted her with an ache as deep and wide as the open spaces out here.

He snapped his eyes back to the road. Danger. The night suddenly seemed to be filled with it, and it wasn't some crazy person he was worrying about. It was himself.

He could do her more harm than some vandal. What she had revealed earlier had told him a lot. He wasn't the only one in this truck with old wounds, not the only one seriously at risk of taking a misstep.

God knew, he didn't want to wound her any more. And he didn't want to go through a replay of the most god-awful months of his life.

She might run. The urge was strong enough that she'd mentioned it, then backed away. All he could do was ensure that neither of them got hurt in any way.

Cassie accepted Linc's hand as she climbed out of his truck beside his ranch house. It was colder, as if the land out here had exhaled the day's remaining warmth faster than the streets in town.

"How'd it get so cold?" she asked, trying to keep this casual. Much as she wanted to fall into his arms, she had decided during the ride that the best thing would be to stay away. He had run cold, then hot, indicating that he had some kind of problem with her. She didn't need to know what it was to realize she needed to keep her distance.

She focused her attention away from him, and tried to quash memories of being held in his strong arms. Tried not to draw a mental picture of those narrow hips and wide shoulders. Tried not to remember the remarkable compliment he had paid her, or the way his blue eyes seemed to heat up when they gazed at her.

The night was suddenly upon them, and although it was cold her internal heat was rising. She couldn't seem to draw enough of the icy air into her lungs. *Don't look at him.* Don't encourage whatever it was that seemed to be filling the short distance between them, that seemed to tug her toward him the way gravity held her to the ground.

"Let's go inside," he said. "I'll make you a hot drink. Then if you want, we can sit out back for a while."

"I'd like that." That sounded safe enough. Sitting outside all bundled up would surely freeze the hot waves of desire that had started to pulse within her. Who could think about sex in the cold, while wearing almost enough clothing for an Eskimo?

Evidently she could, she thought with amusement as she followed him inside.

He left her bag inside the door. "I'll let you pick a room later," he said. Then he led the way to the kitchen, where he made a couple of mugs of instant cocoa.

Outside the temperature seemed to have fallen a bit more. Maybe, Cassie thought, it was just a contrast to being indoors.

He had a wide porch and a number of padded patio chairs that were comfortable. As soon as she settled into one with her mug, he disappeared into the house. He returned a few minutes later with a blanket he tucked around her legs.

"Let me know if you start to feel too cold. I know you just came from a warmer climate."

"Considerably warmer," she admitted. "Occasionally we got down into the low thirties or even twenties, but usually not often enough to get used to it."

"I'd miss the seasons," he said as he settled into his own chair. He put one booted foot up on the railing and looked out into the dark, mug in one large hand.

"I know I did. I wanted to get back to them."

"You hated it?"

"Not really. Not at all. It's just that when I was young, before my mom decided to follow this guy to Florida, I always loved the change of season. Especially autumn. Don't ask me why, but I missed autumn most of all. Down there you usually sense it only by the change in the quality of light. That happens long before it cools down and the leaves change."

"How'd your mom's guy work out?"

"Not too well," she admitted. "It came apart after about six months."

"How did you feel about that?"

"Relieved. He wasn't nasty to me or anything. It wasn't like the horror stories you hear. I just didn't especially like him. He never really tried to like me. I guess I felt tolerated."

He was silent for a while. She realized that he was right, she could see the faint, distant glow from other ranches.

She wondered if it would disappear later, or if they had security lighting.

She heard some soft sounds from the direction of the meadows, but they didn't strike her as disturbed. "Do the animals stay awake all night?"

"No, but they don't sleep like we do. They move around occasionally, and make a little noise."

"It's beautiful out here."

"I think so," he agreed. "Cassie?"

"What?"

"Did you always feel like an outsider, even at home?"

She looked down at the mug she could barely see and felt her chest tighten. "I guess so," she said after a moment. "Doesn't nearly everyone?"

"I don't think so."

"Why did you ask?"

"Thinking about a little girl moving to Florida so that her mother could follow a man she hardly knew. You've changed jobs a lot, too, haven't you?"

"Three different school districts in eight years isn't a lot."

"Maybe not. What are you looking for?"

"I told you. A place like this. Well, a place like what I thought this was."

"You're already thinking about leaving."

She tried to see him, but it was too dark to do more than make out his silhouette. "It crossed my mind. But I'm not going to."

"Why not?"

"Because I really want to put down roots, Linc. *Really.* It's like there's always been this place in my heart where I wanted to live, and life conspired to keep me away from it. I was always in busy metropolitan areas, larger towns.

Places where you could blend in with the walls. I wanted something warmer."

"You can make a community anywhere," he said. "It doesn't have to be geographic."

"I know that. But I want a geographic community. I want to know who lives two blocks over, I want to recognize the people on the streets. I want to be able to greet most of them by name. Most places I've been, you can live in an apartment for a couple of years and barely recognize the people next door. You can rent a house in the suburbs and you'd think the neighborhood was empty. The front-porch culture seems to be gone."

"Not from here," he admitted. "Although those of us out on ranches and farms have to make some effort. It helps, growing up here."

"Are you saying I can't become part of this community?"

"Not at all. It'll happen. You might be referred to as the new teacher for a while, though."

She gave a small laugh. "That I can handle."

"Mainly what I'm trying to get at is that in some ways, even if you live here the rest of your life, you may feel like an outsider. But if you're here a while, most of that will come from inside you."

She thought about that. "You might have a point."

"Maybe." He left it at that.

But he had stirred a memory in her and she recalled a study she had read in one of her psychology courses. "Children who move a lot," she said, "have a tendency not to make the same kind of deep and long-lasting connections that people make when they grow up in one place."

"I know."

"So maybe I can't make deep connections."

"I'm not saying you're broken in some way. If you want to and make the effort, I'm sure you can. Even here, once this mess blows over."

"Why did you bring this up?"

"I was just wondering. I grew up here. The only time I felt like an outsider was when I was away at college, and when I came back I was home. Your experience struck me as different and I wondered how it made you feel."

"Well, now you know."

"And you want to change that."

"You bet I do."

"Then stick around. Don't even think about leaving. It's hard right now, but I can tell you from my own experience, it'll be worth it. Despite the way things look right now, most folks around here are good people."

"I was thinking about that earlier. The way I was welcomed when I got here. I've never before had neighbors I hadn't even met help me move, or bring over meals while I was settling in. That was a wonderful feeling."

"I know, even when you're used to it. They do the same when somebody gets ill."

"Those are the things I need to concentrate on," she said firmly. Then she added, "My hands are getting cold."

"Don't you have gloves?"

"I forgot them. Besides, I don't have any really good ones for here, just some basic, not-too-warm ones I brought with me."

"Let's go inside, then."

In the kitchen, he rinsed out their mugs and put them in the dishwasher. The dishwasher that inevitably reminded him of Martha. Damn. Well, he needed that warning right about now. He needed to get Cassie safely up into one of the bedrooms and close a door firmly between them.

That proved to be easier thought than done. When he turned around, she was slipping off her jacket. The satiny blouse she wore emphasized the way her breasts thrust forward as she held her arms behind her back. And then she shook herself to get the jacket to slide down.

Full breasts, bouncing slightly despite her bra. She seemed unaware that he turned and was looking. The sleeve slipped off one arm and she twisted to tug her jacket around.

Temptation had never come in a lovelier, more enticing package. Her gently rounded shape was generous in all the right places. That little bit of plumpness that she probably hated—the way so many women did—only enticed him more. She would be soft beneath him, curvaceous in his hands. Hips, real hips, not like so many young women who could almost be mistaken for men from behind. His hands imagined how that fullness would feel and he hardened almost between one breath and the next.

He nearly choked with the hunger he felt, the arousal that suddenly pounded through his veins. Who would have thought that watching a woman pull off a jacket could be so erotic? Not he.

Then she turned to hang it over the back of a kitchen chair and he was treated to a full rear view. A rounded butt cased in denim, perfectly shaped. He was losing it.

As if from a distance, almost deafened by the blood hammering in his ears, he heard himself say, "I meant it when I said you're glorious."

Not beautiful, but something far more: glorious.

She turned sharply, surprise on her face. Then he saw her expression melt into one of welcome, her gaze reflecting heat and delight at the same time. And then a flicker of disbelief.

Why she should disbelieve that she was glorious had him beat all to hell, but he was in no mood to question her or discuss it. He chose to respond to her welcome and her heat.

He was through fighting his desire for her.

He was also past finesse. Without a word, he scooped her up in his arms and carried her toward the front stairs.

She gasped. "Linc! You'll hurt yourself."

"Cassie, you seem to have an exaggerated notion of your size." It was true. He was strong, but she didn't feel heavy in his arms. No, she felt good. His breathing grew deeper, his voice thicker, and he managed to say with his last ounce of sanity, "I'm acting like a caveman. Tell me to stop now, before it's too late."

His heart almost stalled as he began climbing the stairs— a wide staircase, thank goodness, unlike many of the older houses around here—and she offered no response.

Then, unmistakably, he heard her giggle softly. "I kind of like troglodytes."

Her answer exploded in his head, filling him with both wonder and a very deep pleasure. Then she lifted her arm and twined it around his neck.

She was his. Just for now, she was his. The heat in him burgeoned, turning to flames that lapped at his every cell.

At the top of the stairs he turned toward his bedroom, the very same room he had used since childhood. He'd never wanted to move into his parents' room. It would have given him no extra space, since all the bedrooms were the same size, and it was loaded with memories. Including Martha, because Martha had taken it over. It had a better view, being on the corner of the house, and she'd even been pushing to have a private bath installed.

He'd considered it, but it didn't get past that before she

left. Since then, the room had been off-limits except when he needed to go in and clean it.

He hesitated a moment, wondering if taking Cassie in there would banish Martha forever, then decided he could find out another time. If there was another time.

Instead he took her to his own room, with its footless queen-size bed, a small desk, a bedside table and a dresser. Furniture, except for the bed, that had been handed down. Only a night-light provided minimal illumination.

He set Cassie down on her feet beside the bed, and bent his head to kiss her. She welcomed him without hesitation, opening her mouth to his, taking his tongue deep inside.

And her curves, ah, her curves. There was nothing to stop him now, and he ran his palms over her, over her shoulder and back, down to that luscious rump, learning every hill and hollow. Rounded softness greeted him.

A soft little moan escaped her, and her hands gripped his shoulders, digging in as if she feared falling. A primitive sense of triumph overtook him as he realized she was his, fully his. She wanted him as much as he wanted her, and he wanted her more than he'd ever wanted anything.

He released her mouth, giving them both a chance to breathe, then dove in again. This time his hands sought other curves. Their tongues dueled in a timeless rhythm as his hand found her breast and squeezed. It was everything he had imagined, full and firm and so damnably cased in clothing.

But as he ran the flat of his hand across the peak of her breast, she arched her hips into his, the message unmistakable. She was ready.

He was, too, but he wanted it to last. He wanted to learn every bit of her landscape, to discover her every secret, to find the promise she offered without even realizing it.

He turned her a bit so that she was bent slightly over his left arm, and tugged her blouse free of the waistband of her jeans. Slipping his hand beneath, he found warm skin softer than satin. She shivered at his touch, and clung harder to his back.

Perfect, he thought. Exquisite. Everything about her, from the scent of her soap and shampoo, to the chocolaty taste that lingered in her mouth. A hint of feminine perfume, and a musky aroma that was strengthening, signaling her need.

He clutched her hip, pressing her side against his throbbing erection for one long, aching moment. Then his hand began to forage along the edge of her bra, seeking treasure.

"Linc..." she gasped, and the sound of her voice pounded in his ears along with the drumbeat of his blood.

Then the phone rang.

Chapter 7

"**D**amn!" He swore sharply as the mood shattered like so much spun glass.

Cassie blinked, feeling the desire vanish as if it had been blown away by an internal tornado. "Linc?" she said, her voice a cracked whisper. Coming back to reality proved unexpectedly difficult.

"I'm sorry. It's well past midnight. It must be an emergency."

She nodded, and was touched when he steadied her as she sat on the edge of the bed. The shrilling phone was on the night table, and he snatched it up.

"Linc Blair." He didn't sound very patient. She watched him, still feeling the hunger even though it had been damped almost to quietude by the startling interruption. She hoped it wasn't an emergency, because if he turned and took her into his arms again, she was going to explode like a banked fire that had only been waiting for fresh fuel.

But she saw his posture change. His shoulders dropped a little. "But he's all right?" Then he said, "Thanks for calling." He put the phone down.

He turned, his face an unreadable mask as if he couldn't decide what he felt. "This couldn't have waited until morning? Like there's damn all we can do about it?"

"What happened, Linc?"

"That was Les. James Carney is in the hospital. He tried to kill himself earlier."

"Oh, my God." As the import of his words hit home, nausea rolled through her in waves and she doubled over. "Oh, my God," she whispered. "Oh, my God."

The bed dipped as Linc sat beside her. He wrapped his arms around her and she turned into his embrace. Shock flowed through her in hot and cold waves.

"He's all right," Linc repeated over and over. "He's all right."

"He's alive," she said brokenly, as tears began to flow. "Alive and all right aren't the same."

"I know, Cassie." His murmur was soothing and pained all at once. "But at least there's still a chance to help him."

"Where there's life there's hope?" She repeated the old saw, then gave way to a sob. "Oh, God, Linc, it hurts. It hurts to know how badly he must have suffered. That he would think of this as a solution."

He held her even tighter, rocking her gently, letting her cry it out. The news about James, she realized, had been like a last straw to the stress of the past week. It was all coming out now, her worry for the student, her uneasiness about the attacks against her. But mostly she wept for James. For all she had been through at times, never had she thought that killing herself was her only way out. She couldn't stand to imagine how that youth must be feeling.

Eventually she realized that she had soaked Linc's shirt with her tears. "I'm sorry," she said thickly, trying to pull away and wipe her face. But he wouldn't let her go.

"Don't apologize," was all he said.

She realized he sounded angry. "Are you mad at me?"

"You? No way. But I'm pretty damn angry with some other people right now. Livid."

Anger hadn't come to her yet. Hurt and fear, yes, but not anger. Even some weariness somewhere deep inside, because this wasn't the first time she had encountered depravity in some people. A teacher soon learned how many children were living in terrible circumstances, how many lived daily with fear, poverty and hunger. The secrets they carried and tried so hard to conceal, yet that were written in their behavior and misbehavior even if they denied anything was going on.

But she'd never had a student attempt suicide before.

Guilt slammed her then, overtaking sorrow. Had she somehow been responsible for this because of her intervention? Because she hadn't just walked away after stopping the bullying in the restroom, but had instead caused those four students to get detention?

What she had seen had been bad enough, but had she made it worse? Knowing the way some people thought, it was entirely possible that they'd bullied James even more to make sure he never spoke about what they had done and were doing.

Her stomach grew leaden, and agitation caused her to jump up from the bed and pace the room. Linc reached over to switch on a lamp, probably so she wouldn't stumble against something, but he remained seated on the edge of the bed.

"Do you know how twisted this is?" she demanded.

"What's twisted?" he asked. "Other than the bullying you and James Carney have been getting."

"That I may have made things worse for James by intervening. What do you do when nothing works? It's like being caught in a spiderweb! I try to protect a student, and it only makes it worse?"

"You don't know that," he said quietly. "Cassie, there is no way on earth you can know if you made things worse. What were you supposed to do? Ignore it? Obviously the bullying has been ignored too much and for too long, because it's evidently going on. Without a crackdown, it won't stop. But you can't blame yourself because you did the right thing."

"I can't? Why not? If my action resulted in that boy being bullied even more, why can't I blame myself? God, I feel like a fool. I didn't even pause to consider when I stepped in that I might make it harder on him. I was stupid."

"No."

"No? Of course I was. I saw something and reacted without considering all the possible consequences. I didn't mediate, I just told the four bullies to get to the principal's office."

"Where Les, and you, would have attempted to find out what was behind all this. Mediation. But you didn't get the chance. James even told you to stay out of it."

"He was right. Look what's happened."

Linc rose. "I'm sorry, Cassie, but I don't agree with how you feel. If nobody ever intervenes for fear of making it worse, we'll never stop it. And right now, you don't even know if it got worse. He may have been contemplating suicide for some time, from what his grandmother told you."

"But what made him do it *now?*"

Linc rose, speaking quietly but firmly. "I'm sure as hell going to find out."

"If anyone will talk to you," she said almost bitterly. A sense of responsibility nearly suffocated her. Breathing had become an effort as her chest grew tight and her stomach twisted. "God, I need to do *something!*"

A useless wish, she thought as her mind and body roiled with reaction. It was the middle of the night. What the hell could she possibly *do* right now? As it was, doing something may have made matters worse for a young man.

"I'll get us some coffee," Linc said. "Then we'll go to the hospital. If the family is still there, we can let them know they aren't alone."

Now she felt guilty in another way. "You have a game tomorrow. Today. This afternoon. You need some sleep."

"It won't be my first sleepless night with a game looming. Let's go."

Soon they were driving down the dark tunnel of the endless night again with a couple of travel mugs filled with hot coffee. Cassie's eyes burned, wanting to shed more tears. But along with guilt, anger had begun to grow in her. A terrible anger, as bad as she'd ever felt.

Logically she knew the people involved in bullying James and trying to frighten her were probably a very small number. Most of the people around here, or anywhere, wouldn't do this kind of thing. Most people were actually decent. They might sometimes be unaware, but they weren't deliberately cruel and wouldn't approve of deliberate cruelty.

That was the point of the antibullying campaign, to raise awareness. To make the students understand that it was happening, and sometimes it got far worse than the minor insults most endured. By making them aware of how tolerating even minor bullying could create a climate that allowed it to grow. Consciousness-raising. It worked.

Especially with students of this age, most of whom usually already felt all alone, and if bullied would probably feel ashamed, as if they were somehow responsible. As if something were wrong with *them* and not the bullies. She knew the feeling all too well.

By making more of them aware, they wouldn't feel alone and wouldn't feel that being bullied was their fault. The other hope was to create such an atmosphere of disapproval for bullying that there would be far less of it.

But all of that would come too late for James Carney. Over and over she reran the incident in her mind, trying to figure out what she could have done differently. Because she was absolutely convinced that she hadn't done something she should have.

No, it wasn't a matter of ignoring what those four students had been doing to James. It was a matter of not doing enough of the right thing. Whatever that right thing was.

She almost wanted to hit her head on the window glass beside her, to try to stir up some new thought. But new thoughts proved elusive, and she seemed to be pretty much stuck in an endless loop of guilt, grief and anger with no way out.

Throughout the drive to the hospital, Linc remained silent. She wondered if he was disturbed by her reaction, or angry that he had to make this trip in the middle of the night. Even though he had suggested it, she wouldn't have been surprised if he'd felt he had no choice, given the way she was taking this.

Or maybe he was angry that she hadn't taken this news better and gone ahead with making love to him. Most of the men she had dated—a small enough sample set to be sure—would have been angry about that.

She couldn't ask him, though. Facing her own cowardice, she realized she was afraid of what he might say. What if he thought she was weird, or overreacting, or just a plain nuisance? He wouldn't be the first.

Linc made good time to the hospital. She hadn't noticed that he had driven any faster, but maybe the trip was starting to seem shorter as she got used to it.

As always, he came around to help her out, a gentlemanly courtesy she had thought long dead.

"It'll be okay," he said quietly. "We're going to do something about this, and most people are going to be very upset if they hear about this."

He was probably right. She was sure he was right. But the family's privacy had to be honored as well.

Her nerves tightened as they walked to the waiting room, where an attendant had told them James's family was waiting. Apparently he was not far enough out of the woods that his family was ready to go home.

As the one who may have started this ball rolling with her intervention last week, Cassie wondered what kind of reception she would receive. She wouldn't be able to argue with them if they blamed her, despite what James's grandmother had said.

James's parents, Maureen and Jack Carney, were alone in the waiting room. They held hands, and while Jack appeared angry, Maureen looked more frightened.

Linc made the introductions—he really *did* seem to know everyone. Cassie gathered her courage and asked how James was, hoping she didn't hear...*as if you care.*

"Unconscious," Jack Carney said. He was a slender man who, unlike many of the people in these parts, didn't look as if he spent a lot of time outdoors. "He's alive, but if he doesn't wake up soon they may have to transport him for additional testing for brain damage."

Cassie's legs turned to water. From what Linc had said of Les's call, she had assumed he was awake. Physically fine, if not emotionally or psychologically. Not facing possible brain damage. She nearly collapsed into one of the plastic chairs. "Oh, no," she said weakly.

"It's bad," Jack said. "It's bad. But we're hoping."

"I am so, so sorry."

Linc slowly sat beside her. "Les made it sound as if James was okay now."

"Okay?" Jack spoke bitterly. "He'll never be okay. He's been bullied everywhere he's ever gone to school. I don't know why. Do you know why?"

Cassie had to shake her head. "He struck me as a bright and very nice young man."

"Who knows why bullies pick their victims," Linc said. "I noticed James was quieter than most, but up until just recently, I hadn't thought of him as withdrawn. Just quiet."

"Of course he was quiet," Jack said. "He's been trying to be invisible for years."

Cassie twisted her hands together, torn between sorrow at what that statement revealed, and anger that James's peers had made him feel that way.

"I should have homeschooled him," Maureen said, her voice raw. "I should have taught him myself and kept him away from all that."

"You had a job," Jack said. He lowered his head, his voice growing heavy. "I had no idea it was this bad. He didn't talk about it. Sometimes the only way we found out was when teachers alerted us."

Maureen looked at him. "Remember third grade? We

didn't know anything was wrong. I'll never understand why the teacher didn't mention the bullying until the end of the year. I'd have taken him out of school then if I'd had any idea. Why didn't James tell us?" She ended on a rising note, then quickly put her face in her hands.

In the midst of her own guilt, Cassie felt Maureen's pain like an added spear to her heart. She rose and went to sit by Maureen. She put her hand gently on the woman's shoulder and tried to find suitable words.

"When they're little, kids often don't tell us things because they think we know already. They endow parents with a kind of omniscience, maybe because they've been caught out so many times when they were being secretive. I don't know, I'm not a psychologist. I just know that it's true. And then when they get older... Mrs. Carney, it's even harder when they get older because there's a tendency to assume responsibility when someone hurts us. All too often we think we must be at fault, and we feel ashamed."

Maureen nodded, but Cassie had no idea if she were really hearing. Probably not. There was too much pain, worry and fear right now.

If she, a teacher who barely knew James and saw him only in class for fifty-five minutes a day, felt guilty about this, she didn't even want to imagine how Maureen and Jack must be feeling. As if she could have. The chasm of horror these parents must have felt exceeded anything in her personal experience.

"I was bullied, too," she said finally, hoping to ease Maureen's mind. "I didn't tell anyone. Not a soul."

Now Maureen turned her head. "Really?"

"Really. It's even hard for me to admit it now. And some bullying...well, it's hard to be sure it's bullying. It has a negative impact, but you're just not sure that person was being intentionally mean, or that you didn't misunderstand. Then there's exclusion. A lot of people don't realize, for example, that selecting students and then telling them to pick a team for some kind of competition, whether it's a race or a spelling bee, can be painfully exclusionary. Believe me, I was always the last person picked for a team when there was a race."

"So you're saying it wasn't that he didn't trust us."

That put Cassie on the spot. She didn't know whether James trusted his parents or not. She had no idea of their family dynamics. "Trust," she said finally, "was probably the smallest part of this. It's so hard for youngsters to figure out what's acceptable, what other people know, and whether they deserve something. By the time they get old enough to start sorting through it, it's become a natural part of their lives, miserable as it is."

Maureen nodded. Then she tugged from her husband's grasp and put her face in her hands. "Please," she whispered. "Please let my baby be okay."

It was a long night. Linc went out and returned with some halfway decent coffee for the Carneys. No one spoke much as they waited for news. As the night waned, though, there was no mistaking the rising level of fear in the Carneys.

And in herself, Cassie admitted. If James didn't come through this, she didn't know how she could ever live with herself.

Sitting there with two people who were plumbing the full depths of hell, she was quite sure they would find it harder, if not impossible. Their tension filled the room like a living, breathing beast.

Finally, just before dawn, a smiling doctor appeared.

"James is awake and he seems to be just fine. He's asking for you."

Maureen burst into tears and hugged her husband. Then they jumped up to hurry to their son's side.

But they nearly broke Cassie's heart when they stopped just long enough to thank her and Linc for keeping vigil with them.

She and Linc walked back to his truck. Cassie knew relief lightened her step and probably Linc's as well.

"I'm gonna take you up on that couch," he said as he put the truck in gear. "We need sleep. We can go back out to the ranch later."

The faint lightening of the day showed Cassie her disabled car again, but Beau had scraped the ugly word off her back window. She was glad not to see it.

Inside, though, when Linc started to turn toward the living room, she took his hand and guided him to her bedroom in back. "You'll sleep better in a bed," she said.

Barely pausing to doff jackets and shoes, they tumbled onto the mattress. For long moments Cassie stared at the ceiling, wondering if anything would ever look the same again, but she was just too tired to evaluate anything. Then Linc rolled over and drew her snugly into his arms. With a sigh, she relaxed against him.

"Sleep," he said. "Everything else can wait a couple of hours."

Her eyes fluttered open to the sound of wind keening. Linc was spooned close behind her, an arm around her waist, and she saw the curtained window. God, his embrace felt good. Before she had time to really enjoy it, or wake enough to wonder why the wind was so loud, he spoke.

"That doesn't sound good," he murmured near her ear. "Let me go find out what the weather is."

At that instant, his cell phone rang. He climbed out of bed, pawed in his pockets and pulled out the phone. "Linc Blair." Then he said, "You're kidding. All right. Thanks, Les."

Cassie snapped upright. "Is James okay?"

"It wasn't about James." He stuffed his phone in the pocket of the jeans he still wore. "You're going to get your wish."

He went over to her bedroom window and drew back the curtains. All Cassie could see was whirling white. She leapt up and went to stand beside him. "Snow? Really?"

"Blizzard. The game's been canceled. They're telling everyone to get home and stay home."

Cassie almost clapped her hands in delight. "I love it!"

Linc gave her a smile. "I'm sure you do. It's early for this kind of thing, though. So, my only question to you is, do you want to head out to my place or enjoy your first blizzard from the safety of town?"

"Will it be safe enough out on the roads?"

"For a while. It's going to get worse, but it just started."

She considered. "I like it at the ranch. I'll bet it's beautiful when it snows."

"Well, come with me, then. I have to go take care of my stock."

Of course he did. She felt almost embarrassed not to have realized he was going to have to look after animals in a storm like this. "I'll help," she announced. "Just let me make a quick change, if we have time."

"I'll make some coffee while you do. Then we're off. It may be a little hair-raising to someone who's not used to it, but the roads will be okay for a while. We're going to get twelve or more inches, though, so if you come you're stuck until we get plowed out. You might want to pack some additional things."

Being stuck with him sounded very good indeed. "I'll hurry."

Okay, he'd lost it. Well and truly lost it. Linc couldn't deny it. He'd had the perfect excuse a short while ago to leave Cassie at home and return to the ranch alone. He could have claimed she would be safer or more comfortable in town. From what he'd learned of her over the last week, he was sure she wouldn't have argued with him. And she *would* be safe for the duration of the blizzard. Even the person who had vandalized her car couldn't be crazy enough to pull something in this weather.

But no, he'd offered her a chance to come to the ranch, where they'd surely be snowed in, and he knew where that was going to lead. Last night hadn't eased the ache one bit, but had instead magnified it. It was sitting in his groin like an irritation, and at the back of his mind like a constant unanswered question.

Reminding himself of Martha wasn't helping at all, either. Cassie wasn't Martha, and while she hadn't put any roots down here yet, and she had even mentioned leaving, some part of him had given in to the hope that she would stay. In short, he had stepped off the dangerous cliff without even really noticing.

That made him stupid, he supposed, but it seemed self-evident now that he was willing to run that risk again because he wanted Cassie. He liked Cassie. Day by day she was worming into his life and his heart and he rather liked her there.

The question had changed. Maybe he was rationalizing his own foolishness, but he was now thinking that he owed it to himself to give this a chance.

It was hard, though, not to know if she felt the same. He knew she wanted him, but did she want any more than sex? It was too soon to ask, if he ever could.

It was sure as hell too late now, he thought. One way or another, this thing between them was going to play out unless she skipped town right after the blizzard, and even by then he might have more of his emotions hanging in the breeze than he would have liked.

Hell, he thought. He'd been fighting his attraction to her since she first appeared on his horizon. He'd never had a chance, he supposed. Not against a need this strong. Well, he'd had a chance, but only back when he was keeping her at a distance. From the minute circumstances pushed them together, this had become inevitable.

Just enjoy the weekend, he told himself. Just enjoy it and then deal with the aftermath. He'd survived it once before, so he could do it again. But whatever the cost, some part of him refused to relinquish the hope, and the experience, of Cassie.

Visibility was bad, though not a whiteout, but the snow hadn't begun to stick on the roads. In the deeper grasses across the fields, grasses that cooled down faster, it had begun to cling, frosting plants in little puffs of white.

"It's beautiful," Cassie said. "It's been so long since I saw snow I'd forgotten. It's started to look as if the world is flocked in white."

"It'll be really gorgeous when the storm passes and the sun comes out. Do you remember all the colors you can see in snow?"

"Prism effect. Barely. I do remember once, though, when I was still living up north, when I realized the snow wasn't white. It amazed me how long I'd spent just glancing at it and thinking it was white, but when I paid attention I saw it sparkled with so many different colors."

"Perception is an amazing thing." It was also a safe topic. "I sometimes wonder how much we miss seeing simply because we box and label things in our minds."

"Probably plenty," she agreed.

Right now, though, they were driving in a white-and-gray cocoon. Even his headlights didn't make it sparkle.

"So this is unusual weather?"

"Believe it. I'm not going to say we've never had a blizzard this early in the winter, but they're rare. And to get so much snowfall at once is rare, too. We're in the rain shadow of the mountains, and they wring most of the moisture out of the air before it reaches us."

"Usually," she said.

He laughed. "Yeah, usually."

By the time they reached his house, the storm had really moved in. The wind was whipping the snow hard enough to sting the cheeks, and blowing it in curtains that occasionally parted to give a glimpse of the leaden sky.

As he turned from pulling Cassie's small bag from the truck, he saw her standing with her head tipped back and her tongue out as if she were trying to catch a snowflake. Except these weren't flakes as much as they were ice crystals.

She laughed, a sound that tugged at his heart, then lowered her head and grinned at him. "This is fun."

It struck him then just how different she really was from Martha. Newcomer? Yes. Could possibly decide to leave? Yes. But Martha wouldn't have been enjoying this storm at all. She'd have been griping about all the things she wanted to be doing instead.

Not for the first time in the last two years he wondered how he could have been so blinded by Martha. If he rolled back the movie of his time with her, her demanding nature popped up over and over again. And he'd been too besotted to realize it. The warning signs had been everywhere, that she wouldn't be content to build a life with a teacher and live on a ranch in the middle of nowhere.

Not for the first time he felt a suspicion that she had seen the ranch as a potential cash cow if he would just sell it and move to a life in a faster lane elsewhere. Hell, it had finally become the bottom line to their relationship, the one that ended it.

She certainly never would have claimed standing out here in the wildly blowing snow was fun. No, she'd have been complaining about the cold, the wind, the way the ice crystals stung. She'd have raced inside to get away from it, then moaned how boring it all was.

Boring was a word that should have clued him in. Martha had used the word often. He was never bored, and really couldn't grasp people who complained of boredom. There was always something to do, he didn't need to be entertained. Nor did Cassie seem to need constant amusement, either. Admittedly, he hadn't been close with her for long, but her reaction to the storm was proving to be a brightly lighted line of demarcation between her and Martha.

Inside, she continued to smile as she rubbed her hands together to warm them. "What do we need to do with the animals?"

"You don't have to help." Martha had sought every opportunity to avoid pitching in.

"I want to. So what do we need to do?"

"Round them in close. The dogs will do most of the

work, but I've built windbreaks with hay they can huddle behind. I need to make sure they're in the right place and can't wander too far. I still need to do their morning feeding, too."

"So they eat more than grass?"

"They're grazers, yes, but they get supplemental food to make up for any nutritional deficiencies, and right now there's not a whole lot of fresh stuff to graze. The horse stalls will need cleaning as well."

"Let's go, then."

"How about a hot drink first? You haven't eaten, either."

"I'm fine. Don't the animals come first?"

Of course they did, but he was concerned about her, too. On the other hand, it was refreshing that she understood the priorities.

Maybe this mistake wouldn't turn out to be as bad as he had feared.

The dogs made rounding up the sheep and goats easy, Cassie realized. With a few whistles and a couple of commands, they began to push the animals toward the rows of hay that Cassie hadn't really paid attention to before.

Nor had she noticed the fencing with gates that Linc closed behind them to keep them in relatively small pens. Well, why would she have noticed? She didn't understand the purpose of a lot of things out here and hadn't even thought about them until she saw them in use.

The blizzard didn't seem to disturb either the sheep or goats. As soon as they were safely enclosed, they settled down and began pulling at the bales that surrounded them on two sides, dining as if nothing was going on at all. She loved it.

Cleaning the horse stalls strained her muscles in new

ways after Linc showed her how to use the pitchfork and shovel. It took a while, but soon the horses had fresh beds of loose hay, and troughs full of fresh water and feed.

By the time they returned to the house, visibility approached zero. Linc clung to her gloved hand as if he were afraid she would wander off or blow away.

Either option would have been possible, she thought as they trudged across frozen ground that was beginning to be covered by little drifts of snow wherever it was uneven. She could see the house only in snatches until finally it loomed over them, too big to miss.

She paused on the porch to look back over a world that had gone completely white, and could hardly see the barn.

"You're not going to have to go out there again, are you?" she asked Linc. "You could get lost."

"Not until tonight. If worst comes to worst, I made sure the horses can make it until tomorrow. I'd hate to leave them like that, but…" He shrugged, the conclusion obvious.

The change between indoors and out was sharp. Warmth, no wind, relative quiet. She could still hear the wind howling and the windows rattling as strong gusts hit, but it was a different world in here, cozy and protected.

"How are you feeling?" Linc asked. "Still as upset as last night?"

"I'm relieved James is going to be okay. I hope his family gets him some therapy, though."

"And the rest?"

She half shook her head. "I don't know, Linc." She held out her arms as he helped her out of her jacket.

"I need to get you some better gloves," he remarked as he took hers and tucked them into the pockets of her coat before hanging it on a wall peg.

"I can do that on Monday."

"No, I meant I'll dig some out. I've got a few pairs in a box upstairs I just never got around to donating."

An especially strong gust rattled the entire house, and she felt a draft snake past her shoulders. She glanced at Linc, experiencing a twinge of uncertainty.

As their eyes met, the air became instantly charged around them. She could almost feel searing heat leaping from her to him. She felt as if the oxygen had been sucked out of the room. Her heart slammed hard, and then an ache clenched her between her legs.

Everything else vanished but this moment, this man, and an arousal that grabbed her so strongly, so suddenly, it swamped her.

She never knew which of them moved. All of a sudden their bodies met, their arms wrapped around each other, mouths came together in a hungry, devouring kiss.

Nothing in her life prepared her for the firestorm that swept through her with staggering intensity. In an instant she became elemental in her need. The trappings of civilization vanished, except for clothing, which had become a hindrance to escape.

His tongue plunged into her like a spear, commanding, demanding, conquering. She wanted to be conquered. She wanted to brush everything away and get to the most basic coupling possible, because she had wanted it for so long, because she feared something might happen to intervene.

She wanted to *know*.

Apparently he felt it, too, or sensed her impatience. His hands slipped down her back to grasp her rump. She felt the world spin, although her eyes were closed, her mouth coming alive to an erotic awareness she had never before experienced.

Then she was sitting on the counter's edge, her thighs splayed, and he nudged his way between them until their loins met, a hard, welcome pressure. Instinctively she arched toward him, wanting more, and as she did she broke the kiss.

He didn't seem to mind. His mouth found her throat, hot and wet, pulling a groan from her. Her head hit the cabinet above but she scarcely noticed. Instead she lifted her arms, grabbing his shoulders and arching into him even more.

As his hot, wet tongue traced fiery lines along her throat and ear, she felt his hands slip up under her sweater. Roughened hands, feeling cool against her heated skin. Close, but not close enough. She wanted to feel those hands everywhere, and her nipples ached for more intimate touches.

She felt suspended on a tightly drawn wire of anticipation, excited by his touches, aroused to an almost mindless state. It had happened as fast as if someone had touched a match to gasoline, and the explosion of hunger and want in her was beyond anything she had ever imagined.

Every cell in her body seemed to be demanding its due. *Touch me, touch me, touch me!* rang like a pounding refrain, pushing her toward a pinnacle. Need lashed her as sharply as a whip, so strong it almost hurt.

She gasped again as he pulled her sweater over her head, and cold air met her skin. Then she felt her bra release her breasts, a sensation that excited her even more.

At last, his palms brushed across her nipples, taunting and teasing, each touch drawing a helpless moan from between her lips.

It was a nearly silent communion, punctuated only by sighs and moans. Hands and bodies did all the talking. She tugged at his shirt, but a gentle grip of his hands stopped her. A whisper of protest escaped her. She wanted so badly to feel skin on skin.

But he stopped her only so that he could bend his head and draw her nipple deeply into his mouth, sucking with a fervor that caused a deep clenching between her legs. With each draw of his mouth, she wound ever tighter until she felt she might snap.

But she didn't snap. She tightened even more, her thighs clamping hard to his hips, her hands pulling at his shoulders, every movement a plea for more.

He moved to her other breast, sucking so hard it was almost painful. With his hands, he pulled her rump closer to the edge of the counter, closer to his staff, its hardness unconcealed by layers of denim. Feeling his need that way made her soar even higher, made her want even more, and she tried to rock her hips against him, seeking the pressure and friction she needed as her mind plunged downward to that point of contact, making it the center of her universe.

Images popped into her mind, the things she would like to do to him, the ways she would like him to touch her. They added steam to the heat that was already burning her like a torch.

With a groan, he released her breast. Before she could protest, as cold air hit her wet skin causing a delicious shiver, he pulled her up against him. Instinctively she locked her ankles behind his hips, and wrapped her arms around his broad shoulders.

The room spun and she realized dimly that he was carrying her upstairs. Burrowing her face against his neck, she found warm skin, a hint of stubble, and licked him as he had licked her.

A muffled oath escaped him and he quickened his pace up the stairs. His evident eagerness was more fuel for the fire that licked at her every nerve ending.

Finesse didn't exist. As soon as he set her on her feet, they tore at each other's clothing, impatient and eager, not caring if they were rough, or if buttons went flying. They were past even noticing in their need to come together.

The roughness and impatience aroused Cassie even more. She now teetered higher on the mountain than she had ever come before, sensing a nearby cliff-edge where she could tumble fast into the oblivion of release.

It was close, so close, and she didn't want to wait anymore. The fuel of suppressed fantasies over the last few months joined the realization that it was actually happening. An explosion was beginning in her, sweeping her away before its force.

They tumbled onto the bed. There was an awful moment when everything seemed to stop, and she started to open her eyes only to see him rolling protection onto his magnificent staff. That hardness was for her.

Another spear of pleasure arrowed straight to her core, then his hands pushed her legs apart and he was there. Oh, he was there. He touched her with his fingers, stroking that velvety slit once, twice, causing her to shudder with delight and need, and then the wonderful moments when he slid into her warm depths, filling her, answering an ache that could be answered no other way, stretching her and completing her.

He moved. The first thrust drew a cry of ecstasy from her. She rose to meet him, needing every bit of him deep inside her.

Then it happened. Fast. Hot. Hard. She shattered into a

million pieces of pleasure that almost hurt. Moments later she felt him thrust one last time, and with a deep groan joined her in completion.

Linc came back to earth slowly, relishing the womanly curves and softness beneath him. Glorious. Better than glorious. Some little corner of his mind whispered that he'd been too rough, though, and he was almost reluctant to lift his head for fear he would see disappointment or hurt in Cassie's gaze.

So he stayed as he was, propped on his elbows just enough to allow her to breathe, his face buried against her neck and the soft curve of her shoulder as perspiration dried, and then the air whispered coldly across his skin.

Outside, the wind keened even louder, like a reminder that he had to face the world.

Slowly he lifted his head. Her eyes were closed, her face turned a little to one side. Fear spiked him. Had he hurt her?

"Cassie?"

Her head turned slowly and her eyes opened a little. Then a smile dawned on her face, a warm, content and happy smile.

"You okay?" he asked, his heart lifting.

"Never better," she whispered. "Never ever."

"Me, too," he said honestly. Then he remembered necessities. "I need to run to the bathroom. I'll be right back."

Holding the condom in place as he withdrew his softening staff, he was glad to realize he hadn't waited too long. God, he never forgot himself like that.

He tugged a quilt over her so she wouldn't get cold, then raced to the bathroom. He wanted to get back to her, to cuddle with her under the covers, and take the time to learn her as he hadn't in the time just past.

He looked back at himself from the mirror, and realized that he had never looked as satisfied as he did right then. Damn, that had been something.

Grabbing a razor, he quickly scraped away stubble that he was sure must have reddened Cassie's skin, then he hurried back down the hall to his bedroom, buck naked in the house's chilly air, with one thought on his mind: *get back to Cassie.*

He had lost the battle and had little doubt that he was going to pay a heavy price. All that caution about a woman new to the area had burned away in his hunger for her. Even more stupid considering what had happened to her. He wouldn't be able to blame her if she decided she didn't want to live in a county where people would vandalize her car and leave dead animals on her desk. She'd even mentioned leaving, then backed away from it.

But the taste of this experience was likely to stay with her for a long time, and if it turned to aversion she'd pack and go. No argument about how it was only a small number of people would change that. Especially since he couldn't actually prove it wasn't everyone, and she hadn't been here long enough to believe it.

But all those thoughts seemed hardly relevant as he hurried back to her side. He could take it. He'd taken it before, from a woman who'd become a huge part of his life for so long. Cassie had only just started to become a part of his days. Separation would be easier.

Or so he tried to tell himself. Not that anything he told himself would change the fact that he couldn't wait to climb back into that bed with her.

She was lying on her side, back to him as he entered, staring at the window that rattled angrily in the wind. "It's really bad out there," she remarked as his footstep made a floorboard creak.

Why did he feel as if she had withdrawn? She was simply looking toward the window. He strode over and pulled the curtain back. Whiteout.

"I'm going to have the check the animals soon." While he cared about those animals, he felt a surge of resentment that they might need him at this time.

"I know."

Something in the tone of her voice made him pivot and stare at her. "Cassie? What's wrong?"

The corners of her mouth tipped up. "What could possibly be wrong?"

Plenty, he thought. And that was no answer. Another stab of fear lanced him. His stomach sank. But if she wasn't going to talk…well, there was only one way he could think to deal with this, to try to get to whatever was troubling her.

Reaching the bed, he pulled back the quilt, revealing her. She astonished him by instinctively covering herself protectively, and looking embarrassed.

"Don't hide from me, Cassie. Please. Everything about you is beautiful. Sexy. Marvelous."

She looked dubious and didn't relax.

Damn! Without another word, he slid onto the mattress beside her, gently opened her arms and moved her until he had her pinned on her back on the mattress. She was startled but she didn't fight.

"I know I was a Neanderthal just now," he said, sweeping his gaze over her. "I didn't let you know how beautiful you are. Hell, I didn't even do a decent job of learning you. Trust me, Cassie, I've been drooling over you for months."

Still she appeared doubtful. "You could have fooled me."

"It was the main reason I avoided you."

"That doesn't make sense."

"It would if you knew." He bent and dropped a kiss on each breast, realizing he was going to have to fess up and hating to reveal his stupidity once again. She squirmed at the touch of his mouth. So whatever doubts she had, they hadn't quieted her desire. Good. He almost smiled.

But then it was time to talk, much as he hated to hash this over. But while he was hashing, he supposed he could be loving her, too. He sucked her nipple, more gently this time, and felt it harden in his mouth. Had anything ever made him feel so good?

He lifted his head. "I was engaged. I'm surprised you haven't heard about it."

Her eyes widened a bit and she shook her head.

"Martha. Anyway, we were engaged, we'd been together for well over a year, the wedding was two months away, and she delivered her ultimatum."

"Which was?"

"Sell the ranch and leave with her. She couldn't stand this place. She was bored all the time, there wasn't anything to do, she didn't like the animals, she thought… Oh, hell, never mind what she thought. I was a fool not to have guessed what was coming long before it hit."

He scooted down a bit and dropped a kiss on the thatch of hair between her thighs, feeling another shiver run through her.

"Why should you have known?"

"Because the push was there almost from the start. She

wanted me to remodel the house. She wanted a master bed-room with a private bath. She wanted new furniture. She wanted a lot of stuff. In fact, I have a dishwasher because of her. Kind of silly for one guy, don't you think? Any-way, almost from the outset she wanted to change things. If I hadn't been so blinded, I'd have to have seen her con-stant discontent."

"Maybe she mostly hid it."

He raised his head. "That's a kind thing to say. Well, hindsight *is* twenty-twenty. And I might see things clearer now because of the way she left."

"Entirely possible." She tugged a hand free from his grip and reached down to stroke his hair.

"Anyway, she wasn't from around here. Like you, she moved here for a job. Clearly this wasn't the place for her."

"So you wanted to avoid another outsider?"

"Bingo. I was drawn to you from the instant I saw you, but I kept telling myself that since you'd probably be leav-ing at the end of the school year, I should just be smart and stay away."

It seemed so incredibly intimate, even to him, to be lying here with his head so close to her most personal places and looking up at her over her body. He liked it a whole lot, and she seemed to be relaxing a bit.

The need was awakening in him again. He licked her in the crease between her thigh and abdomen, and she shiv-ered. "Linc, you are a devil."

A chuckle escaped him. "You love it."

"I can't deny it."

Relief that he'd diverted any continued conversation away from Martha filled him. He didn't want to talk about the past, or about the fear he couldn't quite escape that he would be judged wanting again. That this woman, too, would be unable to tolerate life here. Not now.

Right now he just wanted to sink into her depths, forget all the worries of the past week, forget his fears for her and for the Carney boy, and just focus in this moment with a glorious woman lying in his bed.

He lifted himself a bit and settled between her legs, his face near the apex of her thighs. "If you have any objections to this," he said huskily, "tell me before I offend you."

"No offense. I've never..."

Never? For some odd reason the thought delighted him. He couldn't imagine anyone skipping over these honey-blond curls with their musky scent, but it thrilled him to know he could give her something no one ever had before. He eased her legs farther apart, propped himself on his elbows and gently stroked her velvety petals. As shiver after shiver ran through her, he felt his own body pound its way into renewed need.

His fingers traced her soft flesh, avoiding the very seat of her desire, teasing out the moments, loving her growing excitement. Only when her hips arched up in demand did he lower his head and follow his fingers with his tongue.

She tasted as good as her aromas had promised, and with his tongue he explored every nook of her. Soft moans started to escape her, encouraging him to press on, to stiffen his tongue as he slid it inside her and then dragged it up to her swollen nub.

She cried out, but he remained merciless, flicking her with his tongue until her hips rolled like the sea. The sounds of her pleasure fed his own arousal until he felt as if he would explode.

He felt her crest, heard the cry torn from deep within

her. Still he was merciless, lashing her with his tongue until she was panting and ready yet again.

Only then did he grab a foil packet and rise over her, plunging into her until he could plunge no farther. Her legs lifted, trying to lock around his hips, her hands grabbed at his rump, pulling him in, taking him deeper yet.

They rode the rising tide until at last it tossed them dizzy and sated onto a sparkling shore.

Chapter 8

They rested tangled comfortably together beneath the quilt, her hand on his shoulder, his arms around her. Time passed, quiet except for the wind outside, but finally he stirred.

"This is the best blizzard ever."

She laughed, a delightful sound, easy and free of shadows. "It must be."

"Unfortunately…"

"I know. The poor sheep, goats and dogs are out there."

"You can shower if you like while I take care of them. I doubt I'll be long. Want me to bring you something to eat?" Eating had been overlooked, he suddenly realized, which made him a lousy host.

"I'll get up. I want to help. Besides, being in a blizzard is a rare experience for me. Almost new, even though I can remember some from my childhood."

He enjoyed watching her dress, taking in every graceful movement, drinking in the loveliness that she was con-cealing with each new piece of clothing. He realized he wouldn't have changed one inch of her.

Then, feeling like a gawping kid, he hastened to con-ceal his watching by hurrying into his own clothes. "Let me grab some warmer gloves for you."

It gave him an excuse to run down the hall to the bed-room where he had stored so much of his parents' belong-ings, things he had meant to give to charity but somehow had never managed to part with.

It also gave him an excuse to cool himself down. He couldn't remember ever having been so supercharged with lust for a woman, not even Martha. Ready again so quickly?

It also gave him an excuse to care for Cassie in a small way. Such a little thing to make sure her hands remained warm. He also found a pair of woman's boots—whose? He couldn't seem to remember—and brought them out. He really needed to take this woman shopping for proper winter clothing, he thought, and relished the idea although he wasn't usually fond of shopping.

The boots and gloves fit her well enough and together they stepped out back into a world gone crazy. The wind came so sharply around the corner of the house that she staggered as if from a blow. Only briefly could he make out bits of the hay wall he had built, which he was sure was rapidly disappearing in wind-blown drifts. He also knew in an instant that it was time for wisdom.

"Don't leave the porch," he said. "Stay right here. You could get lost between here and there in fifteen feet and I couldn't promise to find you."

"You can't go out there, either." Her voice rose a little with concern.

"I'll tie myself to the porch. Promise you'll stay here."

"Of course I promise." She looked at him as if she wondered if he thought she was stupid. "I can see how dangerous it is."

"Sorry. I'm just worried. This is a pretty bad whiteout, but I keep a rope in the mudroom just for this."

And if he had known this storm was coming instead of having his head and feelings so wrapped up in Cassie, he'd have strung the rope out and staked it near the fold so he'd have a secure guideline. As it was, if the wind didn't give him a visual break from time to time, he might not reach his animals.

Although he was reasonably certain they were safe, huddled together out of the wind, probably warmed by a layer of snow. Still, he needed to be sure some animal wasn't in distress. He knotted the rope around the porch stanchion then around his waist. Thank God it wasn't that cold, although the wind chill might be deadly.

Then he stepped off the porch into the white and raging storm.

The rat had sickened her, the car had upset and angered her, but now Cassie felt real terror as Linc waded out into that storm. With each step he grew more invisible, and a number of times he vanished completely in whirling snow.

She needed no better object lesson in how dangerous a storm out here could be. There was little to halt the winds in the wide-open spaces once it passed the western mountains. The treeless expanses offered no hindrance to the fury. The blizzards of her childhood had never been this bad. She'd always been able to pretty much see across the street. She had the feeling that if she stepped off the porch, she wouldn't even be able to see her hand in front of her face.

She hoped Linc was dressed warmly enough. In this sheltered part of the porch, it didn't seem very cold until a gust hit her. The wind chill must be fierce, she thought, and he was out there with nothing to protect him but his clothing.

She couldn't remember anyone having mentioned anything about an approaching blizzard, and wondered if this one had somehow managed to come out of nowhere with almost no warning. How likely was that? She didn't know, being new here, and her knowledge of meteorology was limited at best.

She tried to distract herself with random thoughts like these, but failed. Minutes stretched, and along with them her nerves as she waited for Linc. How long would it take? When should she begin to worry? And what should she do if he was gone too long? Follow the rope? She doubted any help could get out here if he got hurt and couldn't get back to the porch.

She closed her eyes, trying to remember the yard between here and the hay. It had been reasonably flat, she thought. Not likely to cause a serious accident. But she couldn't be sure.

Just as she thought she couldn't take it for another minute, the abominable snowman appeared at the bottom of the porch steps. She almost laughed with relief, almost laughed at the way the snow had clung to him, making him even harder to see.

Then he stomped and shook himself, and Linc reappeared with only little bits of snow clinging.

"Everything okay?" she asked.

"Fine." He flashed a smile. "All cuddled up and cozy

under a nice blanket of snow. Did you hear them? A few of them objected to being bothered."

The image made her laugh again, or maybe it was relief leaving her amused. "So they're doing fine but you're not?"

"I'm just cold. That wind is something else." He stepped up beside her. "Let's get inside, warm up and eat. I want to get on with enjoying the best blizzard ever."

The way his blue eyes sparkled at her warmed her all the way to her toes.

Be careful, she reminded herself. No man had ever wanted much more than this from her. Not ever.

Between her own experience and what he had told her about his fiancée, she didn't dare think that Linc would be any different. Sexual attraction had pulled them together, but that was hardly enough to make an enduring relationship. He had plenty of reason not to trust her to stay, assuming he even wanted her to, and she had plenty of reason to expect he'd be like everyone else and drop her.

Just enjoy the weekend for what it was, she told herself. One wonderful weekend, nothing more.

Sunday morning surprised her. When she awoke, she expected to see a world buried in a white blanket. Standing at Linc's bedroom window, however, she saw a world that seemed to have received only a confectioner's sugar dusting.

"Where did it all go?" she asked.

Linc stood beside her and looked out. "It was probably a really dry snow. With all that wind it just kept blowing away until it hit an obstruction and built up. Let's go check the other side of the house."

In a bedroom across the hall, Cassie discovered where the snow was. A huge drift of it had built up alongside the house, reaching almost to the bottom of the second-story window.

"My word!" The sight astonished her. "Does this always happen?"

"Only with high winds and dry snow. This isn't common, though. Usually we get a lot less snow and it's spread over a winter." He laughed quietly. "Sometimes I feel like I shovel the same snow dozens of times."

As he spoke, a gust made snow dance and eddy over the top of the huge drift, sparking little whirlwinds and clouds.

"Could I just climb out the window and slide down it?"

"In your nightgown?"

She turned to him and found his blue eyes sparkling, his face creased with a smile.

"Of course not!"

He laughed. "I wanted to do it when this happened once before. That was so many years ago. I think I was in middle school at the time."

"Did you?"

He shook his head. "Unfortunately from here it looks like it's a solid drift, but it's probably not. First of all, the snow isn't really packed if it's that dry. And secondly, there's probably a pocket where heat from the house has melted it. You could crash right down behind that drift."

"Well, erase that idea."

He laughed again and slipped his arm around her waist, giving her a squeeze. "You're quite an adventurous spirit."

She wondered how to take that. Given that Martha hadn't found it exciting enough here, that might not be a compliment. The thought darkened her mood.

She showered and dressed in jeans and a green hoodie then went down to join him in the kitchen, wondering how this all would end. He had plenty of reason not to trust a woman who had just moved here. She had plenty of reason to expect to be dropped as soon as the sexual heat subsided a little.

They were both fools, she thought wryly, playing with a fire they knew could burn them badly. Wasn't the saying "once burned, twice shy?" Neither of them seemed to have learned that fully.

The kitchen was bright with the morning light. Every now and then a gust of wind moaned around the house, but nothing like the day before. They managed not to get in one another's way as they made a breakfast of toast, scrambled eggs and orange juice, but she noticed that he seemed to have pulled back a little. No touches. No quick little kisses. He had returned to avoiding her. It cast a cloud over an otherwise perfect day.

"I might be able to get you home this afternoon, considering how most of the snow has blown around. The roads are probably pretty clear and I have a plow for the front of my truck."

She looked up from her plate, her mood sinking even more. But before she could respond in any way, he continued.

"I don't really want to take you back. I can't arrange to get your car fixed until tomorrow, so you'd be stuck, and I need to be here later to take care of the animals anyway."

Up and down, a rollercoaster of the heart. He didn't want to take her back, but the reasons had nothing to do with wanting her to stay. Staring at her plate again, she tried to tell herself not to be a fool, not to take everything he said so personally, and for heaven's sake, stop trying to read deep meaning into his every statement. The self-admonishment didn't work.

He spoke again. "We should finish up that bullying presentation."

She still felt deliciously sore and sated from all their lovemaking yesterday and last night, but now he was all business again. It was a pattern she knew too damn well.

"Sure," she said, hoping her voice sounded reasonably normal. Afraid that she might reveal the sorrow that was engulfing her.

God, was she being stupid or what? This man had barely spoken to her for months, and now after little more than a week of working with him and a short period of making love with him, she was this invested?

No way. Not possible. She shoved the sadness from her mind and focused on the really important things, like the antibullying program, like whether they could find out how James Carney was doing, and whether they should include him in their example.

An odd thing happened as they were wrapping up the presentation that afternoon. It was as if her brain had refused to process all that had happened on Friday: the shoving she had endured when they were dancing, the vandalism of her car. Maybe she'd been refusing to accept a lot since she'd found that rat on her desk.

Whatever, a shell seemed to break and it all hit her and hit her hard, as if she'd been living in a fantasy where these things only appeared to be happening. But they were actually happening. Really and truly.

She knew when she went home, whether later today or tomorrow, she was going to be alone with a fear she didn't want to recognize, had indeed been sublimating for the most part.

She had been in some kind of denial, and now denial deserted her.

Breathing became suddenly difficult. She bent over at the table, wrapping her arms around herself, battling down a tide made of equal parts rage and fear.

"Oh, my God," she breathed.

"Cassie? What's wrong?"

"I think…it just hit me. All of it." She had to squeeze the words out as if she were using the last oxygen in the room. Afternoon light was turning golden. The wind still moaned occasionally from outside, but there was no air inside. None. She felt her brain begin to swim.

Linc was suddenly beside her, pressing her shoulders. "Get your head down," he ordered, but gently. "Put it down."

The table was in the way. She felt him turn her chair with surprising strength, then press again until her head met her knees. She gasped for air, feeling her gorge rise at the sickening accumulation of things she had been trying not to think about.

He rubbed her back as she remained bowed over. "I wondered," he said. "You were entirely too calm on Friday. I wondered when this was going to hit you."

She couldn't believe it had taken this long. Memories surged, filling her mind's eye. The rat. The Carney family at the hospital, her car, the confrontations, even that phone call. One thing she knew for sure was that she didn't feel safe. No, she was scared. Everything that had happened was such an overreaction to detentions that at last it really began to terrify her.

Whoever was behind some of this was unhinged.

"Oh, God," she whispered. "He's sick!"

"Sick?" He was still rubbing her back gently. "The guy who vandalized your car?"

"And killed that rat."

He was silent a for a few seconds, then pulled a chair over so that he sat beside her. He resumed rubbing her back gently. "It did cross my mind," he admitted. "It's so out of proportion."

At last she was able to suck in a full lungful of air and then another. But the sick feeling and the fear hadn't fled.

She straightened slowly, realizing that her world had altered yet again. Making love with Linc, discovering so much passion and delight, had been an earthquake by it-self. But now she was having another one.

"I think," she said slowly, "that I've been trying to put it in the category of stupid pranks." Her gaze tracked to him. "All of a sudden I can't do that anymore. Tell me I'm overreacting."

He hesitated visibly. "I can't do that. I wish I could. But even if there's only the merest possibility—and I admit it crossed my mind—it would be really stupid not to be cautious. That's why I didn't want you to be alone. Partly because I was worried about when this would hit you, and partly because I can't be a hundred percent certain it's not going to escalate."

"Then why did you suggest taking me home?"

"Because you have a right to make your own decisions. If you wanted to get home, I'd take you."

She closed her eyes, trying to absorb what felt like a series of blows: realizing that all that stuff last week had been real, that her car was still sitting in her driveway with flat tires, one of which had been punctured, that there really had been a butchered rat on her desk, that a lot of people seemed to be angry with her for turning over the rock under which bullies hid…and that Linc's sole reason for bringing her out here this weekend was protective.

Man. Had she been using his attention as a distraction?

Or had she been totally distracted by his attention? And how could she have so minimized the threatening actions against her? The flickers of fear that had penetrated before were nothing like the full-scale epic of horror and guilt she was feeling right now.

"Cassie?"

It was a question of some sort, but he didn't say what he wanted to know. Maybe it was just a check to see if she were still alive and breathing. Which seemed to be the main part of his interest in her.

He'd offered to take her home, saying it had to be her decision. Nice, except now she was wondering if he thought she hadn't liked his lovemaking and just wanted to get out of here. Or if he was looking for nice ways to get rid of her.

On top of everything else that had just come home in a gut way, she felt too confused to sort anything out. Someone wanted to hurt her. Of that she was now fairly certain. But there was no way to know how far he or she might go. Maybe they just wanted her to quit and leave town. Maybe it would stop there. Or maybe they had some kind of real grudge she couldn't begin to imagine.

"Damn it!" The words exploded out of her as everything coalesced into anger. Anger at least wasn't confused and she almost welcomed it. Rising, she hugged herself and started to pace the length of the kitchen.

"What?" he asked.

"Do you even need me to explain?"

"Probably not," he admitted, "but you might as well get it all out. It usually feels better."

"That depends on how I get it out. Something like this creep is doing…" She let go of that thought, focusing instead on something else.

"Okay, I'm scared. It might not stop with the car. Best

case, this creep leaves me alone, having made his statement of disapproval. Or maybe because word of James's suicide attempt is probably getting around. You'd have to be a cretin not to climb back under your rock in the face of that."

"You'd think."

"Assuming, of course, that people know it might have been associated with him being bullied."

"We know it was. His family knows. They've certainly been talking, and we're going to talk about it at the assembly."

"But that assumes whoever is trying to get me to quit and leave town hasn't got some other axe to grind. Or isn't just out-of-control nuts. And frankly, reacting this way to detentions is so over-the-top. That's what's scaring me. Even one of the student's own mothers just wanted to defend her son. All she did was confront me in the parking lot and insist her son couldn't have done anything wrong. I've faced that before, I'll face it again. That's within the realm of normal reaction. Even the pushing while we were dancing. That was just some people who wanted me to be aware they didn't think that was enough to merit action. I don't think it's associated with the other stuff at all, like the phone call, or the rat and my car. Those exceed a typical response."

"I agree," he said quietly.

She paused her pacing and looked at him. Why did he have to be so gorgeous that she kept wanting to forget everything else? "What you said about the basketball championship. Could somebody really get this heated over something like that?"

"Heated, yes. Enough to make you feel threatened? Not most people."

She nodded. "I agree. But I don't have the pulse of this place the way you do."

"Well," he said dryly, "I do believe most of us left the Wild West and showdowns at high noon behind us."

That caused her a pang. "I wasn't trying to insult your neighbors. It's just that last week you said…"

"I know what I said. I was trying to explain why people might be upset that a star basketball player could be unable to play if he gets another detention. What I said about the rat…" He shook his head. "Cassie, I wasn't trying to minimize it, not really. Yes, kids here are more used to that kind of thing because of hunting and ranching, but to do something like that to send a message…" Again he shook his head. "I just didn't want you worrying needlessly if that was the end of it. Clearly that's not the end."

"So you were just trying to reassure me?"

"Yeah. I was worried about it at the time, and I'm still worried."

"I'm a big girl," she said sharply. "Don't try to shield me or brush things off."

"I'm sorry."

But she didn't want him to be sorry. He was a naturally protective man as she had learned this past week. It had probably been instinctive for him to not want her to get too upset without further cause. "Don't apologize. Just don't do it again."

"Fair enough. So where does this get us? Are you going to pack and leave for other parts?"

"No." Of that much she was certain. She might be frightened of where this could go. Clearly she was the target of someone who was angry with her. But how much of a threat was he? She fought to tamp down the morass of fear that tried to rise again.

Slowly she returned to the table and sat. "I'm mad. I'm stubborn. I'm not going to be pushed around by some coward who makes anonymous phone calls, slashes my tires and uses a dead rat to get his point across. What's more, I was really starting to like this town."

"And?" he asked.

"I'm staying. I'm going to ride it out. I'm not going to turn tail."

"It could get dangerous. I can't promise you it won't. Not after two very obvious threats of violence, that rat and your car."

"They're probably just threats," she said decisively. "But even if they aren't I'm staying. I'm going to keep working to put an end to bullying, and to teach my students the best that I can. I absolutely refuse to give in to a bully, and that's what this guy is."

"Then you'd better get ready to have me around a lot until we're sure this is over."

"I can deal with that." Which was a rather offhand way of skirting the truth: she *wanted* him around. Giving herself an inward shake, she told herself to focus on work, on her job, on her students. It had saved her before.

Chapter 9

They made love again that night, but only once. Cassie didn't know if she imagined that Linc seemed a little withdrawn, but she knew she was tightening into her protective shell again. The passion filled her with melancholy even as it carried her to heights of delight. Barriers that were at least partly hers, and perhaps partly his, seemed to be rising again.

The feeling stayed with her as he took her home in the morning, as he called his friend to come take care of her car while she prepared for school. The magic of Saturday seemed to be waning.

All to the good, she told herself, even as she began to realize that brave words spoken in the shelter of Linc's ranch seemed almost foolhardy now that she was faced with returning to school.

For the first time she felt honestly nervous about going to work, about facing her classes. So far her students didn't seem to have joined the anti-Cassie camp, but what if the antipathy she had experienced on Friday had now reached them? What if she looked into hostile faces?

She'd deal with it, she promised herself. She'd deal with it the way she had dealt with so many things in her life: by ignoring it until it went away. Often that was the only option.

Her first indication of a sea change came from the mechanic Linc had called. When she tried to give him her credit card for the tow he waved it aside.

"No charge for any of this, Ms. Greaves," he said. "Wouldn't want you to think that folks around here would approve of whoever did this."

"But…" Even as her heart swelled with appreciation, she felt guilty. "You need to make a living, too, Morris."

"I'll make one even if I do this. Put that card away."

She was sure her mouth didn't close until her car disappeared down the street on the back of the truck.

"Wow," she said finally.

"Plenty of generous people in the world," Linc remarked. "The ugly ones seem to get the most attention, though."

She couldn't argue with that. The next sign of a shift came before her first class. Les came looking for her, and he was beaming. "You'll never guess what's going on."

"What?"

"Some townspeople, mostly parents, are setting up a fund to help James Carney's family with medical bills and counseling costs. And what's more, the school email and voice mail is full of requests for a special evening assembly for parents to discuss bullying."

"That's wonderful!"

"I told you an assembly was the best way to handle this.

Now we'll get the parents involved. I hardly dared hope we'd get such a response."

"We might not have," she reminded him. "Except for James. Have you heard anything? Linc and I were at the hospital Friday until he was out of danger, but I haven't heard since."

"I called his mother this morning. He should be released today, but she's not planning to bring him back to school." Les sighed, a frown settling over his round face. "She said it was just until he had some counseling, but I don't know, Cassie. This was a terrible thing. People are responding positively, but that doesn't mean we can change the culture overnight."

"I'm sure we can't. But this is a giant step."

A giant step that brightened her morning considerably, as did the students in her classes, who seemed to want to do something, whether it was sending some kind of message to James and his family, or taking on the bullies in their midst. Suddenly it seemed too long to wait until the Friday assembly. Everyone wanted to do something constructive *now*.

Behind that, though, she sensed something else, a kind of uneasiness. It came, she thought, from awareness of their own past transgressions, from the near loss of someone their own age. From guilt and awareness of mortality. Not knowing what else to do, she put her lesson plans aside for the day and just let the students talk, making a mental note that they might need to get the school psychologist in on this.

The day became emotionally exhausting for her as she tried to guide students through their mixture of feelings. Some started out tough, insisting they would never kill themselves over anything as stupid as bullying. Some spoke about how they had been bullied and how it had made them feel. In class after class, a slow consensus was reached: bullying was a bad thing.

She suspected the conversation would go on for days, and she was determined to have it if that was what the students wanted. So she gave them the situation: if they wanted to continue the discussion, they'd have to make up time on the lessons. They voted to make up the work with very few dissenters.

Having allowed them to choose, she was quite certain they would do so. At the end of the day, she was feeling a whole lot better about everything, and already figuring out how to alter her lesson plans for the makeup without pushing the students too hard to keep up.

"Ready to go, Teach?"

She looked up and saw Linc framed in the doorway, his jacket hanging open, his backpack slung over one shoulder.

"It's been a good day," she said as she gathered her last few things.

"You, too? We talked about bullying all day."

Her heart lifted and she returned his smile. "Yes." Then her smile faded. "Why does it always take a martyr to get a point across?"

"People can ignore a lot until they get jolted out of their ruts. How else could we survive?"

That was an excellent point. Walking with him across the parking lot as the afternoon faded rapidly toward twilight, she tried to tell herself not to expect too much, that it would take a long time to really change anything, that after the shock passed it would be easy to forget. "Shock works just so long."

"I know," he said as he opened the truck's door for

her. "That's why I didn't ignore it today. Strike while the iron's hot."

She slid into the seat. "Don't you have a practice?"

"Canceled. We're going to be playing a makeup for the game Saturday. I'll have to get back here by six and we'll play at seven."

"On a school night?"

"Yeah. Only way to prevent messing up the season schedule. Want to come?" he asked as he pulled the truck onto the road.

Since she was feeling considerably better today than yesterday, she actually had to think about it. A football game would be fun, but she had to rework all those lesson plans. And when she tested the sore space inside, the place left by the events of the past couple of weeks, she found it wasn't terribly tender. Her faith had been restored, and she was inclined to figure that nothing would happen that she couldn't handle.

"I need to work on lesson plans," she said. "We're going to get into a real mess with the syllabus if I don't figure out how to space things so the students don't get overwhelmed. I'd better just stay home and work."

"Not afraid?"

She glanced his way and smiled slowly. "Actually, no. Like I said yesterday, whoever did those things is a bully and a coward."

"And today you believe it?"

"Actually, I do. It was like everything changed today. Peoples' opinions seem to have swung around. The bully will probably crawl back under his rock now that people aren't upset."

He was silent as he steered them around a corner. "Probably." He spoke the word slowly. "I don't know, Cassie. I wouldn't have expected anyone to vandalize your car, or put a rat on your desk. Someone has a kink."

"Obviously. Are you trying to frighten me?"

His head shake was quick and certain. "No. I just want you to be cautious. People around here may be experiencing a shift in opinion, but that doesn't mean he has."

She couldn't argue with that, but she felt more confident than she had since this whole affair had started. And despite her burst of fear yesterday, she had begun to realize that the thing she most needed to do for herself was stand up. If she had begun to lose sight of that, her students today had definitely reminded her. They needed her, and other teachers, to help them work through this, and they had shown good hearts for the most part. Turn tail now? No way.

"None of it hurt *me,*" she reminded him, and maybe herself. "All of it was done in a way that would seem to indicate the bully doesn't want to be identified."

She gasped with surprise as they came around the corner. Her car was sitting in the driveway, and it sparkled. "Oh, my! Morris even washed it!"

Linc chuckled quietly. "I told you most people around here are good folks."

He pulled in behind her car, and she grabbed her backpack and climbed out before he could assist her. She walked around her compact and peered inside. "He even vacuumed it! My word!" She touched it. "I'd forgotten it could look this good."

"The key is probably under your doormat," Linc said.

She checked immediately and was relieved to find it. Any mischief-maker could have helped himself if that was a custom around here. Finding the key reassured her even more.

Linc came inside with her. She dropped her bag on the battered couch and faced him, smiling. "It's amazing how fast things can change."

"We've seen a really huge swing since you found those boys bullying James," he agreed. "First all the way down and then up."

"What can I do to thank the mechanic?" she asked him, still thinking about the loving care he'd bestowed on her car for free. "That was really above and beyond. A bottle of wine?"

"Beer would probably go over better. I think he'd appreciate the gesture."

"That's what I'll do, then." Feeling ever so much better, she spun in a little circle. "I can't believe that yesterday I felt like everything was crashing down on me. A weight is gone."

She noticed, however, that he didn't appear quite as thrilled as she was feeling. She glanced away, wondering if she had overreacted yesterday or if she was overreacting now. Yesterday she had been seriously frightened, wondering what kind of attack would come next. Then she had decided that whoever had been bothering her really hadn't done all that much, and what he had done indicated that he was a typical bully, a coward.

She still believed that. Whoever had butchered the rat and vandalized her car had wanted to frighten her, but he hadn't had the gumption to face her directly.

"Do you think I'm being foolish?" she asked finally.

"No." He stepped toward her and surprised her by wrapping her in his arms and hugging her close. It felt so good to be near to him again, to feel as if he weren't holding her at a distance. Last night's feeling that he was drawing away had lingered throughout the day, a subtle sort of ache, a sense of impending loss like a backdrop to all the good things that had happened since this morning. Part of her wanted to pull away, but another part of her took charge and she returned his hug.

"I understand," he said, "that yesterday it all crashed down on you. I'm not quite as sanguine that this bully will settle down now that public opinion is starting to rise against bullying. But maybe you're right. So far he's been a coward, that's for sure. Trying to frighten you without facing you. Typical of bullies."

"Exactly." Reluctantly she stepped back, reminding herself that she shouldn't get in any deeper. He had his reasons for fearing involvement; if there was ever a woman made to fit the bill of what worried him, it was her. She'd been here only a few months, she might decide not to stay.

Her own fault, too, because she could clearly hear herself saying more than once that she should resign and leave. After the rat, especially, she'd been unnerved enough to think about it seriously.

Equally important was that she was certain he had only spent so much time with her because he felt he needed to protect her and reassure her. He seemed like that kind of man, and the sexual attraction…well, little could be built on that. It flared, but it always quieted. She had enough married friends to have observed that.

So they'd been overcome, but that didn't mean she had to put her heart at his feet. Asking to get trampled once again, and this time by a man who had good reason not to trust her, didn't seem bright. If the background ache she'd been feeling was any indication, she was already in too deep. Definitely time to step back.

"Want something to eat?" she asked brightly without quite looking at him. "You've got to eat before the game."

Linc felt her pull away, saw how she avoided his gaze, and wondered what the hell he'd done wrong. Then it struck him: she was pulling away because she no longer felt she needed him.

Why should that be such a shock? Martha hadn't needed him enough to stay. Cassie had needed him since the day when that rat showed up on her desk, understandably. She was a newcomer around here without resources of her own yet. He had stepped up like some kind of hero and she'd welcomed the support and the protection he'd offered.

But now she felt everything was going to be okay. He believed the passion they had shared had been real, but beyond that? Beyond that there was evidently nothing.

He'd been a fool once again. His stomach turned to lead and his mouth soured. Another Martha? Maybe just a different version. But why should he be surprised? Why would any woman who hadn't grown up here want to hitch her wagon to a man who was just a teacher and part-time rancher. There were certainly better prospects out there, even around here.

"No thanks," he said. "I've got something back at the school. Maybe I'll stop by for a few minutes after the game. If anything disturbs you, I'll have my cell phone on, but I might not be able to hear it during the game." He started toward the door, then hesitated, his conscience plaguing him.

"Cassie? Are you sure you don't want to come to the school?"

She shook her head. He wondered why her face suddenly looked a little…wooden? Sad? He couldn't quite read it.

"Thanks," she said, giving him a small smile. "I'll be fine."

He walked out, feeling as if he had just missed something very momentous.

Wishful thinking, he told himself. That's all it was. At some level he'd dared to believe Cassie was different from Martha.

Evidently not.

Some unspoken conversation had just been had, but Cassie was only sure of her part in it. She had pulled back, yes, but she had offered him a meal, something far less dangerous than where that hug could have led. Then he had seemed to want to get out of there as fast as possible.

Mine fields, she thought. They were both full of them. She didn't trust him because he didn't trust her. He had plenty of reason not to trust her, and she had plenty of experience to tell her that trusting a man too quickly led to grief.

An aching sense of fatigue washed through her. Did she really want all this complexity? Not that it appeared she was going to have much choice. She'd pulled back, he'd left. They were quickly crawling back into their safe little shells.

Early twilight was claiming the world and darkening her house. She looked out the front window, saw the streetlights start to wink on from farther down the street. Surprisingly little snow had caught in her front yard, and the sidewalks and driveway were clear. The wind… Remembering the drift outside Linc's house, she walked around, turning on lights for comfort, and looking out windows to see where the snow had ended up.

Mostly in her backyard, she realized. Opening the back door and looking out the storm door, she realized she wouldn't be able to open it. Because of the other houses around, the drift didn't reach her second floor, but it came halfway up the door. From there she could see that most of the snow in this neighborhood had wound up behind and between houses. The street was swept clean, but everything else was buried.

Well, good to know, she thought, that she had only one way out and that was through the front door. She glanced at the clock, saw it was still plenty early, not quite dinnertime, so she pulled out her computer, looked up James's home number and called. His mother answered.

"Hi, Mrs. Carney, it's Cassie Greaves, James's math teacher. How is he doing?"

"Much better than he was. I'm going to be homeschooling him, though."

Cassie didn't argue. There was no good argument. "Is he well enough to see me? And if you want me to, I'd be glad to tutor him at home in math."

There was a definite hesitation, then Maureen's voice thawed a bit. "That would be helpful. I'm rusty on some things."

"Aren't we all?"

"You come over," she said. "You tried to protect him. Might do him some good."

Cassie felt another pang of guilt, as aware as anyone that she might have caused the bullying to worsen by her intervention.

Struggling with the guilt, she grabbed her things and a book she thought James might like to read. Outside, the setting sun outlined the western mountains in fiery red. It almost looked like the sky was on fire.

She was glad she didn't believe in omens.

James and his parents lived in a neat, small house in a neighborhood that looked like it had been built right after the Second World War. Cassie hiked up the drive, feeling the wind cut at her cheeks and try to snake into her jacket.

Maureen Carney opened the door, and greeted her with a tired but honest smile. "Come in, Ms. Greaves. James is in the living room, but I honestly can't tell you how he's feeling. He's been awfully quiet."

Cassie stepped in, noting that the house offered only the smallest of foyers, just enough to step inside and doff a jacket before reaching the doorways that opened off either side.

"James," Maureen called, striving for brightness, "Ms. Greaves is here." No voice answered her, but the woman continued to smile wanly and led Cassie into the living room.

James, looking even smaller than he had before, lay on the couch. He wore a green sweatshirt, and a ripple afghan covered his legs. There was something on the TV, but the volume was low, as if he wasn't really paying attention.

He looked awful. His eyes were sunken, and every line of his face seemed to drag downward. His dark eyes fastened to her, but only briefly.

"Hi, James," she said quietly. "I wanted to see how you're doing. Your fellow students are very upset about you. We talked about it all day."

He hunched his shoulder, as if trying to pull away, but he didn't answer. Cassie sat on an armchair facing him, wishing she knew the right words. Finally, she pulled out the book and leaned forward to place it on his lap.

"I think you'll like it, since you're so good at math. It's full of amusing stories about some great mathematicians."

"Doesn't matter," he said finally in a muffled voice.

She hesitated. Then, firmly, she announced, "It matters. *You* matter. I've seen some real talent in you, and you probably have a lot of talents you haven't even discovered yet. You have a lot to offer the world."

"You wouldn't know."

"Actually, yes, I would. I've been bullied, you know. It made me doubt myself and feel ugly and utterly alone. But here I am, trying to make a difference by teaching. One thing I know for sure, sometimes the biggest contribution any of us makes is a smile and a kind word. You're perfectly capable of that. Don't take your smile away from someone who might need it."

His eyes flickered toward her, then fell away. At least he was starting to hear.

"Your mom says you won't be coming back to school. I'm sorry to hear that, but I understand. I told her I'd be happy to tutor you in math if you like."

"I don't know," he said heavily.

"It's early days," she answered and looked at his mother. The woman was standing out of his line of sight, and right now she looked haggard as she stared at her son. Guilt. How much more guilt must she be feeling than even Cassie? How many times had she hoped her son was silent because the bullying had stopped? How many times had she told herself, and him, that it would stop eventually? And now this, the most desperate cry for help anyone could make, one of utter hopelessness.

She returned her attention to James and decided to take the bull by the horns. "Did the bullying get worse after I stepped in? Because if it did, I am so very sorry."

Now he stared at her. "It never stopped. Never. Like you hadn't done anything. They didn't hit me again, but they didn't leave me alone. They said they were going to get me when they were away from the school."

"Did they?"

"Not really. But they started a page online to slam me. A bunch of people joined in."

Cassie drew a sharp breath and wondered why she hadn't thought about the potential impact of social networking. God, how could she have overlooked that? "How did you find out about it?"

"There was a note in my locker. I didn't want to look, but I did."

She nodded. "I wish I'd looked into that."

"You wouldn't have found it. They didn't use my name or anything on the page. But everyone knew. Everyone was talking about it." His voice, which had been growing stronger, began to fade again. "I'm tired."

"Of course you are. You've been through hell." She didn't think this was a good time to pull punches. "I'll leave you now. But I want you to know I'm very sorry if I made it worse for you, James. But I couldn't ignore what I saw in that washroom."

He turned his face away. "I know. I guess I'm okay with it. You at least tried to do something. You're the first one."

Cassie heard his mother gasp and found Mrs. Carney looked horrified, with a fist to her mouth as if she were trying to hold in a cry.

"I'll come back in a few days," she said, rising.

He didn't answer.

Cassie grabbed her jacket in the foyer and stepped out onto the front porch. Without another word, Maureen closed the door behind her.

Determination grew in her all the way back home. Tomorrow she would address the matter of that social networking page with Les. It didn't matter if it was all happening outside of school. There had to be some way to stop it. But she couldn't imagine what. A sense of helplessness hit her as she pulled into her driveway and parked, a help-lessness so strong she wanted to pound her steering wheel.

Frustrated but determined to at least bring up the issue, she gathered her purse and climbed out of the car. It wasn't terribly late yet, still plenty of time to work on revising her lesson plans. She had to get that done before everything went off the rails.

She wondered how the game was going. She could hear sounds from the direction of the stadium, indicating that a lot of people had come out for the game, cold notwith-standing.

She was on her front step when she remembered she hadn't gone grocery shopping. A glance at her watch told her she had just enough time to at least grab something for tonight and the morning.

She tried not to think about Linc as she climbed back in her car to make the short run. She didn't want to imagine how he looked there on the sidelines coaching the team. She didn't want to imagine that he looked at his cell fre-quently to see if she had called.

She didn't want to imagine him at all, but there he was, popping up anyway. Maybe instead of working on her les-son plans, she ought to dally in the grocery until closing time. Linc would probably be wrapping up the game by then. Then she wouldn't have to waste her planning time by mooning around the house wondering if he'd drop by. The wait would be short by then. If he came.

Dang, she was a fool. Wasting all this time thinking about a man who didn't deserve it if only because he wasn't interested in the long term.

Let it be, she told herself. Let it be. Focus on work. Focus on the bullying program. Focus on the important stuff that she could actually do something about.

But why then did Linc seem as important as all the rest of it? That was the way to pain.

Memories from the past week, and most especially the weekend, insisted on distracting her from the routine chore of grocery shopping. She wasn't apt to get much work done this way.

Sighing, she finally completed her shopping and headed home. She wondered if ever before in her life had her thinking been so scattered and ungovernable. Even to herself she didn't seem to be making sense.

At home she grabbed her grocery bags and headed inside, wondering if a cup of coffee might help her gather the tattered ends of thought and focus.

But as she was emptying the bags, she heard a sound. In an instant her thoughts stopped hopping around and focused intently.

She was not alone.

The itch to get back to Cassie grew more and more overwhelming as time ticked by and Linc kept checking the game clock. At the final two-minute warning, he almost dumped everything on his assistant coach and took off.

All his resolutions not to get involved again, especially with a woman who might move on, had evaporated. And he knew just the moment they had evaporated. When she had pulled back from him, as if to place a distance between them.

He knew he was at least partially responsible for that, and as the evening passed, the need to talk to her increased until it became almost unbearable. He wanted to find out what exactly was causing this sense of distance. He wanted to clear the air, and unless she had discovered she wasn't interested in him, he wanted to tell her that he was willing to take the risk.

Hell, as he tried to keep his focus on coaching, his thoughts kept running to her. Willing to take the risk? Damn, he'd already taken it. Leapt into the fire with both feet.

And now he couldn't simply walk away.

He was troubled, too, by her being alone. Everything she had said about the person who had come after her made sense. The guy—at least he assumed it was guy—clearly was a coward and a bully, unlikely to go beyond anonymous threats.

Unfortunately, whether it was sensible or not, he didn't quite believe it. In fact, the more he thought about all that had happened that day, the more uneasy he got. What if this guy was pushed by the groundswell of support for Cassie and James Carney? What if he felt he was the only one left who would take action in his cause, whatever it was?

Did it even matter why? The threats of violence had been implicit, and sometimes people moved beyond threats to action when they felt pushed.

He should never have left her alone. He should have insisted she come to the game with him. Instead of backing away because she had seemed to want him to, he should have pressed the issue, become a caveman if necessary.

The penalty whistle blew and stopped the game again. He ground his teeth. He was probably overreacting, but he felt strongly that he didn't want Cassie to be alone until they could at least be certain this bully had quit. And he felt equally strongly that they needed to talk.

His insecurity combined with hers might be walking

them both in entirely the wrong direction. Or not. What if she told him to get lost? Well, he'd survived it before.

What was killing him as much as anything was the distinct feeling that he shouldn't have left her alone.

Damn it! He turned to the assistant coach, his mind made up.

Cassie stood frozen, facing the counter and grocery bags, listening intently, acutely aware that there was only one way out of this house because of the snow. The front door.

But perhaps she was mistaken. Straining her ears, she heard nothing. No sound, no movement. A faint rumble that she knew to be the forced-air heater in the basement.

Maybe she'd been mistaken. Maybe a temperature change had caused the house to settle a bit.

But she didn't believe it. The hair on the back of her neck was standing on end with the certainty that she was *not* alone.

Okay, she thought. Okay. Whether she was right or not, the sensible thing to do would be to get out of here. Just grab her keys, her purse, her jacket, like she was going out to get something from the car, and get out of here. Maybe pick up her cell phone and call the cops as she did so?

She uttered a small oath as if she were frustrated, and reached for her keys lying next to her purse on the counter. Her cell phone was in her pocket and she stuffed her hand in to grab it. Just in case, she told herself. Forget the jacket. Just get out the door.

She turned and had taken two steps toward the hallway when the man appeared. Aghast, she instinctively stepped back. He was big, very tall and massive. He wore winter outerwear and a black balaclava completely concealed his face and nose. She wouldn't have known who he was even if she had met him before. He stood between her and her only exit.

"Who are you? What do you want?" The questions escaped her instinctively, even as she backed up another step and her mind ran frantically around wondering what she could use to protect herself. Little enough. Her knives were in a drawer, her heavy pans were in a cupboard. Defend herself with a cloth grocery sack?

"I told you to leave."

It was the voice from the phone call. Maybe. She couldn't be sure of that, and she didn't recognize it otherwise. Her heart hammered so hard that breathing had become nearly impossible. Her mouth grew so dry she could barely speak. "Why?" It was a bare whisper. "I haven't done anything to you."

"You're messing with things you shouldn't oughtta. Upsetting folks. Hurting kids."

"But… Was your son one of those on detention?" A little strength was coming back when he didn't outright attack.

"No."

"Then what?" Desperation filled her, even as a voice kept telling her to remain calm, that he hadn't attacked her yet, that maybe he only intended to frighten her. He was certainly succeeding. *Try to talk him down.* "What have I done?"

When he didn't answer, her fear ratcheted up even more, something she wouldn't have believed possible only a little while ago.

She spread her hands along the counter, trying to look casual, but feeling slowly for the drawer where she kept her knives, never taking her eyes off of him.

He stepped toward her and she froze. "You don't get it," he said. "You had a chance to leave and you didn't."

"But what did I do?"

"You know."

"I don't!" Her fingers closed on the drawer pull. "Did you put that rat on my desk?"

An ugly laugh escaped him. "Bet that shook you."

"It did," she admitted, hoping that agreeing with him would calm him. "It made me sick."

"Good. You shoulda quit then."

Bully, she reminded herself. He was a bully. Even now he wouldn't reveal his face. That must mean all he wanted to do was scare her.

She gauged the distance to the door and his bulk between her and it. If she could get him to move just a little more to the side...

She shifted toward the back door. He instinctively sidestepped that way but shook his head. "You can't get out that way."

So he'd checked it all out. He knew she had only one way to go.

"I'll leave," she said. "Just let me go and I'll get in my car and never come back."

"That chance is gone."

Gone? What did he mean? Then she knew. He wasn't here just to scare her. He meant to hurt her.

As that certainty filled her, extreme clarity settled over her. She could either stand here and take whatever he dished out, or she could do everything in her power to fight him.

Should she grab a knife or try to dart by him? She couldn't tell if he had a weapon, although that probably didn't matter as big as he was. Wrenching the drawer pull, she yanked it open and felt for her big chef's knife. She gripped it tightly and held it high. "Let me go or I'll stab you."

He just stared at her. Then one of his big gloved hands gave a quick twist and he snapped open a switchblade of his own. "You're getting it now."

With no choice left, Cassie charged him.

Linc pulled up in front of Cassie's house, switched off his ignition and hesitated. What if she simply told him to go home, that she was busy, that she didn't have time?

Then he would be a coward for refusing to face it, he decided. A damned coward. Besides, the niggling feeling that the outpouring of support might have infuriated the guy who was trying to frighten her wouldn't leave him alone, either. He'd seen bullies react that way, as if to justify their bad acts by making an even stronger statement.

A strange dynamic, but one with which he was all too familiar.

He climbed out of the truck. At once, though he couldn't say exactly what alerted him, he knew something wasn't right. He scanned the street but it looked normal except for an old pickup parked at the curb a few houses down.

But then he saw the shadows of two figures against the front kitchen curtains. She wasn't alone, and one shadow looked huge. Then he heard an unmistakable, muffled cry.

The clarity persisted. Get out or possibly die. Cassie, deprived of safe options, had no trouble taking action. She charged the man with her knife at the ready.

He reacted a little slowly, maybe because he misread her, and for one brilliant, hopeful moment, she thought she might make it. But just as she passed him, he grabbed her shoulder, shoved and threw her to the floor.

As she cried out, the knife slipped from her hand and she fell facedown, the wind knocked from her.

Oh, God, it was over now. Whatever he had intended, now he was probably mad. Panic filled her because she couldn't draw in air, and without air she couldn't move.

Still struggling to get her diaphragm to work, panic exploded even more as he grabbed her hair and yanked her head back so hard it hurt.

Death was coming. She knew it with absolute certainty.

At the same instant, she managed to drag in a breath, just as the world seemed to be darkening, and she heard a loud slam.

She opened her eyes to see Linc barreling through her front door, head and shoulders low like a football player ready to tackle. Her assailant let go of her hair.

Groaning, ignoring the pain in her neck and abdomen, she rolled over in time to see Linc on top of the man who had attacked her.

Then her entire focus of vision narrowed to the gleaming steel of the switchblade, still firmly gripped in the man's hand.

"Linc..." she barely croaked as she fought to get more air. She had to do something.

Struggling onto her hands and knees, she crabbed her way closer as Linc punched at the guy's head. The hand holding the knife came up, clearly aimed at Linc's side.

"No..." She launched herself with every ounce of strength she had, grabbing at the rising arm. The blade came perilously close to her face, but she didn't care. She had to save Linc.

Using her body's weight, she pressed the arm down. "He's got a knife."

Linc didn't answer, using his energy to punch the guy hard in the right shoulder. A hard punch, one that made the guy squeal. It also made him release the knife.

Quickly, Cassie shoved it away, and when it didn't go far enough, she shoved it again.

Linc let out an explosive puff of air as he took a punch himself from the other side, but he didn't let go of the man.

Cassie, finding energy again, clambered to her feet. She grabbed the switchblade, saw the chef's knife she had dropped and grabbed it, too. With a knife in each hand, she approached the struggling men.

Behind the ski mask, her assailant's eyes widened as he saw the knives in her hands.

"Can you hold him, Linc?" she asked in a voice threaded with ice. "Because I think I'd like to cut his throat."

Linc panted, "No. Call the cops. I've got him."

But all the fight seemed to have gone out of the guy at the sight of the two knives in Cassie's hands, or perhaps because of her icy tone of voice. Linc straddled his hips, legs tucked under the guy, and pressed both his shoulders to the floor.

"I take it you never wrestled," Linc said with something like satisfaction. "Don't twitch or I'll put you in a head-lock you'll never forget."

Later, the police and her assailant gone, Cassie felt near to collapse. Too much, she thought, and it was as if now the threat was past and safely removed, someone had pulled her plug. She was grateful, so grateful, when Linc wrapped her in his arms, held her almost painfully tight and murmured, "God, I was so scared for you."

She'd been scared for him, too, in those moments when he'd tackled the knife-wielding assailant. But as strength drained from her, she knew one thing for certain. There was no place she'd rather be than in Linc's arms. If only he felt the same way.

He offered her no options. He shepherded her back to her bedroom, helped her jam some clothing into a duffel, then urged her out to his truck. She didn't want to be alone, and apparently he didn't want to leave her alone.

Ever the white knight, she thought wistfully. If only he wanted her for more than that, but she had the heart-sickening feeling he did not. Struggling for some emotionally safe perch, she tried not to think about impending loss, tried to think about how she was going to manage to teach today, to help her students, without any sleep at all. Because she could tell there would be no sleep, not tonight.

That didn't distract her, so she tried to focus on her assailant. Anything to get rid of the lead in her heart and stomach. Even those moments of sheer terror.

"Do you think he would have killed me?" she asked finally.

"I don't know. He says not, and I think that's all we'll ever know."

"Yeah." She fell silent, trying to absorb the story that had excused all this insanity. "I have trouble believing his motivation." The man, Stan Bell, was a known alcoholic and ne'er-do-well who had a son on the basketball team. A team that looked like it had a good shot at the championship. Vic Bell, the son, had not been involved in the bullying, so it wasn't as if he might have lost his position on the team.

No, what had driven Stan Bell was that twenty years

ago he had been on a team headed for a championship, a team that had lost because the star player had gotten himself arrested just before the big game. Thus, Stan had been deprived of the win he had counted on, a win that probably would have been the high point of his entire life considering what had followed. All of this because he didn't want his own son to lose his chance at the trophy.

"It seems like an extreme reaction," Cassie remarked, forcing her focus away from the man beside her in the truck. Away from the need to fall into his arms and escape with him to a better place. "Really extreme."

"The man obviously has some serious mental-health issues."

And there it was going to have to stay, Cassie thought with a sigh. The guy was unbalanced. In his own mind he was probably being perfectly rational, but from the outside it looked insane.

"Just be prepared, Cassie," Linc said. "They're not going to be able to charge him with attempted murder. He didn't do enough."

"I know. Gage Dalton told me. He probably won't even go to jail for a whole year."

"Are you okay with that?"

"Do I have a choice? Maybe rehab will help him." She shook her head, wanting to put it all away, at least for now. She hurt, she was tired, and she wondered why she was going home with Linc when it was the stupidest thing in the world for her to do. If he'd wanted her the way she wanted him, he could have had her for the taking at her house. Except for that long, tight hug, there'd been no hint he wanted her.

He pulled up in front of his ranch. She knew he needed

to take care of his animals and she expected him to just usher her inside and leave her while he did that. It would fit.

But he astonished her. He wrapped her in a bone-crushing embrace the instant they stepped inside and whispered in her ear, "I was so afraid I'd lose you."

The sentiment touched her deeply, and she felt the crack in her heart, which had been aching steadily all day, grow wider.

But before she could respond to his embrace, he stepped back and held her by the shoulders, his electric blue eyes boring into hers.

"Tell me the truth, Cassie. Knowing that Bell might be on the streets again soon, are you going to stay or leave?"

There was no lying to that gaze, no evading the demand he was making. She knew exactly what he was asking and why. She also knew that he was making no promises.

But deep inside she knew something even more important: never in her life had it been this essential that she know exactly what she intended, and that she mean it with her whole being. She closed her eyes, to escape his stare, and searched her heart. The man who attacked her would walk these streets again. Maybe in a matter of weeks, maybe next year, but he was going to be back. He might even be crazier and madder then.

But a deep certainty filled her despite everything, and she'd never been more sure of herself in her life when she opened her eyes, met his intense gaze and said, "I'm staying. I'm here for good."

Something in his face softened. "For a while, anyway."

She shook her head. "No, I'm staying. This place has really grown on me. Today I found the kind of community I always wanted to be part of."

"In spite of Stan Bell?"

"Stan Bells exist everywhere. A community that will organize this fast to take care of the Carney family isn't easy to find."

A smile began to curve his mouth. "There's this other thing, too."

"What thing?"

"Me. I wear a few hats, which keeps me pretty busy, I admit. Coaching, teaching, this ranch. But I like my life. I'm not an ambitious sort of guy who wants to set the world on fire. I'm not going great places. I just want to be a good teacher, a good coach and a good steward to my land."

"What's wrong with that? Those are pretty important things. Look at me. I think teaching is a pretty high calling, myself. Now maybe I exaggerate my importance...."

Before she could finish, he hauled her close and silenced her with a deep, burning kiss. "You don't exaggerate your importance," he murmured huskily against her mouth when he let her catch her breath. "Six months."

"Six months?"

"Live with me until the end of the school year. Then if you can still stand it, I want to marry you. Because, damn it, I love you. I know it's fast. I'll give you time. But I've been falling in love with you since I first set eyes on you. I know I tried to stay away, but it was happening anyway. The way you move. The way you talk. You probably don't even realize how much attention I was paying to you. I thought I was being smart, but I was being stupid. I couldn't stop the inevitable. I love you, Cassie Greaves, and seeing you in danger tonight made it impossible for me to pretend any longer."

She felt her heart soar. Fast, maybe it was too fast, but

some part of her knew it with such certainty that denying it would be like cutting out her own heart. "I love you, too, Linc." She threw her arms around his neck, wanting him as close as she could get him, sure that she had at last found her place in life, in the world. With him. Happiness filled her, happiness beyond any she had ever known.

Later as they cuddled in bed together, he spoke. "I'm sorry I rushed in with all that. I suppose I could have chosen a better time, after all that happened to you tonight." He turned toward her, drawing her closer. "But I couldn't wait, Cassie. It already felt like I'd waited too long. When I was at the game, I was thinking I should have said something before I left. I had such a strong feeling we were getting our wires crossed."

"I guess we were," she sighed. "I really didn't think it was possible for anyone to love me. And then you thought I'd leave the way Martha did...."

"We need to learn to talk more. More clearly. Even about things we're afraid of."

She nodded against his shoulder, loving the feel of his skin against her cheek. "Kids?" she asked tentatively.

"Kids!"

For an instant she wondered if she'd asked the wrong question, but then his laugh rolled out, seeming to cover her like warm honey. "Definitely kids. I was going to wait before bombarding you on that. I definitely want at least two. Is that okay?"

"More than okay. I always wanted a large family."

"Well then. I've always wanted to hear kids running around and laughing in this house again."

He swooped in for a hard kiss, then lifted his head, gazing into her eyes. The bedside lamp was dim, but not too dim for her to see he'd grown very serious.

"I want this to be forever, Cassie. Forever."

So did she. Forever seemed like almost enough time.

* * * * *

"I know magic."

"Sure you do."

He studied her with indolent eyes, not saying anything until she recited his address.

His defenses went up. "How do you know so much about me?"

"Like I said, magic." Lauren raised her right hand, palm forward so he couldn't see the driver's license trapped by its edge between her first two fingers.

"I'm not a big believer in magic."

With a flourish, Lauren shook her hand and his driver's license appeared at the end of her fingers. For a moment, Heath didn't know what to say. Before he could recover, she flicked her wrist and sent the plastic rectangle spinning at him.

Heath caught the license in his left hand. His free hand slid down to his pants pocket, then he looked surprised. "You picked my pocket at the morgue."

NO ESCAPE

BY
MEREDITH FLETCHER

First published in Great Britain 2013
by Mills & Boon, an imprint of Harlequin (UK) Limited,
Eton House, 18-24 Paradise Road, Richmond, Surrey TW9 1SR

© Meredith Fletcher 2012

ISBN: 978 0 263 90346 1
ebook ISBN: 978 1 472 00697 4

46-0213

Harlequin (UK) policy is to use papers that are natural, renewable and recyclable products and made from wood grown in sustainable forests. The logging and manufacturing processes conform to the legal environmental regulations of the country of origin.

Printed and bound in Spain
by Blackprint CPI, Barcelona

Thanks for reading!

We're treating you to **TWO** fabulous offers...

Meredith Fletcher lives out West where the skies are big, but still close enough to Los Angeles to slip in for some strategic shopping. She loves old stores with real wooden floors, open-air cafés, comfortable boots, the mountains and old movies like *Portrait of Jennie* while sipping a cup of hot cocoa on a frosty day. She loves action romances with larger-than-life heroes and heroines with pithy repartee. She has pithy repartee herself, but never when she seems to need it most! She's much more comfortable at the computer writing her books. Please contact her at meredithfletcher@hotmail.com or find her at www.whatmakesmyheartbeatfaster.blogspot.com.

For Matt and Alyssa, who found each other.

Chapter 1

"I'm sorry about your friend."

Throttling the urge to scream in rage and pain, Lauren Cooper stared down at the body of Megan Taylor. "She's— She wasn't my friend. We were sisters."

On the other side of the stainless-steel table that supported Megan, the coroner consulted a small spiral-bound notebook. Intensity clung to him like a second skin. He didn't look like a guy who smiled much, but he was handsome and would have had a nice smile when he put himself to it.

Being a coroner wasn't a profession that lent itself to a lot of smiles, though. Not even in Jamaica.

His white lab coat was stretched tight across broad shoulders. The notebook nearly disappeared in his big, callused hands. A faded half-moon scar showed on the left side of his cleft chin. He was over thirty, but not by much. He was six feet plus and lean. His sun-streaked bronze hair was short and neat, professional, but a little long now, a little out of control. Maybe he hit the beach a lot when he wasn't in the morgue. His accent was Southern, somewhere in the lower forty-eight.

Lauren turned her attention from the coroner and focused on Megan. Looking at her lying there on the table was the hardest thing Lauren had ever had to do. Mornings filled with pillow fights, nights packed with shared secrets, all the things sisters did made the reality even more confusing.

Megan's short-cropped platinum-blond hair was tangled with seaweed, and Lauren knew that she would never have wanted to be seen like that. She had to resist the impulse to comb the debris from Megan's hair.

You can't. It's evidence. It's all evidence. Tears burned the backs of Lauren's eyes.

Megan is evidence now.

The thought almost wrung a howl of pain from Lauren. She curled her hands into fists and made herself breathe, made herself push the air out and slowly let it back in. She had to keep the air going out. It was too easy to hold it in.

Looking at Megan's body lying on the table and covered to the neck by the white sheet was a nightmare. She'd been twenty-seven years old, the same age Lauren was. Both of them were similarly built, athletic with curves.

With her fair hair and dazzling blue eyes, Megan had been the one of them that was the light. Dark haired and dark eyed, Lauren had been the shadow. Megan had always fearlessly rushed in, and Lauren had always waited on the outside, watching before she dove in.

That had changed later. Megan had remained fearless, but Lauren had learned to seize the limelight whenever she needed to. Success in her job had depended on that. She was suddenly aware of the silence in the morgue, and that the coroner was staring at her.

She thought back frantically, trying to remember any question she might have missed. There were so many questions swirling through her head right now. "I'm sorry. Did you ask me something?"

"I did. Which of you is married?"

The question surprised Lauren. It didn't seem like the kind

of information a coroner would want. But this was Jamaica. She didn't know how things worked down here. She'd never been to the island country.

"Neither of us is married."

The coroner's eyes were gold with green flakes that stirred restlessly. He didn't blink. "Different last names. Is one of you divorced?"

"No."

"But you said you're sisters?"

"Yes. I was adopted." *Rescued* was more like it. Lauren still had nightmares about the orphanage and foster homes. Her adoptive mother told her those memories would fade, but they hadn't. Lauren had always been thankful for the second chance she'd gotten, and being orphaned once had made losing her adoptive father to a heart attack four years ago even harder. Megan and her mother were all that Lauren had left.

And now Megan was gone.

"You kept your birth name?"

"Yes. It was all I had left of my parents." Lauren had wanted to keep something from them. They had died tragically. It hadn't been their fault that they'd left her. From everything she remembered of them, they had been good people.

"Do you know who Ms. Taylor came down here with?"

"She came by herself." Lauren looked down at her sister. There had been so many wild things Megan had gotten her to do when they'd lived at home and during college.

"Was she in the habit of doing things like that?"

Lauren kept her voice soft. "She liked her adventures."

"Adventures?"

"That's what she called them. Her adventures." Lauren's eyes burned, but she refused to let the tears fall. She wasn't going to do that in front this stranger. She had always been emotionally reserved.

Except with Megan. With Megan she'd always been able to just be herself.

Now that was gone.

"Coming down here by herself was risky."

The flat tone in the coroner's voice stopped just short of insulting, but that somehow made the statement worse. He winced, as if he'd just realized how harsh he'd sounded.

"Sorry. Something like this, it's hard to take even if you've seen it dozens of times before."

The morgue, for all its stainless-steel and tiled-floor impersonality, suddenly seemed too small. Lauren made herself breathe out. *He's just here to do his job. Just answer the questions.* She worked to unclench her fists and failed. She wanted to defend Megan, wanted to explain how her sister loved life and new experiences, and she wanted to lash out at the coroner all at the same time.

"Megan was impulsive." The statement felt naked and indefensible to Lauren's ears. She desperately wanted to make the man understand, but she just couldn't find the words. There *were* words. She knew there were. "She wanted to see Jamaica. She's— *She'd* been going on about it for weeks. This trip was something she'd promised herself when she finished up a project at her advertising firm. This was a celebration. A getaway from the 24/7 life she'd been doing the last few weeks to close the deal."

"So there was no particular reason she came to Kingston?"

"She wanted to come here. For Megan, that was reason enough." Lauren thought back to her discussion with Megan before her sister had left. "There was some movie she'd seen lately. Something about an island cop." She shook her head. "I can't remember anything more than that. She caught a movie on Netflix, and she decided this was where she had to go." She took a breath. "That's just Megan. It's always been Megan."

The coroner made another notation in his book. "Was she meeting anyone down here?"

"No."

"Would she have told you if she was?"

"Yes. When Megan was in *discovery* mode, that's what she called it, she didn't want anyone else around that she knew. She said having a friend along was too limiting. It didn't let her really explore a new environment."

The coroner studied her with those gold eyes. "Would you say you and Ms. Taylor had a good relationship?"

It took a moment for Lauren to answer the question because her voice was thick and felt like shattered glass. "Yes. We did."

"You knew she was here?"

"Yes."

"Who else knew she was coming?"

"I don't know. Lots of people. Megan was people-friendly. That's why she was so good at her job. She kept a Facebook account and updated it regularly. She let everyone know she was taking this trip."

He wrote something else down. "So someone could have been meeting her here?"

"You'd have had to know Megan. If she knew something, or even thought she knew something, she told you. That's how she was."

"Did she have many romances?"

Heat filled Lauren's face, and she glared at the man.

"I didn't mean that the way it sounded. I apologize. That wasn't supposed to come out like that." He waited a moment to see if she would respond. When she didn't, he went on. "I just wondered if there's the possibility that she was currently seeing someone and you didn't know about it."

"No. Not that I'm aware of. Maybe Megan wouldn't tell me about a new guy in her life at the time that relationship started, but I always knew. Megan thought she could hide things like that, but she really couldn't. Not from Mom. Not from me. I knew." Lauren looked down at her sister and wanted to believe that. No, she *did* believe that. She would have known.

The air-conditioning unit cycled, and the cool air washed over Lauren. She wrapped her arms around herself and trembled slightly. Her fists still wouldn't open. She couldn't remember feeling so cold and so alone.

"If Megan had been meeting someone here, I would have known."

"You're certain of that?"

"I'm positive."

"Was Ms. Taylor casually seeing anyone back home? Someone that didn't come along on this trip?"

Lauren tried to keep up, but the questions just kept coming with staccato regularity. The man was like a machine. "No."

"There wasn't anyone she'd started seeing a little more of before she left? Maybe someone she was interested in but not officially seeing?"

"No. Like I said, with Megan, every potential romance was a big deal. I would have known." So would everyone on Facebook. Megan liked being in love. None of her suitors had stood the test of time, though. Megan had liked her diversions, but most of her exes were still friends of hers. That was just how she was. No one would hurt her.

Except that someone had. The dark bruising around Megan's throat testified to that.

"Was there anyone your sister had stopped seeing recently?"

"No."

"Anyone she'd stopped seeing in the past that would hold a grudge?"

"Look." Lauren's tone came out sharper than she'd intended. "You didn't know Megan. She wasn't like that. No one would want to hurt her. Not even an ex-boyfriend. She was the kindest, gentlest, most innocent person I've ever known." A tear fell from her right eye, and she felt it skid down her cheek. She refused to brush it away because she knew that would only open the floodgates.

"Where are Ms. Taylor's—" The coroner stopped himself and offered a correction. "Your parents?"

"We lost our father a few years ago. Mom's not well. She's gone through chemo and isn't able to travel. She asked me to bring Megan back home."

"I see. I'm sorry to hear that." For the first time, the cold, impersonal voice softened just a little.

Lauren took a deep breath and looked at the bruises around her sister's throat. They looked almost like handprints. "Can you tell me what happened to Megan? The police inspector I talked to on the phone wasn't very informative. I'm supposed to meet with him later." She didn't want to know what Megan went through in her last moments. She knew her mom wouldn't want to know, but they had to know so they would be prepared for what was going to happen next. For when whoever had done this was caught. "He said there's going to be an investigation."

"What were you told?"

Again with the questions. Lauren made herself breathe out. "A police inspector, Wallace Myton, contacted my mother and told her that Megan had drowned. When my mother told me, I knew that couldn't be true."

"Why?"

"Megan was a strong swimmer. And she didn't take chances out in the water."

"But you said she was impulsive enough to come to Jamaica on a whim."

Lauren's voice tightened and grew sterner. "I'm telling you what I knew the minute I was told what had happened. My sister did not drown."

He looked at his notebook. "I see that. You called Inspector Myton back and insisted that your sister could not have drowned. You wanted him to investigate your sister's death."

"That's right. The inspector was very polite, but I could tell he didn't believe me."

"He believed you after the bruises showed up postmortem on your sister's neck."

Lauren closed her eyes. She couldn't believe the man had stated that so coldly. "That's when the police knew Megan had been strangled."

"I'm sorry."

Keep breathing. Deal with this. Mom is counting on you.
Lauren opened her eyes and looked back at the man.

"Did your sister know a magician named Gibson?"

The question came so far out of left field that Lauren couldn't help being surprised. "No."

The coroner looked puzzled. "Your sister didn't know Gibson. But I can tell by your expression that *you* do."

"I don't know him. I know *of* him. Everybody who loves magic knows who Gibson is. I've seen him perform." Lauren didn't like the way she suddenly felt guilty. That came from the coroner, not her. She grew more uncomfortable with the questioning, but she told herself she'd never dealt with something like this before and that her answers would help catch whoever had hurt Megan.

"What do you know about Gibson?"

That question was easier to answer. Lauren knew about Gibson. She answered automatically, pulling up the information effortlessly, and was grateful for the change of subject. "The man's a master illusionist. He's up there with David Copperfield. Criss Angel. Doug Henning. Siegfried & Roy."

Frowning, the man shook his head. "I've heard of Criss Angel."

Lauren could tell from the coroner's reaction that he didn't care much for the magician.

"And I thought Siegfried and Roy were lion tamers."

"Magic is a part of their show." Lauren studied him. "I don't suppose you care for magic shows or magicians."

"Magicians are just another type of con artist."

Under other circumstances, Lauren knew she would have argued the point and maybe even gotten angry. Magic and illusion were an art, and shows depended on audiences wanting to be fooled just as much as on magicians and illusionists. For now, though, she just let it go.

"Why would your sister have been interested in Gibson?"

"I don't know that she was."

The coroner reached under the lab coat and took out a photograph. He held it so Lauren could see it.

In the photograph, Megan sat at a table in an elegant club. She held a wineglass in one hand and looked as carefree as ever. The lights sparkled in her blue eyes, and Lauren knew her sister was having a great time. She didn't look frightened or under duress. Her smile was carefree.

The man sitting beside Megan was instantly recognizable. Gibson—that was the only name anyone knew him by—was a virtuoso of illusion. He'd had shows in Vegas and in Europe that were always sold out.

Dark and broody, a wild flip of hair hanging down into his face, Gibson looked mysterious and otherworldly. His persona, if it was a persona, never slipped. In the few interviews he'd done, he'd maintained his distance and hadn't revealed much about himself. No one knew where he came from. He'd just appeared on the magic scene almost as if by arcane means. If it was a shtick, it worked for him.

The black suit was Italian, neatly pressed, and fit him well. In the darkness of the club, he almost seemed to be disappearing into the shadows, as if the darkness around him was drawing him in under its protective wing. His was a hatchet face fleshed out by hard planes and deep-set eyes. A thin beard edged his jaw and pooled in a goatee around his thin-lipped mouth. The pale complexion made him look stark, as if he never saw the light of day.

Lauren had followed his career and had gotten to see him when he'd played at the Cadillac Palace Theatre in Chicago. Megan had bought the tickets and planned their whole night— including a blind date with an accountant for Lauren that was nice but didn't really have any spark.

"Is that Gibson?" The coroner jostled the photograph and broke the hypnotic intensity.

"Yes."

"Ever met him?"

"No."

"Your sister obviously knew him." He put the picture back inside his jacket.

Lauren didn't know what to say to that. She thought for a moment. "That picture wasn't on her Facebook page." She had looked at Megan's Facebook information and updates several times since she'd gotten the news about her sister. Until the night of her death, there had been constant updates and Tweets. "When was it taken?"

"The night she went missing."

Pain racked Lauren. "Megan was reported missing?"

The man nodded. "You didn't know that?"

"No." Lauren focused on her control. She needed to listen. She needed to learn. Her mom would want to know everything. "The first contact we had was Inspector Myton's phone call to tell us—to tell us Megan was gone."

"Your sister was reported missing."

"By whom?"

"A friend she'd made over the last couple days."

"What friend?"

The coroner hesitated, then answered. "A man she was supposed to have breakfast with the next morning. The guy called the police because he didn't feel like your sister was someone who would just stand someone up."

"Megan wouldn't. If she didn't want to go somewhere, she didn't go. If something came up, she called. That's just how she was."

"Then we have to assume she went with whoever did this to her."

Lauren looked down at her sister and shook her head. "No. Megan would never go with anyone that would do something like this."

"Then she didn't know what the guy she was with was capable of."

"How do you know it was a guy?"

The coroner held up his hands. "Her killer had big hands."

An image of someone's hands around Megan's neck squeezing the life out of her nearly brought Lauren to her knees. She thought she was going to be sick. The room spun around her.

A strong hand took her by the elbow and lent her strength. "Easy. Just keep breathing."

Lauren did. She forced her legs to hold her up and concentrated on the door on the other side of the room till the room stopped spinning. "Did you find out where this man was when Megan went missing?"

"He was with friends. Iron-clad alibi."

Iron-clad alibi? What coroner talked like that? Obviously he had been watching too many cop shows. "If the police knew Megan was missing, why didn't they do something?"

"Adults come down to Jamaica to go missing all the time. There were no signs of foul play in her room. The police checked. She just didn't come back to her room that night."

Because she was dead.

"Normally three days have to pass before an adult is presumed missing." The coroner's voice was flat, but she knew he was trying to help her understand what had happened. "Since there was no evidence that she was abducted, the police kept on the lookout for her." He hesitated. "Things happen down in the islands. The police know that, too. Because they were looking, they knew who she was when they found her. Otherwise she could have been here in the morgue for days before anyone knew who she was."

That was a horrible thought. Lauren couldn't bear the idea of Megan lying here in this place of the dead for days without anyone knowing where she was.

The coroner's voice was lower, softer, and the Southern accent was more pronounced. "I'm sorry for your loss, Miss Cooper. But I'm going to get the guy who did this. For what it's worth, I can promise you that. He won't get away with what he's done."

The conviction in his voice startled Lauren. It was raw and hoarse. She looked into those gold eyes and saw the stormy intensity of his gaze. She cleared her throat to make her voice work. "I'm sorry. I didn't get your name."

The morgue door opened, and a rotund man in his fifties stepped into the room with a file in one hand and a mug of tea in the other. He wore dark blue scrubs and a matching surgical hat. A mask hung loose around his neck. He gazed heatedly at the coroner standing beside Lauren.

"What are you doing in here, Detective Sawyer?"

The coroner ignored the older man and focused on Lauren. "Are you okay? Can you stand?"

Not knowing what was going on, Lauren drew away from the man.

"Never mind what you're doing here." The new coroner set his cup down on the nearby counter and grabbed the door. He pulled it open. "You're leaving. Get out of here."

The coroner—*Detective Sawyer*—looked at Lauren, tried to say something, then shook his head and left.

Lauren watched him go and didn't understand anything that had happened, but she was going to find out. She headed for the door, hurrying to catch up.

Chapter 2

You're some piece of work, Sawyer.

Sighing in self-disgust, Heath Sawyer slipped out of the white lab coat as he strode down the hallway from the morgue. His long legs ate up the distance, but he couldn't get out of the building fast enough.

He'd wanted to see the dead woman's body himself, to get a feel for her and how she'd died. Whenever he was working a case, he wanted to know as much as he could about the victims. Seeing them at the crime scene or the morgue helped, but the trade-off was demanding. That kind of intimacy was a lodestone for nightmares. Years later, he could still remember the faces of the first case he'd investigated. He hadn't planned on running into the sister on this one.

But that didn't stop you from taking advantage of the situation when it presented itself, did it?

A wave of guilt assailed him, but he pushed it away. He'd learned to do that on the job, and he was on the job now, even out of his jurisdiction. Hell, he was out of his country.

Memory of the woman's perfume teased at his mind. Lauren

Cooper was holding herself together better than a lot of grieving relatives Heath had dealt with over the years. In fact, she
was holding it together better than he had when he'd found
out about Janet.

He dropped the lab coat onto the counter where an older
woman talked on the phone and entered data on a computer
that had seen better days. A Bob Marley poster hung on the
wall beside a calendar that said, Welcome to Jamaica. Have
a Nice Day.

The woman narrowed her eyes, and her face pinched into a
frown as she watched Heath. "Hey. Hey, you. You come back
here and put that where it goes. I'm not your maid." Her island
accent was thick.

Heath ignored her and headed for the stairs because they
were faster than taking the elevator. He couldn't wait to be outside again where he could breathe. The island temperature was
cooler than it currently was back in Atlanta, but the humidity
was worse. He fished his sunglasses from his shirt pocket and
slid them into place.

The area was dangerous, and that woman—Lauren
Cooper—didn't look like someone used to dealing with dangerous situations. She had no business being at the hospital.
The State Department should have taken care of the arrangements for getting her sister's body back to Chicago.

That image of her standing there beside her dead sister was
going to haunt him. He felt guilty for having noticed how pretty
she was. He didn't know what it was, but there was some indefinable quality about Lauren Cooper that had caught his attention.

Heath forced himself to keep moving. The woman wasn't
his problem. She wasn't his responsibility. She couldn't help
him because she didn't know what had happened to her sister.
He was here looking for a murderer.

The man who had killed Janet.

As the pain and loss took him, Heath closed his eyes and
tried to push it away. He had work to do, and he'd taken a leave

of absence from the P.D. to get it done, to clear the ghosts from his head.

And he knew who his target was. Finally, in the picture of Megan Taylor, he had another link in the chain he intended to hang around Gibson's neck before he dropped the man into the ocean.

Let's see him magic his way out of that.

A trio of young nurses came down the stairs. They chattered in English and a smattering of other languages Heath couldn't identify. And they laughed as they talked about the party they'd gone to last night. He gave way before them and pulled to one side of the narrow stairwell. He nodded a silent greeting.

Then someone's hand dropped onto his elbow and yanked him around. He almost slipped on the narrow stairs, but his left arm came around, hand turning and curling over his assailant's wrist. The move broke the grip at once.

His right hand curled into a fist at his side, and his weight shifted on his knees as he prepared to throw a punch. The response was automatic, drummed into him from years spent on Peachtree and other violent streets in Atlanta while he learned his tradecraft in law enforcement. Mostly, he'd learned how to stay alive. And truth to tell, some of that willingness to hit came out of his Waycross, Georgia, roots, as well.

The identity of the person who had grabbed him surprised him.

Lauren Cooper no longer looked vulnerable and confused. Her dark eyes blazed with fury. Her black hair was cut close and followed the shape of her head down to her jawline and stopped just short of touching her shoulders. He remembered the style was called a bob, something he'd had to learn while taking witness statements.

She was beautiful. He'd noticed that when he'd talked to her in the morgue. Her sleeveless navy blue dress hugged every curve. Tiny silver hoops glinted at her ears, and a small silver cat pendant hung on the slope of just a hint of cleavage. Her mouth was generous, full-lipped, and her chin was strong and

fierce. He hadn't noticed earlier, but there was a small spatter
of freckles across the bridge of her nose. She wore short, black
leather boots with buckles, and she looked as if she wanted to
plant one of those boots where it would hurt.

As soon as that thought struck him, Heath turned sideways
just a little, enough to hopefully allow him to block anything
she might throw at him. He held up his hands in surrender. In
his rumpled suit, one of the charcoal pinstriped numbers he
wore on the job, he felt overdressed for the coming fight, but it
had been enough to get him through the morgue staff.

"Who do you think you are?" Lauren reached out and
grabbed him with both hands.

Pain ripped through Heath as he realized she'd grabbed shirt
and chest hair, and he was pretty sure that was what she'd intended to do. "Hey, take it easy."

"Don't you tell me to take it easy. You just lied to me back
there. Do you get off on doing that?"

Heath grabbed her wrists and tried to disengage her. "Look,
I'm sorry. You don't know what's going on here."

"No. And you're going to tell me." Lauren set herself and
shook him. It wasn't hard to do. On the stairs he was off-
balance, and there was the added problem of him not wanting to hurt her.

Heath scrambled to keep his balance, but one foot slid off the
step, and he had to shift quickly to stop himself from falling.
The woman was prepared for that. As soon as he moved, she
yanked again, pulling him into her and backing into the stairwell railing. He knew her next move was to set herself again,
twist and shove him down the steps. It was what he would
have done. If he'd allowed himself to get in so close to a perp.

So he did the only thing he could do under the circumstances: he let go of her wrists and wrapped his arms around
her, holding on tight. Her muscular body tensed against him,
and he was surprised at her strength. She was five feet eight
inches tall without the boots, and the low heels pushed her up
another couple inches. She smelled sweet, a hint of vanilla and

something else, some kind of berry. He was pretty sure of that, but his senses were swimming.

"Hey. Hey. Hold on."

"No." She pushed against him, but he held on tightly. She tried to knee him, but he turned the blow aside with his thigh.

He put on his cop voice. "Miss Cooper, you need to calm down."

"I *am* calm." She pushed against him, harder. Her short-cropped hair flicked in his face as she struggled. An inarticulate scream ripped from her throat. Then she lifted her boot and drove the heel down his shin and into the top of his foot.

Pain burned the length of Heath's shin, but he held on to her, afraid that she was going to fall down the staircase and get hurt.

Two heavyset orderlies in hospital scrubs raced down the hallway. The woman at the desk urged them on, speaking in French or Chinese for all Heath knew. He was pretty sure it wasn't Spanish. He knew Spanish and Spanglish from the streets.

One of the orderlies grabbed Heath by the shoulders. "Let go of the woman, mon. Let her go now or I'm gonna mess you up."

The other man grabbed Lauren Cooper and pulled her back.

Heath released the woman, then shifted his arm under the arm of the man holding him and forced the man's grip over his head. The guy scrambled and tried for a new hold, but Heath spun around behind him, caught the guy's hand, and twisted it into an armlock behind the man's back. He held the orderly between him and Lauren like a shield. Pain drove the man up onto his toes.

"Okay." Heath made himself breathe normally. "We're all just going to take a step back. Take a minute. Think this through a little. Before somebody gets hurt." The man he held on to tried to break free. Heath moved the arm up just enough to let his captive know he could break it if he had to.

The other orderly hesitated, standing there looking uneasy.

Lauren wrapped her arms around herself and glared at him. She blew a strand of hair out of her face. "What were you trying to do in there? Why were you asking me all those questions? How could you do that to me?"

"Miss Cooper, those are all very good questions, and I respectfully decline to answer them. In a few more minutes, members of the Jamaica Constabulary Force are going to be here, and I don't feel like talking to them. It would be better if we could just agree that our meeting—timing and all—was a mistake."

"A *mistake?* I'm the only one who didn't know what was going on in there."

"Yes, and for that I'm truly sorry. I wish I could have made that easier, but I couldn't." Heath tried to think of something to add, but Hallmark didn't make a card for what he'd done to her. And trying to explain why he'd done what he'd done was just too involved. She didn't need to think about what he knew.

Besides, she needed to pick up her sister and get back home. She'd be safe there.

At least, Heath hoped she'd be safe. Gibson was still out there prowling, and the man was a predator. Heath was the only one who was convinced of that. Given the man's resources, he could disappear and strike anywhere he wanted to, then disappear again.

Losing Janet was proof of that.

Heath leaned close to his captive's ear and spoke softly. "I'm going to let you go now, partner. You just make sure that woman doesn't come after me. And if you come after me, I'm going to hurt you. Understand?"

Reluctantly, the man nodded.

"Good." Heath released the orderly and backed away. Three steps later, when there was no pursuit, Heath turned and fled up the stairs. The woman didn't come after him, and he was a little surprised at that. She didn't seem like the type to give up.

Back at the fleabag hotel where he was staying, Heath took the hotel key card from his shirt pocket and swiped it through the reader. The lock made a *thunk* and the light cycled green.

He put his hand on the doorknob and drew the snub-nosed .357 Magnum from a holster at his back. He'd bought the revolver off an eleven-year-old boy shortly after he'd hit Kingston four days ago. Guns were easy to get. It was answers that were hard.

For a moment, he just held on to the door handle and listened. Nothing moved inside the room. That didn't mean anything. Neither did the electronic lock. The hotel wasn't a security showcase. That was one of the reasons he'd checked in after he'd found it.

Cautiously, he pushed the door inward and followed it inside the room. The hinges squeaked just a little, but he liked that. Besides the *thunk* of the lock, he also had the squeak as an early warning system.

A quick sweep of the room revealed that no one was waiting for him. The hair trapped between the second drawer down and the frame of the chest of drawers told him no one had searched the room.

He locked the door behind him, holstered the pistol, and got down to business. He took off his jacket and threw it on the unmade bed. If maid service was available in the hotel on a daily basis, the sign on the door would keep them out. Maybe. He didn't like leaving anything to chance.

His shin still ached from where Lauren Cooper had scraped him with her boot heel. He cursed softly at the discomfort, but he didn't hold the action against her. He'd deserved everything he'd gotten and probably more.

In the bathroom, he raised his pant leg and surveyed the long, bruised and bloody scrape down his leg. Lauren hadn't been messing around. She'd known exactly what she was doing. *Good for her.*

He returned to his unpacked suitcases and took out a small medical kit. Methodically, he cared for the scrape. On the island, with all the heat and the potential for disease in some of the areas he was traveling in, there was a good chance of infection.

He returned the medical kit to his suitcase and took out a

small wireless printer. After plugging the unit in to the wall, he took out his phone and brought up the images of Lauren Cooper he'd taken while she'd been grieving over her dead sister.

At the time he'd taken the pictures, he'd felt like a heel. Now, looking at the woman's grief-stricken face, he felt even worse. As a police detective, he'd seen more than his share of devastated people, physically and emotionally. He'd been told that in his job as a homicide investigator, he was always meeting people on the worst day of their lives.

Heath sent the pictures over to the printer and took them as soon as they'd come through the unit. The Lauren Cooper he saw in these shots didn't mesh with the wildcat who had met him full-on there on the stairs. He tried to think of how many women he knew who would have tried something like that. There weren't many.

Janet would have. She'd fought her killer. But in the end it hadn't done her any good. He'd killed her just the same. In fact, Gibson had probably enjoyed the struggle.

Realizing the black anger was about to consume him again, Heath pushed it away. He couldn't let that happen. The anger was raw and vicious, worse than any drug an addict could crave. When the anger was in bloom within him, there wasn't room for anything more.

He'd learned that as a kid at Fort Benning, Georgia. His father had been a drill instructor for the army, stationed at the post. Heath had had to take a lot of grief as a teenager, and he hadn't always chosen wisely. For him, the world was black-and-white. That view of things had led him into the military and into the police department later. He loved being a detective, balancing the scales a little every time he broke a case. He'd learned to put away the anger, but since Janet's death, it was back with a vengeance.

He went to the small closet and reached up for the ceiling. Gently, he pushed and popped out the section he'd cut the first night he'd stayed in the room. In the darkness that filled the closet, the cut he'd made couldn't be seen.

Reaching up, he took down the roll of canvas he'd bought from an art store on his way to the hotel. Walking over to the wall near the small desk, he unrolled the canvas and tacked it to the irregular surface. The canvas was three feet wide and eight feet long. The dimensions weren't those of the whiteboard he generally used in the detective bullpen, but the canvas gave him plenty of room to work.

Photographs from crime scenes and printouts from reports were secured to the canvas with double-stick tape. The seven women stared out at him from their pictures. All of those shots were from before Gibson had finished with them. All of them had a photo of a black card with an embossed white rabbit on them. They'd been sent to the various police departments within days of the discovery of the murders.

Below them were crime scene photographs. Some of them were bloody. Sometimes, and the profilers attached to the murders didn't know why, the killer liked to cut his victims. Other times, like with Megan Taylor, he just killed them.

Muriel Evans, the weather girl in Newark, New Jersey, had been shot through the head.

Tina Farrell, the masseuse in Los Angeles, had had her neck broken in a manner that suggested Special Forces training.

The Taylor woman had been the first to get strangled.

The White Rabbit Killer didn't seem like a disorganized killer. He was too methodical, too good at what he did. But an organized killer often used the same weapon. Like the knife.

Janet had been tied up and thrown into a hotel room shower, then had a naked electrical cord dropped in after her. Her death hadn't been easy. Heath still smelled her burned flesh in his nightmares.

So far, the White Rabbit Killer hadn't killed the same kind of victim or in the same city. Not even in the same state. The serial killer was a traveler, but he took some kind of pride or satisfaction in his kills because he always left a calling card behind: a black card embossed with a white rabbit.

At first, no one in the media or in the homicide squads that were investigating the murders knew what the white rabbit meant. Janet had been the first detective to match the white rabbit to the magician Gibson. She'd been the one who'd discovered Gibson had been in all of the cities of the victims during the time they were killed.

But there was no evidence linking Gibson to the murders. And now, even with Janet among the victims, there was still no evidence.

The killer's pace was picking up, though. Only two weeks had passed since he'd killed Janet. His timetable was picking up speed. Either he was growing more confident, or whatever he got from murdering women wasn't lasting as long as it had.

Heath took the pistol out and placed it on the desk. He reached into the small refrigerator near the desk and took out a beer. The air-conditioning in the room was weak and he was already sweating.

In the center of the canvas, Gibson stared out with those malevolent eyes and that mocking smile.

Heath sipped his beer and considered his next move. Gibson was on the island. He stayed locked away somewhere up in the hills. No one Heath had met knew for certain where, and the local police force wasn't being overly helpful in finding the man. They had no reason to interfere with the man's privacy. Or maybe they didn't know.

Gibson wasn't wanted in Jamaica, and he wasn't wanted by anyone in the United States, either. At least, not yet.

Heath's cell phone buzzed for attention. He took it from his pocket and glared at it. The unit was a throwaway he'd gotten in Atlanta before leaving the city and didn't have caller ID, but he knew who it was. Only one person had the number.

Cursing, Heath took the call. "Yeah."

"How's it going down there?" Jackson Portman sounded totally relaxed, but then he always did. An ex-football player and African-American, Jackson's build and don't-cross-me demeanor made him look more like a movie heavy than a homicide detective.

"It's too hot."

"Can't be no hotter than 'Lanta."

"Did you call for a reason? Or are we just gonna talk about the weather?"

"You busting any heads yet?"

"No. Why?"

"Got a call about you."

"From the locals?"

"Nope. I already talked to them. Inspector Myton don't look like he's gonna be a fan of your work anytime soon. Said you had no business bein' up in their business."

"I've heard Myton talk. He doesn't sound like that."

"That's 'cause I'm paraphrasing."

Heath took another sip of his beer. "If it wasn't Myton that called, who was it?"

"A woman. When I first heard her voice a little while ago, I was hopin' maybe you met somebody."

"Overnight?"

"I ever tell you how I met my first missus?"

"Too many times." Heath sat up straighter and looked at Lauren Cooper's picture. "Let me guess who the woman was."

"Sure."

"Lauren Cooper."

"Shocks me how you know that, bro. I mean, you should be a detective."

"I'm working on it. Myton must have told her about me." Heath took another sip of beer. Or the coroner told her. He hadn't cared for Heath, either.

"I don't think so."

"Why?"

"She knows too much about you. Stuff Myton wouldn't know."

Heath stared at the pretty woman in the picture. He'd missed something about her. "Like what?"

"Where you lived. About your sister and her kids. About your gym membership. About me. A lot more than I know about you, actually. That's why I thought maybe you'd hooked up with someone down there and just didn't tell me. Then I realized it was you I was talking about, and I thought maybe I'd call you, check that out. Now you sound like you ain't any too happy to hear from her."

For a second, Heath felt a faint tickle of fear. His sister and his two nephews lived not far from him in Atlanta. He'd been helping out with them when he could since her husband had left her. "I'm not."

Jackson waited a beat. "You want to tell me how Lauren Cooper knows so much about you? Especially if you ain't all chummy and everything?"

There was a knock at the door.

"I'll call you back." Heath picked up the .357 and got up. He walked to the door and avoided the peephole. Quietly, he slid the cell phone into his shirt pocket, then dropped a hand onto the door handle and popped it open just enough to see out into the hallway.

Lauren Cooper stood there with her arms folded. "We need to talk, Detective Sawyer. Now."

Chapter 3

"Are you alone?"

That wasn't the response Lauren expected from the man. She'd expected him to be contrite or defensive, or at least surprised, maybe even outraged that she'd found him, but he didn't seem to be anything more than irritated.

"What?"

"Alone? Are you alone? It's not a hard question to answer." Heath stepped through the door and glanced out at the courtyard in front of the motel room. He held a gleaming black revolver in his right hand, tucking it close behind his thigh so it couldn't easily be seen.

"Yes. I'm alone." Even as she said that, Lauren wondered if coming here alone was intelligent. Now she was wishing she'd gone to the local police. But she also realized that course of action probably wouldn't have gotten anything done. Heath Sawyer might have been there on police business, and even if he wasn't, he hadn't broken any major laws.

Heath grabbed her by the elbow and tugged her through the doorway. Lauren set her heels and started pulling back.

He glared at her. "You came to see me, lady. I didn't come knocking on your door. So either leave or come in. This door isn't staying open."

For a moment, Lauren seriously considered turning around and leaving. That seemed to be the path of least resistance. Except that she'd just seen her murdered sister and she wanted some answers that she felt certain the man in front of her had. Inspector Myton hadn't had many. Then she spotted the canvas spread out on the wall behind Heath.

On autopilot, Lauren stepped into the room, barely aware of Heath shutting and locking the door behind. She kept walking, taking in the photographs and police reports secured to the canvas thumbtacked onto the wall. Her gaze slid over the images of women who were obviously dead, all of them taken at crime scenes.

Then her eyes found the photos of Megan. A feeling of vulnerability descended over her. Sharp pain shot through her stomach. She closed her eyes and took a breath.

Heath crossed over to the canvas and took it down. Despite the speed at which he moved, he was careful with the photos and reports. "I'm sorry, Miss Cooper. You shouldn't have had to see that."

She turned to him. "You're a cop."

His eyes narrowed slightly. "Not a cop. I'm a homicide detective. Something like what happened to your sister? I'm a professional. I'm the guy you call when something like this happens."

Focus, Lauren. She made herself breathe out and put distance between herself and the pain. "Who called you about my sister?"

He hesitated. "Nobody."

"You were here four days before my sister was murdered." Lauren had gleaned that from the receipts in his wallet, which she had pilfered during the physical altercation they'd had at the hospital.

Heath nodded warily, no doubt wondering how she'd known that. "I was."

"Why?"

"I took some personal leave that I had coming. Thought I'd see the sights."

"Did you know she was going to be killed?"

The question rocked him on his heels. Despite his efforts to remain calm, Lauren saw that she'd caught him by surprise.

"No. How could you think something like that?"

"It's a lot easier than you think. Especially since the masquerade in the morgue."

"I went there to get information."

"About what?"

"About whoever killed your sister."

"I thought you had that figured out."

"I believe I do."

Lauren pointed at the rolled-up canvas. "Then tell me what's going on. Explain to me what my sister's picture is doing on that. Tell me who killed her."

He scowled and walked over to a small table surrounded by three chairs. He raised the beer bottle he'd liberated from the small refrigerator in the corner of the room. "Can I get you a drink?"

"No."

Heath sat in one chair and put his feet up in another. He sipped from the beer bottle. "I really would like for you to leave. What's it going to take to make that happen?"

Folding her arms over her chest, Lauren ignored him, keeping her focus on the rolled canvas. She felt confident he wasn't going to try to physically remove her from the room. He'd have already done that if he'd wanted to. And she was certain he didn't want to have anything to do with the local police after the confrontation in the morgue. The actual coroner had been very vocal about Heath's presence there. "Do you think Gibson killed Megan?"

After a brief hesitation, Heath looked at her. "Do you want

me to lie to you? Because what I think doesn't matter." The note
of sarcasm in his voice surprised her. At first she thought it was
directed at her, then realized it was more personal than that.

"I want you to be honest with me. If you can."

"I can. And I think Gibson killed your sister. Getting someone else to believe that can be difficult. I know. I've tried." He
frowned. "A lot of people, evidently, aren't prepared for that
kind of honesty."

Even though she'd asked for the answer, the words hurt. Lauren wasn't as ready to hear them as she'd thought she would
be. Still, she kept her composure. Being weak in foster homes
wasn't something that let a kid survive. She'd learned to keep
her emotions inside and present that hard shell to the world.

"I'm sorry." Heath blew out a breath.

"It's fine."

"No, no it's not. A person shouldn't have someone taken
away from them like that."

Lauren heard the note of wistful hurt in his words, and she
knew that she wasn't alone in her pain and misery. As a foster
child, she'd learned to read tones and expressions and body
language at an early age. That was part of the self-preservation
tool set. "Who did you lose?"

The wince and the slight hunching of his shoulders, like
a boxer who had just taken a blow, let her know her instincts
had been dead-on. This wasn't just a case to the detective. "A
friend."

Lauren nodded toward the canvas. "Is she on there, too?"

He ran a big hand across his stubbled jaw and took a breath.
He didn't bother looking at the canvas. "No."

"Why not?"

"Because that's a visual victimology. My friend doesn't belong with those others. When Gibson killed her, it was different."

"What was different?"

"The motive for the murder. Gibson made Janet's death personal because she'd made her pursuit of him personal."

"How did he make it personal?"

Heath leaned back against the wall. Green flakes stirred restlessly in those gold eyes, but he looked tired. She hadn't noticed that earlier in the coroner's office. Looking at him now, seeing him better, he looked slightly pale beneath the new redness from the sun.

"We worked a homicide in Atlanta. A real-estate agent. Thirty-two-year-old mother of three."

"'We?'"

Heath drained the rest of the bottle and set it on the window ledge. "Yeah. Janet and me."

"She was a police officer."

"Detective. Like me. She was working as lead on the Celeste Morrow murder, working the case with her partner. She used me as a sounding board. We did that for each other when we caught cases where we got stuck and needed an outside opinion. Janet let me have a look at the case." He stared at the wall, but Lauren knew he wasn't seeing it. "We both knew the serial killer was a sociopath. All the traits were there. Random killings. Nothing tying the victims together. But the killings were usually savage."

Memory of the crime scene photos on the canvas played inside Lauren's mind. There had been so much blood. "My sister was drowned. She didn't die like those others."

"No. She didn't. But I learned that Gibson's name came up in the investigation."

"He was identified by the picture she took with him."

Heath nodded. "I've been monitoring Gibson, trying to stay up with him, but he vanishes whenever he wants to."

"Inspector Myton doesn't think Gibson had anything to do with Megan's murder."

"How do you know that?"

"I asked him. He didn't come out and say it, but he let me know he thinks you're obsessed and perhaps not in your right mind."

Heath smiled disparagingly. "Inspector Myton isn't inter-

ested in ruffling any feathers, Miss Cooper. People die down
here all the time. Sometimes they're Americans. Myton ac-
cepts that. Part of the cost of doing business. Eventually all
of that goes away. If Myton can catch someone red-handed,
if that someone isn't so connected that they're practically un-
touchable, he'll put that someone behind bars. I'm convinced
that's the truth." Heath looked at her. "The problem down here
is that money plays. That's the name of the game. If someone
has enough money, they can get away with murder. And a guy
like Gibson has plenty of money." He paused. "He's clever, too.
Otherwise he'd never have gotten to Janet."

Lauren wondered if the two of them had been involved. It
wasn't unheard of, especially with the kinds of hours police
personnel worked. She wasn't going to ask, but something must
have shown on her face.

"We were just friends." Heath looked a little embarrassed,
then hurt followed. "Actually, we were more than that. Janet
was my FTO. Field training officer. She worked with me when
I made detective. She got me started on my investigations, and
she was there during some rough patches."

"I'm sorry for your loss."

"Yeah. Me, too."

Outside the window behind Heath, street noises filtered in.
People walked by. Cars passed on the streets, rubber squeaking on hot pavement. Someone upstairs was playing the television or a music system too loud.

"How old was she?"

Heath scowled. "What?"

"How old was your friend? If she trained you, she must have
been older, right?"

"Eight years."

"Making her forty or so."

"About that." Heath's eyes narrowed, and he looked at her
with increased interest. "Janet doesn't fit on that victimology
board because she called Gibson's lawyers and left a message
saying she knew what he was doing, that she was going to stop

him." Pain turned his voice hoarse for a moment. "I didn't know till afterwards. The lawyers' number turned up on her cell phone records." He drew in a breath. "Gibson killed Janet to prove that he could do it under our noses and get away with it." His voice turned hard. "But that's not going to happen. He's going to pay."

Desperately, Lauren sought to turn the conversation away from Heath's dead friend. She was afraid that he would shut down, and right now she wanted—*needed*—information about Megan's death. "The other women on that—" she pointed at the rolled canvas "—are in their twenties."

"Yeah." Heath sat up a little straighter and looked as if he was regrouping. "They are. Like your sister. Gibson has a thing for younger women. He's older—"

"Forty-three. I know."

He focused on her with new intensity. "How do you know so much about him?"

"I know magic."

"Sure you do."

Still annoyed at Heath and wanting to wipe that smug look off his face, Lauren put her left hand to her temple and closed her eyes as she tilted her head back. "Think of your address."

"You're joking."

"No. I'm going to read your mind."

"You're a mind reader? I didn't know mind reading counted as magic."

Using her right hand, Lauren palmed Heath's driver's license from the wallet she'd taken from him earlier. She opened her eyes, took her hand away, and looked at him. Then she gave the address she'd noticed on the driver's license earlier.

He studied her with indolent eyes, not saying anything.

"Well, is that your address?"

For a moment, he didn't say anything. The defenses went up. She saw that in the way he held his shoulders, the way he tilted his head to look at her. "How do you know so much about me?"

"Like I said, magic." Lauren raised her right hand, palm

forward so he couldn't see the driver's license trapped by its edge between her first two fingers.

"I'm not a big believer in magic."

With a flourish, Lauren shook her hand and his driver's license appeared at the end of her fingers. For a moment, Heath didn't know what to say. Before he could recover, she flicked her wrist and sent the plastic rectangle spinning at him.

Surprisingly, like a cat snapping a moth out of the air, Heath caught the license in his left hand. After he perused the plastic rectangle, his eyes turned to slits. His free hand slid down to his pants pocket, then he looked shocked. "You picked my pocket and stole my wallet at the morgue."

"I *borrowed* your wallet." Lauren reached into her pocket and removed the article. She tossed it to him. Before she'd arrived at his hotel room, she'd photocopied all of the documents at her hotel and left the copies tucked away in her room. Heath knew a lot about her. It only seemed fair that she have the same opportunity.

With the same easy skill he'd shown in catching the license, Heath caught the wallet. He glanced through it quickly. Satisfied that everything was there, he shoved the wallet into his pocket. His eyes narrowed. "Picking pockets isn't a skill most people have."

"It's just a riff on sleight of hand stuff. I work at a magic store."

"Where?"

"In Chicago."

"You sell magic tricks?"

"Yes. I guess you don't know as much as you think you do, Detective Sawyer." Lauren hated that Heath's lack of knowledge about the field made the shop sound pedestrian. "But they're not the kind of tricks you'll find for some kid's birthday party. Professional magicians come there to buy equipment, to talk with each other, and to design new illusions."

Heath leaned his head back against the wall, relaxing a little, or maybe only providing a deception. "Has Gibson ever been there?"

"No."

"Why? Is he that good?"

"I don't know. The guy just appeared on the scene one day and streaked to the top of the heap. A lot of people want to know where Gibson learned his craft. If anyone knows, if anyone is helping craft his illusions, they're not talking."

A frown twisted Heath's features. "People have been trying to figure that out?"

"Sure. The guy's a celebrity in a field where secrets are prized. Every magician wants to know what's in every other magician's bag of tricks. Especially if that magician is as successful as Gibson. The fascination for magic only gets deeper if you're actively involved in the field."

"I'll take your word on that." Heath leaned forward in his chair, dropping his feet to the floor and resting his elbows on his knees. "You've never met Gibson?"

"No."

"Your sister hadn't, either? Until the other night?"

Lauren thought for a moment. "Not that I'm aware of."

Heath nodded. "Somewhere, somehow, they crossed paths. I'd like to know if it was just here, or if it was somewhere else."

"If nothing connects the victims you say Gibson has killed, what makes you so certain he is the killer?" Lauren couldn't believe she was asking that question so calmly, but at the moment she felt dead inside. All of the hurt and pain was pushed back, waiting in the distance like gathering storm clouds. The anger was still there, though. She wanted to know who was responsible for what had happened to Megan.

"Janet and I talked about this case for weeks. I can't even remember which of us came up with Gibson, or how we tripped to the fact that Gibson was playing in each of the cities where those victims were killed. We'd starting checking newspapers in those cities during the time periods of those murders. We found Gibson."

"If you were looking in the newspapers, you probably found a lot of overlapping things."

"We did. But Janet liked Gibson for it."

"Why?"

Heath's lips tightened for a moment. "She was good at what she did. She could make creative leaps that other detectives never got to. Sometimes you get a serial killer who kills over a wide range of areas. Usually he turns out to be a sales rep, or maybe a long-haul trucker. We even considered that, but nothing fell into place. Then we found Gibson. And everything fit. Especially the White Rabbit card."

"Like a magician pulling a rabbit out of a hat."

"Yeah. The guy enjoys playing his sadistic little games. It's his signature. He claims his victims."

"Then why didn't you go after him?"

"We couldn't. We tried making our case to other law enforcement departments, but nobody wanted to go after Gibson. Everything was circumstantial and he wasn't even in-state anymore. Chasing after him would have been expensive, and police departments have budgets that television cop shows don't have to worry about. We couldn't prove that Gibson had any kind of contact with any of the victims. No sightings, no meetings. No forensic evidence. Nothing." Heath looked at her. "Not until that picture of him with your sister. That's the first concrete clue we've had. And it's down here in this place where I have no jurisdiction."

"What are you going to do?"

Heath shook his head as if to clear it and stood. "No more questions, Miss Cooper. I shouldn't have told you as much as I have, but I felt I owed that to you." He folded his arms over that broad chest, and she could still see the lost hurt shining in his eyes.

"You came down here before Megan died." Lauren kept her voice level. "You had a plan then."

"I still do." Heath walked to the door and opened it. "Time for you to go."

Lauren wanted to stay and argue, but she also wanted to stay and comfort him, and be comforted. Detective Heath Sawyer was the only person she knew in Jamaica. She didn't want to be alone, didn't want to have to go back to the hotel room and talk to her mother, but she knew she had to do that. She was already late in doing it.

And she had to make arrangements for taking Megan home.

She nodded and walked to the door, pausing only a moment to look at Heath. "Thank you for being honest with me. It…helps."

He winced at that but didn't say anything about his earlier duplicity. "Have a safe trip home, Miss Cooper."

She turned and walked toward the elevator.

Downstairs and out of the building, Lauren slid behind the steering wheel and set her purse in the passenger seat. She felt the vibration of her phone inside while she was reaching for the keys to the car. She checked the caller ID.

Mom.

She hesitated only a moment, then put the phone back in her purse. She knew her mom would be worried, but Lauren didn't want to try to talk to her until she was in her hotel room. There, at least, she would have some privacy.

After sliding the phone back into her purse, she glanced back at the hotel room where Heath Sawyer was staying. The curtain was pulled slightly to one side, and his profile shadowed the light.

Resolutely, Lauren put the car into gear and pulled away, but she couldn't stop thinking about Gibson. Imagining him as a serial killer seemed like some kind of fantasy.

So was the idea of never seeing Megan again, but that one was dark and terrifying.

Chapter 4

At the window, Heath watched Lauren Cooper drive away and vanish into the dark streets, only realizing then how late it had gotten. Only a few blocks over, a neon fog pooled above an area near a beach where the tourists gathered. Over there the music would be too loud, college kids and twentysomethings just out in the world would be dancing and celebrating summer, beer and liquor would flow, and no one would know that the White Rabbit Killer had taken another victim.

Maybe knowing wouldn't even slow them down. They were there to party.

Pensive and irritated, Heath thought about grabbing his jacket and heading out into the cool night, just blowing through an evening by trying to sink into the magic of the island. That would have been wasted effort, though, and he knew it. If things went well, he'd only end up more restless than ever. If things went badly, he could end up in a fight. He knew himself, and he knew the dark mood he was in.

It had been years since he'd exhibited that kind of behavior, but he knew he was next door to it now. He could feel the techno trance of the club music in his veins. That was where he would gravitate to. Trance, industrial heavy metal, something that would bang through him, something that would amp him up even more.

Country music would be worse. Those songs were loaded with pain, and he'd do his best to drown it. He'd done it before. The only reason he'd become a cop was because he hadn't known what else to do after four years with the Marines right out of high school. He hadn't wanted the military life his father still enjoyed, but he'd wanted something physical, something where he'd make a difference. He'd taken the police exams, thinking that if the cops didn't want him, he'd re-up with the military.

Atlanta P.D. had taken him, though, and he'd found work that he could do that wasn't the same thing day in and day out. He didn't see himself as a hero. He was a guy who helped paint that thin blue line between the civilians and the savages. He'd liked busting heads, maybe a little too much.

Detective Janet Hutchins had taken an interest in him. She'd seen that he had an eye for investigation, didn't just take the first answer he was given, and that he checked the facts. She'd gotten Heath groomed for his detective's shield, then partnered with him for three years till he made Detective 2nd and got a junior partner of his own.

That was two years ago. The junior partner had been Jackson Portman.

Heath turned away from the window and pulled out his cell phone. He pulled Jackson up on speed dial, then punched the call through. It rang only once before the connection was made.

"There you are." Jackson sounded relieved.

"Here I am."

"Thought you were gonna leave me hanging just when things were getting interesting."

"No."

"You still got company?"

"No. I need you to do something for me."

"Sure. First, tell me about Lauren Cooper. That's how this favor thing works. You do something for me, I do something for you. How did that woman know so much about you?"

"She read my mind."

Jackson snorted derisively. "Bro, the stuff she knew, even you don't know without checking. What's your gym membership number?"

Heath didn't say anything because he didn't know it. Case numbers he knew, phone numbers of snitches he knew, but not so much numbers involving his personal life.

"Well? Time's ticking." Jackson whistled, an off-key version of *Final Jeopardy!*

Heath grimaced, knowing that once Jackson was armed with the facts of what had happened, his partner would never let it go. "Back at the hospital when I was checking out the murder down here, I bumped into Lauren Cooper. She's the dead woman's sister. While we were in a heated discussion, she lifted my wallet."

"Lifted your wallet." Jackson sounded hollow, as if he couldn't believe what he was hearing.

"Yeah, it means she picked my pocket."

"I know what it means. Just surprised you'd slip up like that. It ain't like you, bro." Some of the colloquial accent was gone from Jackson's words. He was deadly earnest now. "You really don't have your game, Heath. You should come back home. Let's sit down and sort this out. We still own one of the White Rabbit murders."

"Two. We own two." Neither of them mentioned Janet's name.

"Come home. We have enough to buy into the investigation and leverage some muscle from the captain. Let's dig into it together. If I have to, I'll get some leave and we'll work the investigation together."

"The investigation is down here. This is where Gibson goes

to hole up. He's got a place down here. I found it. I just can't get close to it."

"All right. That's something we didn't know. How did you find his place?"

"Gibson made a mistake. The dead woman took pictures of his house and uploaded it to her Cloud. I got a chance to look at the data dump from her iPad, accessed the pictures, and found the house."

"So he took the woman to his house?"

"Yeah."

"Can't the locals get a search warrant?"

"Gibson says he put the woman in a cab, waved goodbye, and he never saw her again."

"Uh-huh. And they decided not to press him on that?"

"They don't have any proof that that wasn't what happened."

"They find the cab driver?"

"No."

"They look?"

"Myton says they did, but this is a tourist area. A lot of people take cabs every night."

"You think the locals are protecting him?"

"They're being careful. Gibson is rich. They don't want to ruffle any feathers until they have a lock."

"You did mention this guy is a probable serial killer? Probably gonna kill again?"

"Yeah. The cops here I've been talking too aren't big fans of the American justice system, and they're even less happy about Georgia detectives wandering in off their beats to poke around in their business."

"That would be a problem. So tell me about Lauren Cooper. Did she look hot to you? 'Cause from what I'm looking at here, she looks seriously hot."

"Can I quote you on that to your future second missus?"

"Lord, no. That woman's jealous enough."

"What are you looking at?"

"Her file. Since she called in, knew so much about you, I

thought it was only fair we know stuff about her. Only expected to get a hit on her from the Chicago DMV. That's where she told me she's from. Turns out she's had a little bit of a record."

That surprised Heath, but then he thought about how easily she had picked his pocket. Even on his worst day, he wasn't the easiest guy to pull something like that on. "What record?"

"Breaking and entering and assault. From what I see, she broke into a guy's apartment and punched him out in Chicago three years ago."

"For what?"

"Says here she claims the guy stole an illusion she was working on. She's some kind of magic designer or something. The guy claimed that they came up with this thing together, that there wasn't a clear title to anything. The judge dropped the hammer on her because it was a home invasion. She ended up doing some community service—magic shows at old folks' homes and orphanages—and had her record expunged. Are they serious about the magic thing?"

"She does magic."

"She must be good at it if she can lift your wallet. 'Course, her looking like she does, I could see how you got distracted."

Heath ignored that. "Actually, the magic angle is what I want you to look into. Gibson picked up the woman down here. She'd taken her sister to a magic show Gibson put on in Chicago. Check and see if any of the other victims had a connection to magic in any way. Maybe Gibson is culling from a more select group than we thought."

"Looking for relatives of people who jones on magic?"

"Yeah."

"I'll have a look." Jackson hesitated for a moment. "Something you told me when you first started training me to work homicide—stay detached. Look at everything from the outside. The minute you crawl inside of an investigation, you lose all perspective. I'm gonna tell you now, because you're my friend and I love you like a brother and you're likely gonna be my best man when I wed my second Missus Portman, that you're all kinds of up inside of this investigation. The captain came out asking what did I know about you impersonating a coroner. I told him I didn't know nothing."

"I can't be detached from this one. Gibson killed Janet. Look into those cases and let me know what you come up with regarding the magic angle." Heath broke the connection and tossed the phone onto the rumpled bed. He got a fresh beer from the refrigerator and stood at the window looking out again, trying to figure out what his next move was going to be.

Instead, to his surprise, he couldn't keep his thoughts away from Lauren Cooper and how she'd felt struggling against him. He closed his eyes and could smell that berry vanilla scent again. Then he forced his eyes open and sipped his beer.

There was a thread here. Nobody killed that clean. He was going to find it, and he was going to use it to strangle Gibson.

"There." From the backseat of the Jaguar X351, Gibson pointed at the low-rent hotel off the beaten path of the city. "Pull into the parking lot."

In front of him, behind the steering wheel, Roylston re-settled his bulk, looking like a steroid-infused earthquake in motion. Dressed in a black business suit, his skin dark and his head shaved, he could have passed for a native to the island. Only the Boston accent marked him as an outsider. During the three years he'd been with Gibson, Roylston hadn't ever spoken much, and never mentioned anything personal. As far as Gibson knew, the bodyguard/chauffeur didn't have a life outside of protecting him.

But all three of the live-in security specialists who tried to manage Gibson were like that. None of them wanted to get to know him, and they didn't want him to know anything about them. They got paid to watch over him, protect him and try to rein in his "impulses."

Escaping the watchdogs that had been with him throughout his life had been the initial part of the Game he played now. He'd avoided his protectors when he was a boy, escaped them at times for glorious bits of freedom, but in the end he'd always let them catch him in order to satisfy his father. Even at forty-three, Gibson didn't want to completely escape his father's attempts to control him. That was the very best part of the Game.

That particular thrill was even better than the killing, which he relished.

The bodyguards tended to be compliant with him. They didn't want his father to know when they lost him, so they covered up most of his escapes—except for the ones that were too egregious.

His father covered for him as well, trapped by his desire to keep his corporation protected and to have an offspring to carry on his name. Gibson had robbed the man of that as well by choosing his stage name. Still, his father held out foolish hope of someday controlling him. The man was trapped, simply couldn't let go of the selfish dream.

That was the very best part.

Roylston glanced up at the hotel. "This is where that Atlanta detective is staying."

The fact that the man knew so much of his business irritated Gibson. He rested his elbows at his sides, curled his elbows and steepled his fingers under his chin. "I know that."

With obvious reluctance, Roylston guided the sedan into the parking lot. The headlights flashed against the parked cars in the lot. "This is dangerous."

"Of course it's dangerous. I wouldn't visit if it weren't dangerous. The circus doesn't really come alive until the aerialists perform without a net, until the lion tamer sticks his head inside a lion's mouth. Death hovers there, just a *snap* away. And the potential of that is what keeps the crowd on the edges of their seats." Gibson smiled and leaned over to the window so that he could look up.

Atlanta Detective Heath Sawyer still stood at the window. His shadow was a blurry image behind the curtain.

"You know I'm close, don't you, Detective?" Gibson smiled

at that thought, savoring it because he knew that closeness was making the man's wounds hurt even more. When Gibson had killed the female detective in Atlanta—*Janet,* her name rolled so invitingly across his tongue—he had known her death would push the man to go the distance. Gibson had considered killing both of them, but in the end he'd decided not to. Having a *mortal enemy* was a delightful concoction that he'd never thought of.

Heath Sawyer didn't worry Gibson. He had lawyers and riches that would keep the police far from his door. And if the man got too bothersome, it was never too late to take care of that loose end.

After a couple of minutes, the shadow at the window went away.

Gibson waited for a short time longer, enough to make Roylston uncomfortable. Then he leaned back in his seat again and addressed the driver. "Let's go."

Roylston had the sedan rolling within the next heartbeat. "Any particular destination?"

"Downtown, I think. I want to see how the revelers are doing." Gibson took a California ten dollar gold piece from his pocket and rolled it across his knuckles. The coin leaped and flew like it was a living thing. He closed his hand on the coin, folding the fingers in with his other hand, then opened his hand again to reveal that the coin had vanished.

He smiled at the smoothness with which he worked. He was good and he knew it. The Atlanta detective could disappear just as easily when the time came.

Until then, there was the Game to play.

Back in Lauren's hotel room, the phone call to her mother didn't last too long. Chemo wore her out and left her in a fog. Plus, it was so late that Lauren had woken her up when she'd called. Her mother had insisted that she call when she returned to her room. Their conversation had been sad and groggy and disjointed, and had finally trickled off when her mother no longer had the strength to maintain it.

The doctors said she was improving, that this round of drugs was battling the cancer back into submission. She wasn't supposed to undergo any stress during this time. That wasn't going to happen.

After leaving Heath Sawyer's room, Lauren had had to return to the morgue to finish paperwork she'd left undone earlier when getting to know more about Heath Sawyer. She'd worked in a numb state, just plodding through the information, borrowing a computer to get information she didn't know, and contacting the insurance company as well as the State Department.

All of that had been exhausting.

Now, she couldn't sleep, and it was two o'clock in the morning. She kept seeing Megan laid out on that table, so impersonal, so still, so cold to the touch. But the memory was confusing because Heath Sawyer was also there. No matter how hard she tried, she couldn't get the man out of her mind. She could still feel the strength of him when she'd fought him, still see the indomitable will in his green-flaked gold eyes and the set of his stubbled chin.

But she remembered the pain in them, too, when he'd told her about his old partner. Lauren remembered that image of him the most, that vulnerability that she'd seen that she was sure he would deny.

There was something more behind that pain, though. Heath Sawyer had been hurt somewhere else along the way, too. She could sense it in him even though she couldn't yet put her finger on it. It was the same way she could take apart an illusion. Something was there just behind the curtain. If she spent enough time around him, she would have it.

That was why many of the illusionists who frequented Mirage Magic in Chicago where she worked insisted on giving private shows for her as they perfected pieces of their performances. If they could fool her, they could fool anyone.

Lauren didn't think that was true, but it was nice to hear.

Warren Morganstern, the semiretired magician who had started the business over forty years ago as a supplement to his performances, told her that she had an eye for magic. More than that, though, she had a love for magic. She wanted to believe that magic could happen, and that made all the difference.

Seven years ago, when Lauren had been in college, she'd answered an ad in a newspaper for a part-time position at the magic store. When Megan had found out about it, she'd teased her unmercifully, till Lauren had finally gone and applied, knowing she was going get turned down, just to shut her sister up.

Then magic had happened. Lauren had gotten the job at Morganstern's shop. She'd never asked how many other people had applied or what had made her application stand out among the others. Seven years later, she had taken over the store, allowing Morganstern to completely retire from performing, though he kept active in the business to socialize with the other magicians.

Since Lauren had started working there, she'd also started booking some of the acts, and she'd gotten successful at that. After a couple of years, she had doubled the store's business, and Morganstern was giving serious thought to moving to a larger building.

Lauren hadn't thought of the job as permanent, but she couldn't think of anything else she'd rather do. She loved magic. She loved the possibility of what-if.

For a while, she tried to relax and go to sleep. Her flight tomorrow didn't leave till the afternoon. Her mind wouldn't stop spinning with everything that had happened.

Finally, she gave up trying to sleep, sat up in bed and got her laptop computer out of the bag. She logged on to one of the community boards that she used for the magic store and started asking questions about Gibson.

Someone out there had to know who the man was. Lauren

still didn't believe the man had killed Megan, but someone had. Heath Sawyer seemed to be the only person really digging into the investigation. Lauren thought that if she could prove the killer wasn't Gibson, maybe Heath's attention would refocus on the case from a different perspective.

Lauren was not going to let the killer go free if she could help it.

Wearing skintight surgical gloves, Gibson took out one of the specially embossed cards he'd had made when he first decided to kill. Ordering the cards anonymously from Thailand was simple. He'd used a drop box at a box store, an online pay service that accepted cash up front, and ordered from a large printer that did a lot of volume in special jobs. He knew the police investigators had tried tracking the origin of the cards he'd sent to claim his kills, but they hadn't been able to do that.

Still seated in the rear of the luxury car, with Roylston looking on, though he was pretending not to, Gibson played with the card. Even with the gloves on, his skills were amazing. The card appeared and disappeared with lightning quickness.

Tiring of the game, he slid the card into an envelope he'd gotten straight from a box, affixed the address label he'd cut from an image he'd downloaded from the police department's website. He added a picture of the young woman who'd been recently killed, a picture of her in the water not far from where her body had been discovered by two young Germans looking for a romantic section of the beach. He pulled the paper from the sticky strip, made sure there were no fibers clinging to it, and sealed the envelope.

When he was finished, he waved to Roylston, who pulled over to the public mailbox in front of the seedy hotel where Heath Sawyer was staying. Gibson thumbed down the window and leaned out for just a moment, knowing there were no security cameras on the premises to catch him in the act.

He popped the letter through the slot, then sank back in his seat as Roylston guided the car through the parking lot like a big shark. Gibson hummed to himself and took out the gold coin again, rolling it deftly across his knuckles, almost mesmerizing himself as the gleaming metal caught the reflection of the neon lights.

Chapter 5

You shouldn't be here. Heath told himself that again and again as he stood on the fringe of the crowd at the graveyard service. *You should be back in Jamaica trying to find Gibson.*

In the end, though, he'd had to come to Chicago to attend the Megan Taylor funeral. Part of the reason he'd felt the need to be there had to do with the investigation. The other part was the guilt that he still felt for deceiving Lauren Cooper. He didn't know how he was going to make up for that, so he concentrated on the investigative area.

Once the police departments in the various cities had realized they were working a serial killer after the White Rabbit cards had started coming in, they'd gone out to the victims' families and friends and gotten as many pictures and as much video as they could. They'd combed through those images and video footage, the same way he and Janet had done.

No one had ever seen Gibson.

That didn't mean he hadn't been there, though, and it was that hope that had brought Heath to Chicago.

At least, that was what he told himself, but he knew he

wanted to see Lauren Cooper again, as well. The woman had
left quite an impression on him.

She sat there beside the coffin with an older woman that
Heath assumed was her mother. The woman appeared frail
and exhausted, leaning on Lauren for physical and emotional
support. Big sunglasses crowded the woman's face under the
broad-brimmed hat. Heath had noticed the lack of eyebrows
and the wig at first sight and had known she was taking chemo.

Beside her, dressed in black, her head bare and bowed,
Lauren held the older woman's hands in one of hers and
wrapped her thin shoulders with her free arm.

It was a good day for a funeral, which was an odd thing to
think, Heath admitted to himself, but he did. He'd attended
many funerals when it had been raining or so muggy you could
drown in your own clothes. The sun was shining, the trees were
green and vibrant overhead, blocking the early afternoon sun
and dropping a green tinted haze over the cemetery. A gentle
wind blew to stir things up, but even then the grounds were
quiet enough that the preacher's voice rang out.

A lot of people had turned up for the funeral. That was one
of the things that Heath had noticed during his attendance at
the funerals of murder victims, and of his own family. There
were always more people at a young person's funeral than at an
older person's burial. Common sense said that an older person
would have made more friends and more solid relationships. In
actual practice, more people attended the funerals of the young.

Death was a new experience for young people, and it was
scary at the same time. They didn't know how to act, and when
an older person passed, they were always a generation or two
away. Death didn't seem so close. So they came to funerals because it was a social event and because it was something new.

Now you're being cynical. Heath took in a breath and let
it out. He was tired. He still wasn't sleeping well because the
frustration clamored inside him. But over the past three nights,
the last one in Jamaica and the two since, he'd had nightmares,

too. He still had the ones involving Janet, but Lauren Cooper was in there now as well, and he didn't know why.

The worst one had been when he'd stood by helplessly while Gibson put Lauren into one of those boxes magicians always used, locked her down tight, then broke out the chain saw. In practice, magicians routinely passed swords, guillotines and chain saws through those boxes. No one ever got hurt, though. But in the dream, Lauren had screamed in pain, and blood had cascaded to the floor. Heath hadn't been able to save her.

A creeping chill climbed Heath's spine. He was dressed in a black suit, fitting in with the other attendees, but he suddenly found himself wishing he'd brought a jacket.

And a gun.

His own sidearm was back in Atlanta, and the revolver he'd bought in Jamaica was still there in that hotel room behind the air vent cover. Getting a pistol while in Chicago was too problematic.

He'd slept in his rental car down the street from Madeline Taylor's home. That was where Lauren had been spending her nights. She had her own apartment, but she'd stayed with her mother. Heath had gotten a police scanner from a pawn shop and tuned it in, then grabbed as much sleep as he could during the night while watching over the two women. In the mornings, he'd tailed Lauren as she'd gone about making arrangements for her sister's funeral.

He'd gone back to stakeout mentality, sitting on a person of interest and hoping for the best. There was no reason to think Gibson would be there, but the killer's habits were accelerating and no one knew why. Sometimes they just did. The adrenaline rush the killer got from killing wore off faster and faster.

Taking shelter behind the tree where he stood, Heath raised the small digital camera he'd brought with him from Jamaica, part of his investigation go-bag he had for when he had to move fast. He focused the camera quickly and took another round of shots, getting as many of the faces as he could. He'd get more when the people came by to pay their last respects at the grave.

Identification would come through Facebook and online college and high school yearbooks.

"Hello." The voice came from behind him, neutral but authoritative.

Heath knew at once that he'd been busted. Slowly, keeping his hands on the camera, he turned around.

Two men, one black and one Hispanic, stood there just far enough apart that they couldn't both be gotten easily, but they were still right there to help each other. Neither of them had their hands on their guns, but their jackets were open, and their hands were open and ready.

"Hi." Heath released the camera with one hand but kept the now-empty hand up and clearly visible.

"I'm Detective Green with the Chicago police department." The black man's eyes were invisible behind black Ray-Bans. His hair was cut short, barely showing against his skull. A small, narrow mustache framed his mouth. "This is Detective Hernandez. We need to see some ID."

Heath didn't bother asking why. If he'd been Green, he'd have asked him for identification, too. In fact, in different instances on some of the cases he'd handled, he had asked to see identification from people who hadn't seemed to fit at funerals and other events.

"Sure, Detective. Right-hand pants pocket. I'm going to move slow."

The man nodded.

Heath forked his wallet out and passed it over.

Green opened the wallet, then looked at Heath again. "Says here you're from Atlanta. You're a long way from home."

"I've got some more identification for you if you'll let me get it."

"Slow."

This time Heath reached inside his jacket and brought out his badge case. He passed it over. Green flipped it open and found Heath's shield.

"What are you doing here, Detective Green?"

"The deceased was the female victim of a violent crime. Those go down, usually it's the husband, a boyfriend or an ex. Sometimes a family member. A funeral can bring out the worst in people. The captain thought we might drop by, make sure everybody stays safe." Green looked up. "Are you on the job here, Detective Sawyer? Something the Chicago police department should know about?"

"I've been working the White Rabbit killings."

Green nodded toward the funeral party. "This was one of those?"

"Yeah. Jamaica P.D. hasn't made it official yet, but it is. They got the card two days ago."

"I haven't heard anything about it."

"Jamaica has better control over their news services than we do here."

"If they can keep that quiet, they do." Green handed the wallet and badge case back.

"It won't last forever."

"No, it won't." Heath put away his things, managing it one-handed because he was still hanging on to the camera.

"Does the family know?"

"I told the sister when I met her down in Jamaica. I don't know if she believes me."

"You tell her about the card?"

"No. I haven't talked to her since Jamaica."

"Probably something you should do."

Heath hesitated. "We didn't really get on while we were down there together."

Green lifted an eyebrow, but he didn't ask about that. "Tell you what. I'll call Jamaica, confirm the White Rabbit connection, then I'll have a word with the sister. Professional courtesy."

"I'd appreciate it."

"If you find out anything further, Detective Sawyer, let me know." Green passed across a business card, pausing briefly to write a cell phone number on the back. "Looks like we're all interested in this now. I've been following the White Rabbit case and know what happened in Atlanta."

Heath took the card and slipped it into his jacket pocket. "I'm sorry it went down like that with your detective."

"Me, too."

"But you must have been getting close to the guy, right?"

"We thought so." Heath knew he couldn't drop Gibson's name. The department would rake him over the coals for exposing them to a lawsuit like that.

"We'll get this guy." Green gave Heath a brief flicker of a grin. "It's what we do." He nodded and kept moving, his partner a silent shadow behind him.

Keyed up all over again, face-to-face with how Janet had been lost so quickly, Heath tried to put his emotions aside and concentrate on doing his job. When he turned back, though, he saw that Lauren Cooper was headed straight for him, and she didn't look happy to see him.

At first, Lauren hadn't believed that Heath Sawyer was there. She'd noticed the police detectives as they'd been circulating the funeral. She didn't know what they were doing there, or if someone from the police department always showed up in a situation like this, but she knew that Heath Sawyer shouldn't have been there.

From the disappointed look he gave her, she knew he wasn't happy that she had seen him. For some reason, that lack of appreciation made her angrier and more confused. She had felt livid, surprised and excited to see him all at the same time. That was something she didn't want to do. Her emotions were too confusing now.

He cleaned up really well. The black suit was clean and pressed and fit him nicely. It made him look a lot different than he had in the casual business attire he'd worn while masquerading as a coroner. He was clean-shaven, his hair moussed and in place, and the pair of Oakley sunglasses would have gotten him on the cover of *GQ*. His tie was knotted perfectly.

Lauren stopped in front of him and folded her arms, looking up at him.

Heath gave her a small, crooked smile. "By the time I realized you had spotted me, it was too late to retreat."

"Do you feel the need to retreat, Detective Sawyer?"

"Yes, ma'am." His Southern accent was more pronounced
now, or maybe she was so used to the native accents around her
that something different really caught her attention.

"What are you doing here?"

"Miss Cooper." He spoke calmly to her, and that infuriated
her even more. She was burying her sister, and he was butting in, catching her off guard the same way he had down in
Jamaica. "Maybe this isn't the best time to talk about this."

"Did you have another time planned?"

"No."

"You came here because you thought Gibson would be here,
didn't you?"

He hesitated a moment before answering. "I did."

Lauren sipped her breath and made herself speak rationally.
She glanced over her shoulder to check on her mother. Madeline Taylor was doing fine at the moment, having some final
words with her brothers and sisters. The closeness of those
family members had made Lauren feel the slightest bit out of
place, something she hadn't experienced in years.

She looked back at Heath. "I read over the newspaper stories
about the White Rabbit killings. All of them. They're all different. Different women. Different ways they were killed. Different times of days, weather conditions, a lot of things are
different. I've also done a lot of reading on serial killers the
last few days."

Heath didn't say anything to that.

"Most serial killers kill the same kind of victim in the same
way with the same kind of weapon. The killing is an orderly
series of events." Lauren couldn't believe she was talking so
nonchalantly about such a horrible subject. The reading had
been hard, but she'd always been good at research.

"There are different kinds of serial killers." Heath's voice was flat, no-nonsense. "What you're describing? Those are ritualistic killers. Guys who have hang-ups about something or a particular kind of person. There are also compulsion killers. Guys who don't know why they kill other than whatever satisfaction they derive out of it. Gibson is an organized killer, always in control of the victim, in control of the encounter area. He plans out his killings, but he doesn't do the same thing over and over again." He paused. "Magicians don't always pull the same tricks over and over again, do they?"

Lauren thought about that, surprised by the question.

"I've seen some of those guys work when Janet and I first started looking into Gibson as our doer. Some magicians work the same patter and stunts. Some try to come up with new acts every time you see them. But it's all about the magic, about the performance."

"Do you think that's what Gibson is about? The performance?"

"You know his magic better than I do. Which kind of magician is he?"

It only took Lauren a moment to realize that Heath had a point. Gibson did a round of shows, then he dropped out of the public view. When he reappeared months later, he had a whole new elaborate production ready to go. Sometimes the show was intimate magic for a group or a pay-channel broadcast. Other times it was escapology, a feat that taunted human endurance or even death itself, such as when he'd sat in an immersion tank for over seven minutes before breaking free of his shackles. He was well short of other magicians' time, but anytime a feat like that was done, it was impressive. The pay channels had eaten it up. Another time, he'd levitated himself in an effort to get out of a notoriously haunted house that burned down around him while malign spirits tried to keep him within the fire. Lauren didn't believe in malign spirits, but the performance had been nerve-racking all the same.

No one knew what Gibson would do next.

"He doesn't like to repeat himself."

Heath didn't say anything to that.

"You could be wrong, you know." Lauren spoke pointedly, getting her words across like hammer blows. "You're focusing on Gibson because he was in a photograph with Megan. The whole time you're doing that, telling Inspector Myton that Gibson is Megan's killer, the real killer could be getting away."

Heath's clean-shaven jaw bunched, and the muscles stood out in sharp relief. His words were soft. "Gibson is the killer, Miss Cooper. Maybe if more people believed me, we could put him where he belongs more quickly. Either way, I'm going to get him. You can bet the farm on that."

"There's nothing to tie Megan to the White Rabbit Killer."

He hesitated. "Yeah, there is. Two days ago, Inspector Myton received a black card with a white rabbit embossed on it. The Kingston police just aren't telling anyone yet." He looked past her. "You should go back to your mom. She probably needs you."

Looking over her shoulder, Lauren checked on her mother and saw that most of the family members had gone. She couldn't just leave her mother sitting there at the gravesite. Hurting and feeling guilty about being gone so long, she turned back to address Heath.

Only he wasn't there. He was already several long strides away from her, moving with deceptive speed through the graveyard.

Lauren considered going after him, but she didn't know what else to say. He was set on his course, and there was nothing she could do to break him of that.

He's not your problem. She concentrated on that, then turned and walked back to rejoin her mother.

Chapter 6

"You need to eat, Lauren. I can fix you something if you'd like."

"I'm all right, Mom. You should rest. Or, if you're hungry, I can make you something." Lauren perched uneasily on the edge of the couch in the living room where she'd spent the best years of her life. She didn't know what to do with herself. She was exhausted from the funeral, but she knew she couldn't rest. Thoughts of Megan's murder and Gibson kept whirling around inside her head. And Atlanta, Georgia, detective Heath Sawyer was in those thoughts way too much for any degree of comfort.

"No, honey. I'm fine." Her mother didn't look fine. The days since Megan's murder had sapped energy from her that she didn't have to spare. Her skin was pale and blotchy. Now that they were back home, at the house where Lauren had finished growing up in, her mother had taken off her wig, pulled on a crocheted cap to cover her bald head and sat in her favorite chair.

The television was blank, but the street noise drifted in through the closed windows. Outside, children played in yards, celebrating the arrival of summer and the end of school. Lauren didn't have many of those memories of playing in the neighborhood at that age. She'd been older when she'd arrived, but she could remember the other, younger kids in the neighborhood doing that. Whitman Park was only a couple of blocks away.

Lauren sat on the couch and felt alone. As heavily medicated and as tired as her mother was, she was barely there. The pain between them was so raw that it couldn't be touched.

After a little while, her mother slept in the chair. Unable to sit there any longer, Lauren got up quietly and retreated to the kitchen to fix a cup of tea. It felt good going in the kitchen, finding everything in its place where it had always been.

What was unaccustomed was the silence. Even after her dad had passed away, there had always been joy in the house. Megan had been the center of it, of course, because she had been the chatterbox. Lauren hadn't realized how silent the house could be without her sister.

The tears came while she waited for the water to heat. For a time, she let them fall, grateful that she'd been composed throughout the service. She didn't like showing emotions in front of others. She'd never felt comfortable doing that.

A few minutes later, the kettle whistled. She took it from the stove and dried her tears, then filled a cup and added a tea bag. As she waited for the tea to steep, she walked through the house, finally going upstairs to the rooms she and Megan had lived in when they'd been there.

Megan had been the first to leave, the first to get a "grown-up" job because Lauren hadn't been able to let go of the job at the magic store. She hadn't been ready for freefall among strangers then, and magic was—and still remained—her passion. There was something about magic, something about the illusion of being something else, or maybe *someone* else, that appealed to her in ways nothing else did.

Megan's room had been a mess after she'd departed in a whirl of excitement, littered with cast-off clothing, keepsakes from junior high, high school and college, books and rock star posters. It had taken Lauren and her mom three days to clean everything up, and they'd threatened to box it all up and send it to Megan to deal with, but neither of them wanted to think about finding the boxes sitting in Megan's apartment unopened when they went to see her.

The bed was neatly made. Trophies lined one wall. Pictures of Megan as a cheerleader, a business leader and in speech competitions, as well as on family trips and vacations, covered the wall. A person could stand in the middle of Megan's room and watch her grow up in the spotlight. Lauren had always thought that was weird, the growing up part. As for the spotlight part, there just hadn't been any other place for Megan.

Lauren's room, on the other hand, had been freshly cleaned and neat the day she'd left it. She'd stayed in the house till she'd gotten through college, to help her dad with her mom's first bout with cancer. Then, when the job at the magic store had become full-time, once Mom's cancer was in remission, Lauren had moved out and claimed her own space.

Even four years later, that apartment still felt like a temporary way station, a brief shelter from the turbulence that had claimed the rest of her life. Nothing before had been permanent. *This,* this had been home. And now it was withering away.

She sat on the edge of her bed and glanced at the walls. Compared to Megan's, they were empty. The Taylors had adopted her when she was eleven, young enough that she could share a lot with Megan, but old enough that she could never really escape the experience of getting shuffled between foster homes.

Pictures of her at that age and older were on the walls. She'd played softball and ran track and swam competitively. All were sports more or less recognized for individual effort. Only in the family photos did she look like a team player, and that was primarily because Megan had always been right there to pull her in.

On the chest of drawers, Lauren's early magic kits sat in boxes and pouches, as if a magician would be along any moment to put them to use. Lauren was surprised that her mother hadn't thrown them away, but Mom had always maintained that magic was the one thing that seemed to make Lauren come alive. A magician had to have an audience, she'd always said, and that was when Lauren had shone.

Lauren had let her believe that was true, but the actual truth was that she had sat in her room and performed magic all the time. Megan had watched in fascination at times. On other occasions, Lauren had used her tricks to bother Megan when she was on the phone. Especially after she developed an interest in boys. It was hard to focus on a conversation when coins and scarves and other small items kept appearing and disappearing.

Walking over to the chest of drawers, Lauren picked up the white-tipped black magic wand. It had been her first. When it was popped the right way, it became a bouquet of flowers. When she'd been eleven, she'd thought it was the coolest trick ever.

Now she just wished it had real magic in it so she could bring Megan back.

"What do you know about Gibson?"

Warren Morganstern lifted his head from the deck of cards he'd been shuffling and regarded Lauren. He was in his seventies, comfortably possessing a potbelly and a wrinkled face that still showed all the handsomeness of the posters Lauren had seen of his magic days. His hair was iron-gray and neatly parted on the left. Laugh wrinkles surrounded his blue eyes. He wore a pressed white shirt with the sleeves rolled up to midforearm. His jacket dangled from the back of his chair. A steaming cup of coffee sat to his right on the small table.

He eyed Lauren. "How are you doing, kiddo?"

"I'm okay." Lauren leaned on the load-bearing pillar behind the table. She knew she didn't look good. She hadn't slept well last night. Her mind was too full of Megan and Gibson and Heath Sawyer. Everything was getting twisted up in there.

"You don't look okay." Morganstern's voice was gruff and hoarse, an old man's voice now and not really strong enough for stage shows. He still had the hands and reflexes of a master, though. He just needed an assistant who could carry on the verbal part of the act. Lauren had been that assistant a number of times.

"Thanks."

"I call 'em like I see 'em, kiddo." Morganstern waved at the chair on the opposite side of the small card table.

The magic store had four little rooms where magicians could rehearse tricks and illusions. In those rooms they could practice with the tricks to see if they would work for them, or they trained with other magicians to make the trick their own.

After a brief hesitation, knowing that Morganstern was wanting to talk to her and knowing that she didn't feel like talking to anyone, Lauren went around the table and sat.

Morganstern shrugged. "I thought about coming by, after the funeral."

"I'm glad you didn't."

"I know. You always liked to be alone with the hard stuff." Morganstern shuffled cards again. "Your mom okay?"

"With the cancer or with Megan?" Lauren knew she sounded angry. She *was* angry, but she didn't mean to take it out on Morganstern.

He didn't flinch, though. He'd known her too long. "Both."

Lauren let out a tense breath. She loved that she didn't always have to be polite with Morganstern, and that he didn't take it personally when she wasn't. "She's doing okay."

"You asked about Gibson. I'm assuming we're talking about the magician, not the guitar." His eyes twinkled just a little.

"Yes."

"Something on your mind?" The cards danced in Morganstern's capable hands, flitting from palm to palm like flickering doves.

"I need some time off."

Morganstern nodded. "Sure, sure, kiddo. Me and the missus expected that. That's why I'm here this morning. Take all the time you need. We cleared our schedules, not that there's

much to clear these days. That's what retirement is all about."
He smiled.

"I don't know how much time that will be."

Morganstern shot her a curious look. "It's okay." He paused.
"You just do what you gotta do."

Lauren paused, not knowing how much to tell him. Warren
Morganstern was a good man. He'd looked out for her for years,
another father figure, but this one had led her into a realm of
make-believe possibilities and a way of forgetting so many of
the bad memories.

"One of the last people Megan saw down in Jamaica was
Gibson."

Morganstern nodded and reshuffled the cards. He laid them
on the table in a row, then made them dance from side to side.
"How'd that happen?"

"I don't know."

"Did Megan tell you about it?"

"No."

"Seems like that's something she would have told you
about."

"It is. I think she just didn't get the chance to."

Morganstern nodded and was somber and silent for a moment. "Something must have happened pretty quick for her not
to tell you something like that."

"I know."

"So you're wanting to talk to Gibson? See if he knows anything about…your sister?"

"Yes."

Morganstern shrugged. "Gibson isn't exactly a helpful man.
As far as I know, he doesn't have any friends. No one in the
business here that I know, and I know a lot of people."

"But he has a home down in Jamaica?"

"Rumor would suggest so. He spends a lot of time down
there."

"Why?"

Morganstern sighed. "I don't know, kiddo. Most magicians

like a place they can retreat to in order to design their illusions. Operate under the radar till they get the bugs worked out. I can make a few calls, see what I can find out."

Lauren nodded, getting more comfortable with her course of action. She couldn't sit back because the police weren't obviously going to carry the investigation very far. "I need this to be kept quiet. I don't want Gibson to know anyone from the magic community is looking into him."

"All right." Morganstern frowned. "I gotta say, I don't like the idea of you going down there and talking to that guy. Especially not if you think you gotta do everything on stealth mode."

Lauren looked at him and saw the worry in his face.

Morganstern hesitated a moment, then started talking. "Ten years ago, when Gibson was just starting out on the circuit, before he blew up and got network attention with those street magician YouTube spots, he had a reputation for being hard on female assistants." He shrugged. "That doesn't make him a killer, but I don't think he's a nice guy, either. You've seen what fame does to some people—makes them think they're living in a whole different world than the rest of us."

"You think that's what Gibson believes?"

"I don't know, kiddo, but I think it's something you should keep in mind. And now that I think about it twice, this is probably something you should tell the police about and just walk away."

"I'm not going to do that." Lauren was silent for a moment, thinking about Heath Sawyer and his vendetta. "There's a police detective from Atlanta. He lost a friend, another police officer, to the White Rabbit Killer."

Morganstern's eyes narrowed. "You're saying Megan was murdered by that guy?"

"It hasn't come out yet, but the local police handling the investigation in Kingston have received a White Rabbit card."

Morganstern swore softly.

Lauren went on, divorcing her emotions and speaking mechanically. "Heath and his friend had worked the White

Rabbit murders together, and they were narrowing the focus on Gibson. Everywhere one of those murders was committed, Gibson had been playing a venue."

"Have the police questioned him?"

"No. They don't have any evidence against him, nothing that ties him to the murders."

"Then why are you so interested in Gibson?"

"Because he was one of the last people to see Megan alive. He could have seen something that will lead the police to the killer."

"If that was the case, why doesn't he come forward?"

"Maybe he doesn't know he saw anything. Maybe he doesn't want the publicity. Either way, he's got enough lawyers to keep the police away from him."

"What are you planning to do?"

"I want to ask him about that evening he spent with Megan. I want to know where they went, who they saw, anything that might help with this investigation."

"You're not an investigator, kiddo."

"I know. But Heath Sawyer is, and he appears to be a dedicated police officer. He's blinded himself, though, totally focused on Gibson."

Morganstern shook his head. "You can't do that. You focus on the magician, you miss the trick."

Lauren reached across the table, took the deck of cards from Morganstern and shuffled them. "We know that. That's why I want to go back down there and talk to Gibson, find out what he knows. I think if anyone can find out who hurt Megan, Heath Sawyer can do it. I just want Heath looking at everything." She raised the cards in a tight stack in one hand, then made pulling motions with her other hand.

As if by magic, one of the cards levitated from the deck. The new card was one of a collector card series featuring magicians. This one was of Gibson, showing him in his patented black leather jacket and black turtleneck. A white dove nested in his cupped palms. He was stone-faced, mysterious, and no one could tell if he was going to release the dove or break its neck in the next moment. Lauren had never thought that before, but she did now, and the prospect chilled her.

Morganstern grinned in appreciation then clapped. "Good job, kiddo. I never saw you slip that card into the deck. Very smooth."

"That's because you were focusing on the magician."

The next day, Lauren boarded a flight that was going to be the first leg of her return to Kingston. She stored her carry-on in an overhead bin and took her seat next to the window. She preferred sitting there because she got the most privacy.

She opened her iPad and brought up one of the books she'd bought on the subject of serial killers. After her meeting with Morganstern, she'd returned home, found her mother resting, and spent the evening getting familiar with the books available on the subject. If Heath Sawyer was right about Megan being murdered by a serial killer, Lauren wanted to know more about the murderer.

She'd read for hours last night, wishing sleep would come, then had been taken by surprise when she'd been awakened by her cell phone's alarm chirping into her ear. After a hasty goodbye, she'd left her mother in the house with a promise to return soon and no word at all of where she was going.

Trying to go back home or to work was out of the question. Her mother believed it was that strong sense of responsibility that had propelled Lauren through life that had made her leave. If she'd known where her daughter was actually headed, Lauren knew her mother would have held on to her.

At least, there would have been a huge fight and lots of tears on both sides, because Lauren couldn't let the issue go. The horrible death Megan had suffered wouldn't leave her thoughts.

After takeoff, Lauren settled in and read as much as she could. The author reduced the sociopathic savagery inherent in most serial killers to a clinician's report that held almost no emotion. According to the author, law enforcement personnel who chased serial killers had to learn to tune out their own feelings.

She couldn't help wondering how police investigators could shut down emotionally like that. Heath Sawyer certainly hadn't, and Lauren was willing to bet his ex-partner hadn't, either.

Or maybe things were different when the killings were personal.

Lauren quickly negated that, as well. Heath Sawyer had been involved in the hunt for the White Rabbit Killer before his friend's murder. Reading the newspaper reports of the murder last night had left Lauren shaken, but she'd also gained a greater understanding of Heath's motivation.

The White Rabbit Killer hadn't been satisfied with killing Detective Janet Hutchins. The murderer had ensured the funeral would be a closed casket service. Some of the photographs associated with the story had featured Heath Sawyer in them, as well.

One of the things that had surprised Lauren was the amount of dedication "organized" killers devoted to the craft. Those killers pursued, "trolled" for victims of a specific type and tended to repeat their crimes, doing them over and over again as if seeking perfection. In fact, according to the book, that need to reach a "perfect" murder compelled some of the murderers.

Lauren couldn't help but think how similar that single-minded purpose was to a stage magician planning out the perfect performance. That thought disturbed her because she could see how someone like Gibson might fit the profile. She had made a list in the notes function on the iPad, then quietly ticked them off.

She rolled her neck and suddenly became aware of a familiar cologne. Her pulse sped up, and she felt self-conscious. Trying to remain casual, she glanced over her shoulder and caught Heath Sawyer leaning on the overhead bin and looking down at her.

He wore jeans and a dress shirt with the sleeves rolled to midforearm. His hair looked as if he'd run his fingers through it with a little mousse and hoped for the best. Stubble gleamed on his chin. Fatigue showed in his face, but his gold eyes gleamed as the green flakes moved restlessly.

"That's not exactly light reading there, Miss Cooper." His voice was flat and carried an accusatory note.

Lauren pressed the home button and shut down the tablet. She didn't have anything to say, and she wasn't going to give him any ammunition to work with.

After a moment, when he realized she wasn't going to answer him, Heath frowned. "Do you mind telling me where you're headed?"

The trip had a flight change. "Yes."

Heath waited, but she didn't answer. "Yes, what?"

"Yes, I do mind. Very much."

Heath dropped into the unoccupied seat.

"Happy?" Lauren tucked her iPad into the pouch of the seat in front of her.

"To see you? No. You're not stupid, that's why I can't believe you're acting that way." Heath took in a breath and let it out. "Going back down there is the worst thing you can do."

"Really? And where are you headed? I'm betting it's not back to Atlanta."

Heath took in a deep breath, and she knew he was holding back his instinctive response. "If you go after Gibson, you might get hurt."

For a moment, Lauren almost softened. He was worried about her. Despite all the anger and frustration that he was feeling, she believed his concern was real. But she couldn't back off. "According to you, no one can get close to Gibson. So why worry?"

"Your sister got close to the guy."

A sharp stab of pain lanced through Lauren and momentarily took away her breath.

"Look." Heath ran a hand through his hair. "I'm sorry. I didn't mean to go there." He sighed. "What I'm trying to say is that your mother has already lost one daughter. She shouldn't lose both of them."

"She won't." Lauren knew it was pride that made her say that, but she wasn't going to be made afraid, either. She wasn't going to take chances. Not like Megan had.

An older airline hostess with elegant makeup and a no-nonsense attitude parked herself in the aisle beside the seat Heath had taken. She folded her hands in front of her and gazed steadily at Heath. "Is this man bothering you, miss?"

"No, I'm not bothering her. I'm trying to save her life."

The hostess glanced at Lauren. "She doesn't appear to be in any jeopardy. We have an air marshal riding this flight with us. If you don't return to your assigned seat, I'm going to get him."

Growling inarticulately, Heath heaved himself up from the seat and walked to the rear of the plane.

The hostess peered at Lauren. "Will you be all right? Is there anything I can get you?"

"No. Thank you. I'm fine."

The hostess hesitated for just a moment longer, then retreated.

Leaning back in her seat, Lauren concentrated on breathing and relaxing. But she kept thinking about Heath, his intensity and his desire to capture his friend's killer. She hadn't realized it before, but she knew then that she was afraid for him.

"She's there?"

"Yeah, I'm looking at her now." Heath stood in the middle of the crowd at baggage claim. The carousel whirled and displayed a seemingly endless supply of suitcases and bags for the travelers.

Lauren Cooper stood on the other side of the carousel and pointedly avoided looking at him. She looked small and alone in the press of people around her. Most everyone else in the crowd was paired up or part of a larger group. Overall, she appeared vulnerable, like the way he remembered her from the day they'd met in the morgue.

"What is she doing there?" Jackson Portman sounded as irritated as Heath felt.

"She's not down here for the sand and surf."

"You want to know what I think?"

"No." Heath scanned the baggage for his suitcase.

"I'm gonna tell you anyway. I think things are crazy enough with you down there on your own. With Lauren Cooper there, too? Things are just gonna get crazier. That's what I think."

"Maybe while you've got your head clear from all that thinking you can find out where she's going to be staying down here."

"How am I supposed to do that?"

"Call her mother. Tell her you're following up on some leads about her daughter's murder and that an investigator needs to talk to Lauren."

"You want me to lie to her mother?"

"Yes."

"See, now this is when you carry this whole partnership thing too far. You don't lie to mothers, man. They know stuff. Part of the stuff they know is when you're lying. Santa Claus powers ain't got nothing on mother powers."

"I know stuff, too. If I don't keep an eye on Lauren Cooper, she's going to end up in a lot of trouble. And since I'm going to be watching Gibson, too, my life would be simpler if I knew where she was staying." Heath reached down for his suitcase, caught the handle and took it from the treadmill. "Don't make me do all the heavy lifting."

"Couldn't you just follow her? You being a detective and all?"

"I'm going to. Call the mother. Get back to me." With his suitcase in one hand, Heath headed for the outer perimeter of the crowd. He glanced over his shoulder and saw that Lauren had a skycap handling her bags. *Bags.* Evidently she was planning on staying for a while.

Heath's gut clenched at the thought of the danger she was

going to be in. She wasn't thinking straight. She'd just lost her sister. And she wasn't trained for anything like this.

She hadn't seen him yet, so he headed straight for the exit doors, intending to get a cab so he could follow her. He could return later to pick up the rental he'd arranged. He stood in line waiting.

A moment later, Lauren walked through the doors with her luggage in tow. And she walked directly to a waiting private car. Realizing she had arranged for the pickup at the airport ahead of time, that she was about to get away, Heath tried to get through the crowd.

Unable to reach the car in time, Heath stepped out in front of the vehicle as it drove away. The driver barely acknowledged him and might even have run him down had he not stepped back. Frustrated and feeling a little panicked, almost the way he'd felt when he'd driven to the hospital after he'd been told Janet had been admitted, he watched helplessly as Lauren Cooper vanished.

Chapter 7

Baking in the midday tropical heat, relishing the cool breeze that streamed in from the ocean, Heath tried in vain to find a comfortable position in his rental car. After hours spent seated there, though, comfort seemed to be impossible. He'd parked near the public beach close to Gibson's villa.

A stone wall ran around the perimeter of the estate, marking off a large chunk of private landscape filled with palm trees that stood up like a child's pinwheels, bougainvillea and other flowers that Heath couldn't identify. Although the stone wall was at least three hundred years old, maybe older, it was covered with the latest in high-tech security. There was also on-site security with at least nine guards that worked in rotation. Heath had figured that out on his previous visit and reconfirmed that during the two days since his return.

Between Heath's vantage point under a copse of palm trees and the mansion three hundred yards away, people lounged on the beach. Most of them were tourists, pale skin showing pink from the sun. But there were a few fishermen on a short wooden pier who seemed more interested in telling stories and drinking beer than in catching anything. In the middle, a spirited volleyball game took place between what looked like college-age guys and girls. They called out encouragement and derision to each other, and that was punctuated by sharp barks of laughter. Out on the water, a few small sailboats with brightly colored sails glided toward the horizon.

Heath pulled at his shirt to allow a breeze in, then cleaned his sunglasses to get the sweat streaks off the lenses. He pushed the sunglasses up again and picked up the binoculars lying on the passenger seat. He trained the binocs on the mansion.

C'mon, do something. You can't just want to sit in that house all day and all night. Heath raked the house from side to side and top to bottom, searching in vain for Gibson. For the past two days and both nights, there had been no activity at the villa. Nobody went in and nobody went out. Heath still didn't know Gibson's schedule. Inside the house, the man was invisible and unknowable.

Frustrated, Heath started to put the binocs away, but a familiar figure caught his eye. He adjusted the magnification and brought in the woman lounging on a chaise on the outer edge of the volleyball game. He wasn't sure what had caught his attention, maybe the set of her jaw, maybe her hair or maybe the fact that she was watching Gibson's villa with the same intensity he was.

But he knew her in a heartbeat. Lauren Cooper sat in the chair wearing a white bikini that set off a figure that had more curves than Heath would have guessed. Her skin looked smooth and satiny, with just enough of a tan to blunt the sun's harsh rays. She wore her hair pulled back under a floppy hat. Large sunglasses obscured the top part of her face, but he knew it was her. Her tablet lay on her taut stomach.

Unable to stop himself, Heath drank in every inch of her, for a moment forgetting the White Rabbit murders, Janet and his frustration at being unable to break the case. Lauren Cooper was beautiful, and lying there she looked even more vulnerable than he'd thought she was.

During the past two days, her whereabouts in Kingston had remained a mystery. Jackson Portman's conversation with the mother hadn't gone well. The woman hadn't known where Lauren was, and she'd been surprised that her daughter wasn't at home or at work, so Jackson had only succeeded in agitating her.

Since his return to Kingston, Heath had set up surveillance on Gibson. He'd expected to spot her somewhere along the way because he knew she wouldn't be able to stay away from the magician. But he hadn't seen her, and he had begun to worry that something had already happened to her. Even though seeing her there irritated him, he felt relieved at the same time.

Lauren reached down for a bottle of water she kept by the chaise and sipped the contents through a straw. Heath relished the smooth play of toned muscle under her skin as she shifted in the chair.

At least she wasn't trying to bum rush the front gates. On the first day of surveillance, Heath had halfway expected her to do that. When he'd thought of that, he hadn't known what to fear more—her alerting Gibson or getting accepted inside.

Lauren got up without warning and dropped her tablet into the big beach bag beside the chaise. She folded the chair, grabbed her bag, and headed toward a small parking lot a short distance away.

Caught up in the undulation of her hips, Heath took a moment to realize what had gotten Lauren up and moving. He switched the binocs back to the villa just in time to see the wrought-iron gates part and a sleek black Jaguar sedan patiently waiting like a predator. Once the gates were open, the luxury car slid through like a bullet.

Heath scanned the car as he reached for his keys and started his rental. The engine turned over smoothly and caught. The vents blew hot air into the side of his face.

The Jaguar's windows were tinted so dark they looked like sheets of oil. Heath caught only a glimpse of the driver, a powerful-looking man named Deke Roylston. Roylston was a hard case who was no stranger to breaking the law, but his record was spotty over the years. The man had worked as a mercenary in his younger days before settling in as Gibson's bodyguard six years ago.

Nothing in the paper trail connected Roylston, but he worked for a professional security service based in Seattle, Washington, and had been on permanent assignment in Kingston for the past six years. Poking into the security company's background hadn't been easy, and Heath hadn't learned much. They were a high-end executive protective service used to providing bodyguards to corporate personnel and celebrities.

Heath put the transmission in drive and wheeled his vehicle around, taking up the pursuit back to Kingston. As he drove, he adjusted the .357 Magnum partially concealed under his right thigh. Thankfully, there was some tourist traffic on the road. He was able to tuck in a couple of cars behind the Jaguar. When he glanced in the rearview mirror, he caught a glimpse of Lauren behind the wheel of a nondescript white compact rental as she slid behind a car behind him.

Then she was gone from sight, but Heath could still feel her back there. He snarled a curse. *Get your head back in the game. One thing at a time. Focus on your guy. Take him out and everybody's safe.*

That was what he had been doing when Janet had been killed, though.

Trance music played over the Jaguar's sound system, filling the rear seat with techno sounds and synth. The female singer's voice sent chills rippling down Gibson's back.

Gibson steepled his hands in front of him and stared through the windshield at the sun-blasted road ahead of them. "Is he back there?"

Even though Gibson was sure Roylston already knew the police officer was tailing them, the big man checked the rearview mirror anyway. "Yes."

Gibson smiled and felt satisfied. "Good." The acknowledgment was double-edged, intended more to irritate Roylston than to respond in polite fashion.

"Out here, you're vulnerable." Roylston looked back in the rearview mirror, locking eyes briefly with Gibson. "There's just me. You'd be safer back at the villa."

"Others will be waiting at the restaurant."

"There's miles to go between here and there."

"Lighten up, Deke. You should be enjoying this. A game of cat and mouse like this? You should be eating it up. When you stopped killing people for pay to protect me, some part of you must surely miss the excitement."

"No."

"Not even a smidgen?"

"You haven't been in that position, being out in the jungle, not knowing when the next step is gonna be on a mine, or if a sniper has you in his sights from a thousand yards away. That's not fun. That's hell."

"You could have chosen another career."

"The pay was good."

"Not that good. You enjoyed what you did. And you enjoy what you're doing now. You enjoy being around me."

"You cause too much trouble."

"For which you're paid quite handsomely. Never forget that. And never forget that I've looked into your files. You were no saint. You took your pound of flesh and your pleasure where and when you wanted to while you were over there. Maybe you've even done that here."

Roylston didn't reply.

Gibson put his arm on the rests and drummed his fingers in time to the music. He stretched his legs out, enjoying the little pulse of adrenaline singing through his blood.

Roylston drove on in silence for a time, but he couldn't keep his thoughts to himself. Gibson knew the man was going to break his silence by the way he held his shoulders. That was another game just the two of them played.

"You're pushing this cop too far."

Gibson folded his arms behind his head and radiated the perfect picture of indolence. "Do you think so?"

"Yeah, I do. You shouldn't have killed his partner."

Gibson smiled. "Maybe you shouldn't have let me. As I recall, that happened on your watch."

Roylston grimaced and his voice thickened. "Maybe you're pushing *me* too far, too."

"Really?" Gibson feigned surprise.

Roylston started to say something, then closed his mouth and focused on the road.

"Do you ever wonder why you got saddled with me?"

Roylston made no reply.

"I think it's because you had some indiscretions of your own. I think you were assigned to me to do penance for philandering with my father's ex-fiancée. A good security man should know better, shouldn't he?"

Roylston glared at him in the mirror.

"You pretend you have a moral compass, but you don't. Not really. Everybody is out to get what they think they want. Whatever captures their attention, whatever new thing they think their heart desires. Most of them end up unhappy and they don't even know why."

"Killing those women makes you happy?"

This time Gibson's smile was real. Excitement flared through him because he knew he'd penetrated the bodyguard more than he ever had before. "Yes, actually it does. I love knowing their lives are mine to do with as I please. That I have that much control over someone else. And I know that you know what I'm talking about. You've been there, too. But that's not the best part."

"Then what is?"

Gibson rolled the coin across his knuckles. "What makes me happy is making my father unhappy. I kill those women because I know he fears me getting caught and embarrassing him. So I kill the women and you people have to clean up the mess. When you can find the victims, which you haven't always been able to do. That's the game I play with my father. He chose you to watch over me because he doesn't care for you after the philandering incident. Working with me is your penance, but you'll never be able to pay that off. My father doesn't let people out from under his thumb. You have to make your own way out from under."

Roylston drove on for a short time in silence. The outskirts of Kingston were just ahead, buildings suddenly filling the empty expanse of jungle and beach. Hotels and business centers in the New Kingston area looked white and stark against the blue sky.

"Your old man's gonna get tired of playing games with you one of these days."

"Do you think so?" Gibson relished toying with the man.

"I would."

"You're not my father. To him, I'm irreplaceable."

"Seems to me he replaced your mother pretty quick when the time came."

Anger burned bright and ember hot, and Gibson felt the heat rising to his face. The coin disappeared from his hands, and the .45 ACP Derringer pistol he carried appeared as he leaned forward. He pushed the barrel against the base of Roylston's skull.

"Don't talk about my mother. *Ever.*" His voice was a cold growl, breath that blew over a wood rasp.

"Pull that trigger and we both die."

"No. If I pull this trigger, you die. *Maybe* I'll die." Then Gibson laughed, palmed the pistol again, made a fist, then slowly opened it to show that it was empty as Roylston watched him in the rearview mirror. "I could take my chances with the car's safety features." He leaned back in the plush seat. "Or I can just wait till you're asleep some night in your room, step in and blow your brains out." Smiling, he laced his fingers behind his head. "Your successor can clean up the mess."

Roylston shifted uncomfortably in the seat. He cleared his throat, but he didn't say anything.

"Let me worry about Detective Heath Sawyer." Lackadaisically, Gibson gazed through the side window out at the approaching line of the metro area. "You just sit back and enjoy the show."

Chapter 8

Oyster Rose Restaurant catered to the affluent tourist class. It occupied an old, converted warehouse three blocks back of the ocean, but the second-floor veranda offered a good view of the coastline and the sunsets over the city. The original architecture had been kept for the most part, but a lot of work had gone into the interior.

Heath had heard of the restaurant since he'd been in Kingston, but he couldn't remember where he'd first learned about it. The business was one of the high-traffic destinations for tourists, and it was expensive and hard to get reservations for. A couple dozen people sat in the waiting area to one side of the building. Servers brought out drinks, ensuring that guests would run up a profitable tab before they ever got a table.

After Gibson had arrived at the restaurant, Heath had parked in a lot across the street from the lot where the driver had left Gibson's car. Then he'd followed at a safe distance. Neither the driver nor Gibson paid him any attention, and he thought they were unaware of him. There were enough people in the restaurant even in the afternoon that Heath felt certain he could blend in while escaping notice.

Gibson was either a regular at the restaurant, or the owners were fans or he had a reservation. As soon as he arrived, one of the hostesses wearing a shimmery flowered dress that clung just enough to hint at the curves lying beneath went to him and guided him to a table with a good view of the harbor.

Laughing and joking with the hostess, Gibson took the offered seat. Roylston sat opposite him. The table was positioned just far enough away to discourage conversation with other guests. A few of them recognized the magician or at least thought they did. Heath could tell that from the body language of the guests as they leaned in to talk quietly among themselves.

Gibson ignored them and contented himself with the iPad he'd brought with him. He made no attempt to talk to Roylston. The bodyguard sat languidly in his chair, but his eyes roved over the other diners, and his jacket, tailored to disguise the pistol Heath was certain was holstered under his right arm, was left loose.

A stool opened up at the end of the bar. Heath stepped up and took the seat, still able to watch Gibson's table.

"Hi. What can I get you?" The female bartender on the other side of the bar was petite and had her hair up in dreadlocks.

"Beer. Bottled. Domestic is fine." Heath took money from his pants pocket and paid her when she handed him the beer dripping ice water. The bartender went away as Heath sipped his beer. The ice-cold beer hit the back of his throat and felt like heaven. He ran the chilled bottle across his forehead.

Televisions hanging in different areas of the restaurant broadcasted baseball and soccer games. Other televisions offered continuous advertisements of activities and scenery around the island.

Heath watched Gibson, but he kept an eye out for Lauren, as well. He'd seen her car a couple of times on the way into Kingston and he didn't think she'd gotten lost. Of course, it was possible. He was also afraid that something had happened to her, that maybe Gibson coming into Kingston was just a feint to draw her out so that some of his bodyguards could seize her.

You're seeing conspiracies everywhere. Stop. Take a breath. It's entirely possible that she got lost. Heath sipped more of his beer.

A server brought drinks to Gibson's table. A mixed drink for Gibson and coffee for Roylston. Gibson continued to be amused by whatever he was looking at on his iPad.

Heath hated the way Gibson grinned at whatever he was checking out on the device. He thought of how he'd seen Janet, of how he hadn't been there when she'd needed him. And he thought about how Lauren Cooper had looked down in the morgue when she'd gone to identify her sister.

Nobody should have to hurt like that.

And the guy who was responsible for that pain shouldn't get to enjoy his life.

That wasn't going to happen.

Before he knew he was moving, Heath pushed away from the bar and threaded through the tables with single-minded focus. He was barely aware of bumping into people, but he didn't care.

Roylston noticed Heath's laser-beam approach immediately. The big man stood and crossed his arms over his broad chest, putting himself out there as a human roadblock between Heath and Gibson.

Gibson gave no indication that he'd even noticed the bodyguard's movement.

"All right." The bodyguard's voice was gruff and low, just threatening enough to be a vocal speed bump. "That's far enough. You take another step and you're going to get hurt."

Anger stirred inside Heath. He wasn't worried about getting hurt. In fact, getting hurt might even feel good. When his temper flared back as he was playing sports, it felt good to hit and to get hit.

Heath kept coming, stepping into the bodyguard. Roylston

put his hand on Heath's chest to stop him. Lifting his left arm, Heath batted the man's hand away and took another step.

At the same time, two large men at tables on either side of Gibson stood and reached to their hips. Their jackets kept the weapons concealed, but Heath knew immediately they were carrying.

"Detective Sawyer." Gibson's voice was cool and crisp. He lifted his gaze from the iPad, pushed the device onto the table, and steepled his fingers as he rested his elbows there. He smirked, and his dark eyes glowed with magnetic intensity.

Heath made himself breathe and work through his anger. He still wanted to smash Roylston down, if that was possible, and go for Gibson. But that wasn't how he was going to make his case. All he wanted to do here was rattle Gibson's cage, shake the man up and let him know that not everyone was just going to walk away from what he'd done.

"What can I do for you?" Gibson sipped his drink and leaned back in his seat.

"I just wanted you to know that I haven't gone away, that I was still here turning over rocks."

Gibson leaned back in his seat, totally at ease. "Should I feel threatened? Be impressed by your single-minded intent? Maybe even be proud of your stubborn insistence?" He grinned. "What do you want from me?"

Heath grinned back, a thin, mirthless expression tight on his face and feeling as if it had been frozen there. "I just want the truth about those murders."

Gibson sipped his drink again. "Careful, Detective. You're in a public place. You're coming awfully close to slander."

Nearly all the afternoon crowd had paused their lunches to observe what was taking place. A few families had left their tables and were edging toward the door.

Heath felt bad about that, but he couldn't stop himself. He was barely able to control the white-hot fury that threatened to explode from him. That night of horror, trying to deal with Janet's husband and kids, was indelibly marked in his mind.

And thinking about how Lauren Cooper seemed to be determined to involve herself with Gibson pushed him past the point of no return. He didn't want her to get hurt.

"No slander here, but I'll make you a promise." Heath's voice was stronger and colder and harder than he would have believed. "You're not going to get away with what you've done."

"Hollow words, Detective." Gibson took in an easy breath. "You can't prove I've gotten away with anything."

"I will."

A little round man wearing a suit and a frown walked to Heath's side. "Please, sir, I must ask that you leave the premises. Otherwise I will be forced to summon the police. I am sure neither one of us wants that."

Heath didn't want that. He didn't know how much it would take to get him thrown out of the city, but he definitely wanted to stop short of that point. If Lauren was going to insanely continue her observation of Gibson, Heath wanted to pull all of the man's attention to himself and hope that the woman escaped notice.

"Sure. I'll go." Heath locked eyes with Gibson, but the magician just returned his attention to his iPad. "But I'll be around."

A gold coin suddenly appeared in Gibson's hand, then rolled across his knuckles and disappeared in a twinkling.

Seething, barely under control, Heath turned and left the restaurant. Roylston and his two companions didn't return to their seats till after Heath had stepped into the street and headed for the parking lot. Two of the restaurant staff followed him, both of them good-sized guys who probably handled aggressive guests.

Heath swore at himself. He had intended to play the surveillance cool. Just watch and learn. But thinking of Lauren Cooper getting involved and perhaps getting hurt because she didn't know any better had thrown him off his game. The woman was going to cause all sorts of problems for—

From the corner of his eye, Heath caught sight of a familiar figure walking into the restaurant.

Lauren had ditched the beachwear for a lightweight dress that accentuated her figure. Heath realized that the only way she could have possibly gotten dressed that quickly around here was changing in the car on the drive over. He hadn't been at the restaurant that long. Imagining her changing her clothing in the car was distracting, and by the time he'd realized she was still moving, she was inside the restaurant.

Heath tried to follow, but two staff members stepped toward him. The bigger one shook his head.

Disgusted with the situation, Heath held up his hands in surrender, then turned and jogged across the street to his car. He unlocked the door and climbed inside, then picked up his binoculars and followed Lauren Cooper's progress through the restaurant.

She looked beautiful…and too vulnerable.

Walking through the restaurant was a performance. Lauren focused on that, telling herself that again and again as she closed in on Gibson's table. She didn't take a direct route because that would have drawn too much attention and possibly put the man on the defensive. She wasn't sure exactly how she wanted to approach Gibson, but she thought if she could get him talking, maybe she could learn something.

She paused at the bar long enough to order a glass of wine. From her vantage point, she had a clear view of Gibson. The man seemed consumed by his tablet, pausing every now and again to tap on the surface, presumably sending emails.

He didn't look like a killer. Lauren had tried to picture Gibson as that, as the man who had taken Megan's life, but she couldn't. The man was magic, capable of captivating an audience and doing the impossible right before everyone's eyes. The magicians who gathered at the magic store spoke of Gibson with awe and envy. Many of them didn't understand how Gibson had hit the public eye so easily. His connections with the media had seemed equally as magical.

She sipped her wine, barely tasting it.

Screwing up her courage, afraid that Gibson was only there for drinks and would soon get up and leave, Lauren left the wine on the bar and headed in the general direction of the bathroom.

On the way there, Gibson pierced her with his stare.

For a moment, Lauren was afraid that Gibson had somehow recognized her. Megan had carried photos of them together in her purse. If Gibson had killed Megan, he might have gone through her things. There was nothing in the White Rabbit files that had indicated any such interest, though. The man had simply killed his victims. Except for Detective Janet Hutchins. The killer had taken his time and tortured her.

This is a performance. Perform. Lauren forced herself to smile and turned to face Gibson. She turned off all her feelings of loss and pain and battened them down deep inside herself the way she had when she'd been in the foster homes. She'd learned how to perform there first, and she'd learned how to be invisible even in a crowd.

She crossed the distance to Gibson's table and held out a hand, holding her clasp purse in her other hand. "Gibson? *The* Gibson? The magician?" She put as much "ooh" and "ahh" into her voice as she could, surprised at how easy it was even under these conditions. She was a fan of his work, after all.

The man seated at the table stood and put a hand out to block her advance, stopping just short of actually touching her. "I'm going to have to ask you to stand back, miss."

"I'm sorry. I just couldn't help myself." Lauren continued to look at Gibson. "It's just that I'm one of your biggest fans. I saw the show you did in—" she started to say Chicago, then realized that might remind him of Megan and make him cautious "—Minneapolis two years ago." She had seen the Chicago show in person, with Megan, but she had watched the Minneapolis performance on HBO. "I still can't figure out how you made that big Humvee disappear."

Gibson plucked a speared olive from his drink and leaned

back in his seat. He popped the olive into his mouth and bit down. "It was magic, of course."

Lauren forced herself to grin like a loon. "Of course it was." She looked at the table. "I'm sorry. I didn't mean to interrupt your lunch."

The big man took his hand back but didn't sit. He kept his face neutral and never took his gaze from her. "Mr. Gibson prefers his space."

"I understand. I don't mean to be a bother, but I didn't know you were here. Are you performing?"

Gibson shook his head and flashed white teeth. "No. A bit of a vacation actually."

Lauren smiled. "This is a great place for a vacation." Several of the nearby guests kept track of the conversation with obvious interest.

Gibson's gaze traveled up and down Lauren, and for a moment the cold appraisal in his dark eyes made her want to shiver. Part of his interest was sexual, she recognized that, and she squelched her immediate impulse to walk away. There was something dirty and hungry in Gibson's attention, and that surprised her.

This man killed Megan. The thought rocketed through Lauren's head with iron-clad conviction. She didn't know precisely what had caused her to suddenly believe that, but she did.

"It is." Gibson dropped the plastic spear from the olive back into his empty drink glass. "You should enjoy your time here. Now, if you'll excuse me, I think that's my lunch." He pointed over her shoulder.

Turning slightly, Lauren found one of the servers waiting patiently behind her with food on a tray. Lauren stepped back out of the way. "I apologize for coming over."

Gibson ignored her, focusing on the server as she placed the salad, soup and seafood dish on the table in front of him. "Not a problem. I'm glad you enjoyed the show. I look forward to bedazzling you in the future."

Dismissed, Lauren started to go. She had never in her life

tried to approach a man like that, hoping to get herself invited to his table. Getting sent on her way in such a cavalier fashion actually stung in spite of all the other mixed feelings about Megan. It also frustrated her because she didn't know how she was supposed to get close enough to the man to find out more.

"Miss."

Lauren turned back to Gibson. He held up an empty hand, then turned it, closed it and opened it again. A silver coin lay in his palm.

"A memento, perhaps?" Gibson held the coin perched at the end of his thumb and forefinger.

"I'd love one." Lauren made herself smile as she reached for the coin. The metal felt cold and hard against her skin. She closed it in her fist. "Thank you. I'll be looking forward to your next show."

Gibson nodded, but his attention was already on the meal in front of him.

Lauren headed back to the bathroom feeling miserable but turned and walked out of the restaurant a different way than she'd entered. She felt miserable because seeing Gibson there, so nonchalantly going on with his life even if he hadn't killed Megan—which Lauren no longer believed—bothered her deeply. She wasn't going to just walk away and accept things, but she didn't know what she was going to do to change things, either.

A large shadow fell over Lauren as she used the key fob to open the locks on her rental. She checked the reflection in the window glass to see who had made the shadow. She thought it might be the big man who had been sitting with Gibson. That guy had looked as if he was no stranger to violence.

She turned around with the keys clenched between her fingers, ready to strike out if she had to. Her other hand held her clasp purse, but her fingers had already started lifting the door handle.

Heath Sawyer stopped only a few inches away, just short of

touching her. The heat from his body radiated against her, and the smell of his cologne and natural musk filled her nose and made her senses dance. God, why did the man have to look so good? She had never been so captivated by a man she'd spent so little time with.

Part of that was blunted by the angry set to his mouth and jaw. His sunglasses hid his eyes. When he spoke, his voice came out as a half growl.

"What do you think you were doing in there?"

"I was trying to prove you wrong about Gibson. I thought if I talked to him, maybe I could find out something that you and the local police haven't been able to discover about Megan's death." Anger poured out of Lauren and she directed it at Heath. "You were so sure of yourself that I thought you were too locked in to know what you were doing."

"He's the guy who killed your sister."

Lauren took a breath. "I know."

Heath had started to say something. Now he paused, thought for a moment, and closed his mouth. The blank lenses over his eyes hid any clue as to what he was thinking. "You know he's the guy? Did he say something to you?"

"Like, 'I did it? I killed your sister, and I killed all those other women'?" Lauren shook her head and crossed her arms. She was on the verge of tears, and she didn't like that. Crying was a weakness. It didn't solve any problems, and often it only made them worse. If she could have gotten in her car and driven away, she would have been all right. Heath Sawyer had just caught her at the wrong time. "No, he didn't say anything like that."

"Then what did he say?"

"He gave me this." Lauren handed over the coin she'd gotten from Gibson. It was a two-headed disc that featured Gibson on stage on one side and an empty stage on the other.

Heath took the coin and looked at it. "What's this?"

"One of Gibson's tokens. He uses them in his magic act in front of audiences. Hands them out so people can flash them around, tell everybody they've seen the amazing Gibson." Lauren heard the vitriol in her words and was surprised. Only a short time ago she'd been a Gibson fan intending to prove the magician's innocence.

"He gave this to you?"

"Yes."

"Why?"

"Because he's a jerk. Because he thought I was his Number One Fan and this was consolation prize because I didn't get to talk with him more." With deceptive ease, Lauren plucked the coin from Heath's fingers, then rolled it across her knuckles, exposing the sides in rapid syncopation. "See how Gibson seems to appear and disappear? It's an optical illusion if you learn how to roll the coin right."

She popped the coin into the air so that it spun and caught the bright sunlight. Then she caught it in her palm, closed her hand and turned it over, palmed it smoothly with her other hand while she acted like she was pointing to her hand with her forefinger. When she opened her hand, the coin was gone.

Stone-faced, Heath looked at her. She was suddenly aware of how close they were, and it was almost like he was giving off enough gravity to pull her into his orbit. For a moment, she wanted to just lean in and give herself over to him, let him put his arms around her and tell her everything was going to be all right. She wanted comfort from him like she hadn't wanted anything in a long time.

Instead, Heath remained those few inches away. "You need to stay out of this. You don't know what you're doing. You don't know how much danger you're exposing yourself to."

That rekindled the anger inside Lauren, and she gave herself over to it. "You don't get to tell me what to do."

"Believe me, it's not a privilege. You're interfering with police business."

"What police business?" Her voice came out louder than she'd expected and drew the attention of a small group of passersby. "This isn't your turf, Detective Sawyer. You don't have any more right here than I do, and you definitely don't have the right to tell me what I can and can't do."

"Somebody needs to. You're out of control."

"Out of control?" Lauren clamped her jaw on a torrent of swear words only because some of the people walking past had small children in their care. She lowered her voice with effort. "I'm not out of control."

"Yeah, you are." Heath cocked his head to one side. "You should be home, not here."

"What would I do there?"

"Grieve. Go back to work. Take care of your mother. From what I saw at the funeral, she needs someone there with her right now."

The sudden guilt felt like salt rubbed into a wound. "Leave my mother out of this."

His face softened a little and his voice gentled. "You can do more good there than you can here."

Lauren knew the argument was a good one, and that it was probably true, but she also knew she couldn't walk away from the investigation into Gibson. Maybe Megan would have gone with the magician anyway that night, because he was a good-looking man, but she'd been made more vulnerable by Lauren's interest in him. She couldn't leave while Gibson was loose. She didn't like feeling helpless, and she didn't appreciate Heath pointing that out. "Like you're doing so much good here. Why don't you go home and grieve over your partner? Maybe that's what you should be doing."

Too late, Lauren knew that what she'd said was too much. It was more than she'd intended, just spewed out of painful vindictiveness. Despite the sunglasses, the hurt showed on Heath's face. She wanted to apologize, but she didn't know how to start and was convinced that, at the moment at least, any apology would do no good.

His voice turned cold and hard. "If you keep interfering with Gibson, you're going to get yourself hurt."

Lauren couldn't back off. She wasn't going to be cowed or

sent to her room like that little girl she'd been. She'd come a long way since those days. "Maybe if I do, you'll catch him this time."

Heath snarled inarticulately and turned away from her. He never looked back as he crossed the street to another parking lot.

Lauren got into the hot car, turned the engine on and set the air-conditioner on high. *Great trick there, Lauren. Alienate the only guy who might be able to help you.* She leaned her head on the steering wheel for a moment, then she centered herself, put the car in gear and headed back to her hotel. She didn't know where else to go at the moment.

Chapter 9

The next two days passed like vague memories of the first. Lauren set up on the beach with a view of Gibson's villa and kept watch. The magician stayed put. A few of his men went into the city, always in pairs. On the second day, Lauren followed them and discovered they were evidently taking downtime away from the villa, visiting restaurants and strip clubs. The Palais Royale Night Club seemed to be the favorite.

During that excursion, Lauren noted that Heath had evidently had the same idea or had followed her. He always positioned himself where he could watch over her and the villa, and that irritated her because it meant he didn't trust her to keep herself safe.

When the two bodyguards went into a club called the Bronze Parrot, Heath followed. The reggae beat swirled out over the street as hucksters in front of the bar shouted out to passing pedestrian traffic and cars.

The thought of Heath watching dancers gyrate inside the club bothered Lauren more than she wanted it to. He was just there observing the two bodyguards. She knew that, but the idea of him inside the club chafed her.

She briefly considered following him into the club, then put it out of her mind. Her beachwear wasn't appropriate attire for the place, and she had nothing suitable to wear into the club in the back of the car. In fact, she hoped she had nothing suitable to wear there at all.

She turned the car around and retreated to the villa, telling herself that she was going to catch Gibson leaving, and Heath would miss out.

That didn't happen. She spent the day watching the villa, and nothing stirred. Hours later, Heath followed the bodyguards back and resumed his observation post.

As she sat in the chaise and listened to the sound of the gentle waves lapping at the coastline and the laughing voices of the volleyball players, Lauren used her iPhone to access Twitter. She'd keyed in Gibson's name as a trending topic. Unfortunately, since *Gibson* was the only name she was able to enter and *Gibson Magician* didn't pull up Tweets any better, she had to sort through a lot of entries.

Shortly before sundown, she received an email from Morganstern.

Lauren,

I've just heard from Sinclair that Gibson will be at a nightclub called the Bright Blue Calypso tonight. Sinclair's cousin is a travel agent who handles reservations for Gibson's agent, Devon Walters. The information should be good.

I hope that you are well. We are doing fine here, and I must say that being back in the store is exciting. I've seen a couple of illusions that I think are going to astonish audiences when they're revealed. I can't wait to show them to you on your return. And I must say that you should come home soon. Viv and I worry about you.

Your mother is fine. I've been to check on her myself. She

is concerned about you down there, but I'm sure you've already heard from her regarding that.

Be safe and come home soon.

The Amazing Morganstern ☺

Lauren smiled at the email and quickly dashed off a reply, thanking him for the information and reassuring him that she was quite all right, just still not ready to come home.

As she was finishing that off, an email from her mother arrived. The email was short and to the point, talking briefly about her recent visit to the doctor and how everything still looked hopeful, and that she missed her and wished she would come back home, though she understood the need to do something.

If I weren't laid up with chemo, I would be there with you. I think I've read far more detective novels than you have. LOL

The attempt at humor brought a tear to Lauren's eye. She wiped it away as the cool, salt breeze ran across her and made her realize how late it was getting. She emailed her mom to let her know she was fine, then closed down the email app on her phone and glanced back at the villa. Lights glowed in some of the windows.

The problem was getting to Gibson. The bodyguards kept the man too closely supervised. They were like stage assistants, visible and invisible as needed, but the focus remained on Gibson.

Realizing that gave Lauren another idea. Maybe she couldn't separate Gibson from his bodyguards, but she might be able to separate one of the bodyguards from their employer. And she thought she knew how to do it.

She was going to need help, though.

Getting to her feet, she folded the chaise and carried it and her water bottle to her rental, stashing everything in the trunk. Then she walked back toward Heath Sawyer's car.

* * *

Heath noted Lauren's approach at once and appreciated the smooth roll of toned flesh as she made her way to him. His heart felt firmly lodged in the back of his throat as he noted the swell of her breasts and the cleavage captured by the yellow-and-orange swirled string bikini she wore today.

He'd watched her earlier, and he'd ended up paying far too much attention to her. That was part of the reason he'd decided to tail Gibson's bodyguards into Kingston earlier that day. The other part was because he knew she would watch Gibson. Eventually whatever she learned, he would know. Whether they liked it or not, they were working together.

She wore her dark hair swept in an updo that left her neck long and beautiful...and too vulnerable. Heath couldn't get the memory of the bruises around her sister's neck from his mind. She'd pushed her yellow sunglasses up into her hair, and the look totally worked for her, even though he was certain she hadn't consciously chosen to make a look. She only wore mascara and eyeliner. Her skin glowed from being in the sun all day.

He didn't let his guard down, though.

She came to a stop a yard away and crossed her arms. "Gibson's supposed to go out tonight."

That irritated Heath. She wasn't supposed to be better informed than he was. "You're sure?"

"Yes. He has a reservation at Bright Blue Calypso tonight."

"What's that?"

"A nightclub." She gave him the address as he reached for a pad lying in the passenger seat next to the binocs.

He finished writing the address and looked up at her. "Why are you telling me?"

"I thought maybe we could work together."

Heath was shaking his head before she finished. "No. Not a chance. There is no *we*."

She shrugged. "All right." She turned around and walked away.

"You need to stay away from there."

Lauren tossed him a wave over her shoulder but never missed a step.

He watched her go, mesmerized by the way her hips twitched, thinking that he wished that she wasn't so hard-headed.

The Bright Blue Calypso Club featured soul-driven calypso music, which was no shock, but the elegance of the club surprised Lauren. It was located on the bottom floor of one of the downtown office buildings and existed within its own bubble.

The crowd was wild and fun, and the dance floor stayed packed. Bright blue lasers shifted and danced through the darkness filling the upper reaches of the high ceiling. The sound system rocked the house and the music was live from a colorfully dressed band on a well-lit stage.

Sitting at a small table against one wall in the club, Lauren sipped her beer and watched the front door. It was 8:17, probably still early for Gibson. The table that had been reserved for him still sat empty in front of the band.

Lauren didn't think Gibson would be there just for the music, so she puzzled over what would bring him to the club. She wore a strappy mini black cocktail dress that hit her at midthigh and black heels, and wore black bangles on her right wrist. The bangles looked like polished ebony and caught the light when she moved. They were a distraction she planned to use. She kept her hair moussed back. thinking that she looked a lot different than she had when she'd confronted Gibson in the restaurant.

Her stomach fluttered nervously as she considered what she was about to do. She'd never done anything like this, and what she was prepared to do could easily land her in jail.

You'll do fine. Easy-peasy. You've worked an audience before, and this isn't much different.

Except that what she planned on doing was illegal. Failure or success, she was going to be in a lot of trouble if she got caught.

The fact that Heath Sawyer hadn't yet shown up further

unnerved her. He had seemed liked the reliable type, and she got frustrated with herself for thinking that—for *counting* on that—when it was evidently not true.

She sipped her beer and watched the door.

At 8:32, Gibson strolled through the front door with his primary bodyguard. The big man came ahead of Gibson and scanned the premises, one hand resting lightly under the fold of his coat.

As usual, Gibson was dressed all in black, wearing a black leather jacket over his turtleneck. His hair was neatly combed, and he looked like a lord who had stepped into a night out with the provincials. A small smile played on his full lips for a moment, then he was distracted as a small feminine figure wriggled up under his arm.

Lauren's heart sped up and fear turned cold inside her as she studied the young woman.

She was in her early twenties, if that, and looked as if Gibson had cut her out from one of the college groups vacationing in the city. She had chestnut-colored hair that had been teased into wild abandon, a shocking pink mini-dress with a broad black belt and a figure meant to be sheathed in it. She gazed around the club with wide-eyed innocence, but she carried a smartphone in her right hand, and she was already photographing the sights.

Lauren looked at the young woman. She wanted to go over to her and tell her to get away from Gibson, but she didn't know if that would do any good. More than likely, it wouldn't. She pushed aside the fear for the girl. If everything she had planned worked out, Gibson wouldn't be taking anyone home anyway.

One of the cocktail servers met Gibson and his party and led them over to the reserved table. The girl squealed in delight and hugged Gibson fiercely. Her pink nails flashed across her smartphone and Lauren felt certain that Tweets were going up by the dozen. Maybe that alone would be enough to prevent her from ending up another victim.

Gibson sat at the table with his primary bodyguard. Two

others took up positions nearby. Both of them were middle-aged, hard-bodied and alert, but one of them had an eye for the women. His hair was moussed back, and he had an arrogant body language. He was good-looking and he knew it, and that attitude was already drawing women to him.

Lauren chose him as her mark. She finished her beer, took the empty bottle and placed it onto the tray of a passing server, and walked toward the bodyguard. As she swept the dance crowd, she spotted Heath Sawyer on the other side of the room. He was dressed in a casual sports jacket, slacks and a pullover that allowed him to effortlessly fit into the younger crowd. She was surprised at how much he had changed.

Evidently her appearance caught him off guard as well, because he had to look twice to recognize her. She knew he had her when he frowned and shook his head, waving slightly to tell her to break off contact with the bodyguard she was plainly walking toward.

The club catered to everyone, from the college-aged vacationers to the senior set. Picking a likely victim from them was harder, but Lauren finally decided on a man and woman in their fifties. The woman obviously didn't care for the way some of the girls were dressed and kept making comments to her husband, who was already three sheets to the wind. She would be the type to squawk the loudest when something went wrong.

The man paid in cash when the drinks came, reaching inside his jacket to pull out his wallet.

Lauren timed her passage by the man as a server came along at the same time. They had to navigate the narrow space between tables.

"Oh. I'm sorry. I wasn't watching where I was going." Lauren stepped back and *accidentally* tripped herself, bumping into the man and falling against him.

Even though he was inebriated, he made a valiant attempt to rescue her. She ended up having to save herself but also managed to end up sitting halfway in his lap.

"My word!" The wife's voice was loud and shrill, the perfect kind of voice to draw attention. "Perhaps you've been drinking too much."

"Actually, it's the heels. I'm not used to wearing them." Lauren gave a wan smile and lifted one heel to show off the tall spike. The heels were taller than she normally wore because she was fairly tall already, but she was comfortable in them. She used them in her occasional magic act. "I'm sorry."

"It's okay." The man held on to Lauren. "I've got you. No worries."

The woman smiled and patted Lauren on the hand. "You poor thing. The shoes are beautiful, but perhaps in the future you should stick with ones you can manage."

"I will." Lauren acted as though she had difficulty getting to her feet, and the man gently nudged her up. She waved her right arm, and the bangles slid and gleamed in the light. While the man was helping her, she slipped her hand inside his jacket and glided the wallet free. She twisted it and hid it beneath her clutch. "Thank you. My name is Clarissa."

"Wonderful name." The woman nodded in approval. "My name is Ruth Beebe. This is my husband, Ralph. We're on holiday from Melbourne."

"I thought I recognized that accent." Lauren focused on Ralph. "Thank you for rescuing me, Ralph."

"No worries, miss. No worries. Quite enjoyable, actually." The man gazed after her and smiled hugely, drawing ire from his wife.

Glancing across the room, Lauren saw that Heath was sitting at his table, but he was now accompanied by two college women who were talking with animation. Irritation flared through Lauren, and she pushed it away because she had a man to frame.

In less than five minutes, she'd picked the pockets of three other men. She walked over to the bodyguard, who was hitting on an elegant woman with coffee-colored skin and a French accent. Lauren stepped in behind the man at the bar and ordered a glass of wine. While she waited, she tucked some of the captured wallets into the bodyguard's jacket without him noticing.

After paying the bartender, she started to walk away with the glass of wine in her right hand. With her left hand, she opened the first wallet she'd gotten and dropped it on the floor as she bumped into the bodyguard. Ralph Beebe's identification and credit cards were loose in the fold where she'd left them. When the wallet it the floor, the contents scattered.

Lauren instantly knelt down. "So sorry. Let me get that for you."

The bodyguard ignored her at first, then noticed the woman he'd been chatting up wasn't enchanted by his reluctance to help out. He knelt down, too, and began gathering the credit cards. "It's okay. Not my wallet."

Lauren picked up the driver's license that plainly showed Ralph Beebe. She glanced over at Ralph with a look of shock. "Ralph, how did your driver's license get all the way over here?"

Ralph shook his head. "Can't be my wallet."

Lauren held up the driver's license. "This is you." Beside her, the bodyguard had frozen, not sure what he'd gotten involved with.

Ruth slapped her husband on the arm. "Don't be an idiot. Check your wallet."

Ralph shook his head. "It's not mine, I tell you." He reached into his jacket, then looked surprised. "Hey! My wallet is missing!"

Right on cue, Ruth leveled her arm at the bodyguard, pointing at him in accusation. "That man has my husband's wallet! He stole poor Ralph's wallet! Security! *Security!*"

"Hey, wait a minute." The bodyguard stood and raised his hands. "I didn't do anything. I don't know where that wallet came from."

Ruth and Ralph got up from their seats and came over to examine the wallet. Their voices rose, drawing the attention of everyone nearby. Guys in black T-shirts with Security stamped on them rushed toward the group.

Okay, your work here is done. Quietly and quickly, Lauren eased out of the crowd, barely avoiding the security people as they closed in. She headed for Heath's table, trying unsuccessfully to ignore the young women sitting with him.

The two women glanced at her, too, then shut up and tried to make themselves smaller. One of them looked as if she wanted to say something, but the other woman yanked on her arm and whispered something in her ear. Together, they got up and left, taking their drinks with them.

Heath remained sitting, his attention riveted on the situation rapidly escalating at the front of the club. "What did you do?"

"I'm still trying to find out who killed my sister. Are you interested, or are you taking the evening off?" Lauren knew it was a cheap shot and wasn't necessary, but adrenaline was flooding through her body and she couldn't keep quiet.

Heath remained calm and spoke in a level tone. "What did you do?"

Lauren stood there but didn't look back. "Unless I miss my guess, that bodyguard is about to be arrested for being a pickpocket."

"You framed him with that wallet."

"And with others that are going to be found on him when the police come."

"Why?"

"To separate him from the others. I got him away from them. Do you think you can find out when they let him go?"

Heath was silent for a minute, thinking, watching her with those green-flaked gold eyes. "Yeah. I can do that."

"Then maybe we can find out more about Gibson." Lauren walked toward the exit then, not wanting to be recognized by Ruth and Ralph. She still felt bad about getting them involved in the situation. She just hoped it would be worth it and that Heath could seal the deal on his end.

Chapter 10

"She framed this guy with wallets she'd pickpocketed from other club guests?" Jackson Portman sounded incredulous at the other end of the phone connection. "And nobody tripped to that?"

"Yeah." Heath sat behind the wheel of a van he'd "rented" from the same uncle of the kid who had sold him the gun. He'd also paid to have the vehicle detailed and "lost" after he'd finished using it for tonight's soiree.

Jackson laughed uproariously. "Buddy, you have *got* to bring this woman back to 'Lanta. I want to meet her."

Irritation flared through Heath. He didn't want to be around Lauren Cooper any longer than he had to, and he wished she wasn't here now. Mostly. She had a lot of brass, and she was beautiful. "No, you don't want to meet her. She's trouble."

"Trouble? Sounds like she set up a situation where you can have a little personal session with one of Gibson's errand boys."

"She framed him for stealing."

"Says the guy who's patiently waiting outside the city lockup to kidnap the same man. Even in Jamaica they frown on kidnapping a lot more than they do stealing. Or framing someone."

Heath knew he couldn't argue that. He'd gotten the van, duct tape and a black hood for that very purpose. "I can't let the opportunity pass by. But that's only if the guy gets out on his own. If he has one of the other men pick him up, things will get harder."

"You gonna back off if that happens?"

"No."

"Okay, now this ain't so funny." Jackson's voice grew more serious. "One guy, with surprise on your side, I can see how you might think you can get this done. But these guys are military trained, Heath, not the chowderheads we deal with on the street. They ain't nobody to jack around with."

"Yeah, I get that." Heath fingered the lead-filled blackjack lying on the seat beside his thigh.

"You and me have done some cowboy stuff before, buddy, but it was only as we needed to."

"Need to do this now."

"I know you feel that way."

"Not just feel, *know* I have to." Heath stared through the bug-smeared windshield at the exit from the police lockup. It was three in the morning, and the streets were dark in this section of the city. "I'm not getting any closer to Gibson doing this any other way."

"I know, I know. Believe me, I feel you. Where's your girl?"

"She's not my girl." The response came out hotter than Heath expected.

"Touch a nerve there, partner?"

Heath sighed. "She's complicating everything. It is hard enough watching Gibson, trying to figure out what he's doing, without trying to look out for her, too. She doesn't know what she's doing, and now I'm getting stretched thin trying to guess what she might do, too. This thing tonight caught me completely off guard."

"I like what she's doing so far."

"I don't."

"Maybe you need to take the crankypants off and accept the fact that she gave you this guy."

"For all I know, Gibson's going to send a small army down here to get him."

"Crankypants and Debbie Downer. You're falling apart. No matter what, she made something happen tonight. Changed the status quo. You and I both know that's worth something."

"I know."

"You got a guy on the inside of the jail there who's gonna let you know the score on the release?"

"Yeah. FBI agent I talked to when I got down here gave me the name of a jailer that can be bought. Information can be hard to get down here. Sometimes persons of interest pursued by the FBI get *accidentally* released before the agents can pick them up."

"Sounds like the system works both ways."

"It does. I'm just hoping tonight that it works my way. Since the man is from out of country and there's home field advantage, I'm thinking I have a good chance."

"I seen this guy's jacket." Jackson sounded intensely serious now. "Guy's a killer. All of Gibson's so-called security people appear to be."

"They have something in common. Only they kill for money. Gibson kills for something else."

Adrenaline flowing into his body and his pulse rate quickening, Heath spotted his target. "Showtime."

Jackson's chair squeaked at the other end of the connection. "I wish I was there, buddy."

"Me, too."

"Let me know when you're outta the fire."

"Yeah." Heath folded the phone and put it into his pocket. He reached into the passenger seat for the black full facemask and pulled it on. Only his eyes were visible. He fisted the blackjack and opened the door. He'd already extracted the courtesy light from the dome so the vehicle's interior remained dark.

He slipped across the street and hid in the shadows with the blackjack lying along his leg. The exit from the building was just around the corner. A car sped along the darkened street, the pools of light from the headlights momentarily tearing holes in the night.

The man, Vincent Sisco, reached the sidewalk talking on a cell phone. "Yeah, yeah, I'm out. Send somebody to get me." He lifted his head and looked around. "Yeah, well, he ain't *here*. I'm here, but he ain't here, Roylston. I know 'cause I'm standing out here tired and hungry and there ain't nobody else out there." He swore. "I'll call him. He's probably at a joint nearby."

Sisco put his phone away for a moment, then stood long enough to light a cigarette behind cupped hands. He inhaled deeply and blew smoke out as he walked away from Heath. He was cursing as he punched numbers on the cell phone.

Heath followed quickly, hating the fact that the man had gone away from him instead of coming to him. Tension rattled through him as he closed the distance faster than he would have liked to. He stepped carefully, avoiding making any noise, but men out on the battlefield developed a sixth sense about being hunted. Heath's own combat readiness had saved him more than once in Atlanta's alleys.

Vincent Sisco evidently had the same internal warning system. Heath knew that he'd made no noise, that the shadows were falling the other way from the streetlight up ahead, but Sisco turned toward him anyway and dropped into a martial arts crouch.

Heath could hear Jackson's mocking voice in his head as he squared off with his intended prey. *Last thing you needed tonight, brother, a Jackie Chan wannabe.*

Only Sisco wasn't a wannabe. He had the skills, and he wasn't shy about using them. The bodyguard threw a short left jab at Heath's throat, going for the soft spots, not the face. Heath got his right hand up in time to block the blow with his forearm. The impact partially numbed his arm all the way to the elbow.

Sisco followed up with a roundhouse right kick into Heath's side that knocked the wind from his lungs and might have cracked a rib or two. The guy was *fast*. Even as Heath got himself set, the guy unfurled a left snap kick aimed at his groin. Sidestepping to his right, synching into the man's frenetic rhythm, Heath dodged the kick, then avoided the short jab at his throat again, managing to catch Sisco's arm in his left and holding on to it.

Before his opponent could yank his arm free, Heath hammered Sisco's shoulder with the blackjack. The limb went limp in Heath's grip, and he released his hold on it. Face racked with pain, Sisco raised his right leg in another roundhouse kick, this one aimed at Heath's head. Heath blocked with his left arm, feeling the pain digging deep into his side, then brought the blackjack down onto Sisco's thigh.

The man cried out in pain. When he dropped his leg down again and tried to get it to take his weight, the limb crumpled beneath him, and he fell forward. Instinctively, Heath caught the man, roping an arm around the man's chest, then was fighting for his life again as Sisco jabbed fingers at his eyes.

Heath jerked his head, avoiding the cruel fingers, and head-butted the man in the face, feeling Sisco's nose snap. As the man staggered back on his one good leg, Heath swung the blackjack again, catching his opponent under the ear this time.

Sisco's eyes rolled white, and he fell. This time, Heath let the man fall, not wanting to touch him again until he was certain Sisco was unconscious. As the man lay there, a car came around the street at the end of the block, the lights gleaming against the office buildings. The vehicle cruised slowly while the brake lights lit up intermittently.

On the ground beside Sisco, the dropped cell phone started ringing.

Heath had no doubts that the car slowly coming this way was Sisco's ride. Unwilling to give up his prize so easily, Heath scooped up the phone, dropped it into his pocket, and pulled Sisco up over his shoulder. Before he could start back to the parked van, the car's engine accelerated, and the vehicle braked to a screeching halt out in the street beside Heath.

"Hey!" The driver got out and stood behind the open door. He aimed a large pistol across the top of the car. "Stop right there!"

Heath turned slowly, not certain what his next step was. If the jailers came out of the building, things were going to get even worse.

Another engine roared to life, then Heath watched in disbelief as the van he'd acquired for the night jumped into motion and sped straight at the car. Panicked, the driver whirled and fired two shots at the approaching van, which was gaining speed.

The van plowed into the car, knocking it back several feet. The driver went backward and down, firing one more shot into the air, then he was hanging on to the door as the car skidded back the way it had come.

Heath stared at the bullet holes over the van's driver's side window, totally expecting whoever had been driving to have been shot. Instead, Lauren Cooper's head popped up and looked frantically around as the van rocked to a stop.

Her wide eyes focused on Heath. "Get in!"

My God, you're crazy! Heath couldn't believe she had just done what she'd done, but he started moving on autopilot. The adrenaline spiking his body gave him extra strength and speed, and he jogged over to the van. He popped the side door and shoved his unconscious burden inside, clambering over the man a moment later.

"Are you all right?" Lauren twisted around in her seat and looked at him.

"Me? That guy was shooting at you." Heath flailed out a hand for the roll of duct tape, caught it, then rose on his knees and peered through the windshield.

"I know." Lauren looked at the unconscious man on the floor of the van. "Are you kidnapping that man?"

Heath rolled Sisco over and pulled his hands behind his

back, then started taping his wrists together. "No, I'm wrapping him for Christmas."

"You can't just kidnap him!" She stared at him in disbelief.

On the other side of the windshield, the driver started getting to his feet. The interior light streaming from the car revealed his search for the pistol he'd dropped.

"You going to let him start shooting again?" Heath pushed himself to his feet and crouch-walked toward the front two seats.

She shoved the transmission into Reverse and floored the accelerator. The van's engine had demonstrated more power than Heath had expected, and he guessed that this wasn't the first one his contact had supplied for nefarious purposes.

Caught off guard, Heath lost his footing and smashed against the windshield. Before he could recover, Lauren straight-armed him in the side, hitting the same injured ribs the captured man had given him. He cried out in pain just as the driver fired two more shots. One of the rounds punched through the windshield and whistled through the space where he'd just been. The other whistled off the van's nose.

The jail's door opened, and uniformed men peered outside. They had automatic weapons and brandished them with authority.

"Halt!"

Heath dropped into the passenger seat and grabbed for the safety belt. The van started slowing. He pulled the belt around him and stared at Lauren. "What are you doing?"

Both hands on the steering wheel, Lauren looked at the jailers. "They're the police."

"Yeah, they are. And they're going to be really interested in what we're doing out here. Especially after they find out about him." Heath jerked his thumb over his shoulder.

"I didn't kidnap him."

"I don't think they're going to be happy with people driving over pedestrians in the street, either."

"That guy started shooting."

"Go!" Heath placed his foot on top of hers and floored the accelerator again, hoping she kept control of the vehicle.

Startled into action, Lauren looked back over her shoulder and somehow managed to keep the van between the buildings and shot across the intersection. Cars narrowly missed them. Horns blared and brake lights flared ruby all around them.

"Now forward."

Lauren took her foot off the accelerator and placed it on the brake. Once the van had stopped, she put the transmission into Drive and looked at the traffic light in front of them.

Heath gazed around, wondering what she was seeing. "What are you waiting for?"

"The light's red."

Despite the fear that was thundering through him, Heath couldn't help laughing. Sometimes that happened when things got tense. During those times, Jackson Portman swore that Heath was insane.

The laughter evidently touched a nerve. Lauren shoved her foot down on the accelerator and swerved to the right, narrowly avoiding locking bumpers with a car in the oncoming lane. She also cursed at him. "There's nothing funny about this."

Heath shifted in the seat, trying to find a comfortable position because the ribs were aching something fierce at the moment, but that pursuit was made even more impossible by the safety belt and Lauren's erratic driving.

"I know, I know. Sorry. But it was kind of funny at the time."

Lauren got the van straightened out, and they hurtled down the street for two blocks. Then she forced her breath out and spoke without looking at him. "The police are going to be after us. I don't want to be arrested. And I don't know where I'm going." Her voice sounded ragged and hard.

"It's okay. I do." Heath knew she was on the verge of losing it. Truthfully, he didn't know how she'd done everything she'd already done. He'd had a lot of experience in the military as a soldier and in Atlanta as a police officer and detective. His younger years hadn't been spent without incident, either. "I know where we're going."

"Okay." Lauren took a breath and relaxed a little.

"We're going to be fine. At the next intersection, take another right."

"Okay."

"And you can slow down a little."

Lauren nodded and eased off the accelerator. She made the turn, and Heath kept watch for any signs of pursuit.

Chapter 11

"I can't believe you *kidnapped* that man." Lauren stood with her arms crossed in an alley in a part of Kingston that she knew she wouldn't have visited during the daylight. She was certain rats patrolled the overflowing garbage bin, and from the raw stink that filled the air between the warehouses near the harbor, she felt positive that bodies had been left there.

She didn't want to be there. More than anything, though, she wished she could stop shaking. Now that everything seemed to be over, now that there was no more shooting and it looked as though they had escaped police pursuit, she felt as if she was going to be sick. She didn't want to think about how close the bullets had come.

Bullets. She couldn't believe she'd even thought that.

"Me?" Heath slid the van's side door open with a rasping squeak that sounded loud enough to broadcast for miles. He was irritatingly cool and collected by comparison. "You framed this guy and got him arrested. You wanted me to talk to him, right?"

"Yes. *Talk* to him. Not kidnap him." Lauren hadn't envisioned that Heath would act so directly.

"Seriously? How was I supposed to get him to talk to me?" Heath sounded as if he was torn between anger and incredulity. "This guy is a trained mercenary and works for a man we think is a serial killer, and he gets busted for something he *knows* he didn't do, and somehow that's going to persuade him to become my best friend so he'd reveal all his boss's dirty secrets?"

Lauren hesitated, knowing, even though the kidnapping was beyond what she had imagined Heath would do, what she had imagined had been close. "I thought maybe you'd rough him up a little."

"'Rough him up?' How, exactly, is that different from kidnapping him?"

Lauren glared at him, for the moment hating the logic he was insisting on. "It's not *kidnapping*. It's…different."

Heath snorted and leaned in to check his prisoner. The man was still unconscious.

Worried, Lauren leaned in. "Are you sure he's breathing?"

"Yes, I'm sure he's breathing."

"You hit him pretty hard."

"I didn't hit him any harder than I needed to. I know what I'm doing."

"You routinely kidnap people?"

"No, I don't routinely kidnap people. But I've subdued perps before, and I've knocked out a few guys."

Lauren didn't know how to react to that.

Heath pulled back out of the van and momentarily his body was pushed up against hers because she hadn't noticed him shifting until he was there.

Pressed against him, Lauren felt the tension in him, felt the hard planes of his back and the taut muscles of his shoulders. She'd gotten the impression of strength when she'd struggled with him at the morgue, but he felt different now. There was something more feral about him. At this moment, he fit in this alley and in this dark part of the world.

Shocked a little, Lauren drew back and stumbled. Heath caught her by the shoulder, hand moving so fast that she didn't even see it in motion. His steely fingers stopped just short of biting into the flesh of her upper arm.

"Are you okay?" The anger was gone from his voice now, only concern sounded in there, and those green-flecked gold eyes softened.

"Yes. I'm fine." She wanted to shove his hand away, but he guided her a couple steps back to the driver's seat.

"Why don't you sit down? I suspect tonight has been a bit much."

"It's my first kidnapping." Reluctantly, Lauren sat. Once he was sure she was settled, Heath pulled back and looked at her.

"You didn't get hurt when you crashed into that car, did you?"

She shook her head. "I don't think so. I don't feel hurt. I just got light-headed there for a second."

"Adrenaline overload. You'll be all right in a few minutes." Heath reached into the back of the van and handed her a bottle of water. "Here. Drink this."

Almost childlike, Lauren uncapped the bottle and drank. Her lips quivered, and some of the water dribbled down her chin.

Heath stood in front of her, watching over her and the— *their*—prisoner. "How did you get there tonight?"

She stared at him. "Do you really think we have time to go into this now?"

With a nonchalant air, Heath leaned against the van. "We have to wait for Sleeping Beauty to wake up."

"You're just going to question him here? In the alley?"

"Yes. I don't want him to know for certain who has him. Which is why I was wearing this." Heath plucked the black mask from his back pocket. He frowned as he regarded her. "I don't want him to recognize you, either." He reached back into the van, pulled a strip of duct tape from the roll on the floor, and strapped it across the man's eyes. "When he wakes up, I'm going to ask the questions. You keep quiet. Gibson and his security people might guess that I had a hand in this, but they don't need to know about you. Now, how did you get there tonight?"

Lauren shot him a look. "The police arrested him. He was going to jail. I figured you would be here, so I came along."

"To do what?"

"To see if you…talked to him."

"What were you going to do while I *talked* to him?"

"Wait. Then talk to you and find out what you'd discovered."

Heath held up a Baggie that contained a cell phone, wallet, coins and paper money and keys. "Not much. Guy travels light."

Lauren studied the bag. "That's a smartphone. He's probably got numbers and maybe even an itinerary on it."

"That's why I took it."

"Then they'll know that you know." Lauren shook her head. "You should copy whatever information you find there, then put the phone back so he won't know you've looked at it. That way—" She stopped when she realized Heath was just looking at her. "What?"

"Are you sure this is your first kidnapping?" He was smiling at her.

She grimaced impatiently. "The kind of trouble we're in, and you think this is funny?"

"It kind of is, yeah. You're the one with the big idea of talking to this guy, now you just want to give him back. For all you know, this guy helps Gibson kill his victims."

That hurt. For a moment Lauren had a brief vision of Megan struggling against her captors in the water. Heath was right. Even if the man hadn't helped Gibson, there was little doubt that the man knew what kind of monster he had for an employer.

"Sorry." Heath shook his head. "My partner thinks I've got a twisted sense of humor. At the wrong times. Janet used to say the same thing." He took the smartphone from the Baggie and started it up.

The view screen lit up, standing out brightly in the dark

alley. Several small eyes in the garbage reflected the illumination. Lauren tried not to think about that.

"The phone's pass-code protected." Heath growled and started to drop the phone back into the Baggie. "I'll have to keep it and see if I can get someone to scrape the information off the SIM card."

"Do you think you're going to find anything on that card?"

"Don't know till I try."

"I can't see this man leaving pictures of previous murders on his phone." A chill chased through Lauren. "Or even taking pictures of something like that."

"Men like Gibson, men like these mercenaries, they're not wired like your average person, Lauren. That's something you need to know about them." Heath frowned at her. "Especially if you're going to continue to play in their sandbox."

"I'm not playing in their sandbox. I'm trying to find out who killed my sister."

"I know." Heath regarded her levelly. "Something else you should know—I'll do *anything* it takes to find the man who killed Janet and those other women. And I won't let anyone stand in the way."

The wind slipping through the alley seemed to drop a few degrees as she looked at him. She knew that he meant it. If she hadn't been convinced that Gibson had killed Megan, she would have been worried that Heath might let his pain and loss blind him to the point that he would persecute an innocent man. But she was convinced of Gibson's guilt, as well.

The unconscious man inside the van rolled slightly, moaned and turned his head.

Heath put a finger to his lips, then turned his full attention to the prisoner. He knotted a fist in the man's shirt and jerked him up to a sitting position in the open van door.

"Sisco, do you hear me?" Heath's voice was calm and flat, barely loud enough to carry.

"Is that you, cop? You got that redneck accent I can hear.

You better kill me, 'cause when I get loose, I'm gonna kill you." Sisco leaned forward and spat at Heath.

Heath easily dodged, then yanked the man hard to one side, banging his head against the door frame.

The man cursed and started squirming in pain, and Lauren felt even more scared when she realized the man knew who Heath was.

Heath waited till the man's cries subsided. His voice remained level when he spoke. "Nobody said you were getting out of this alive, Sisco. If you don't answer my questions, I'm going to put a bullet in your head and drop you out in the ocean. The crabs and the gulls can finish off what's left of you."

Lauren knew that Heath wouldn't do that; at least, she trusted him not to do that, but the threat made everything worse.

"Roylston will know you grabbed me, and he'll figure I told you everything I know. He'll kill me if you don't."

Lauren thought she was going to be sick. She hadn't thought about that possibility at all.

"Then you've got nothing to lose by telling me what you know."

Sisco shook his head. "Man, you grabbed the wrong guy. You wanted the whole story, you shoulda grabbed Roylston. All I know is that Gibson likes killing women."

"And you just let him? Is that what you're saying? You just let him kill those women?" The words were out of Lauren's mouth before she knew she was going to speak.

Sisco sniffed. "I know that perfume. You're the woman who's so free with everybody else's wallets." He shook his head and winced. "I gotta say, that was pretty slick the way you set me up. Never saw it coming. Did you put her up to that, cop?"

"Tell me about Gibson."

"What's to tell?"

"Why does he kill the women?"

Sisco shrugged. "Guy's sick. Twisted. If you've been in

the military, you've seen guys like him. Probably seen them in Atlanta, too."

Lauren couldn't help herself. "Why are you working for him?"

"Money's good, and Gibson doesn't kill as many people as other employers I've had. You ask me, this is one of the easier assignments I've had. Roylston makes this operation run like goose grease on ice. Keeps us all tight and right."

At the end of the alley, a car rushed by, then brakes squealed and white reverse lights flared to life. An engine roared as the car pulled back to the alley, then changed directions and raced down it.

Smiling, Sisco looked in Heath's direction. "That'll be Roylston. He keeps tabs on everybody. Hope he doesn't kill you too quick."

Instinctively, Lauren ducked down, and it was just ahead of a fusillade of bullets that struck the rear of the van. Broken glass tumbled from the windows. A man hung out the window of the approaching car and fired repeatedly.

It took her a moment, but she thought she recognized the bodyguard who had been sitting with Gibson at the restaurant a couple of days ago. The muzzle flashes highlighted his face for a moment before she ducked below the door and lost sight of him.

The bullets ricocheted off the van and the building walls. At least one of them crashed through Sisco's head in a spray of blood, and he fell back inside the van.

Warm wetness splashed against the side of Lauren's face. She reached up and wiped at it. Her fingers came away stained with crimson, and she almost screamed.

Heath pulled Lauren's upper arm, getting her into motion and keeping her low. He pushed her to keep her moving. "Keep going. Get to the end of the alley. I'll be right behind you."

Frightened, Lauren did as she was told because she couldn't think of anything else to do. Bullets whined off the wall overhead and crashed through the trash cans.

Then heavier *cracks* punctuated the automatic fire. Lauren glanced back over her shoulder and saw Heath firing from behind the open driver's door. In the next instant, he turned and charged toward her, easily overtaking her and grabbing her by the arm again.

"C'mon!"

Lauren ran, somehow matching him stride for stride till they reached the end of the alley. Heath paused at the corner with his back against the wall. Without looking, he opened the revolver and shook the hot brass into his hand, dropping it into his jacket pocket and bringing out new shells, inserting them into the cylinder, then snapping the cylinder closed again.

Peering around his shoulder, Lauren saw the other vehicle had stopped in front of the van, unable to proceed any farther. At least two men climbed out of the car because their weapons flickered lightning on both sides of the alley. Neither of them appeared to be in any hurry to pursue Heath and Lauren.

Heath whirled around and looked at the street as a taxi came up it. He grabbed Lauren's hand and pulled her out into the street, waving to cut the taxi off. She assumed the driver didn't see the gun in Heath's hand, because the vehicle came to a stop beside them.

Opening the door, Heath pushed her inside. Instinct took over, and she climbed in willingly. Heath dropped into the seat beside her and addressed the driver, giving him the name of a club downtown.

Lauren turned to him as the taxi pulled away from the curb and the two shadows halted at the alley mouth. "Where are we going? We need to go to the police!" That caught the taxi driver's attention, and he glanced up at the rearview mirror. "We can't just—"

Heath leaned in and kissed her, taking her breath away and shorting out her senses. She wanted to push him off her, might have even tried, but he twisted in the seat and wrapped his arms around her, holding her tight. The immediate panic passed, and she gave herself over to the kiss, losing herself in it. A fire ignited in her belly, and she knew it had been there for the past couple days. Fear swirled into hunger, and she lifted her hand and cupped the back of his head, pulling him in close because having him there made her feel alive, and she knew she'd come close to not being alive.

He opened his mouth, demanded access to her, and she gave it willingly, surprised at the appetite that threatened to consume her in a rush. He tasted sweet and strong and masculine, and he growled as his own need flowered within him, too.

His hand drifted down her body, pulling her closer, drifting farther down till he cupped her hip and held on tight. She put her other hand on his jaw, feeling the rough, sandpapery stubble that covered his chin. For the moment, all that mattered was having him close, but that was triggering a greater need in her she didn't want to address.

Out of air, needing to breathe, Lauren pulled back from Heath. After a quick breath, he came after her again, but she noticed that the taxi driver was paying more attention to the rearview mirror than to the street. The shadows must have hidden the blood on her face.

"No." Lauren slid a hand over his mouth and blocked his attempts to kiss her again. "No."

Reluctantly, Heath pulled back against the seat as if it took all his strength to do that. "Okay." Lights from passing streetlamps and businesses that were still open flashed in his gold eyes and caught on the green flakes. "Maybe we can talk about the other thing later."

Not trusting herself to speak, Lauren nodded.

Once they arrived at the club Heath had suggested, he paid the driver and took Lauren's hand. They walked three blocks through the downtown party area and stayed in the shadows. Heath kept checking behind them, but he didn't act as if anyone was following them.

At the corner, he flagged down another taxi and told the driver to take them back to the jail.

Chapter 12

Surprisingly, there was no real activity at the jail building. Lauren had expected a gathering of police cars, emergency vehicles and fire trucks as there were in movies and television shows. Instead, only a spray of broken glass marked the area where she'd driven the van into the car.

Heath caught her looking around and squeezed her hand. "The police won't be here. They'll be working the murder in the alley."

"The murder." Lauren repeated the words and still had trouble wrapping her mind around it.

"Yeah. Those guys murdered Sisco. They were there to take out everyone."

"That doesn't make any sense."

"They were trying to kill us. Sisco was just collateral damage. We got lucky."

It wasn't just luck. Heath had gotten them moving quickly, too.

"What are you driving?"

Mechanically, functioning on fumes of adrenaline now, Lauren pointed out the compact rental she'd arranged.

Still holding on to her arm as if they were out for a night on the town, Heath walked them over to the vehicle. "Let me have your keys."

Lauren thought briefly of arguing with him, of telling him she was capable of driving, then she decided it wasn't worth the effort. She handed the keys over. Heath opened the passenger door and put her inside, then slid behind the wheel, and they were off.

At the hotel where Lauren was staying, Heath pulled the car into the outside parking lot, then got out with her and led the way toward the building. The hotel was set back from the main streets, and darkness surrounded them. On previous nights, the darkness hadn't bothered Lauren, but now it felt almost threatening as she crossed the short expanse of pavement to the side entrance.

She was walking better, more focused. "I can make it to my room."

"I can walk you." Heath was distracted, looking all around them.

No one was in the mezzanine when they entered the hotel. Lauren's stomach clenched as they crossed the open area, expecting to be apprehended at any moment. She felt almost relieved when they stepped into the elevator.

Heath's hand hesitated over the buttons. "What floor?"

"Five." Lauren glanced at her reflection in the stainless-steel panels that covered the doors. She had something on her face. Her skin felt tight. Automatically, she reached up to brush at her cheek.

Heath caught her hand and trapped it gently. "Don't."

She looked at him, swallowed hard, and tried not to freak out when she realized what the dark splotches were. "I've got his blood on my face."

"Not for long."

That wasn't any kind of answer. Lauren wanted it *off.* Now. She clenched her fist and willed herself not to touch her face, but she couldn't help glancing down and seeing more blood spattered over the black pullover she was wearing.

"Just stay calm. We're almost there."

She made herself nod, but her breathing was strained.

"Where's your room key?"

Grateful for something else to think about, something else to do, Lauren slipped the key card to her room from the back pocket of her jeans. She handed it to Heath and let him guide her to one side of the door.

"I need you to stay back just a minute." He had his pistol in hand, covered by the loose folds of his jacket, when he slipped the key card through the slot. When the light flashed green, he pulled the lever down with his left hand and leaned a shoulder into the door. He relaxed a little and turned to her. "Okay." He stepped to the side so she could enter. "Does anything look moved? Touched in any way?"

Lauren entered the room and looked around. Her suitcases were in the closet, her iPad on the desk on the charger, and her clothing was hung as she'd left it. "No. Everything's fine."

"Good. I don't think they know about you, but I didn't think they'd have a tracker on Sisco, either. I don't want to be surprised again tonight." Heath slid the pistol back into the holster on his hip.

Pausing in front of the mirror at the vanity, Lauren looked at herself, shocked at the blood that marred the side of her face, her neck and her hair. She didn't know how the taxi drivers had missed seeing that. Then she thought maybe the man hadn't and that the Kingston constables were already en route.

She grabbed a handful of tissues from the box in the vanity and started scrubbing at the blood on her cheek, but it wouldn't come off because it was dried. She started to shake then, and she scrubbed even harder.

"Hey." Heath stood behind her. "Calm down."

"Calm down?" She glared at him in the mirror, unable to

stop scrubbing. "I've got someone's blood on me. It's in my *hair*."

"It'll wash out." Gently, Heath took her hands and kept her from scrubbing. "Take a shower. Everything's going to be all right."

She looked at him, wishing she could believe him, but he had blood on his face, too. Both of them had been *so* close to dying. She closed her eyes and saw the man getting shot again, his head snapping back, feeling the warm wetness on her face.

"Get some clothes. Take a shower. You'll feel better."

Lauren just looked at him, not believing that he thought a shower was going to fix everything. When she didn't move, he went to the chest of drawers and began searching through them.

Watching him paw through her underwear broke her out of her trance. "What are you doing?"

"You need clothing."

"Stay out of there."

Heath ignored her, emerging with a pair of panties, sweat pants and an oversized T-shirt, all things that she liked to lounge in and sleep in. He handed them to her. "Here."

Not knowing what else to do, Lauren took the proffered clothing.

"Shower." Heath gave her a gentle shove to get her moving.

"Aren't you leaving?"

Heath looked at her and spoke softly. "No. I'm not leaving. I'm going to be right here."

For a moment, Lauren remembered the kisses in the taxi. Her body still thrummed with excitement, but it was mixed in with the residual aftereffects of the near-miss in the alley. She felt confused, not certain what Heath's motives were.

He turned from her, though, and walked to the window. He stripped his jacket off and dropped it onto the chair by the small table, then moved a chair so he could more easily peer out the window as well as watch the news on the television he angled his way.

Not knowing what else to do, lost amid all the conflicting

emotions, Lauren retreated to the bathroom. She took off her clothing with shaking hands, feeling terribly cold all of a sudden. Then she stepped under the shower spray and turned it up as hot as she could bear. For a long time, she just stood there and let the wet heat seep into her. She turned her face up to the spray and let it run through her hair, not looking down to see if the blood was sluicing from her body.

With her eyes shut against the shower, she kept seeing the gunfire again and again, but mixed in there, she kept feeling Heath's lips pressed against hers.

"Heath?" Jackson Portman sounded tense. "Buddy, I was about to give up on you getting back to me."

"Told you I'd call." Heath sat in the chair looking through the window out at the parking lot. Nothing was moving. The street out in front of the hotel only had occasional traffic.

"Get anything?"

"Gibson is our guy. The man we took down tonight—Sisco—confirmed that Gibson is killing the women."

"Wait a minute. *We?*"

"Yeah. Lauren worked herself into the snatch. Saved my butt, actually, but everything went sideways on us." As Heath relayed the story, he couldn't help thinking about Lauren in the shower. The water ran steadily, and he knew it was tracing every curve. He kept thinking about the kisses in the taxi, as well. He'd kissed her to shut her down, to keep her from speaking. At least, that was what it had started out being. At the end there, he wasn't sure what that was about, but she had seemed to be getting into it.

"This guy Roylston was the one that pulled the trigger?"

Heath played the scene over in his mind again. There had been too many variables in play. He hadn't been expecting to be found, hadn't been expecting Lauren to be there, and he hadn't expected everything to turn so violent so quickly. His first instinct had been to get Lauren safe, not identify the shooters.

But he felt certain he'd seen Roylston's face revealed in the muzzle flashes.

"Yeah, I think so. Things happened pretty fast once they arrived."

"Sisco getting dropped like that is gonna send a message to the rest of Gibson's bodyguards. They're all expendable."

"I know, but something about the shooting doesn't feel right."

"What do you mean?"

"Back at the jail, Sisco's partner came to pick him up. If he'd been worried about Sisco talking, he could have opened fire on both of us."

"Maybe Lauren ran the van into him before he could."

"No. He had time to shoot. He was trying to protect his partner. Doesn't make sense that he would kill him so easily a few minutes later."

"His partner probably got picked up by the police out in front of the jail. He probably wasn't even there, so he didn't have a say."

"Maybe not, but his response felt different than those guys back in the alley. Roylston and his crew came to kill somebody."

"Could be you triggered that reaction out of Gibson by confronting him."

"This wasn't Gibson. He's too interested in gaming me. He's a guy who wants to taunt every chance he gets, then slide the knife in slow. If you met him, I bet you'd read him the same way. This thing tonight was a burn. Roylston, if that was him, was happy to sacrifice one of the bodyguards in an attempt to get me."

"That doesn't make sense."

"It does if Roylston doesn't like the way Gibson is dealing with me. The guy's got the money and the connections, Jackson. He could be in the wind, gone too far and too fast for me to follow. My pockets aren't as deep as his. He could leave me at the starting gate. Instead, it's like he's baiting me."

"All the more reason to regroup and bring it home, buddy."

"I know. I'm giving that some serious thought." Heath gazed back at the bathroom. "I need to get Lauren clear of this whole mess before she gets hurt."

"Good. Because I'd like you to come home, too."

Heath peered out into the darkness, but he wasn't seeing it. He was seeing that crime scene with Janet. "This guy killed Janet. I can't let him get away with it."

"He's not going to get away with it, bro. You know you've got the right guy. Now it's just a matter of police work."

"Police work's not going to reach from Atlanta."

"We'll find something. We'll keep turning things over till we do."

"You and I both know that the captain put everything we could into that investigation. There was nothing at that scene that ties to Gibson. We don't even know what his real name is, and without probable cause, we won't be able to get it. We haven't been able to get through his lawyers."

"I know, but I also know all of this takes time."

"I'm putting pressure on him here. Things are happening."

Jackson sighed. "You're gonna get hurt there, Heath. That woman is going to get hurt. You don't want that to happen."

Heath didn't reply, but he knew it was true. Protecting Lauren Cooper was becoming very important to him.

"You put enough pressure on Gibson down there that you almost got killed. This guy isn't going to let anyone interfere with his games, and he's got a group of heavy hitters working for him. You've seen their rap sheets same as I have. They're not guys you want to meet in dark alleys."

"They won't get me again like that. The tracker surprised me."

"Heath, the next time Roylston surprises you, it might be from behind with a bullet into your ear. Step back from the ledge. Get some perspective."

Everything Jackson said made sense. Reluctant as he was, Heath knew it was the right thing to do. "Okay."

The water in the bathroom stopped running.

Heath sat up a little straighter. "I've got to go."

"Fine. Give me a call in the morning. Let me know when I can expect you here."

"Will do." Heath hung up the phone and sat in the darkness crowding the room.

"I'm not leaving." Feeling somewhat refreshed from the shower, Lauren stood in front of Heath. She hadn't known what to expect when she stepped out into the room, but she had certainly not expected him to still be there, though she hadn't liked the idea of him leaving. She just thought he would have.

Heath sat in the chair at the table. His elbows rested on his knees as he leaned toward her. "This isn't about just you leaving this time, Lauren. It's about *us* leaving. It's not safe here. Gibson or Roylston or someone else will be gunning for us."

"You mean, they'll be gunning for you. They don't know I was involved."

"You don't know that."

"They're not here." Lauren hung on to the outrage she felt. That emotion was the only thing getting her through the residual fear left inside her. "If they knew about me, I think they'd be here right now."

"Maybe. And maybe they're biding their time because the heat is on them right now because of Sisco."

She shook her head. "You're not going to scare me. I'm not going to let you."

"Now is the time to be scared." Heath spoke in a level tone that Lauren hated. He was making too much sense. "This response tonight, it was way more than anything I figured would happen. Gibson is hitting hard and fast."

"That's fine. That's what we want him to do, right?" Lauren knew she was right and held to her conviction. "Come at us and make a mistake?" She thought hurriedly. "In fact, can't that shooting in the alley be used against him? Aren't the police going to investigate him because one of his people was killed?"

A chill ghosted through her as she said that. She wrapped her arms around herself to stay warm. The heat from the shower was already leaving her, but she was still hypersensitive to Heath's presence.

He pointed at the television. "Gibson's people have already got their story in place. Sisco was grabbed outside the jail by persons unknown. Gibson's lawyers say he doesn't know anything about it and random acts of violence aren't his responsibility. Since Gibson has nothing to do with the case, he's not going to get involved."

"What?" Lauren couldn't believe it.

"The police can't do anything but question Gibson about his employee. There's nothing to tie Sisco's death to him."

"Gibson's people killed that man."

"Maybe."

"I saw Gibson's bodyguard there. He was the one firing the gun. I can testify to that."

"Are you sure it was him?"

"Yes. You saw him, too."

"I saw a guy that looked like him. Without physical evidence that concretely says Roylston was there, it would be our word against his. A good attorney will bring up the fact that the alley was dark, that bullets were flying, that the headlights were in our eyes. Those are all things you can sell a jury on, if it ever got past a judge, and you can bet Gibson's attorneys won't let it go that far."

"If we go in, we can tell them he was the one that killed Sisco. If Roylston knows we've identified him, he might get scared. He could plead out and tell the police Gibson sent him there to kill Sisco in exchange for a reduced sentence."

"Did Gibson send Roylston there? That's a jump. This could be something Roylston did on his own to protect his security perimeter. Or maybe Gibson sells Roylston out and says Roylston was working on his own. Again, this might not roll back over onto Gibson. On top of that, Roylston's a mercenary. He's not going to be able to work in his field if he gives up his employer. He gets paid to take the hits. I think he's going to like his chances of running free better than a trial."

Frustrated, Lauren realized that was true.

"Even if the police believed us and arrested Roylston, he'd be out on bail and gone before his trial. Either he'd be out of the country, or maybe Gibson would hire someone else to take him out, if he didn't trust him to keep his mouth shut." Heath's voice remained a soft growl. "Even worse than that, if we offer testimony about what Sisco said and the fact that Roylston *might* have been there, we'd have to explain what we were doing there in that alley."

Lauren closed her eyes in defeat. She hadn't thought of that.

"We'd have to admit we kidnapped Sisco. The police know the man was taken. We'd end up in jail before Gibson did. And I don't think anyone would be interested in testimony from admitted kidnappers working on an agenda to pin your sister's murder and my partner's death on Gibson."

"So we're screwed, is that it? We know Gibson did it and we can't touch him." Anger crept up inside Lauren and outweighed the residual fear that caromed inside her.

"Sisco said that Gibson killed those women. But for all we know, he was lying. Maybe he was the killer and was framing Gibson, and Roylston just executed him tonight to put an end to everything. There might not be any more White Rabbit killings."

Lauren pinned him with her gaze. "Do you think the killing is going to stop?"

Heath returned her gaze full measure for a moment, then he blew out a disgusted breath and shook his head. "No. Whoever killed Janet and your sister and all those other women, he's gotten a taste for blood. Could be he's always had it. Whatever the case, it's not going away. I don't believe Sisco was the killer."

"So we're just supposed to pack up and leave? That's your answer?"

Heath spoke softly, rationally, and that came close to infuriating Lauren. "Leaving is the best thing to do." He paused and shook his head. "Believe me, I don't like it any more than you do."

"What happens to the next girl that Gibson goes after?"

"We need to regroup, find a new way to go at this."

"You're just giving him time to kill again. You've already said that his timetable is accelerating. How many women can he kill while we're regrouping?" Lauren answered before Heath could. "I don't know if you can answer that, but I can tell you this—even one person is too many. You can leave if you want to, but I'm staying."

Slowly, Heath stood and came over to her. "You're a stubborn woman."

"No." Lauren looked up into his eyes, and she remembered the kisses in the back of the taxi. For a minute she thought he was going to try something like that again. "I'm just right, and you know it."

"You are right. So we'll play this out until we've got the answers we're looking for or we're in jail." Heath looked at his watch. "You should get some sleep. Tomorrow's going to start early."

He walked over to the bed, and Lauren briefly thought he intended to stretch out on it, which didn't sound as awkward as it should have. Instead, he pulled a pillow from the bed and crossed the room to the couch. He lay down, kicked off his shoes, and placed the big revolver under his pillow.

"What are you doing?"

"I'm not leaving you alone tonight. That's not happening."

Lauren wanted to protest because she didn't like the idea of Heath invading her space, but she also didn't want to be alone. Reluctantly, she walked to the bed and stripped off the top blanket, then gave it to Heath, surprising him. He didn't say anything, though, and Lauren was glad. She didn't know what he would say, and she definitely didn't know what kind of reply she would make to anything he said.

She returned to the bed, pulled the blanket and sheet back

and crawled in before shutting off the lamp. Darkness enveloped them and quietness filled the room.

For a long time, she lay there listening to Heath breathe. After a few minutes, his breathing deepened, and she knew that he had gone to sleep. She felt tired and she wanted to go to sleep, but memory of the shooting and the way Heath had kissed her in the back of the taxi danced in her head, keeping her alert and thinking until sleep finally claimed her.

Chapter 13

Bright sunlight slanting through the heavy curtains woke Lauren. She shifted in bed and tried to doze off again, but then she spotted Heath Sawyer's lanky body overrunning the small couch at both ends and knew she wasn't getting back to sleep anytime soon.

He slept like a kid, on his back with one arm folded over his eyes. Sometime after he'd gone to bed, he'd taken off his shirt and lay there naked to the waist. His body was hard, his chest was broad, chiseled from working out, and the sight of that smooth, bronze skin awakened a hunger in Lauren that she'd never felt before. She made herself look at his face, but she couldn't maintain her concentration.

Giving up, she got out of bed as quietly as she could, knowing that he needed his sleep. He'd been putting in a lot of hours watching over Gibson, and that had gone on for days before she had joined him.

He turned slightly on the couch, and the blanket drifted farther south. That movement caught Lauren's attention, but his shirt hung by itself on the back of a nearby chair, so she guessed that he was still partially dressed. However, the scar on his left side was revealed. It was pale white with age, but stood out against the tan skin and was at least five inches long. She knew it wasn't from an appendectomy, because it was on the wrong side and ran too vertical.

The scar and the tan both made her curious because she wanted to know where he'd gotten them. The tan looked real, gotten from working outside, not from a tanning bed, and a homicide detective didn't often have cause to take his shirt off at work.

Blood spatters had ruined his shirt. Lauren felt a queasy roll in her stomach just for a moment, then she forced the feeling away. She was surprised that no one had noticed the blood last night, but it had been dark. There was no way Heath was going to be able to walk around in daylight without someone calling the police.

And staying in the hotel room all day, as intriguing as that seemed given the sparks that had flared between them last night, wasn't something Lauren was prepared to risk. The hunt for Megan's killer was complicated enough without pursuing whatever that had been, and she was more than willing to admit it was a mistake brought on by adrenaline.

She knew she needed to get out of the room, away from Heath Sawyer, and clear her head. A brief shopping spree would serve as a good distraction.

Lauren grabbed khaki pants and an orange pullover that she knew fit her nicely and flattered her figure. She headed to the bathroom.

Heath's cell phone woke him with a start. He rolled over on the couch, feeling the aches from sleeping in the cramped space, and grabbed the cell from the floor by the couch. He pulled it to his ear. "Hello."

"Good morning, Detective Sawyer. Sleep well?"

At first, Heath didn't recognize the caller because he'd never before heard him on the phone. "Who is this? How did you get this number?"

"It wasn't hard. I got your friend Janet's number, too."

"Gibson." Heath recognized the carefully enunciated words and laid-back tone then. Gibson was giving a performance.

Heath threw the blanket off and sat up on the couch. He pulled his gun from under the pillow and looked at the hotel door. The interior locks were no longer in place. A trickle of fear snaked down his spine. He glanced over at the bed and saw that it had been made.

Lauren was gone.

Heath got to his feet and shouldered the phone. He walked toward the bathroom, fearing what he might find in there. Even though it didn't make sense that Gibson or his men could have gotten into the hotel, much less known where it was, it also didn't make sense that they would kill Lauren and leave him alive.

Except now he's playing games with you. He's moved into a new phase of his killing.

"You can call me whatever name you want to. I'll answer to it."

Heath rounded the corner to the bathroom with his revolver at the ready. He peered into the room, but it was too dark to see the shower. Flipping on the light switch beside him, his pulse beating at his temples, he looked at the shadows created by the white shower curtain.

There was no blood on the floor. If Lauren had been killed like Janet, there would have been blood everywhere. Heath crossed the room and whipped the shower curtain back. When he saw that it was empty, contained none of the horrors he'd imagined, he let out a long breath.

"What do you want, Gibson?" Turning from the shower, Heath padded barefoot back into the room, looking for some indication of what had happened to Lauren.

Since the bed was made, he felt she'd left of her own volition.

The neatly made bed also made him realize how soundly he'd slept. He'd stayed the night to protect her. Some bodyguard.

"I regret having missed you last night."

"You didn't miss me. Your people missed me. They didn't miss your buddy Sisco. I didn't see you there last night, so I suppose you keep your killing to women." Heath gripped his pistol tightly and looked around the room, finally turning and spotting a note on the mirror of the vanity outside the bathroom.

Went shopping. Back soon. L.

Shopping? Heath held back a curse and kept himself calm with effort. Last night should have taught Lauren the danger they were in.

"You made a mistake last night." Gibson's anger was apparent in his tone.

"No, I didn't. It's just going to be a matter of time till I bring you down."

"That's what your partner thought, didn't she? It didn't work out for her. It won't work out for you."

Gibson broke the connection before Heath could reply. He checked the view screen and only saw Unavailable there. He tried to reconnect the call, but it kept failing out. Cursing, wishing he knew where Lauren Cooper was, he called Jackson Portman.

"Yeah?" Jackson sound tired.

"Catch you at a bad time?"

"Tell me you're on a plane for 'Lanta and I'll get to feeling better quick."

"Gibson just called me."

"Why?"

"To gloat. Do me a favor—dump the phone records on this number and see if you can trace the phone number that called me this morning. It'll be the only incoming call today. You probably won't get anything, but it's worth trying."

"I can do that. When are you headed home?"

"Not now."

"Seriously?"

"Lauren says she's not leaving. I can't make her go." Heath took a breath. "And it's not just her. I can't leave this thing unfinished, either. We've poked Gibson enough that we've got a reaction."

"'We?' That woman's not a partner, buddy. She's not even a cop. She's a civilian. You're letting her get in harm's way. That's not like you."

"If I leave, she's going to stay. I can't let her stay without protection."

"That's not your problem."

"Would you leave?"

Jackson swore.

"Yeah, I didn't think so. I'm going to protect her, and I'm going to get the answers Janet's family needs."

Jackson was quiet for a moment. "Listen, Heath, you and I both have been around the block a time or two. We know there isn't an answer for what happened to Janet. Gibson's a predator, pure and simple. He kills because he wants to."

"Then I'm going to find a way to put him down. I've got to try to give them that. I owe it to them." Heath stared out the window at the tourists walking the street in front of the hotel. There were enough of them that he guessed one or more of the cruise ships were in the harbor.

"Okay. I'll dump this number, see if we find anything."

"Thanks."

"Where's Lauren Cooper now?"

"I don't know."

"Well…that's not good."

"I know." Heath picked up his shirt from the back of the chair and noticed the dark bloodstains all over it. There was no way he could walk around in that shirt without getting the police called. "Get back to me when you can."

"I will."

Heath punched the phone off and slid it into his pocket. He took the shirt to the vanity sink and poured soap all over it, then started washing it by hand. Anxiety thrummed in him. He stared at the mirror. What could she possibly have been thinking?

Blood ran down his fingers and swirled in the sink.

Gibson stood out on the stone veranda at the back of his villa. From that point he had a breathtaking view of the ocean and the harbor in the distance. It was beautiful there early in the morning and at night when the stars filled the sky. Women he'd taken there had all been in awe of the sky and sea.

He sipped champagne and stood there in the clothes he'd worn last night. He'd fallen asleep in the chair in his office, watching some of his best performances and admiring his smooth skills while awaiting word from Roylston.

For a time he'd been enraptured by his performances. Audiences loved him and clamored to know how he did his magic. At least that was what they said. In truth, and Gibson knew this was the truth, they didn't want to know how he did those amazing feats. They wanted to believe. No one did it better. Not Copperfield, not even Houdini himself.

The gold coin twinkled in the morning sunlight as Gibson rolled it across his knuckles. Magic had been his salvation. He'd found it as a child, watching performers and learning their tricks. Nothing about the rest of his life had satisfied him, not the riches, not the cars, not even the women.

Not until he'd learned how to kill. That was the greatest trick of all: the disappearance of another's life. He still didn't know where a person went when they vanished on the other side of death.

He'd been fifteen years old when he'd first killed. The nineteen-year-old girl he'd been dating had told him she was pregnant, obviously planning to burrow her way into the family money because she'd figured out who he really was and had come after him. She'd surprised him with her announcement, telling him while they'd been in a hot tub in a rented hotel room they'd gotten with his father's money.

Gibson had lost control then. At first. He'd clamped his hands around her neck and shoved her under the water. She'd screamed, but her screams had only come out as bubbles that made no sound. She'd fought, and she'd carved furrows down his arms. The scars were still there, grayed out over the years, but reminders all the same. Now he didn't think of them as scars. They were badges, commemorations of his performance.

After a time, too short a time, she'd stopped thrashing and had lain quietly, almost floating. The water had stilled, and he'd studied her face, so slack, so surprised. The blood from the cuts along his forearms had threaded the water with streams of scarlet fog.

That was where he'd been when his father's security people found him after he'd called his father. Years of therapy had followed, but Gibson had worked on his magic in those places, teaching himself more and more. He'd even taught himself to hide his bloodlust from trained observers till he was finally discharged from their care. Everything was illusion.

The girl whose life he'd taken was still presumed a runaway. That had been over a quarter century ago. His father knew how to make things disappear, as well. Gibson had to give the old man that. He respected that. But there was nothing his father cherished about him except the fact that he was the old man's only child and he knew it.

A sailboat ran with the wind out on the horizon, the white sails bright against the gray-green sea and the azure sky. Out on that boat, people would be partying. Probably there would be young people, young women.

The dark hunger stirred restlessly inside Gibson's belly and wormed up to his heart. He embraced the hunger and felt it blossom inside him. Little more than a week had passed since he'd last killed. Normally he didn't feel the need to take a life again so quickly.

But things had changed when he'd killed the woman detective in Atlanta. She had been so smug, so sure of herself, when she'd finally gotten him on the phone. She'd told him that she wanted him to come in for questioning, and Gibson had known she'd thought herself somehow clever enough to trip him up.

She'd been stupid. Gibson's father had tried to break him over the years, and the old man hadn't managed that, either. If he couldn't do it, no one else could.

That woman had been surprised, too, when he'd caught up with her. She'd been alone in her house. Her husband and their two sons had been at a baseball game. A cop's salary didn't provide much in the way of a security system, and her husband didn't make much more than she did. Gibson had been getting past security systems much more sophisticated for years.

He'd arrived at her house shortly after the husband and children had gone. After he'd stolen her away, he'd had hours to kill her in the rented hotel room, and he'd taken his time.

He closed his eyes and remembered, and the salt air around him reminded him of the stink of her blood. He hadn't been able to hear her scream the way he had some of his other victims. There had been too many close neighbors. He'd been forced to cut out her vocal cords first.

Gibson relished the memory, knowing it would always be his. Then the morning heat on his face took him away from that time and brought him back to the veranda.

He realized he was no longer alone.

Turning, he found Roylston standing there with a tube in one hand. The man looked somewhat fatigued from staying up all night.

Gibson sipped the champagne. "Well?"

"The cop's not at his hotel."

The news irritated Gibson. After last night's debacle and the calls from the police about Sisco, he'd hoped to at last put an end to Heath Sawyer's threats. He'd called the man to distract him while Roylston and his team closed in on him.

"You're sure?"

"Yes. We broke into the room and took a look around. We found this." Roylston opened the tube he carried and pulled out a rolled poster. When he spread it, Gibson saw the photographs of the women he'd killed on display there.

Of course, not all of the women were there. Only a small sampling of those whose lives he'd vanished were represented there. Heath Sawyer and his dead partner hadn't figured out everything. Gibson hadn't started sending the White Rabbit cards until the past few years. Just to make the trick more interesting and to build an audience.

"Then where is he?"

Roylston shook his head. "I don't know. His car was there, too. We found it in the parking lot. He's not driving it."

Heath's disappearance irritated Gibson. The man was a loose cannon. Gibson didn't think Heath could do anything to him other than make life somewhat uncomfortable, but he wanted the man out of the way at this point. "Did you trace the van he used last night?"

"We did, but we didn't have any more luck than the police did. The van has been used in some criminal activities before. Tracked its VIN number to some impounds regarding drug deals and theft, nothing else. It's a scab vehicle. Somebody rented it or sold it to the cop off the books."

"Then find that person."

"We're looking."

Gibson felt like exploding at Roylston, but he knew it wouldn't do any good. The man would only point out that killing the woman detective had caused all their current grief. And that maybe attacking the last woman so close to home hadn't been smart. He'd already mentioned those things. Gibson didn't want a replay.

He turned his back on Roylston. "Let me know when you find Sawyer. And put that poster in my office. I want to keep it. It'll make a fine souvenir."

Roylston stood there for a moment, and Gibson knew the man was angry. The cop had shown him up last night by getting away. Roylston wasn't used to being outfoxed. As much as anything, the man's professional pride was going to keep him tracking the Atlanta detective, and he wouldn't rest until he was in the ground or at the bottom of the ocean.

"Sure." Roylston walked away, his footsteps receding until they were covered over by the sounds of the surf.

Over the past few years they'd been together, Gibson had wondered if the day would come that Roylston would leave. After all, the man had helped cover up some of the murders over those years. He or his team had found the bodies Gibson had left behind and disposed of them. That was one of the primary reasons Gibson had started mailing in the White Rabbit cards. He'd wanted to claim his kills, to have people see those performances.

In the end, though, Gibson knew Roylston wouldn't leave. He'd stay, not out of loyalty, but because Gibson's father paid him well enough to stay no matter what Gibson did.

Gibson drained his glass and embraced the restless hunger that grew larger inside him. He would kill again.

Soon.

Chapter 14

Lauren held her bag of purchases in one hand while she used the key card with the other. The locking mechanism *thunked* inside the door, and the light cycled green. She pushed the door open and found Heath Sawyer standing at the vanity sink with his wet shirt in one hand and the big revolver in the other. His face was hard and cold.

His voice was a growl when he spoke. He lowered the revolver to his side. "Where have you been?"

Squelching the angry retort that sailed to the tip of her tongue, Lauren entered the room and allowed the door to close behind her. "I left a note."

"You shouldn't have left this room."

"We needed some things." She walked past him to the table on the other side of the room. "No, let me rephrase that—*you* needed some things. I went out to take care of it while you were sleeping."

"You could have woken me up!"

Lauren looked at the gun meaningfully. "Waking you might not have been the safest thing to do." She couldn't believe she'd felt so safe in his arms last night. Right now he looked cold and distant.

"Going out there by yourself was stupid."

Hurt and angry, Lauren looked at him and folded her arms. "Waking you so you could accompany me in that shirt would have been even more stupid."

Glumly, he looked at the sodden mess in his knuckled fist. The cloth dripped onto the carpet.

"Wash that shirt all you want. That blood's not coming out of that material. Or those pants."

Heath grimaced. "This is only the third time I've washed it. It's getting cleaner."

"With all the blood and the wrinkles you're going to have, you're going to look like an accident victim. You'll draw attention, and I don't think you want that." Lauren reached into the shopping bag and took out a pale blue lightweight long-sleeved, tapered dress shirt, khaki slacks, underwear and socks. She tossed the clothing to Heath, who dropped the soaked shirt in the sink and managed to catch everything. "I got you a matching jacket, as well."

"Suits aren't really my thing."

"I could tell that by the suit you wore to Megan's funeral. If those guys come hunting us again, you should look different. I thought maybe something more upscale might work. I have clothing that doesn't scream beach bunny."

"I kind of liked the orange-and-white bikini."

Feeling her cheeks flame with embarrassment, but pleased that he had noticed, Lauren tried to ignore him. She gestured at another bag. "I also picked up shoes and a belt. They were all out of gun holsters, so you'll have to make do."

A brief grin flickered in those green-flecked gold eyes. "Sounds expensive."

"It was. You're going to pay me back." She stared at his chest, at the interesting scar on his side, and made herself turn away from him. "Go shower. I also brought breakfast."

For a moment, she thought he was going to argue, but she

heard him pad away. The bathroom door closed. After a few minutes, during which she couldn't help imagining him taking his clothes off and what the sleek lines of his body would look like, the shower came on, and she knew everything she'd imagined was about to turn glistening wet.

Then she remembered the bag of toiletries she'd picked up for him, too. She knew delivering them to him could wait, but she couldn't help picking up the small bag and going to the bathroom door. She hesitated a moment, then knocked.

"Yeah?" Heath's voice rose over the sound of the shower.

"I forgot. I got you a razor, some shaving cream and a few other things you might need."

He didn't say anything.

"I can leave them out here, or I can open the door enough to put them in the room."

"Put them in the room."

Opening the door just a few inches, resisting the urge to peer around the door, she reached into the room and placed the bag on the sink. Although she didn't look toward the shower, the mirror and the angle gave her a good view.

The translucent shower curtain only softened the hard planes of his body a little. On the other side of the barrier, Heath looked nude, but he didn't look naked. The room smelled of soap, and the air was thick with humidity. Steeling herself, Lauren withdrew.

She sighed in frustration, returned to the table, and focused on the bag containing the breakfast she'd picked up at the market. Detective Heath Sawyer was just too attractive for her own good.

Heath stood under the heated spray of the shower and wondered what he'd gotten himself into. *She's not your partner. She's a civilian. You're letting her get in harm's way.* Jackson's words haunted him.

He ducked his head under the spray and told himself that

he didn't have a choice. He wasn't putting her there. She was putting herself there. All he could try to do was keep her alive.

He kept thinking about how she looked. Those khaki pants she'd worn hugged her hips, and that orange top was on the verge of driving him crazy. Her clothing wasn't revealing, was tasteful, but it showed off just enough of her body that he wanted to see the rest of it.

He growled at himself and turned the water on cold full blast, till all he could think about was the cold. He almost froze to death before he could get those kinds of thoughts of her out of his mind.

After drying off, he wrapped a towel around his waist and stepped in front of the sink. The small bag of toiletries sat to one side. He fished out the shaving cream and razor first, then lathered up and managed to scrape his face smooth without nicking anything.

She'd bought deodorant, facial cleansing soap, toothpaste and toothbrush, mouthwash and a few other things. Heath didn't know what all of it was, but Jackson Portman would. The man was a metrosexual to the *n*th degree. Guys who got on the wrong side of him were often surprised by how nasty he could be in a dustup.

Heath administered what he could figure out, then dropped the towel and got dressed. He looked a lot different when he was finished. Once he transferred all of his personal effects from his cast-off clothing to his new clothes, he bundled up the pants and socks and stepped out of the bathroom.

Lauren wasn't in the room. She was at the table on the balcony that overlooked the harbor. She'd changed clothing, too, evidently in the room while he'd been in the bathroom showering, and that definitely stirred thoughts in his mind. She now wore a dark orange ruffled sundress with spaghetti straps that hit her midthigh.

The balcony was tiny, hardly tourist-worthy, but it held a small round table and two chairs under a faded umbrella decorated with seahorses. All of the red ones had bleached out to a dirty gray, but enough of the color remained to show what they had been.

"That may not be safe out there." Heath picked up the soaked shirt and added it to his pile of discards, rolling it in the center and putting it in one of the empty plastic bags.

"If anyone is looking for us, they didn't find us so far. I don't think they're going to find us this morning."

"You don't know that."

"I'm not eating breakfast in that room."

Heath pulled on socks, then stepped into a pair of brown shoes that went well with the pants. He added the slim belt and picked up the .357 on his way to the balcony.

The table held a selection of foods in cartons. He recognized the pineapple and watermelon and bananas and breadfruit. He'd had the ball-shaped fried dumplings before, and he knew that the other two servings held meat. There was also a small pot of coffee from the room's coffeemaker and a carafe of orange juice. He picked up a plastic fork and one of the disposable plates.

"What's this?" He pointed at the yellow clumps in one carton.

"Ackee and saltfish. Ackee is a fruit. Very subtle flavor that complements the salted cod."

"You've had it before?"

"I have. Not everything has to be steak and potatoes."

"I look like a steak and potatoes guy to you?"

She wore large sunglasses, so he couldn't see her eyes, but her lips quirked up at the corners. "You do."

"Okay. What's this?" Heath pointed to the carton that held what looked like fish and tomatoes.

"Sweet and sour fish. Mackerel sautéed with onions and tomatoes. I picked all of this up at the Pegasus Hotel."

"I'm paying for breakfast, too?"

"No. *I'm* buying breakfast." The sunglasses centered on him. "You saved my life last night."

"I think we actually saved each other's life." Heath pointed his fork at the cartons. "You want to divvy?"

"I thought you were old enough to feed yourself."

"When somebody lays out a spread like this, I get intimidated." Heath rolled up his sleeves while she sorted out the cartons. "Manners aren't my strong suit. Maybe you could have guessed that, too."

"You look good in those clothes."

"Thank you." Heath felt a little self-conscious at the compliment. He knew he turned women's heads every now and again, but they didn't compliment him on the way he was dressed. His eyes, his hands, those were the usual things. "You look good, too. How did you get the sizes right?"

"The shirt was easy. I just checked the shirt you'd been wearing. I did the same for the shoes. The pants were a guess."

"You guess pretty good."

"I help outfit a lot of stage magicians. Extra pockets. Hideouts. Things like that. I have to know sizes and what you can do with them." She finished putting food on her plate.

Heath looked around and smiled. "You've got the view. The table. The food." He tapped the fork against the empty plastic flower vase glued to the table. "I'm surprised you didn't get a table setting, too."

With a small grin, she spread her hands, and a bright pink hibiscus appeared in them. She stuck the flower stem into the neck of the vase, and it sat there.

"Now you're showing off." Heath frowned at the flower. "How did you manage that?"

"The flower?" She looked terribly innocent.

"Yes, the flower."

She shrugged. "Magic. Don't you believe in magic?"

"No."

"Maybe you should start." She picked up her fork and speared a pineapple chunk.

"You are missing a candle, you know?"

An arched eyebrow rose above the sunglasses lens. "You believe in candlelight dinners?"

"I do. Easier to believe in than magic. And you can have steak and potatoes by candlelight. Does that surprise you?"

"What do you think?"

Heath forked a helping of ackee and saltfish into his mouth and chewed. It was surprisingly good. "Actually, I don't think you get surprised by a lot."

She didn't say anything, just kept eating for a moment. Then her expression sobered. "What are we doing after breakfast?"

Heath hated that the casual flirting had been set aside. It was easy to believe, just for a little while, that he was in the Caribbean with a beautiful woman that might be the least bit interested in him. More than that, it was a pleasant diversion from the dark thoughts that had plagued him for the past few weeks since Janet's death.

"After breakfast we're going to my hotel room."

"That could be dangerous if Gibson's people are watching your room."

"Let's hope I see them before they see me. I have equipment there that I can use."

"It might be safer to get more somewhere else."

Heath shook his head. "My files are there, too."

The two men watching Heath's room weren't any of the bodyguards from the villa, but they weren't Kingston policemen, either. They were both African-American, decked out in casual wear and likely carrying concealed weapons. Judging from the tattoos and the scars and the way they manned their positions, they had military backgrounds.

Even though she wasn't trained for such things, Lauren was used to watching people and figuring out what they were about. Living in foster homes had taught her that, and everything she had learned told her these men were dangerous.

She sorted through the tourist brochures hanging on one wall, selected a few, then walked back out of the hotel. Heath, dressed in the lightweight jacket and amber-tinted sunglasses, waited in her rental in the parking area adjacent to the hotel. He reached across and opened her door.

Lauren climbed in and sat, pulling the door closed. "Someone's watching, but they're not any of Gibson's regular bodyguards. From the looks of them, they're military."

Heath's eyes narrowed. "What is it with Gibson and these military guys? There has to be some connection."

Lauren shook her head. "I don't know. Like I told you before, Gibson is almost a nonentity in the magic circles. He just... appeared, and he vanishes whenever he wants to."

"I know. Janet and I tried tracking him back through taxes, but all we ever reached was a legal firm that backed us off. We never got enough evidence to get a warrant to leverage the attorneys."

"What about the attorneys? Do they have access to people like Roylston, Sisco and the others?"

Heath looked at her in surprise. "Janet and I never thought to ask about that."

"Might be worth it."

Heath nodded and used the cell phone he'd purchased after leaving Lauren's hotel this morning. Lauren kept watch on their surroundings while he talked.

"Hey. Do me a favor. In the White Rabbit file on my computer, there's a listing for the attorneys Janet and I tracked Gibson back to. Run a background check on those people, see if you turn up any ex-military or paramilitary connections." Heath folded the phone and put it away. He looked up at the hotel.

"What are you thinking?"

"That my hotel room didn't have any alarms on the windows."

Looking out her window, Lauren spotted the fire escape snaking up the side of the building. "That's not a good idea. If there are people watching the lobby, you can bet there's someone watching the room."

"Yeah. From the outside. I'm not going in from the outside."

Heath slid the revolver from under the seat and tucked it into the back of his pants. "Keep a lookout here. If you see something suspicious, call me on my cell."

Worry knotted in Lauren's stomach, but she knew better than to argue. It would only be wasted breath. "Good luck."

Heath left the vehicle, and Lauren slid over behind the steering wheel. She watched as he walked to the rear of the hotel and started up the fire escape. Keeping an eye on Heath and the front door of the hotel was hard, but she managed.

Chapter 15

At the fourth floor landing on the fire escape, Heath paused and hunkered down. He peered through the sliding door, unable to see through the drapes.

Drawing back an arm, maneuvering so his back was to the sliding door, Heath thrust his elbow into the glass and broke it. Turning back around, he used his jacket so he wouldn't leave fingerprints on the pieces and plucked out enough fragments to allow him to stick his hand through. Again using the jacket, he unlatched the door, opened it and strode through with the .357 in his hand.

His clothing lay strewn all over the room. The drawers were pulled out and dumped onto the floor. Someone had taken the poster of evidence. He cursed the theft and walked to the table where his gear was. The travel bag containing spare rounds for the revolver, restraints and other gear sat open under the table. His computer was gone.

A maid stepped out of the bathroom carrying folded towels. She wore earbuds that connected to an MP3 player hanging around her neck. Her black hair was pulled back in a ponytail, her skin was dark and she looked as if she was in her mid- to late twenties. The maid's outfit didn't flatter, but she had a hard, lean body.

"Oh. Sorry." The woman spoke with an accent. "I didn't think anyone was here."

Heath started to reassure her that he meant no harm, then he realized she was carrying folded towels *out* of the bathroom, not into. More than that, she was supposedly cleaning a room that looked as though it had been burglarized.

He reached for the gun, sweeping it up as she fired a pistol of her own from under the towels. Bullets whipped by Heath and jerked at the curtain folds. The sliding glass door shattered and fragments tinkled against the floor. There were no gunshots, only liquid *thwips* that told him she was using a silencer.

Throwing himself sideways onto the bed, Heath fired twice. The shots sounded incredibly loud inside the room, and he knew they were going to be joined in seconds.

The woman staggered back, dropping the towels and the pistol. She leaned back against the wall beside the bathroom and bit her lower lip in pain. Her left hand covered her right shoulder. Blood soaked into her blouse.

Holding the .357 on the woman, Heath engaged the secondary locks on the door. He walked toward the woman. "Who are you?"

She glared at him, eyes narrowing. "Room service."

"Tell me one that'll make me laugh or I'll put another bullet in you." Heath reached for the MP3 player, held it in one hand, and managed to stick one of the earbuds into his ear.

Men's voices carried over the frequency, not music. "That was a heavy-caliber pistol."

"That woman had a silenced nine, man. That's not her."

"On my way up. You watch the lobby."

"I will. If you see our target, give me a yell. I'll cover your six."

Heath pocketed the radio in his jacket pocket. "We don't have a lot of time to get to know each other, and my dance card looks pretty full, so I'm going to ask you one more time. Who are you?"

She shook her head. "Nobody you would know. I was contracted to kill you."

"By who?"

"By the man I work for. I don't ask questions. He pays me not to ask questions."

"Do you know Roylston?"

"I don't know anybody by that name."

"Let me see your arm."

Reluctantly, the woman lifted her hand. The bullet had hit her in the shoulder, sliding in under the clavicle and over the top of the scapula. She had some rehab ahead of her, but she wasn't in any serious danger of bleeding to death.

Taking advantage of his distraction, the woman attempted to knee him. Heath blocked her with his own knee and shoved her back hard enough to bounce her off the wall. He screwed the .357's barrel into the side of her neck. "Don't."

She froze, mouth hard and set, her eyes fluttering as if she expected him to pull the trigger at any moment.

Heath reached down for one of the towels and draped it over her injured shoulder. "Keep the pressure on to stop the bleeding. Have your friends get you to a hospital."

The woman hesitated, then nodded. "Thanks." She was a total professional.

Heath picked up her pistol by the barrel, dumped it into the equipment bag, zipped it up and hoisted the bag over his shoulder as he sprinted for the fire escape.

Even with the window rolled down, Lauren only thought she heard gunshots. It wasn't until people started running out of the hotel lobby that she had confirmation. She turned on the ignition, listened to the motor catch and glanced anxiously at the fire escape. She wasn't sure what she was going to do if Heath didn't appear there soon.

But he did.

He came out of the room and rapidly descended the stairs two and three at a time at a headlong pace that threatened to throw him off balance. By the time Heath reached the second floor, a man stepped out of the fourth floor room brandishing a large pistol. Lauren recognized him immediately as one of the two men she'd spotted in the lobby.

Leaning over the fire escape railing, the man fired three shots at Heath. The bullets ricocheted from the metal fire escape and from the hotel wall. The *spang* of metal on metal rang loudly. Heath threw himself over the second-floor landing and dropped the final story to the pavement, catching himself on one hand and bent knees. Turning, he brought his gun up and fired four times.

The return fire struck the fire escape around the gunman on the fourth floor, causing him to duck back to cover.

Lauren put the car in gear and sped closer to Heath, throwing open the passenger door. Heath tossed the bag into the backseat and climbed into the vehicle. He flicked the revolver open, shook out the empties, and started feeding new cartridges into the cylinder.

"Go! Now!" His gaze roved the street as Lauren wheeled the car in a tight turn and headed for the street. She floored the accelerator and held on to the steering wheel, hoping no one stepped out in front of her and a lane was clear in the street when she arrived there.

Bullets hammered the pavement around them. One cored through the roof of the car and knocked a hole in the floor next to Lauren's left foot. Another round took out the back glass. Then she turned hard right, screeching out onto the street. The car fishtailed wildly, and she fought the wheel.

"Straighten it out! Straighten it out!" Heath's hand flashed out and covered hers, holding the steering wheel tight. "Hold steady! Get the car under control first! Just like you would on slick ice!"

Lauren didn't know how he could speak so calmly. She wanted to scream, but she didn't have the time. The comparison to ice locked in for her, though. She was used to Chicago winters, and sometimes the streets felt the same way this out-of-control slalom felt. She stopped fighting the wheel and the car settled into place.

"Good. That's it."

Heath wasn't even looking at her. His attention was riveted on the street.

"What are you doing?"

"Guys set up like that will have a chase car set up, too, if they wanted to seriously cover the hotel. I want to find it before it finds us."

Lauren glanced in the rearview mirror and saw a dark sedan roaring up behind them, dodging in and out of traffic. "There it is! Behind us!"

"These guys are good." Heath turned in the seat and brought the pistol up in both hands over the car seat. "Cover your ear if you can. This is going to get loud."

Taking her right hand from the steering wheel, Lauren covered her right ear and waited tensely, grateful that the traffic in front of her was light. She pulled to the left, dodging around a Jeep, then popped back into the correct lane just as a cargo van rushed at her, horn blaring.

Glancing back in the rearview mirror, she saw the chase car was closing on them. Her heart thudded painfully, and she willed the car to go faster, but the engine just didn't have any more to give.

Heath opened fire without warning. Six thunderous booms filled the car, and Lauren lost most of her hearing.

"Turn right." Heath was beside her, yelling into her ear, and still he sounded as if he was a long way off. "Head into town. We have to find a place to lose this car." He emptied his pistol again and started reloading.

Looking up into the rearview mirror again, Lauren saw that the chase car was falling back. Gray smoke billowed from under the hood and green fluid rained between the front tires.

A few blocks farther on, the adrenaline aftershock hit Lauren, and she thought for a moment she was going to be sick. But she kept breathing, kept forcing her way through it, and she gradually calmed down.

"Are you okay?" Heath was looking at her so she could partially read his lips. When he'd at first leaned in, she'd thought he was going to kiss her again, and she knew she would have welcomed that. It was disappointing when she realized he was just trying to talk to her.

"Yes. I'm fine. Are you all right?"

"I'm good. Keep driving. I'll give you directions."

"All right."

"In the meantime, I need you to call the rental agency and tell them your car has been stolen."

"What?" She shook her head. "The police will start looking for it."

"The police are already looking for it." Heath pointed at an alley. "There. Pull in there."

Obeying, Lauren drove the car into the alley. No one was around at the moment.

"Stop here."

She did, but she couldn't help looking back through the broken window, knowing that the police were going to drive up behind her at any moment. "We can't stay here."

Heath was already getting out. He paused to pick up the empty casings from his revolver, counting them silently—or maybe just too quietly to be heard through the deafness in her ears—till he was satisfied with the number. He slid them into a pocket and looked at her. "Get out."

Lauren got out.

"Walk to the end of the alley and flag down a taxi. Hold it till I get there."

Lauren started walking, almost up to a run in the short distance. She glanced around, afraid that a taxi wasn't going to be nearby, then she spotted one coming up the street. She waved a hand to flag down the driver. She turned to call out to Heath, but he was already headed in her direction. Behind him, the rental car suddenly sprouted flames underneath it.

"What did you do?"

Heath took her by the arm and walked down the street away from the mouth of the alley. "I cut the gas line and lit a match. I want that car to be as confusing as possible for the forensics team when they get here. Did you call the rental company?"

"No."

"Do it. Tell them you got up and went out to get your car while you were shopping at the Jubilee Market on Orange Street. You left the car near the park there. When you went back to get it, the car was gone." Heath helped her into the taxi and climbed in after her.

The young driver turned around and took one earbud out. "Where to, mon?"

"Jubilee Market."

"Sure, sure. Have you dere in just a minute, mon." The driver replaced the earbud, bobbed his head in time with the music and pulled out into traffic.

Heath continued talking calmly. "The police will probably want to talk to you. I know I would if I was investigating this mess. All you have to do is tell them the same story." He looked at her. "Can you do that?"

"Yes."

"If you can't, we're going to get busted. They can't do anything to us in the long run because they can't prove that we did anything wrong, but they can send us home." Heath paused. "Unless you're ready to go home."

"No."

Heath threw an arm around her and gave her a hug. The driver looked at them in the rearview mirror and smiled, then went back to his music.

"Do you have the car keys?"

Lauren was surprised that she'd thought to get them in all the excitement, but she had. She showed him the keys.

"You can't have those." Heath took them from her, then

separated them from the ring and began dropping them out the open window as the taxi raced along the street and sirens sounded behind them.

The taxi driver let them out on Orange Street, and Heath walked with her for a short distance. "I'm going to be around, but I don't want our names entered on the same report, okay?"

Lauren nodded.

"You were here, shopping, alone."

"Then where are the things I've been buying?"

Heath pulled her to one side where a small group of street artists were selling paintings. "Buy from people like this." He pointed at a painting with seahorses and held up twenty dollars. "People that just take cash and don't do printout receipts. You're looking for vendors surrounded by a crowd of tourists. Make small purchases. Knickknacks. Don't buy big and don't spend a lot of money, and you won't even be remembered." He looked at her and smiled. "At least, not by these people."

"Are you flirting with me?" Lauren was surprised at how calm she felt moving through the tourist crowd jamming the market. And she understood about the buying, too. It was all misdirection for whatever audience they drew.

His grin grew bigger. "Maybe a little. Breaking the law and getting away with it kind of makes me reckless."

"I thought you were a law enforcer, not a lawbreaker."

"You don't know everything about me."

A young woman in island dress nodded, took his twenty dollars and handed him the seahorse painting. Heath gave it to Lauren, who took it and crossed over to another booth that was selling small, colorful purses. She bought one and kept moving.

"Do you have enough money?" Heath kept pace with her.

"Are you offering to give me more?"

"Well, I did get you shot at this morning."

"You still have to pay me for that suit, mister. I don't want you claiming poverty later." Lauren moved quickly, seeking out other tables and wares.

Heath chuckled. "You're awfully calm."

"This is a performance. I do performances."

"Are you going to be okay with the police?"

Lauren stopped at a table that sold shell jewelry. She didn't know who she was going to give the necklace and bracelet to when she returned home, but she bought them anyway and quickly moved on. "They're not sending me home, I can tell you that." No matter what it took, no matter what she had to do or how many times she was going to have to risk her life, she wasn't going to let Gibson get away with killing Megan. That wasn't happening.

Chapter 16

Thirty-seven minutes later, Lauren sat on a bench in the shade while sipping a strawberry juice drink when Inspector Wallace Myton came strolling up in an ill-fitting suit. Two uniformed patrolmen trailed at his heels.

"Ah, Miss Cooper, I hear that you have suffered misfortune." The inspector was shorter than Lauren, in his early fifties, and had warm, coffee skin. The unmistakable accent of the island echoed in his speech. He was balding and kept the sides shaved to salt-and-pepper stubble, and his neat mustache matched the color. In spite of his small stature, he had a long neck that had always put Lauren in the mind of a turkey during her dealings with him. He wore a light blue suit.

"Inspector Myton." Lauren looked up at him. "I'm surprised to see you."

"Are you?" Myton tapped a cigarette against the back of his hand.

"I just called in about my car being stolen." Lauren's heart beat faster and she struggled to remain calm. *It's just a performance. If you blow this one, they're going to send you home, and Megan's killer may never be found.* Thinking about her sister steadied her, gave her purpose and direction. She wasn't going to fail. She refused.

"So I heard. The rental agency called the police department, you see."

"I thought you only worked homicide investigations."

"I do." The inspector put the cigarette between his lips, then lit it with a book of matches. He inhaled, then let out a long stream of smoke. "Sometimes I work very hard to *prevent* them."

"Are you here to take my report, because there isn't much to tell, actually. When I went to the parking lot with my purchases, my car was gone. So were my keys. They were in my purse."

"A tragedy."

"I'm just glad it wasn't my car. The rental company said they'll send me another one."

Myton waved at the bench. "May I sit?"

Lauren put some of the bags onto the ground and made a place for the inspector. The two patrolmen continued to stand nearby.

Myton sat and started poking around in the bags. "My wife often comes out here. She likes little things like these. They bring her joy, but I fear we are running out of places to put these things."

Lauren started to worry that she'd gone overboard in buying. Heath had helped, and they'd ended up with quite a haul.

The inspector looked at her. "I hadn't taken you for a collector of amateur arts and handcrafts."

"I'm not." Lauren smiled. *Performance.* "And I have a small apartment. Most of what you see here is going to be given to people I grew up with in foster homes. When you move around like that, you end up with a lot of brothers and sisters."

Myton smiled. "Yes, I suppose you would." He gestured with his cigarette. "And you are close to these other brothers and sisters?"

"Yes."

"Like you were with Megan?"

Lauren let the smile disappear from her face. "No. Not as close as I was with Megan." She gave the inspector a hard look. "Why would you ask something like that?"

"Forgive me. Perhaps sometimes I am insensitive. I am a very inquisitive man. In part, it is what makes me good at my job."

Unable to reel in the anger that the inspector had ignited, Lauren lashed back. "If you're so good at your job, Inspector Myton, why haven't you found the person that killed my sister?"

"I have touched a nerve."

"Yes, you have."

Myton shrugged. "Such is the nature of this business that I do. Sometimes I must ask the hard questions. Like, would it surprise you to know that your stolen vehicle was involved in a shootout at a hotel only a short time ago and later burned in an alley?"

"After hearing how my sister died, I'm not much surprised by anything these days." Lauren kept her face unreadable.

"Then you deny that you were involved?"

Lauren waved at the bags of purchases. "I've been shopping. I noticed the car was missing. I checked for my keys. They were also missing. I was told the market was notorious for pickpockets."

"So it is." Myton took another hit off his cigarette and expelled smoke. "These *thieves* who took your keys, I think they must have been very lucky to find your vehicle in all those that are parked around here."

"Not if they saw me leave it and decided to take my keys."

"So you were a prospect targeted by these people?"

"I don't know."

"Because I have to ask myself, why would a thief take your car, then go to a hotel and start shooting?"

"Maybe he didn't have cab fare."

Myton laughed at that, and the sound was genuine. He pointed his cigarette at her. "That is a very funny answer."

"Who was shot at?"

"Alas, that is also a question to which I do not have an answer at present. But soon, perhaps. I am still working on things." Myton stood and brushed ashes from his suit coat. "I am a very patient man, Miss Cooper. Eventually all answers come to me. I'll bid you good day, and I hope that your next experience with a rented vehicle goes much smoother than your first."

"Thank you."

Myton started to walk away, then he stopped and looked at her. "You know, you have never said what you are doing back in Kingston."

"Vacation."

"I would think, given the circumstances, there would be better places to vacation."

"Not at the moment."

Myton dropped his cigarette to the pavement and crushed it out underfoot. "Have you seen Detective Heath Sawyer since you've been back?"

Lauren thought about that for only a second. There was no right answer, and she thought it was better to go with the lie than an admission at this point. "No. Why?"

"Because he is still here, too. I thought it wouldn't be too much to presume that the two of you might run into each other."

Lauren didn't say anything. A midsize car glided to a stop in front of the bench. The driver wore a cap that advertised the rental agency Lauren was using. He got out with a clipboard and searched the surroundings till he spotted Lauren.

"Miss Cooper." The driver smiled and waved the clipboard. "I have your car."

Lauren got up, grabbed some of the bags, and headed for the car. The driver opened the trunk, then scurried over to help her. Myton gestured to the two uniformed patrolmen. They stepped in and helped transfer purchases, as well.

Once she'd signed the rental form, the driver told her that he would take a taxi back to the agency. Myton came over to hold the door open to allow Lauren to slide behind the steering wheel, then he closed the door.

"Have a good day, Miss Cooper. Please be safe."

"Thank you, Inspector." Lauren put the car in gear and pulled into traffic. Her cell rang almost immediately.

"Hey." Heath's voice sounded laconic, as if getting shot at and burning cars was an everyday thing. Maybe back in Atlanta it was.

"Hey." Lauren's clenched stomach relaxed a little when she heard him.

"Good performance. Very nice."

"So what do we do now?"

"Standard police work." Heath didn't sound happy about that. "We watch, we learn, we hope we catch a break. Gibson is rattled now. He's trying to manage his situation because I'm making him uncomfortable. With your help, though he doesn't know that. What I'd like to do is find out who the new players are and what they're doing here."

"You said you didn't recognize any of them."

"I didn't, but you're not the only one that can pick up things that don't belong to you. I picked up the weapon the *maid* used at the hotel. I'm going to run her fingerprints, see if we get a hit. She was an ice-cold pro. Somebody will know her."

"Do I need to circle around and pick you up?"

"No. I'm in the taxi four cars behind you."

Lauren glanced in the rearview mirror and counted back cars till she spotted the taxi. Knowing he was there made her feel safer, not as alone.

"I'll meet you at your hotel. Wait for me in the lobby."

Heath sat at the desk in Lauren's hotel room and worked on the captured pistol. He'd gotten some mechanical pencil lead from the gift store in the hotel lobby, chopped it fine with a razor blade purchased from the same place, and turned it into a fine powder. A brush from a small cosmetic kit, also bought for an unconscionable price, allowed him to dust the graphite onto the pistol's surface.

The natural lighting from the balcony door provided plenty of illumination to see the latent friction ridges on the weapon. Using transparent tape, he lifted the prints, then affixed them to a sheet of typing paper that the gift shop had carried.

"Who knew the gift shop was one-stop shopping for your own CSI lab?" Lauren sat in the nearby wingback chair and watched the proceedings with avid interest.

Heath went in search of another print, this one off the magazine. "A very pitiful excuse for a CSI lab."

"It seems to be getting the job done."

"I hope. And I hope she has a file."

Lauren kept working on her iPad. Heath didn't know what she was doing, but when she wasn't watching him, she was very intent on the device. She looked up again. "You're different than I expected."

"How so?" Carefully, Heath extracted one of the bullets from the magazine. When he dusted it, nothing came up. He hadn't expected to net any results because brass could get lost during a shooting. Keeping up with ejected casings could be too problematic. The woman had been a professional. She would have used gloves to load her weapon. Dusting the bullet had been to confirm his impression, and it had.

"I knew you were a tough cop. I could tell that from the first time I met you."

"During which time you were thinking I was a morgue attendant."

She frowned at him.

"Okay, maybe that's too soon. Blame it on tiredness."

"You slept later than I did."

"True."

"No, I knew you were tough."

"Had a lot of experience with tough cops, have you?"

A ghost of a smile turned up her lips, and for a moment he

could see the little girl she might have been. "I grew up in foster care for half my life. Of course I knew tough cops."

"Any outstanding juvenile warrants?" Heath affixed another print to the paper. He had eight of them so far, which he thought was a good number.

"All of them have aged out, Detective."

"Then you're safe." Heath reached down into his equipment bag and took out the camera he'd brought with him. He took several hi-res photographs of the prints, then sent the images to Jackson Portman's email at the P.D. Whoever had broken into his hotel room had stolen his computer, but the camera was Wi-Fi capable. "So how am I different?"

"You're more thorough than I thought you would be. And you know a lot about your job."

"I have to know a lot about my job. It's what I do." He looked at her while waiting for the uploads to cycle. "How many coin tricks do you know?"

"Disappear? Appear? Change? What kind of coin?"

Heath grinned. "I guess neither of us learns just one trick, do we?"

"I suppose not."

Heath glanced at his watch. It was after two. "We missed lunch, and breakfast was too long ago. It's going to take my partner a while to run down these prints, if he's able to. Let's assume the restaurant in this hotel is adequate. Do we do room service or dine there?"

Lauren thought for just a moment. "Let's eat in the dining room."

The decision was disappointing. Heath enjoyed his time alone with Lauren, probably more than he should have. He stood, wiped the graphite from his hands and picked up his jacket.

She smiled at him. "It'll give you another chance to show off your new wardrobe."

"A limited wardrobe, it seems, since recovering my other

clothing is going to require me talking to Inspector Myton and his people."

"Maybe you can go shopping with me this time."

"I'd rather have a root canal."

Only a few people were in the dining room when Lauren and Heath arrived. They took a booth in one corner and looked at the menu for a while.

Lauren didn't know what Heath was thinking. His face didn't give away much about what was going on inside his head. She watched him over the top of her menu, and for just a short time, she imagined what it might be like to actually be out for a meal with him.

He was attractive, and it wasn't just the physical aspect. Not just the tough cop, or even the thorough cop. He was…attentive. He watched things, really saw them. And he saw people, too. She knew that she aggravated him. He didn't like the fact that she didn't listen to him, but he respected it. When the situation was bad, he trusted her, too. Even when it was circumstances that he knew Lauren had never been involved with.

Not a lot of men would do that. Especially not rugged, tough, thorough homicide detectives. She decided that maybe she'd been wrong about him in the beginning, except that she knew she was right. Under prevailing circumstances, Heath Sawyer could be a complete jerk. That was just how he'd been made. It was going to take a woman with a lot of patience to put up with him. Lauren had never been patient for anybody outside of herself and her family.

He looked up at her without warning, and their eyes met. He smiled inquisitively.

Lauren broke the awkward silence quickly. "What are you having?"

"They have steak. They have potatoes. I'm a happy guy."

She laid her menu aside. "Aren't you going to ask what I'm going to have?"

"Sure. What are you going to have?"

"Maybe you should guess."

"Nope."

"Why?"

"Because, even if I get it right, you'll just say that's not what you're having and tell me you're having something else."

Despite herself, Lauren grinned. She knew she would have done exactly that.

"This lady has been busy." Jackson Portman spoke over speaker function while Heath's phone sat on the desk. Lauren's iPad sat beside the phone. Jackson had sent his findings to a Dropbox account Heath had activated to receive the file.

Lauren sat beside Heath, but he was asking the questions. She stared at the hard-faced woman in the photo. The image had been captured in three-quarter profile. She'd been wearing combat fatigues and a helmet. She carried an assault rifle in her arms. Her eyes were dead and flat.

"Who is she?"

"Name's Suzana Veslin." Jackson spelled it out. "She's a mercenary. A high-end operator out of the Balkans. Interpol has conflicting reports about where she's from exactly. They believe she was sold into human trafficking and fought her way out with a toothpick. After that she learned how to use knives and guns. I have to tell you, amigo, you went up against this one and came out on top, you're better than I think you are or you got lucky."

"It's always good to be good, but it's better to be lucky."

Lauren couldn't believe Heath was passing off whatever had happened inside that hotel room so casually. A chill tightened her stomach at the thought that he had come so close to getting killed.

"Who's she working for?" Heath slid his fingers across the iPad, changing out the first image for others that showed Veslin in military gear in other places.

"Hard to tell, bro. Some of the big corporations have used her to get back hostages, but Interpol says she's been used on dark ops most of the time. She's taken hostages, killed people, all the bad stuff."

Heath reached the end of the images, then started over. "Doesn't make sense. A guy like Gibson wouldn't have access to people like this."

"You've gone up against his people." Jackson's voice was tense. "You can't deny what you've been dealing with. Veslin isn't quite to Roylston's pedigree, but she's close."

"Any connection between Roylston and Veslin?"

"None that I can find. None that Interpol and a half dozen other international agencies know about. By the way, I'm getting some heavy interest from some of those people. They want to know why I'm asking."

"Tell them you're curious."

"Yeah, because that'll satisfy them."

Heath tapped the desktop irritably. "There's a connection somewhere. We just have to find it."

"I know. I'm looking. You guys just need to watch yourselves down there."

An hour later, Heath was cleaning both his weapons, the revolver he'd gotten and the 9 mm he'd picked up from Suzana Veslin, getting them ready to use. While he'd been doing that, he'd been watching Lauren. She sat cross-legged on the bed, fingers working intermittently on the iPad. She'd changed out of the sundress, much to Heath's chagrin, and into cargo shorts and a tunic top, which wasn't bad. She'd also pulled her hair back into a short ponytail. He admired the way she worked, full-blown concentration, no holding back. He wanted to ask her what she was working on, but that would have meant direct interaction and would have robbed him of the chance to watch her. When she moved, she was smooth and graceful, and he liked the curves and lean tautness of her body. She was made well. There was no other way to put it.

She looked up at him and caught him staring, almost like earlier in the dining room when he'd looked up from the menu and caught her looking at him. For just a moment, everything felt awkward. Then she smiled at him.

"Want to guess where Gibson is going to be tonight?"

That caught his attention, and the awkward moment fled. "Have you turned into a mind reader for real now?"

"No. But I know where he's going to be."

"Where?"

"Have you heard of Agony House?"

Heath thought for a moment and finally came up with it. "Some kind of haunted house?"

"Yes." Lauren's smile grew wider. "Supposedly a *very* haunted house with a long and bloody history. They're having a fundraiser there tonight for a children's nonprofit organization."

"Why do you think Gibson will be there?"

"Because I see it in the crystal ball." Lauren turned her iPad around, showing him a Twitter page. She tapped one of the entries with her forefinger.

I'm gonna be at a haunted house 2nite with the Amazing Gibson! Check out Agony House!

A tiny url was provided after the announcement. Lauren tapped it and the iPad linked to a website dedicated to Agony House. In the center of the page was Gibson's photograph.

Chapter 17

At 8:00 p.m., Agony House was lit with baby spotlights that picked up the color from the ocean out front and the sky above that tinted the white exterior blue. The original house had been built in 1817 by a sugarcane plantation owner for his new bride, and that was only part of the story. Lauren had told Heath the rest of it while they'd gotten ready for the soiree, and he still couldn't believe everything he'd heard.

The house had been remodeled several times over the years, but in 1957, Prudy Cranmer, a small-time Hollywood actress who had married big-time money, purchased the estate. Several films had been shot there, most of them low-budget thrillers and a few horror movies.

The actress had left Agony House to her granddaughter. These days Agony House continued to be, according to Lauren, a place of mysterious happenings and curiosity.

Heath stood in front of the hotel and felt dwarfed. Fountains sprayed up from a half dozen pools, three on either side of the wide stone steps that led up to the main lobby from the beachfront plaza. Several of the guests talked about the rumors of ghosts and offered testimony as to what they would do when they found one tonight.

Heath drifted in with the herd and paid the price of admission at the door. Lauren was already inside, and he felt uneasy without her in his sight. The past couple days had been filled with close calls. Tonight wouldn't be any different.

Inside the hotel, Heath found an alcove that allowed him to watch everything while staying somewhat in the background. Everyone had gathered in the main room to await the start of the show. At the bar set up in the corner, Heath paid for a bottled beer and returned to his post.

At 8:45, Lydia Cranmer, the granddaughter of the actress who had initially purchased Agony House, put in her appearance. The lights were dimmed, and a baby spotlight dawned at the top of the long stairs. No one had been allowed access to the upper floor yet.

A hush fell over the crowd as they waited expectantly.

"Ladies and gentlemen, my name is Lydia Cranmer, and tonight you are my guests." She smiled at the crowd. "Welcome to my home. Welcome…to Agony House." She threw an arm theatrically into the air.

A laser light show suddenly erupted, and bright colors blazed around the ceiling. The kaleidoscope of neon lights whirled faster and became a blur.

Then they disappeared, and the lights went out, leaving the grand room doused in shadows. The blue light glowing outside created just enough illumination to allow people to see a few feet into the cottony darkness.

The crowd started whispering, wondering if this was part of the show. A few of the women grew scared, and a few of the men did, too. Heath was convinced it was all theater, but he was frustrated that he didn't know where Lauren was. He hadn't liked the separation aspect of the plan.

The baby spotlight came on again, and this time it picked up Lydia Cranmer halfway down the stairs, standing quietly at attention. "Many of you are first-time arrivals here at Agony House, and many of you are returning guests. It is good to see those of you who have returned, and I look forward to meeting new friends."

Gradually, the lights came back up, but they remained soft, a buttery-yellow that allowed deep shadows.

"The history of this house goes back to 1817, when plantation owner Benjamin Hervey built a magnificent home for his young bride, Abigail.

"Six months later, her husband was dead, and no one knew the cause. It didn't take long before talk of voodoo started every tongue wagging. When Abigail first came over to Jamaica, she'd suffered a dangerous fever that had been cured by a woman who practiced medicine. Her name was Tante Simone and she was reputed to be a *mambo,* a female voodoo priest.

"They say—though it was never proven—that Tante Simone taught Abigail as much about the dark arts as she did about the healing ones. They say—though this, too, is disputed in legends and stories—that Abigail took her husband's life because he had taken her from her home and caused the drowning deaths of her family during an ocean voyage to visit Abigail."

Heath sipped his beer and watched the crowd.

"Eight years into Abigail's widowhood, a storm struck Agony House and caused massive damage. It looked like Abigail was going to lose her house because she couldn't afford to rebuild it. So she sought out a rich suitor named George Bascombe—seduced him through voodoo, some said—and brought him home. Repairing the house drained the man's wealth, and it was said Abigail stole Bascombe's life."

Lydia waved to the back of the hotel. "The graves of Abigail, her husbands and some of the slaves who died here have been relocated, but they still exist. During the day, or tonight, if you dare, you're welcome to visit the cemetery. Just don't take anything. No keepsakes or mementos." She paused. "You can never be sure of what might follow you home. There are reports, never verified, however, of visitors to Agony House that returned home and found they'd brought a ghost with them. The dead still live here among us, after all. Every now and again, they reveal themselves to us."

Inside the house, everyone was silent.

Even though Heath knew most of the story from Lauren's briefing earlier, he discovered he felt a little uneasy. He chalked the feeling up to knowing that Gibson was going to be there.

"Tonight, Agony House welcomes a most special guest." Lydia smiled at the crowd. "I know you've all heard of the Amazing Gibson, one of the foremost magicians in the world these days."

A few of the people surrounding the crowd started clapping, but Heath thought maybe they were hotel employees salted among the rest of the guests because they appeared to be sober and not cowed by the retelling of the legend. The other guests picked up the applause till the grand room vibrated with the thunder of it.

The lights went out again, then a detonation exploded sharply enough to make Heath's eardrums ache. A pall of gray fog rolled onto the top of the stairs. When the baby spotlight flared to life again, going almost nova in its intensity, the bright light hit the fog and turned it into a white cloud.

Then Gibson stepped through it, clad in his trademark black suit. He regarded the audience quietly, then held up his black-gloved hands. Putting his hands together, he moved them as if he was kneading dough. Something white appeared between his fingers and grew rapidly. His hands suddenly shot up high over his head and separated.

A white dove exploded from his hands and beat its wings frantically, causing the audience to duck before the bird flew through the main doors and between the hotel employees who held them open. The lights came on in the hotel so the bird could be more easily seen.

When the audience turned back to Gibson, he breathed flames into the space over their heads. Then his hands plucked unseen things from the air, and he tossed shining silver discs into the crowd. Gleefully, the audience grabbed the coins or chased them on the floor.

Heath knew without looking that they were the signature coins Lauren had told him about earlier, the ones with Gibson on one side and him vanished on the other.

Finished with his coin trick, Gibson spread his hands in invitation and nodded graciously.

Lydia climbed the stairs to join Gibson. "Ladies and gentlemen, tonight Gibson has graciously agreed to act as your host for the tour. He, too, knows much of the history of this house."

Gibson took her hand and kissed it, bowing slightly. "I know some of the house's history, but I don't know it all. You are the expert in that area, dear lady. I am but a shadow from a passing flame." He turned over his hand, and suddenly he was holding a lit candle.

The audience clapped appreciatively as Gibson held the candle aloft briefly before handing it off to an assistant who stepped over to him.

Heath finished his beer and handed the bottle off to a passing server.

Lydia took Gibson's arm and waved to the audience to come up the stairs. "Come along. The original Agony House may be gone, but its memories live within these walls."

Hesitantly, then with growing speed, the audience followed.

Finally, at the end of the forty-five-minute-long tour, with Gibson doing sleight of hand tricks and extolling the history of the house, they ended up at the library.

"Come inside." Lydia waved to the group, urging them to step into the large room. "This is the most completely salvaged room in Agony House. The walls, the floor and the books were rescued from the original house and moved here, where they have stayed ever since. Several of our guests have often claimed to have seen Benjamin Hervey in this room."

A clutch of plush sofas occupied a baroque area rug in the

center of the room. A writing desk sat to the left, on the opposite side of the room from the massive wall of books.

So far Gibson had given no indication of seeing Heath, and Heath believed that was because the man was so intent on soaking up the attention. The guy was definitely a glory hound around an audience, and that need for attention also explained the White Rabbit cards he mailed after the murders. Going into seclusion must have been hard on him.

Or maybe that was when he picked his next victim and prepared to deliver his next trick.

Gibson swung his arm to take in the room. "Imagine her, if you can, sitting in this room, locked away with stories of outlandish monsters and ghosts. Perhaps even a premature burial or two." His candle winked out and the room was shrouded in darkness.

An eerie female voice spoke in a heavy accent from one of the back corners of the library. "You don't have to imagine her in this room. You can hear her if you wish. If you have the nerve."

A chill crept up Heath's neck, and he had to check a shiver.

A small flame dawned in the corner and was reflected on the writing desk there. The desk faced the wall, and the light illuminated the figure sitting in the chair. She was dressed in a black mini-cocktail dress that showed off her figure, a hood over her head, and thigh-high black boots.

Heath's radar went off with a sonic boom inside him as he took in the trim figure, the legs encased in black lace stockings. Even though he had spent a lot of time with her the past couple days, it took him a moment to recognize the woman.

Lauren.

His mouth went dry at the sight of her, and he couldn't help staring. Then, somewhere in the dim recesses of his totally blown mind, he realized that they could both be in a lot of trouble.

Lauren tilted her head just enough for the candlelight to illuminate her mocking smile and left her eyes a mystery. "Do you wish to speak to Abigail?"

Lydia made her way to the tour group, which had evidently decided to keep a respectful distance. The candlelight managed to pick Gibson out of the crowd, as well. He looked like a malevolent shadow, and only the hard planes of his face stood revealed. His eyes were black pits above sharp cheekbones.

"I demand to know who you are." Lydia stood her ground, but she stood it a few feet away from Lauren.

"My name is Mistress Tereza." Heath couldn't believe the voice belonged to Lauren because it sounded so different.

"You're not supposed to be here. You're trespassing."

"No, I *am* supposed to be here. I was called by Abigail."

Hesitantly, Lydia turned to look at Gibson. The magician stood stock-still in the shadows and made no response.

Okay, she just blew his mind, too. Heath thought that was funny, but he was too anxious over the trouble Lauren might be in to enjoy the moment very much. But mostly he was drawn to Lauren, unable to decide if she was more sexy or more spooky.

"I'm going to call security." Lydia started to walk toward the door.

"If you do, you'll miss what Abigail came here tonight to say. You know that she talked to your grandmother, but has she ever talked with you? Would you forego that opportunity?"

Heath held his breath, knowing that Lauren had to be running a bluff.

Chapter 18

Lydia stopped at the library door, then walked back into the room. "All right, prove it."

Lauren spoke in a whisper. "Be careful challenging the spirits, Ms. Cranmer. Your grandmother warned you about such things. There are too many evil presences still associated with this house to risk their anger."

Face blanching a little, Lydia stepped back.

With every eye on her, Lauren walked to the coffee table in the middle of the room. She pointed to the sofa on the other side of her as she sat. "Please, sit. Together, Abigail and I will reveal to you that story."

Heath's breath was tight in his chest. He didn't know how Lauren was going to pull this off.

A few of the women in the tour group urged Lydia to sit when they saw that she was reluctant. Finally, probably more out of being a good hostess than anything else, she sat.

Lauren pulled two lighted candles from the air and set them at opposite sides of the coffee table. Heath knew the candles had to be the result of sleight-of-hand, but he hadn't seen them coming till they were there. She'd gotten his wallet without him knowing, though, so he knew she was good. Just not this good.

With the candles in place, Lauren looked at Lydia. "This knowledge isn't just coming from me, Ms. Cranmer. Abigail has touched those of your party. They have the answers, not me."

Drawn by the soft voice and the promise of a brush with the supernatural, the crowd hovered closer. Only Gibson, Roylston and Heath remained back, and the magician's attention was resting solely on Lauren.

"Do you remember when your grandmother told you she'd seen Abigail?" Lauren focused on Lydia.

"Yes."

"Good." Lauren waved an arm over the coffee table. Fire leaped from her fingertips for just a moment, blinding Heath for a second. When he blinked to clear his eyes, he saw that a small crystal ball had appeared on the table.

The audience murmured in appreciation and there was scattered applause.

"Please." Lauren looked at the crowd. "This is not a spectacle. Do not offend the spirits." She focused on one man in a loud Hawaiian shirt and khaki shorts. "You, sir, you know part of the date when Prudy Cranmer revealed to her granddaughter the conversation she had with Abigail. Tell me the month of your birth."

The man hesitated for just a moment. A stocky woman beside him slapped him on the arm. "Tell her, George." She turned to Lauren. "Oh, for Pete's sake, now you know what I have to deal with on anniversaries. His birthday is August ninth."

Lauren smiled and nodded her thanks. "August is the correct month, is it not, Ms. Cranmer?"

As if dazed, Lydia bobbed her head. "August, yes."

"But the ninth is not the correct day, is it?"

"No."

Heath kept an eye on Gibson, noticing the magician stood

ramrod straight. Finally, he shook his head. "This is just cheap theater, Lydia. Don't buy into this."

Agitated, Lydia glanced back over her shoulder at him.

Gibson grinned and shook his head. "This is just a show. Vaudeville, nothing more."

"Is that what you truly believe?" Lauren locked eyes with the magician.

"Yes."

"So you do not believe in the spirits?"

Gibson grimaced and Heath wanted to grin. The magician had stepped right into that. "Of course I believe. I came here tonight to show these people the spirits that walk through this house."

"Then do so. Give me the date when Prudy Cranmer told her granddaughter of her visit from Abigail."

Shaking his head, Gibson grinned again, but there was no mirth in the expression. "You have the floor, *Mistress Tereza*. Why don't you do the honors?"

"Because I cannot do this thing without you." Lauren stood and held out her hand. "Take my hand."

Gibson held up his gloved hands. "I don't do that."

"Is there someone here that you trust?" Lauren turned a hand over toward Lydia. "Our hostess, perhaps?"

"No, I don't think so."

"There must be someone."

Gibson jerked a thumb over his shoulder at Roylston. "Him. Him, I trust."

"Very well." Lauren moved her hand over in Roylston's direction. "Take my hand."

The bodyguard looked at Gibson, who nodded. Gibson watched everything as Roylston took Lauren's hand. Heath tensed, thinking that the bodyguard or Gibson might recognize her from the other day, but she looked so different, and the lights were dim. Still, Heath's hand wasn't far from the gun holstered at his hip.

"Now, take Mr. Gibson's shoulder with your other hand."

A grimace twisted the magician's face. Obviously he preferred "The Amazing" to "Mr."

Roylston looked at his boss, and Gibson nodded again. Gingerly, the bodyguard rested his hand lightly on the magician's shoulder.

Lauren looked at Gibson. "I need you to first clear your mind. Empty it of everything."

Gibson looked impatient and gave a quick nod. "Mind's cleared."

"I do not think you have cleared your mind." Lauren continued looking at him. "I will ask Abigail to speak louder to you."

He shook his head. "You're not going to blame the failure of your little parlor trick on me."

"I will not fail because you will not fail Abigail. She will not allow it." Lauren turned back to Lydia with a small envelope in her hand. "Ms. Cranmer, please take this envelope. Inside is a card. Write down the date that your grandmother talked to you about Abigail's visit. Just the day, not the month."

Lydia reached into her clutch and took out a pen and wrote quickly.

"Please put the card back into the envelope and await further directions." Lauren turned to Gibson. "They say that you can touch the spirit world, that you too can know the unknowable. I only need access to your power for a moment."

Gibson didn't say anything.

Lauren handed him a card and envelope.

Gibson immediately took the card out and examined it. "It's blank."

"For now, yes, but you are going to write on it with your mind."

"I am?" Gibson smirked in disbelief.

"You and Abigail will write on the card."

"Okay, what am I supposed to do with it?"

"Hold it to your forehead and concentrate. Very hard. Use your abilities. You have the power. Talk to Abigail."

Gibson closed his eyes just for a moment while holding the

card to his forehead. Then he opened the envelope and revealed the blank card. "I don't see anything written here."

"Patience. Trust the spirits. Everything is as it should be. Please give the card to this man." Lauren pointed to Roylston.

Gibson didn't move for a moment, and Heath guessed that the magician was thinking of refusing. But the audience was watching him, putting him on the spot. He had to play his part. The performer in him demanded that. He handed the envelope to Roylston.

Lauren reached for the envelope, managing to get her thumb and forefinger on the envelope for just a moment before Gibson caught her wrist. The magician's grip hurt because pain flickered through her eyes for just a moment.

"I don't think so, Mistress Tereza. That envelope stays right there."

With a nod, Lauren released the envelope. "As you wish." She turned to Lydia. "Please use one of the candles and burn your envelope in the fireplace."

Lydia rose with the candle in one hand and the envelope in the other. The audience watched in quiet fascination. In a moment, the envelope was crumpled ash on the fireplace floor.

"Now, Ms. Cranmer, I need you to take the envelope from this man and take it to the coffee table."

Lydia walked over to join them. Roylston looked at Gibson, who nodded, then released the card. The magician followed the hostess to the coffee table.

Lauren walked to the fireplace and dabbed her finger in the black and gray ashes. She sat on the other side of the coffee table and looked at Lydia. "Open the envelope and lay the card on the table."

Lydia did.

Gibson smirked and waved at the card. "It's still blank."

Without a word, Lauren smeared the ashes across the card. "Blow the ash away, Ms. Cranmer."

Heath knew that Gibson realized he'd made a mistake. As careful as he'd been watching, he'd still been taken. He stood and walked through the crowd. Roylston and another man fell into step with him as they went out of the room.

"The sixteenth!" Lydia held the card up in amazement. "The sixteenth!"

Lauren spoke calmly. "Was that the day, Ms. Cranmer?"

"Yes. Oh, my, yes, it was." She looked at Lauren. "How did you know?"

Lauren shook her head. "I did not. Abigail did." She smiled and touched the other woman's shoulder. "You have spirits that live here, harsh and unkind spirits, but you are under your grandmother's protection."

By the time Lauren returned to her hotel room, she'd partially come down from the nervous high from the performance, but her blood was still singing through her veins. She had noticed Gibson leaving the library at the end of the reveal. The man hadn't broken stride quitting the premises. That still made Lauren grin.

Chaos had erupted at the Agony House after that, and Lauren had demonstrated all the knowledge she'd picked up from the internet that afternoon. She'd always been a good student, able to absorb material quickly. Lydia Cranmer had been frazzled to a degree, gobsmacked by the "spirits talking," and—to a degree—devastated that Gibson had deserted her.

Heart still thumping, Lauren walked out onto the patio and looked out over the city. She hated being alone in her moment of glory. She and Heath had taken different cars from the Agony House to make sure they weren't followed. Heath had tailed her for a while to make sure no one showed any undue interest. When he'd been satisfied, he'd called her and told her to return to the hotel.

She'd expected him to follow her there. He hadn't.

Leaning on the balcony, Lauren thought about her performance. She'd always been reluctant to put on shows, though Morganstern and some of the other magicians who frequented the shop had urged her to. Megan had even begged her to try for one of the amateur nights in Chicago.

Always before, Lauren had told her sister, her mother, Morganstern and everyone else that she was satisfied selling magic supplies, that she didn't crave the limelight.

After tonight, Lauren knew that was a lie. She'd never felt more alive than in front of that impromptu audience in the Agony House library.

Someone knocked on the door.

Lauren crossed the room and peered through the peephole, spotting Heath out in the hallway. She opened the door and let him in. "Hey."

He smiled at her, looking at her from head to toe, taking in the costume she still wore. She'd forgotten she still had it on. "I have to say, I didn't expect this."

Lauren put on the accent again. "What? Mistress Tereza?"

"So who is this?"

Grinning, Lauren pirouetted. "This is a personality that I sometimes do in the magic shop. For private shows with friends. I told you, I like to do magic."

"You pack that everywhere you go?"

"Actually, I brought it in case I needed to change my appearance. I figured I'd break the pieces up and use them with other outfits. Mistress Tereza wasn't scheduled for an appearance."

"Good thing you brought it. You put Gibson in his place." Heath frowned. "You want to tell me how you pulled that off?"

"Which part?"

"Let's start with the envelope thing. You never touched the envelope."

"Correction, I touched it. With this." Lauren dug in one of the hidden pockets of the hood she wore and produced a bit of wire that looked like a folded paper clip. The loop was just big enough to fit over her thumb. In the center of it was a small numeral 16. "I touched the card hard enough while Roylston was holding it to indent the card enough to leave an imprint that the ashes could reveal. Like your fingerprint kit you made."

Heath nodded. "I never saw that wire."

"Neither did anyone else. I'm good at sleight-of-hand."

"My wallet and I know this. So how about the guy with the August birthday?"

"His wallet knows I know sleight of hand, as well, but he doesn't. I had to pick the pockets of seven guys before I found one that would work."

"I never saw you in the crowd."

"You weren't supposed to."

"If you'd been wearing this outfit, I would have noticed you."

"I wasn't wearing this outfit." Lauren sat on the edge of the bed while Heath took the wingback chair. She couldn't help crossing her legs and watching the sharp attention Heath gave her. That pull that existed between them was back, and it was stronger than ever. She wanted him to come for her, and if he did, she wasn't going to turn him away.

"All right, how did you know the date?"

"That was from research I found on the internet. When she was a little girl, one of her favorite singers died on that date. Prudy Cranmer told Lydia Cranmer that maybe Elvis would come talk to her the way Abigail came and talked to her. That was in an interview with the both of them back then."

"August sixteenth?"

"August sixteenth, 1977."

Heath thought for a moment, then shook his head.

"Seriously? You don't remember when Elvis Presley died?"

"I wasn't even born then. Neither were you."

"My mom *loves* Elvis. Megan and I used to try to tease her about it, but she would never budge. When we got to be teenagers, we watched a few of his movies and the *'68 Comeback Special*. We got it then. Bad boy looks and rock and roll."

Heath showed her a perplexed grin. "I don't see you as an Elvis fan."

"Then what do you see me as?"

Caught off-guard by the question, Heath shook his head. "I don't know, Lauren. I've never met anyone like you. I think

I know you, then you do something that I would have never thought you would do. Like tonight. You were incredible."

Lauren smiled at him. "Doesn't seem to have gotten us any closer to catching Gibson, though."

"You don't know that. Guys like Gibson, they're used to operating by their timetable. You took that away from him tonight. You stole his thunder. He's not used to that. Tonight could have been the crack that will trip him up somewhere along the way."

They were quiet for a moment.

Heath looked at his watch. "I should be going."

That surprised Lauren. "Where are you going to go? Your hotel room is a shambles. The police are probably looking for you to talk to you about that." She took a deep breath, discovering that the air in the room suddenly seemed thin. "You're safer staying here tonight."

"I know, but you may not be."

Smiling, feeling a little more certain of herself, Lauren got up from the bed and walked over to him. "I can take care of myself." She leaned in close and kissed him, felt the soft heat of his lips pressed against hers, his stubble raking her chin, then—as if by magic—she pulled him effortlessly to his feet and led him to the bed.

Once he was on the bed with her, there was no turning back. He was insatiable, and his hands roamed over her body, stripped away the Mistress Tereza outfit and ignited a heat in her she'd never before experienced.

She relished the weight of his body pressing hers down into the mattress, felt the hard certainty of his erection against her thigh. Gasping, longing, feeling her need growing stronger and stronger, she pushed his pants down over his hips. She grasped his erection in one hand while his lips pressed against hers and his fingers found the molten core of her sex.

He stroked her and teased her till she was shivering and thought she couldn't take any more. Then relief came, bursting the tension that had swelled up inside her. She shook and was lost in bliss. Then she opened her eyes and looked up to see him smiling down at her.

Rolling to her side, Lauren pushed him over, pausing only long enough to reach into the nightstand for the marital aid kit that came with the room. She unrolled a condom over him, taking her time with the task, massaging and grasping till she knew she had him on the edge of control.

She leaned down and kissed him, then looked into those green-flecked gold eyes as his senses spun into overload. "Not so calm now, are you?"

He didn't reply. He just pulled her over on top of him in an inarticulate growl. He slid in instantly and started trying to move. Lauren pressed her hands against his chest, stilling his movement. Then she began to ride, feeling his hard length fill her each time she rose up and sank back down. He struggled to hold back, but she knew he couldn't, and she gloried in her ability to drive him past the point of control. She felt his release, felt him go stiff, then relax.

She lay there, enjoying the feel of his body against her. She rubbed her hands over his shoulders, just wanting to be next to him. Instead, he lifted her up bodily and rolled her over onto her back again. Then he was driving into her, hard as ever, and this time the pace was relentless. Her senses shattered and spun and fell into a world she'd never before seen.

Chapter 19

The shrill ringing of Lauren's cell phone woke her the next morning. Snuggled up against Heath, she didn't want to answer it, but as soon as the cell quit, it started ringing again. Grudgingly, she rolled away from the warm man beside her, who still somehow managed to sleep blissfully unaware, and grabbed her phone from the nightstand.

"Hello." She glanced at the bedside clock and discovered it was 9:12 in the morning. Not many people had her personal cell number. She expected to hear her mom's voice.

"Tell me you are the Mistress Tereza that visited the Agony House last night."

"What?" It took Lauren a moment to place Warren Morganstern's voice because she didn't think she'd ever heard the man that excited.

"Mistress Tereza. You know, spooky girl of magic and mystery. Your act."

"I don't have an act." Lauren sat up in bed, realized she was naked and felt self-conscious even talking over the phone. She pulled a sheet up to cover herself.

"Well, lady, you better get one together because I think you're going to need it."

"What are you talking about?"

"You worked the Agony House last night in Kingston, right?"

"I wouldn't say I worked it."

"I've seen the video. I'm saying you worked it."

"Wait. What video?"

"Somebody in the crowd was filming while you were supposedly channeling some ghost named Abigail. They uploaded the video to YouTube. It's going viral, kiddo, and getting lots of attention. Piling up hits like you wouldn't believe. It's called 'Mistress Tereza at Agony House.' Some people are calling it 'Mistress Tereza Out Magics the Amazing Gibson.' Like I said, getting lots of attention. Professional magicians envy this kind of publicity."

Still not believing what she was hearing, Lauren climbed out of bed with the sheet wrapped around her. That, of course, woke Heath, and he gazed at her with sleepy interest. Even staying in bed till nine, neither of them had gotten much sleep. The night had consumed them.

She picked her iPad up from the desk, sat down in the chair, and brought up the YouTube website. She entered *Mistress Tereza,* thinking that would be enough, and found videos advertising things that she would never have done. Although some of them looked interesting enough to think about doing with Heath. She added Agony House and Jamaica, just to be on the safe side, to the search.

"Did you find it?" Morganstern sounded impatient.

"I did." In disbelief, Lauren watched her performance, split between seeing the video and reliving those moments last night. The residual rush she got from watching those events transpire filled her with excitement.

Heath sat up, reached for his pants and pulled them on, then padded over to join her.

"It's a great bit, kiddo. You remember Ernie Barber?"

"Yes. He's a booking agent for some of the magicians."

"Yeah, and he's already called me, wanting to know if I know who Mistress Tereza is. He's called a lot of people. Getting out there on the grapevine." Morganstern laughed. "I told him, sure, I know who she is. So he wants to meet. If this video continues to go viral. And Ernie and I both think it will because you pants Gibson in it. There's a lot of buzz behind this."

Lauren looked at the hit counter and couldn't believe the number she was seeing. "This many people have watched the video?"

"Yeah, it's great. Just goes to show you—you can be good all day, but none of it counts until you catch a break. You've been good for a while, you just haven't believed it. Looks like you're catching your break now." Morganstern paused. "So when are you coming home? This could be good for you."

"I don't do shows. You know that."

"Well, you did one last night, kiddo. I've watched it a dozen times this morning after one of the guys texted me about it. It's a good bit. Not terribly original, not flashy, but there's a lot of heart in the way you sold the story and that performance."

Yeah, that's because I was trying to get a chance to talk to Gibson, but that didn't work out well. She'd hoped to at least get an audience with the magician.

"Too bad you can't tweak Gibson's nose again." Morganstern chuckled. "*That* would be something to see."

The comment got Lauren to thinking, and she was certain Heath wasn't going to like it at all. "Can I ask a favor?"

"What?"

"I need some gear."

"What kind of gear?"

"Straitjacket. Escapology stuff. I'll send you a list."

"We gonna see Mistress Tereza again?"

Lauren watched the video play through again and saw areas that she could tighten up if she ever did it another time. "Yeah, I think you will."

Morganstern hesitated. "There's one thing, kiddo. The escapology is good, and I know you've been working on some stuff, and you're good with the straitjacket, but it's dangerous if you don't have a trained crew around you."

"I know. I'll be careful."

"Send me the list. I'll get it out to you posthaste. I gotta go. I gotta call some more people." Morganstern hung up.

Placing the iPad back on the table, Lauren looked up at Heath. He looked worried as he watched the YouTube video.

"That's from last night." He rubbed his stubbled jaw with a big hand.

"It is."

"So what's going on?"

"The video is going viral. Warren just told me it's getting a lot of notice in the magic community. Mostly because Gibson gets shown up in it."

He switched his attention to her. "So what's this equipment you're asking for?"

"An escape I've been working on. A riff on Houdini."

Heath frowned. "What?"

"Oh, it's something that's sure to get Gibson's attention, but you're not going to like it at all."

"I don't like this."

Two days later, Lauren climbed the mainmast of a motor-sailer they'd rented for the stunt. The sun was bright and the ocean was relatively calm around them, rolling in gentle swells that lifted and lowered the boat. Festive balloons tied all over the rigging strained at their tethers and made the boat look like a flowering plant.

Connected through a radio channel, Heath stood on the beach two hundred yards away. He was near his usual observation spot to watch Gibson's villa. He watched Lauren through binocs and suffered through the churning of his stomach.

For the past two days, he had helped Lauren get the equipment ready, charter a boat and arrange for a film crew. In between those times, they'd constantly been in bed getting to know each other as lovers. Even now, staring at her in her Mistress Tereza outfit, all he could think about was getting her back into bed.

Except right now he was also thinking that she could get burned to death in the next few minutes. He really didn't like what Lauren was planning to do.

"Don't watch." Lauren sounded a little out of breath as she climbed the mast. "And Kadena loves this."

Kadena was the videographer Lauren had picked for the shoot. He was a young Jamaican who talked about himself in the third person and totally got on Heath's nerves. However, he was also a good videographer. Heath had liked his work.

"Yeah, well, Kadena isn't going to be swinging from the end of a rope in a straitjacket. He doesn't get a vote."

Lauren laughed. "It'll be fun. I've done this dozens of times. It's all about timing. I've just got to be out of the straitjacket before I run out of air."

"I might feel a little better if you'd told me you'd done it thousands of times."

"I only have to do it right once today."

Lauren sat on the yardarm of the mainmast for a moment. People on the shore and in the boats started snapping pictures. The young Jamaican sailor who had accompanied Lauren to the top of the mast started cinching her up in the straitjacket.

Feeling more and more uneasy by the minute, Heath swiveled the binocs toward Gibson's villa. He dialed in the magnification and spotted Gibson out on his veranda, dressed in black, his arms folded and not looking happy at all. Evidently someone had gotten word to him about the escape.

Shifting the binocs back to the motorsailer, Heath watched as Lauren, wrapped in the straitjacket, walked along the yardarm. Balancing itself was a feat. A bungee line was attached to her right ankle.

Several people in the boats and on the beach were pointing. They all recognized the straitjacket.

"Oh, my God! She jumped!" The speaker was female, but

Heath didn't know who it was. He was watching Lauren plummet toward the water. She bounced four times before settling down into a low-hanging arc only a few feet above the sea level.

The Jamaican sailor who had strapped Lauren into the straitjacket leaned down over the bungee cord with something in his hand. A heartbeat later, flames raced down the length of the cord toward Lauren's bare legs.

Heath cursed. She hadn't told him about this part of the act. "Lauren. *Lauren.*"

She didn't respond.

Holding the binocs in one hand, Heath sprinted for the motorboat he'd rented for the day. Even with it, he knew he would arrive too late. Then, just as the flames started twisting around Lauren's legs and black smoke trailed from the bungee cord, the tether that held her to the boat came free and she dropped into the sea.

Clambering aboard the motorboat, Heath cranked the engine over and accelerated away from the beach. Only then did he realize the ocean around the motorsailer was congested, and he wasn't going to be able to get through to Lauren. He yelled curses as he tried to bump through the other vessels.

Long minutes passed as Heath watched helplessly. Then, finally, looking like a drowned cat, Lauren surfaced. She waved to Kadena. A cheer swelled up from the onlookers. Music chugged from the motorsailer's onboard PA system, a swirling and intense calypso grind infused with heavy metal. Several young people dove into the water and swam toward Lauren as she swam toward the motorsailer.

Heath relaxed, then grew tense again as police patrol boats arrived with whirling light bars and intermittent blasts of sirens. The other boaters were cheering and screaming in disbelief in a half dozen different languages.

Before Lauren could reach the motorsailer, a police boat powered up to her. A man threw out a life preserver and ordered her aboard. Heath cursed. The police were another thing they hadn't figured into their plan.

* * *

"What are you in for?"

Sitting with her back against the wall and her arms folded, Lauren stared at the bleak walls of the jail cell for a moment before turning to her bench mate and answering. "Setting myself on fire and jumping off a boat in a straitjacket."

The older woman sitting at the other end of the bench was heavyset, her head wrapped in colorful scarves. She stared at Lauren for a moment before speaking again, placing a hand over her heart. "It is a man what has done made you do these things, yes?"

Lauren smiled at that, still caught up in the adrenaline afterglow of pulling off the escape. "More or less."

"And you in love, too." The woman laughed. "I can done see it in your eyes. Girl, you are in a stewpot full of trouble."

A female jailer in a neatly ironed uniform stepped to the bars. She smiled a little. "If you ask me, I think what you did was pretty cool, but you done broke the law."

"I know."

"Someone posted bail for you." The jailer opened the door. "Come on. Time for you to go."

Lauren got up and stepped through the door. She didn't realize till she was in the hallway how restrained she'd felt in the cell. She also felt bad that Heath had arranged bail for her, though that was nice, too, because now Gibson would probably discover that they were working together.

The jailer led her to a back room and motioned to a small iron-barred security window where a gnarled man sat in a police uniform. Lauren hadn't had many personal effects when she'd gone into the water, only her driver's license. The man on the other side of the window had her sign for it, then slid it across in a manila envelope.

"Thank you."

The man nodded and pointed to the computer on his desk. The screen was turned so Lauren could see it. "That boy that shot your escape did a good job. Good thing, too, because you better not do that again in this city."

"I know."

The man shook his head and smiled. "Saw you at the Agony House, too. Quite the show, quite the show."

"Thank you." Lauren followed the jailer to the back of the building and ended up stepping through the door she was shown and out on the street where she and Heath had taken Sisco captive days ago. The sun was already going down. She'd been questioned and processed and kept waiting for hours. She'd begun to think that she would be spending the night in jail. She checked both sides of the street.

Heath Sawyer wasn't there waiting for her.

Roylston was. He was dressed in a nice suit and wore wrap-around sunglasses. "Mistress Tereza?" He looked at the phone in his massive hand. "Or should I say Ms. Lauren Cooper?"

Feeling a little frightened, Lauren focused on the man. The luxury car she had seen him driving Gibson around in sat at the curb. Another man in a suit, one she didn't know, stood beside the vehicle.

"Whichever suits."

Roylston smiled, and there was nothing pleasant or welcoming about the expression. "Gibson would like to meet you. If you're interested."

For only a heartbeat, Lauren hesitated. The plan was to entice Gibson with another video of Mistress Tereza, then meet him at their convenience. Not be swept away. She looked around the street again but didn't see Heath anywhere. She thought of Megan and how more proof was needed to name Gibson as her murderer.

No way was Lauren going to let Gibson walk on that.

No way.

She nodded. "Sure. I've been wanting to meet him. I wanted to tell him that night at Agony House, but he disappeared before I knew it."

"Gibson is like that."

"Maybe you could pick me up at my hotel in half an hour?" Lauren pulled at the outfit. "I smell like I took a bath in the ocean. I'd like a chance to clean up."

"Gibson is quite insistent about meeting you now. Don't worry about how you're dressed. There is a selection of clothing at the villa. Gibson often entertains guests. I'm sure you'll find something to wear."

Lauren still hesitated.

Roylston's smile faded a little. "I'm afraid the offer will expire. Gibson's time is very valuable."

Taking a breath, Lauren nodded. "All right. Let's go." As she approached the car, Roylston opened the rear door. When she got inside, the big man slid in beside her and closed the door.

The other man got in behind the wheel, put the car in gear and rolled into traffic.

Lauren craned her head over her shoulder and looked back at the street, still not seeing Heath.

"Expecting someone?" Roylston sat calmly beside her.

Turning back around, Lauren faced forward. "I thought maybe the media would be around."

"They're in front of the building. Gibson talked to someone in the police department and all parties concerned agreed that it would probably be best if you quietly disappeared."

Lauren didn't think the choice of words was by chance, and a shiver passed through her. She clamped down on the fear that prickled within her, trusting that Gibson wouldn't just spirit her away from the jail and kill her. Even he couldn't pull that off.

Chapter 20

Seated in a café across from the jail, Heath looked at the bail bondsman he'd recruited to get Lauren Cooper out of jail. "What do you mean she's gone?"

Denroy Paul was an earnest young man who hadn't quite escaped the laid-back attitude of the island. He was six feet tall and slim, his hair done in dreadlocks, and he had a very white smile that he liked to use a lot. He wore slacks and sandals and a white short-sleeved shirt.

"Just that, mon. I go there looking for this woman. I ask about her like I always do." Denroy shrugged. "Then the jailer, she tell me Lauren Cooper already be gone, mon. Someone else bailed her out." He grinned. "Must be you not the only one interested." He nodded. "I seen them videos, mon. Very good-looking woman."

Heath curbed the angry retort that landed at the tip of his tongue. "Did you find out who paid her bail?"

"Gibson. The mon who is the magician. You know him?"

"Not as well as I'd like to. How long ago did Gibson post her bail?"

Holding his forefinger and thumb an inch apart, Denroy shook his head. "Missed her by that much, mon."

Heath got up from the table. "I owe you anything?"

Denroy opened his hands. "Not me, mon. I didn't do nothing for you."

"Thanks." Heath hustled for the door, almost running by the time he got there.

Twenty-three minutes later, certain he'd violated every traffic law in Kingston, Heath pulled to a stop at his observation point on the beach up the road from Gibson's villa. A sand cloud ghosted gray around him, and campfires carved holes in the darkness that had settled over the beach. His heart ached when he thought of Lauren in Gibson's power.

During the whole drive, he couldn't help remembering Janet Hutchins and how he hadn't been there in time to save her from Gibson. That guilt had nearly eaten Heath alive over the past couple weeks. But he knew that he hadn't let Janet down. She hadn't had time to call for help when Gibson had gotten to her. She'd been gone before Heath had known.

He adjusted the binocs and swept the house. The luxury car's headlights dimmed in the circular driveway, then the dome light flared on. Heath's breath caught at the back of his throat as he watched Lauren step out of the car and walk up the steps leading to the house.

Standing at the window, fingers pulling the drapes slightly aside, Gibson stared down at his latest prey. She wore the same outfit she'd worn when she'd accosted the tour in the Agony House, only now she looked somewhat tawdry and bedraggled. She was still beautiful. There was no taking that away from her. Natural beauty always shone through.

His hunger to kill coiled like a dark thing at the back of his mind. He felt it sitting there, waiting to consume his senses when the time came. This time the hunger felt different, more alive and vital than it had before. It felt stronger, so much like it had felt the night he had killed the woman detective.

Only this felt much more pleasurable. The anticipation was almost sexual, and the desire turned physical.

She had offended him. She had seized the limelight that was supposed to have been his at the Agony House. The tour had been his to direct that night, and she had derailed his efforts.

And now, today…

He turned from the window and glared at the large computer screen on the inlaid desk that anchored his private sanctorum. The YouTube video of *Mistress Tereza* was frozen at the point that the woman was entering the ocean while flames clung to her legs.

The flames were an illusion, though. Gibson knew she had protected her flesh, and the fire only burned the fumes of the chemicals. There was heat, yes, but no scorching. Escaping the straitjacket while in the water was impressive, though. Gibson had never wanted to do something like that too much, though he'd done some of it in his early career. Escapology was too much physical labor. He preferred illusions, making an audience think they knew what they were seeing.

That was what made him great. That perception that others had of him.

The room was a trophy chamber of his successes. Framed pictures of performances and his meetings with celebrities filled the walls. This was his world now, not his father's. He had gone much further than his father had ever believed he would in his career, and Gibson reveled in that knowledge, even though his father would never acknowledge his success. Knowing that there was so much of it to ignore made that success even sweeter.

At the computer, he brought up the closed circuit television system he had hidden throughout the house. He watched as the woman entered the villa on Roylston's heels.

Gibson stood in the dark and awaited his call to tonight's performance. The hunger coiled and uncoiled inside him.

* * *

Desperate, Heath threw himself from his car and went around to the trunk. He wore the .357 on his hip in a holster, but he'd stored the 9mm he'd captured from the woman in his hotel room in the trunk. Since then, he'd also gotten extra magazines and a shoulder holster from the kid who had sold him the revolver.

In the shadows under a palm tree, Heath strapped the 9 mm under his left arm, then pulled a black windbreaker on to hide the weapons. He shoved the extra magazines into the thigh pockets of his cargo jeans, then pulled on a black ball cap to cover his hair.

After closing the trunk, he jogged down to the beach and ran along the dark water. Trying to approach the villa across the light-colored sand of the beach would have made him stand out. Since the moon wasn't up, the ocean was inky dark, and he knew he was nearly invisible against it. He jogged, his feet sinking into the wet sand with liquid crunching noises.

With someone in their midst, Heath felt certain that the villa's flesh and blood security would draw closer to the core, leaving it to the electronic surveillance to watch the perimeter. Those systems weren't fail proof. During the days he had scouted the villa, Heath had felt certain there were weak points. Trespassing would have made any evidence he'd obtained that way illegal, though. So he'd kept his distance.

Tonight, all bets were off. Lauren wasn't supposed to have bearded the monster in his lair. They were supposed to have coaxed Gibson out.

He ran, his muscles warming up against the chill coming in from the sea.

The house had seemed large and ornate from outside, but once Lauren was inside, she was overwhelmed by the opulence. Chandeliers, art, plush furniture, woods, marble and window treatments that looked as though they'd been ripped from designer catalogues filled the rooms she saw as Roylston escorted her to the back of the house.

Lauren's fear had grown when she'd entered the villa's gates, and it was everything she could do to control it as she followed the bodyguard. She made herself think of Megan, but that was a double-edged sword because that memory was as filled with terror as it was with resolve to see her sister's murderer caught.

She followed Roylston up to the second floor to a door. The bodyguard indicated the door. "Everything you need will be inside. Feel free to choose whatever you wish."

"Thank you." Lauren stepped through the doorway into a large room that contained a vanity and two large closets filled with women's clothing.

"Sure." Roylston pointed to an intercom on the wall. "If you need anything, just ring. When you're ready, let me know and I'll come get you."

"All right. Thank you." Lauren watched the man close the door, but she still didn't feel alone. She took a deep breath and tried to release the tension that she felt inside her.

She couldn't help wondering if this was what Megan had been treated to, as well. Then she knew that wasn't the case. No matter what had happened between Gibson and Megan, Lauren knew her sister would never have put up with something like this.

Yet, here she was, prepared to put on clothes Gibson had provided for his "guests." Curious, Lauren looked through the closets, wondering what kind of clothing Gibson had chosen, and wondering, too, at the women whom he brought back to the villa. During the time she and Heath had watched the villa, no one had brought a woman onto the premises.

Growing up in foster care, Lauren had endured her share of hand-me-downs, but this was a more exotic collection than she'd ever seen. The clothing wasn't all "play" wear either, though there was an assortment of that, too: catsuits and wispy lingerie. But there was also a choice of casual clothing, beachwear and cocktail dresses. There was even a range of sizes and lengths.

Lauren picked a pair of snug-fitting skinny-legged jeans and a close-fitting pullover because that outfit provided the least amount of loose material that could be used against her if she had to fight for her life. She didn't think that would be the case. Too many people knew that Gibson had bailed her out of jail. He wouldn't dare hurt her, would he?

She took the clothing to the bathroom in the rear of the room.

Sipping from a snifter of brandy to hold the darkness in him in thrall for a while longer, Gibson watched the woman strip in the bathroom. Her body—her shape and her form and her nudity—wasn't what excited him. It wasn't even the vision of what he would do to it. What fascinated him most was the knowledge that he was about to have more power over her than anyone had ever had before.

Onscreen, the woman stepped into the shower but the heated water had fogged the windows to the point that she seemed like an illusion on the other side of the translucent glass.

He hummed in anticipation, knowing it wouldn't be much longer now. She was going to pay for upstaging him.

Chapter 21

Plastered up against the seaward wall of the villa and drenched in the darkness, Heath felt his phone vibrate in his pocket. He slid it free, thinking that Lauren might be calling him from inside the house.

Instead, Jackson Portman's face showed on the view screen.

Heath debated answering the phone, but this late in the evening with everything going on, he knew that his partner wouldn't call unless there was serious need.

"Yeah?"

"I think I know who Gibson is."

The information surprised Heath, but not the fact that Jackson had stayed with the search. "How?"

"I kept backtracking Sisco's employment to a place called Blackheart Solutions. Heard of it?"

"No."

"Don't feel bad. Neither had I until I dug in. Turns out Blackheart Solutions is a company that specializes in computer software. They get a large part of government contracts every year. Providing encryption and stuff like that."

Heath gazed up at the tall perimeter wall. "I got a thing here, Jackson. Maybe you could pick up the pace a little."

"Blackheart Solutions is owned by a man named Julius Bleak. Guy knows congressmen and presidents by their first names. He also has a son, Terrence, who is forty-three years of age. Terrence has a history of violence against women. Two charges of rape and aggravated assault in Seattle. Both cases were dismissed with prejudice because Terrence Bleak's daddy used his leverage to get the charges dropped. I had to really look for that information to get it. Terrence was nineteen and twenty-two at the time. Then Terrence vanished. No history. A few years later, Gibson starts hitting the magic circuit. How do you like that?"

"Less and less by the minute, buddy." The anxiety inside Heath reached shattering levels. All he could think about was Janet and how he hadn't been there for her. "I've got to go. I appreciate everything that you've done."

"Let me know how everything works out?"

"Definitely." Heath couldn't tell Jackson his situation. His partner would have tried to talk him down, and Heath didn't have the time for an argument. He hung up, then looked up Inspector Myton's phone number and placed a call to him.

Myton was slow to pick up, and when he did he sounded half-asleep. "Hello?"

"This is Heath Sawyer."

That perked Myton up immediately. "Where are you, Detective Sawyer? I have some questions I'd like you to answer. It seems your hotel room was trashed, and there was a shootout in front of the building that has me puzzled."

"I'm at Gibson's estate."

"Really? What are you doing there?"

"I'm saving my friend. You need to hurry." Heath hung up, turned to the security wall and walked to where the ocean lapped at the perimeter. Over the years of constant assault, the salt water had chipped away at the mortar holding the stones together, leaving hand and foot holds. He started climbing, hauling himself up as quickly as he could.

Lauren followed Roylston back down to the first floor, then to a library much like the one at Agony House, though designed on a less ambitious scale. The shelves held books and DVDs on magic, and glass display cases held dioramas of famous magicians performing legendary tricks and escapes.

Fascinated, she stopped in front of a display case that held a scene of Houdini talking to a gypsy woman seated at a table with a crystal ball. The magician had hold of the table and was yelling at the woman, who was terrified.

"Houdini didn't believe in the spirit world." Gibson had come into the room behind her without her knowledge.

"That's right." A chill passed through Lauren, but she suppressed it. She couldn't help thinking that she was looking at her sister's murderer, and that she was standing more or less helpless inside his house.

"Would it surprise you to know that I first got involved in magic because I wanted to speak to my mother?"

"I've never read that anywhere."

"I've never told anyone." Gibson gazed at the diorama. "My mother died when I was very young. I've missed her my whole life."

"I'm sorry to hear that."

Gibson shrugged and smiled. "She chose to leave. Committed suicide." He shrugged again. "At least, that's what my father tells me. He's a very powerful and influential man, so that must be true, don't you think?"

"I wouldn't know."

With slow, deliberate steps, Gibson crossed the room to gaze intently at the diorama. "Who are you, Mistress Tereza—or should I call you Lauren Cooper, since you were booked under that name—that you would come into my world and seek so strongly to attract my attention? I feel that I should know you."

Lauren was surprised to discover that Gibson still hadn't

recognized her from the encounter in the restaurant days ago. "I'm a struggling magician trying to make a name for myself."

"And you choose to do this by confronting me on my turf?"

"I didn't mean any harm."

Gibson looked at her then. "Not even when you stole the show from under me at the Agony House?"

"I didn't expect you to be so confrontational. I was going to use someone else in the audience to finish the trick, but when you stepped in so hard, it had to be you."

Shrugging, Gibson lifted a hand, and a gold coin danced across his knuckles like a leaf flowing down a river, smooth and effortless. The deep yellow color of the metal winked in the light. "I couldn't let you just steal the show like that. Then, I couldn't stop you."

"I thought maybe we could work together."

"If you know anything at all about me, you know I don't work with a partner."

"I wasn't trying to be a partner. Just a warm-up act."

"And the death-defying leap from the ship into the ocean while in a straitjacket today?"

"That was to get your attention."

"Was it? Because I think it was to capitalize on the success of the video currently going viral across the internet." Gibson smiled, and there was no humor. Malice gleamed in his dark eyes.

"A little publicity never hurts."

"This publicity? It's going to hurt you." With his other hand, Gibson snapped a card into the air.

The card whirled like a Frisbee as it crossed the distance to Lauren. Without thinking, she plucked the card out of the air.

"Very good reflexes." Gibson seemed genuinely amused.

Lauren turned the card over and saw the white rabbit there.

"After the police find your body, I'm going to mail them that card." As he strode toward her, Gibson's hands came from behind his back. In one of his hands, he held a long knife.

* * *

Heath clambered over the security wall without setting off an alarm, then dropped to the ground and ran toward the main house while staying in the shadows. The sweet, heavy scent of the bougainvillea filled his nose and almost made him sneeze.

One of the security guards emerged from the house and went to the car parked in the circular drive. The engine started with a smooth growl. The guy rested behind the steering wheel with the dome light off, the instrument panel glowing in his face. Another guard stood at the door to the house and talked on his cell phone.

Stealthily, knowing there was no turning back at this point but feeling certain that Lauren's life was in danger, Heath crept up on the man. Just behind the door, he whispered only loud enough for the driver to hear. "Move and I will kill you."

The man slowly started to raise his hands.

"Put your hands on the steering wheel. Let's not invite your friend before we need to."

After a brief hesitation, the man grasped the steering wheel.

"Is the woman still inside the house?"

"Yes."

"Is she still all right?"

"She was. She's with Gibson in the library."

A sharp feeling of relief flooded Heath.

"Doesn't mean she's going to stay that way, though. Gibson's been in the mood to kill her since she showed up at that house. You're the cop, right?"

"Yeah."

The guy pressed a hand on the horn as he shoved out of the car and rounded on Heath, catching him off guard. His hand slammed into Heath's chest because Heath didn't want to fire immediately. Thrown off-balance, Heath staggered back and watched the man bring up a pistol.

Heath squeezed the .357's trigger and felt the pistol buck as a bullet whipped past his ear. His round caught the man in the chest, and he followed it with a second round that cored through the man and shattered the door window behind him.

The man at the door brought up his pistol and took a defensive position inside the house.

Keeping a lid on the panic that filled him, not wanting to think that he was going to lose the woman he was almost certain he was in love with, Heath yanked the falling dead man out of his way and slid behind the steering wheel. Shots blasted through the windshield and tore into the passenger seat as he pulled on the safety harness. He slammed the transmission into Drive and pressed his foot down on the accelerator.

The high-performance engine thrust the car forward. Heath laid the .357 in the passenger seat and steered with both hands to bring the car on a direct path with the front of the house. He hoped the front end stayed together long enough to get him where he was going. Otherwise he was a dead man and Lauren was going to brutally die.

The front tires jerked and juddered as the car raced up the wide steps, but they navigated the incline with less trouble than he'd anticipated. The whole vehicle shook and shimmied, but he managed to hold it on course with one hand while he picked up the revolver with the other.

When the car hit the front of the house, the airbags deployed. Even though he'd prepared for the impact, even though the seat belt clamped like a vise around his chest, the face plant against the airbag rushing up at him robbed Heath of his senses.

Chapter 22

Savage joy filled Gibson when he saw the fear in the woman's eyes. That look, that palpable feel of the connection to his audience during the final performance he would give them, was an elixir that never failed to transport him out of the ordinary world. Drawn by that fear, he closed on her, eager to open her up and let the blood hit the ground.

It would be the first time he had killed in the library in front of so many of his childhood heroes. He didn't know why he hadn't done so before. No one could stop him. Nothing could get in his way. He was invincible.

The woman, Mistress Tereza, cowered before him, giving ground as he backed her toward the fireplace. She reached out and toppled a diorama of Doug Henning's performance in *Spellbound.* The display smashed across the wooden floor in front of Gibson. He snarled inarticulate curses at her. The diorama could be replaced, but he hated the idea that anyone could touch his things.

He lifted the knife and strode toward her with greater speed. Then Roylston's mocking voice halted him. "Hey, Terrence."

In disbelief, stunned to have heard *that* name here in this house, Gibson turned toward his bodyguard. *"What* did you call me?"

Twenty feet away, Roylston stood framed by the door. He held something in his left hand and a pistol in his right. He flicked his left hand forward, and a cylindrical shape flew through the air to land at Gibson's feet.

It was a cigar.

Gibson glared at Roylston. "What is the meaning of this?"

Roylston smirked at him. "Your old man just called me. He's having another son. He doesn't need you anymore to carry on the family name." He raised the pistol to fire.

Panicked, filled with fear for himself for the first time in years, Gibson flung the knife he held. It flickered through the air like quicksilver and caught Roylston in the neck.

With a look of shock, the big man clamped a hand to his neck and pulled it away covered with blood. The pistol fell from his nerveless fingers.

Cursing, knowing that Roylston wouldn't be acting alone, Gibson raced over to pick up the pistol. He gripped it and turned around, determined to get out of the house. But first, he was going to take care of the woman. He started to turn back around, but something that sounded very much like a bomb went off at the front of the house. Security alarms screamed to life throughout the villa.

Grimly, Heath clawed back up from the thready darkness that was trying to suck him down. He forced his head up and lifted the revolver at the same time.

The man who had been hiding behind the door rose up like a ghost from the grave, covered in plaster and mortar dust that pushed into the house in a large, roiling cloud. He fired at the car, his hand suddenly filled with a muzzle flash.

Taking deliberate aim, Heath put two rounds into center body mass, following through on muscle memory he'd gotten while in the military and from hours spent on the shooting range.

The bodyguard stumbled back and fell.

Looking around, his head feeling as if it was about to shatter from all the security alarms, Heath realized the car had gotten wedged in the suddenly enlarged doorway. The doors were stuck, and he couldn't open them.

He tried to free himself from the seat belt that felt as if it was crushing the life out of him, but something had to have been broken in the locking mechanism during the crash. He had to fish out his pocketknife and cut himself free.

Breathing hurt. Moving hurt. But Heath leaned back in the seat and kicked the windshield out of the car, then turned around and crawled out after it. He almost fell when he stepped off the front of the car, but he retained his balance and flipped the revolver open, ejecting the four spent shells and replacing them with fresh rounds. He snapped the cylinder closed with a flick of his wrist and moved on into the house. He didn't know where Lauren was, but the need to find her consumed him.

He started moving toward the stairs, then heard a shot from the right. "Lauren!"

The only thing that held the fear at bay inside Lauren was the knowledge that her sister's murderer stood in front of her. Incredulous, she'd watched Gibson throw the knife with deadly accuracy, but by that time her fingers were already closing around the fireplace poker.

When Gibson went after the fallen bodyguard's pistol, Lauren had gone after him. She ignored the reluctance she felt for what she was about to do and instead stoked her rage over losing her sister. Her hands curled around the poker.

Gibson lifted the pistol and turned around, and Lauren swung the poker off her shoulder in the flat arc that her adoptive father had spent time teaching her for softball. The poker caught Gibson alongside his jaw, and bone cracked loud enough to hear in between the frantic bleats of the security alarms.

Stumbling to the side, Gibson tried to bring up the pistol again. Stepping forward as though she was meeting a fastball pitch, Lauren swung once more, only catching Gibson on the arm that he instinctively raised to defend himself. The blow drove him to the side and down to the ground.

Lauren moved toward him and raised the poker over her head, intending to bring her weapon down on Gibson's skull. He looked up at her, his face streaming blood. All she had to do was swing and he would go away forever. She knew that.

But she also knew that wouldn't bring Megan back. Nothing would bring Megan back.

Screaming in frustration, Lauren crashed the poker through the diorama of Houdini exposing the fake spiritualist.

"You should have killed him. You know you wanted to. At least you would have had that."

Drawn by the wheezing voice, Lauren turned around to discover Roylston once more on his feet. The knife was still in his neck. He hadn't removed it. And he had another pistol in his hand. He waved the weapon at Gibson. "Go ahead. Bust him up like a piñata. If I do it, it won't mean as much to me. Just the end of a long, tiring job. But you? You'll get something out of it. He tried to kill you."

"He killed my sister. He killed Megan."

Frantically, Gibson shook his head in agony. Blood dripped to the floor. He pointed at Roylston.

"Megan Taylor? The woman drowned down here?"

"Yes."

Roylston chuckled despite the pain he was in. "No. That was me. This idiot tried to kill her that night, but she fought him off and got away. It was just one more case of me having to clean up his mess. Then he sent that White Rabbit card to the police. Claiming his kill. Feeding his vanity." He swallowed with effort and chuckled again. "That's funny. You coming down here, taking him on—bringing him to this, really, and it was for something that he couldn't even do right."

Gibson tried to get to his feet.

"No, you just stay where you are, you sick psychopath. I'm going to let Mistress Tereza have one more—"

Gunfire erupted somewhere in the house.

Roylston glanced back over his shoulder. Seizing her chance, with her sister's killer once more in front of her, Lauren raised the poker and raced at the bodyguard. Some sixth sense must have warned him of her approach, though, because she knew he didn't hear her. When she swung, he turned around and caught the poker in his left hand as he lifted the pistol to point at her face.

Heath zeroed in on the sound of the gunshot and came up on Roylston from behind. Over his shoulder, Heath spotted Lauren standing in front of the man, almost dwarfed by his bulk. Roylston was still holding on to the poker that Lauren had obviously swung.

Another gunshot boomed inside the room, and this time Roylston staggered back and sat down on the floor. Then he fell backward, and the thousand yard stare in his eyes revealed that he was dead.

Lauren turned, still not seeing Heath, and looked back into the room. There, kneeling on the floor, Gibson struggled to get to his feet. His jaw hung strangely, but he pointed a pistol at Lauren, and his intentions were clear.

Unable to get Lauren clear of the situation, Heath stepped into the library with both hands on the .357. "Drop the weapon, Gibson." Heath didn't want to risk the man accidentally discharging his weapon by shooting him. "Only chance you're going to get. Otherwise I make you disappear."

Gibson blinked to focus on Heath, then nodded and slowly lowered the pistol, leaving it on the floor and lacing his fingers behind his head.

Heath reached down and untied Roylston's bloody tie, surprised to find the knife lodged in the side of his neck, then used it to tie Gibson's hands behind his back. He glanced up at Lauren, who looked as if she was ready to fall down.

"You okay? You hurt?"

She shook her head. "No. I'm fine." Studying him with concern, she crossed over to him and touched his face. "You're bleeding."

"I'm okay."

"You don't look okay."

"It's been a long day." Holding the pistol to the back of Gibson's head, his knee still firmly planted in his quarry's back, Heath reached out his free arm and held Lauren tight. "I'm really glad you're alive."

"Me, too." She leaned down and kissed his bruised lips.

Sirens screamed in the distance. Lauren pulled back.

Heath grinned. "That will be Inspector Myton. We're going to have a lot of explaining to do."

It was a *lot* of explaining. Hours passed by while Lauren sat in an interview room and talked with Inspector Myton. She had told him, then two successive investigators, an edited version of what had happened at Gibson's villa. They had agreed to leave out Sisco's kidnapping and the encounter at Heath's hotel. If the inspector wanted to pursue those events, he'd have to do it without their help.

"Well, Miss Cooper, it certainly is a most interesting—and most curious—story you and Detective Sawyer have to tell." Inspector Myton once more sat on the opposite side of the table in the interview room.

Lauren sipped her water and didn't say anything.

"I must admit, there are parts of your stories that bother me. Missing pieces, mostly." The inspector smiled. "But I am willing to let many of them go at this point. After all, the nefarious White Rabbit serial killer was brought in on my watch, was he not?"

The goodbye at the airport was hard. Lauren held on to Heath as her flight to Chicago boarded. He would be returning to Atlanta on his flight within the hour.

She'd never felt a person who completed her more than Heath Sawyer outside of her family. She didn't want to let go of that feeling. But the murders of Megan and Janet had been the only things holding them together. Freed from the shadow of the White Rabbit Killer, both of them could go back to their very separate lives.

Lauren forced herself to be neutral, to not think about the end of everything and to concentrate on the good they had done. As Heath had said, there was no telling how many lives they had saved. She cleared her throat to speak. "So how much trouble are you going to be in back in Atlanta?"

Heath shook his head. "I went way over the line. I don't know. The captain doesn't like problems, and Gibson's testimony about his father's security people are going to bring his father down, too. That guy's in tight with several government agencies." He frowned. "It's going to end up being a big deal. That's not my fault, but the captain's gonna blame me for it to a degree. It's how he is." He looked at her. "What about you? Are you going to be okay?"

"Yes." Lauren took a breath. "It's not going to be the same without Megan, but Mom and I will get through it. We got through losing Dad, too. You just don't forget, you know?"

"I know."

The airline representative made the last call for the flight to Chicago.

Lauren reached down for her carry-on. "I've got to go."

Heath nodded. "Have a safe flight, Lauren." He stepped forward and kissed her lightly on the lips. She wanted to hold on to him, but she couldn't and she knew it. Giving in to that weakness here would be hard because she knew she had to get back to take care of her mother.

And Heath had his own life.

He let her go, and she turned around and walked toward the entrance to the boarding tunnel. She didn't look back because she didn't want him to see the tears in her eyes. Leaving was hard enough without both of them being miserable.

Epilogue

"Ladies and gentlemen, late from her last showing in Kingston, Jamaica, may I present the lovely and mysterious Mistress Tereza!" Warren Morganstern's announcer's voice was strong and loud, carrying over the PA system in the small room in the magic shop.

Once Lauren had returned home, Morganstern had insisted on hosting a show for her. They had spent the past two weeks getting everything ready, and even though she'd done every trick on the slate hundreds of times and the show was primarily invitation-only to a select audience, Lauren still felt nervous.

She hadn't ever done a real show before, only bits and pieces as interludes and warm-ups for real showmen. She launched into the table magic first, doing old tricks with occasional little personal flares that brought oohs and ahhs from the audience.

Her mother had a front-row seat and looked better than she had looked in months. The doctors had said she was in full remission. Her mom told her that she believed Megan had reached back and taken the cancer from her as a final gift.

Lauren didn't know what to believe, but she was glad to have her mom healthy.

One of the finales of the act was the disappearing cabinet. It was an old trick, too, but she'd always enjoyed it.

"Ladies and gentlemen." Morganstern was really laying it on as stage hands brought the seven-foot tall cabinet onto the stage. "As you can see, this is a simple box. A plain wooden construction of humble origins. But Mistress Tereza is going to make magical history here tonight for your viewing pleasure as she disappears from this very box."

A drumroll sounded as the box came to a stop in center stage, and that surprised Lauren because they'd never discussed that. Still, clad in her black outfit, she walked to the box and bowed, then she opened the door to show the audience that it was empty.

Only it wasn't.

Heath stood inside dressed in a tuxedo and top hat, and looking more handsome than she'd ever seen him. He winked at her, then stepped from the box toward her holding a magic wand. She stood there, not knowing what to do.

Then, with a flourish, Heath waved the wand and it turned into a bouquet of flowers. He took her into his arms and kissed her long and hard, and the sizzle of their magic spun through her body. When he drew back, she was breathless.

The crowd hooted and hollered, and from their reactions, Lauren knew Morganstern had roped them all in on the trick. Even her mother, who was clapping in delight.

"I wanted to let you know that I had a little magic of my own." Heath grinned down at her.

She smiled back. "You always have, mister."

"What would you say if I told you Chicago's finest is looking for a detective?"

Lauren repressed a smile with real effort. "Atlanta is willing to let you go?"

"It's not up to them, and they don't have the same benefits package as this city."

"Chicago's always been one of my favorites."

"We'll have to talk then. Until then, I hear you're going to disappear in this box." With theatrical aplomb that was only a little awkward but endearingly so, Heath waved to the waiting box.

"I am. But only for a little while." Lauren stepped into the box and started to close the door, then she opened it, reached back for Heath and pulled him inside with her. "I'm not letting you out of my sight tonight."

The audience rolled with laughter, evidently hearing everything over the PA pickup.

Heath held her tightly. "I've never really disappeared before."

"It's easy. I'll teach you how." Lauren leaned in and kissed him, then closed the door.

And they disappeared.

* * * * *

A sneaky peek at next month...

INTRIGUE...

BREATHTAKING ROMANTIC SUSPENSE

My wish list for next month's titles...

In stores from 15th February 2013:

❑ Gage – Delores Fossen

& Mason – Delores Fossen

❑ Alpha One – Cynthia Eden

& Internal Affairs – Alana Matthews

❑ O'Halloran's Lady – Fiona Brand

& Seduction Under Fire – Melissa Cutler

❑ Colton's Deep Cover – Elle Kennedy

Available at WHSmith, Tesco, Asda, Eason, Amazon and Apple

Just can't wait?

Visit us Online

You can buy our books online a month before they hit the shops! **www.millsandboon.co.uk**

0213/46

MILLS & BOON® Book Club

2 Free Books!

Get your free books now at
www.millsandboon.co.uk/freebookoffer

Or fill in the form below and post it back to us

THE MILLS & BOON® BOOK CLUB™—HERE'S HOW IT WORKS: Accepting your free books places you under no obligation to buy anything. You may keep the books and return the despatch note marked 'Cancel'. If we do not hear from you, about a month later we'll send you 5 brand-new stories from the Intrigue series, including two 2-in-1 books priced at £5.49 each and a single book priced at £3.49*. There is no extra charge for post and packaging. You may cancel at any time, otherwise we will send you 5 stories a month which you may purchase or return to us—the choice is yours. *Terms and prices subject to change without notice. Offer valid in UK only. Applicants must be 18 or over. Offer expires 31st July 2013. **For full terms and conditions, please go to www.millsandboon.co.uk/freebookoffer**

Mrs/Miss/Ms/Mr (please circle)
_____

First Name
_____

Surname
_____

Address
_____

_____
                                        Postcode

E-mail
_____

Send this completed page to: Mills & Boon Book Club, Free Book Offer, FREEPOST NAT 10298, Richmond, Surrey, TW9 1BR

Find out more at
www.millsandboon.co.uk/freebookoffer

Visit us Online

0113/I3XEb